I0749614

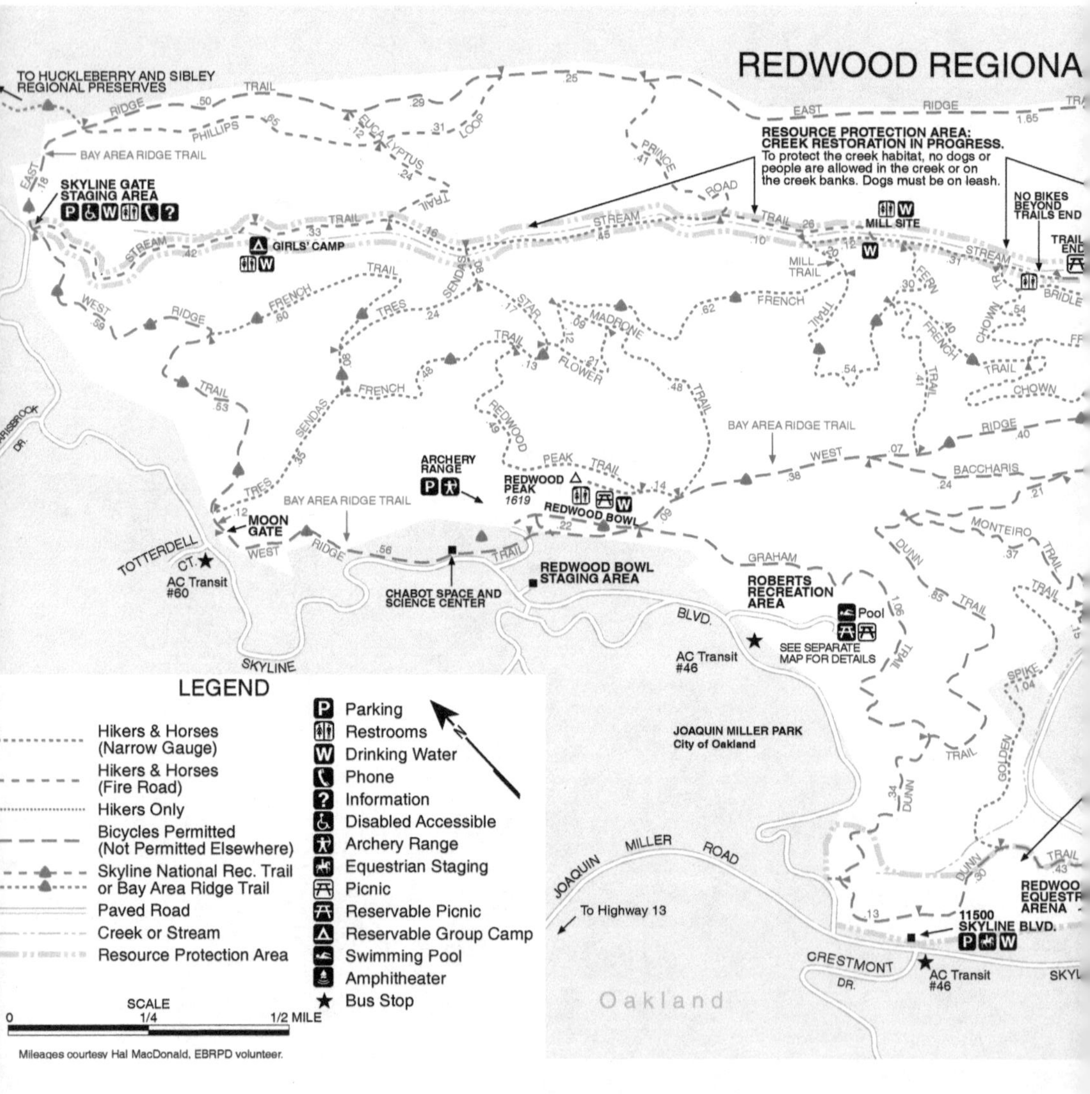

REDWOOD REGIONA
TO HUCKLEBERRY AND SIBLEY REGIONAL PRESERVES
SKYLINE GATE STAGING AREA
BAY AREA RIDGE TRAIL
GIRLS' CAMP
RESOURCE PROTECTION AREA: CREEK RESTORATION IN PROGRESS.
To protect the creek habitat, no dogs or people are allowed in the creek or on the creek banks. Dogs must be on leash.
NO BIKES BEYOND TRAILS END
MILL SITE
ARCHERY RANGE
REDWOOD PEAK 1619
REDWOOD BOWL
MOON GATE
TOTTERDELL CT.
AC Transit #60
CHABOT SPACE AND SCIENCE CENTER
REDWOOD BOWL STAGING AREA
ROBERTS RECREATION AREA
Pool
SEE SEPARATE MAP FOR DETAILS
AC Transit #46
JOAQUIN MILLER PARK
City of Oakland
JOAQUIN MILLER ROAD
To Highway 13
11500 SKYLINE BLVD.
CRESTMONT DR.
Oakland
REDWOO EQUESTR ARENA
LEGEND
Hikers & Horses (Narrow Gauge)
Hikers & Horses (Fire Road)
Hikers Only
Bicycles Permitted (Not Permitted Elsewhere)
Skyline National Rec. Trail or Bay Area Ridge Trail
Paved Road
Creek or Stream
Resource Protection Area
Parking
Restrooms
Drinking Water
Phone
Information
Disabled Accessible
Archery Range
Equestrian Staging
Picnic
Reservable Picnic
Reservable Group Camp
Swimming Pool
Amphitheater
Bus Stop
SCALE
0 1/4 1/2 MILE
Mileages courtesy Hal MacDonald, EBRPD volunteer.

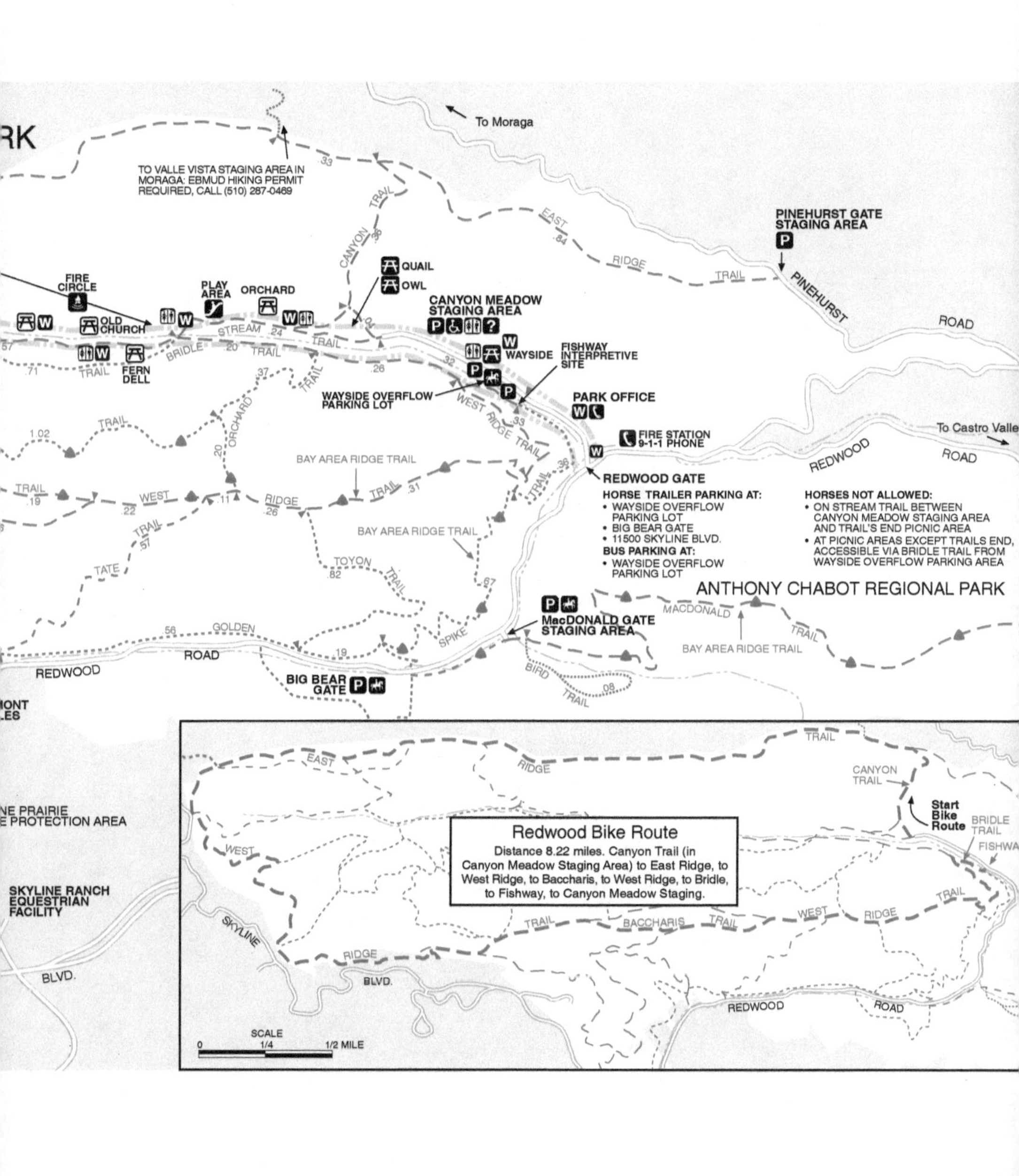
To Moraga
TO VALLE VISTA STAGING AREA IN MORAGA: EBMUD HIKING PERMIT REQUIRED, CALL (510) 287-0469
PINEHURST GATE STAGING AREA
PINEHURST
ROAD
FIRE CIRCLE
PLAY AREA
ORCHARD
QUAIL
OWL
OLD CHURCH
FERN DELL
CANYON MEADOW STAGING AREA
WAYSIDE
FISHWAY INTERPRETIVE SITE
WAYSIDE OVERFLOW PARKING LOT
PARK OFFICE
FIRE STATION 9-1-1 PHONE
To Castro Valley
REDWOOD GATE
HORSE TRAILER PARKING AT:
• WAYSIDE OVERFLOW PARKING LOT
• BIG BEAR GATE
• 11500 SKYLINE BLVD.
BUS PARKING AT:
• WAYSIDE OVERFLOW PARKING LOT
HORSES NOT ALLOWED:
• ON STREAM TRAIL BETWEEN CANYON MEADOW STAGING AREA AND TRAIL'S END PICNIC AREA
• AT PICNIC AREAS EXCEPT TRAILS END, ACCESSIBLE VIA BRIDLE TRAIL FROM WAYSIDE OVERFLOW PARKING AREA
ANTHONY CHABOT REGIONAL PARK
BAY AREA RIDGE TRAIL
MacDONALD GATE STAGING AREA
BIG BEAR GATE
REDWOOD ROAD
SKYLINE RANCH EQUESTRIAN FACILITY
BLVD.
Redwood Bike Route
Distance 8.22 miles. Canyon Trail (in Canyon Meadow Staging Area) to East Ridge, to West Ridge, to Baccharis, to West Ridge, to Bridle, to Fishway, to Canyon Meadow Staging.
Start Bike Route
SCALE
0 1/4 1/2 MILE

DIABLO'S SHADOW

MARK W. DANIELSON

NIGHT SHADOWS PRESS

This book is fiction. All names, characters, places, and incidents are products of the author's imagination or are used fictitiously. In other words, I made it all up. Any resemblance to actual events or locales or persons, living or dead, is coincidental.

First Edition

10 9 8 7 6 5 4 3 2 1

Printed in the United States of America

Library of Congress Catalog Card Number 2008928904

ISBN 978-0-9799167-5-5

Night Shadows Press, LLC
8987 E. Tanque Verde #309-135
Tucson, AZ 85749-9399

To Lyne

Special thanks to my wife Lyne for her unconditional support and tireless determination to make this book everything it is. I love you.

To Bob Middlemiss and Joan Hansen. Thank you for all you have done for me and other mystery writers.

To Ron and Michele Gerbrandt. Many thanks for your wonderful book jacket design.

To my brother Paul. Thank you for your beautiful photo of Mount Diablo from West Ridge Trail.

To my daughter Brooke. Thank you for taking the wonderful photo of me with Lucy.

Finally, many thanks to the East Bay Regional Parks Police for their assistance in researching this book, and to the East Bay Regional Parks District for letting me reproduce their map.

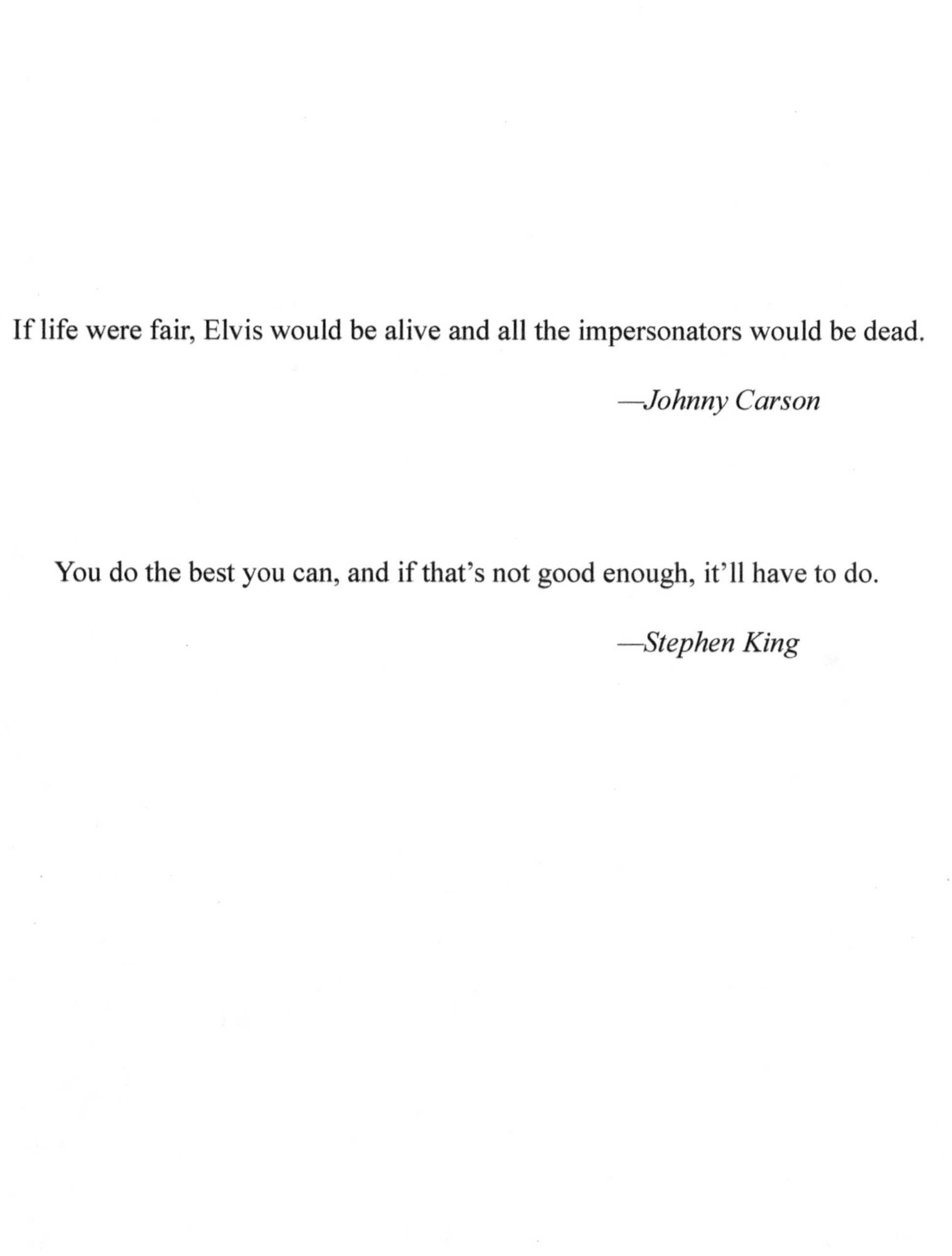

If life were fair, Elvis would be alive and all the impersonators would be dead.

—*Johnny Carson*

You do the best you can, and if that's not good enough, it'll have to do.

—*Stephen King*

ONE

The returning fog helped snuff the Sunol hills inferno. Slowly, the air cleansed, and on October tenth, the Golden Gate Bridge glistened in the morning sun. But an approaching cold front left Oakland's Redwood Regional Park jarringly deserted. The stalker grew restless. And then a young girl giggled...

Advertising executive Randy Connifer held his car door open for daughter Kerri. Though eager to spend time with her, he couldn't help fretting over his ten AM business meeting. He kissed her, closed the door, and ran to the other side of his shiny BMW. He had just enough time for their walk, drop her off at school, and then grab a latte before his business meeting. This account had the potential of elevating Bay View Advertising Agency to icon status. The belief pleased him very much.

His six-year-old rolled down her window and waved to her mom. In his mirror, Amanda Schaefer was waving back from her Oakland hills porch. She looked pretty as ever, but her heart was cold. Toward him, at least. He breathed easier after he pulled away from the curb.

Wednesday mornings with Kerri were always special, but today's crisp air would make their hike exceptional. He couldn't wait to get started. He smiled warmly at her. "It's a perfect day for a walk, isn't it?"

"It sure is, Dad." She watched out the window, randomly smacking her lips. "Can we get some cocoa afterwards?"

"We'll see."

She pressed the button and her window slid shut. The car quickly warmed once the draft was sealed. "I bet a lot of people will be taking pictures today, huh, Dad?"

"Maybe."

He contemplated his upcoming meeting. Two years of courting Wilson Industries was about to pay off. Slack times had hit his business hard, and a contract with Wilson could triple his income.

She toyed with her hair, just like Amanda. She also shared her mother's fine features. Lately, it seemed that everything Kerri did reminded him of his loss. Only a heartless woman could break their family apart like this. Her blue eyes smiled back at him. He rested his palm against her cheek and said, "Have I ever told you I love you?"

She giggled. "Only a million times."

"Then I guess I'm starting my second million." They both laughed at that one.

Skyline Boulevard traversed the Oakland hills, which predominantly ran east and west. From Amanda's house, the woods was to their right; San Francisco Bay their left. Thankfully, some influential people had the foresight to safeguard green space for future generations. Now, a series of connecting regional parks preserved much of the East Bay's forest.

Redwood Regional Park was their favorite, encompassing a labyrinth of trails. One of Kerri's most beloved spots was the bench on West Ridge Trail that overlooked Mount Diablo. Standing four thousand feet above sea level, the Devil's mountain was the tallest peak in the Bay Area. Diablo was one of the few to ever receive snowfall, but that was quite rare. Today, the mountain cast ominous shadows that pointed toward the park.

"Hey, Dad. Do you think there's any snow on Mount Diablo?"

He grinned. A series of cold fronts had brought brisk temperatures to the Bay Area, but while the damp air may chill bones, the climate remained deceptively mild. "Honestly, Kerri, I can't remember the last time it had snow."

She pouted, wrinkling her button nose, pondering his answer. "What about a rainbow? You think we'll see a rainbow today?"

More weather was on the way, but for now, the sky was clear. She loved rainbows, and must have painted three a week. "I suppose anything's possible, right?" She smiled at him enthusiastically. "Let me know if you see one, okay?"

The narrow, winding road led them to Redwood Regional Park. This magical place allowed him to share his love of nature with his daughter. He and Kerri had hiked all of the park's trails where ever-changing vistas made them forget that six million people lived on the bay side. Kerri had no idea how blessed she was living here.

The Skyline Gate entrance to Redwood Regional Park was curiously deserted. He had never been the first to arrive, and looked for signs that the park was closed. Not seeing any, he took the parking spot closest to East Ridge Trail and shut off the engine. "It looks like we have the park to ourselves." He climbed out and inhaled the eucalyptus scent, finding its effect more invigorating than a Starbuck's. "Let's go, kiddo."

"I'm right behind you, Dad."

A punch on his key fob locked his doors. After tucking it in his pocket, he took her hand and read the latest notice on the bulletin board.

> **MISSING FEMALE CHOW DOG!! ANSWERS TO "PURINA". FORTY POUNDS, BROWN FUR, NO COLLAR. LAST SEEN NEAR LAKE CHABOT, HEADING TOWARD REDWOOD REGIONAL PARK. PLEASE CALL 510-555-1745. REWARD!**

Randy empathized with the owner. Regardless of the circumstances, losing your pet was heartbreaking. Too bad people can't mimic a dog's unconditional love. He kneeled down, smiling as he zipped up Kerri's jacket. "How should we get to Eucalyptus Trail? East Ridge or Phillips Loop?"

She gave a dour expression to warn him he was in trouble, and then placed her hands on her hips to drive her point home. "You know where the lookout bench is, Dad. Let's take East Ridge all the way. I want to see snow."

"Sweetheart, the lookout bench faces Sunol. You can't see Mount Diablo from there."

"No, Dad. I know you can see it from there. I've seen it."

She was confused, but their time was limited, so rather than argue, he led her up the East Ridge fire trail that was wide enough for two vehicles. Kerri had walked every path, so there was no way he could cut their walk short without her knowing. Less than a half mile in, he checked his watch. "Kerri, I'm not sure we have enough time to make it to the bench. You have school and I have an important meeting."

She grabbed his hand and tugged hard. "Come on, Dad, we can make it. I *know* we can. Run!"

He broke into a trot, but quickly stopped. College football had ruined his knees. Now, even fast walks hurt. He nearly fell when she yanked on his arm again. After catching himself, he sensed something was hiding in the bushes. Oddly, there were no birds today. Not even a lizard. An eerie sensation came over him. He had never felt so paranoid.

She tugged one more time. "Come on, Dad. Walk faster." When he refused to speed up, she let go of his hand and sprinted up the trail.

"Kerri, wait!" She spun around, pouting, arms folded across her tiny chest. He caught up and took her hand, fighting the urge to spank her. "You know I can't run, and it's more fun walking together anyway. Let's see how far we get, okay?"

"Okay." She automatically assumed the lead.

Sunshine speared the forest, but the air smelled like rain. The Weather

Channel predicted it, but not until later this morning. The forest canopy obscured the western sky. This time of year, anything was possible. Hopefully, the rain would hold off until they were done.

Sandstone wrinkles caught his eye and he pointed them out. "This dirt reminds me of rhino skin. What do you think, Kerri?"

She glanced at the washed-out trail and shrugged. "I guess. Come on, Dad. Let's go."

He smiled, dreading what she'd be like as a teenager. But her determination came from being focused, not spoiled. Her teachers loved that quality in her. He thought about her mother and realized all three of them were over-achievers. But while high standards had benefits, they also created friction. Were all their disagreements fight-worthy? When Kerri kept tugging, he cupped his hand over his ear. "Listen. Do you hear that? It sounds like the beach."

Her rolling eyes reminded him he had asked her that question too many times. But for him, the leaves' resonance stirred up memories of his father saying, "Listen to the wind, Randy. When it blows like this, the forest becomes a waterless beach." Dad was right. This was the same sound he heard when he was a child. So why couldn't Kerri hear it? Probably because she knew the nearest beach was miles away, and they always crossed a bridge to get there.

Kerri huffed. "Can we *please* go now?"

Her plea brought him back and forced a smile. "All right, but stay close."

He tucked his hands in his pockets, watching her run ahead. It seemed there was no stopping her. Then again, there was no reason to.

Proceeding east, giant Monterey pine and eucalyptus trees yielded to live oaks and madrones. At the lower elevations, colossal redwood trees laid a needle carpet that nurtured lush ferns. Overgrown raspberry, Scotch broom, and poison oak shrubs obscured most of the park's views of Mount Diablo. It would take a while to reach the bench, and time was running out.

Kerri noticed something on the trail and squatted to inspect it. She picked up a twig and poked curiously at the matted gray object. "What's this, Daddy?"

He recognized it and immediately kicked it aside. "That's what's left of a mouse. I'm guessing an owl ate it. Don't ever touch stuff like that."

"You mean that's owl poop? *Yuk*!" She tossed the stick into the woods and yanked a Kleenex from her pocket. She wiped her hands, wadded the tissue, and handed it to him.

"Gee, thanks."

Suddenly that creepy feeling returned. Clouds stole the sun and narrowed their path. The rustling leaves and clanking branches sent a chill up his spine. He scanned the forest for anything unusual, but saw only foliage. Oddly, his daughter wasn't bothered in the least. "Kerri, we don't have time for hide-and-seek today, so stay close to me, okay?"

"Sure, Dad." She grinned and marched forward, staying a few steps in front of him.

Randy expected her to take off at any moment. That twinkle in her eyes announced her intentions. She couldn't help herself. She was like a thoroughbred in a starting gate. Besides, hide-and-seek was one of her favorite games, and she loved making him find her. He loved it, too. Just not today.

A skyward glance confirmed that storm was building. By the time he looked back, she had stretched her lead by twenty yards. "Kerri, wait." He limped along, thankful that she stopped to look at something. "Hey, cutie, what did you find?"

"Ladybugs. Look at them all. There must be hundreds of them."

Her enthusiasm eased his tension. He stood over her, mesmerized by the colony where hundreds of tiny beetles jockeyed for position on an old wooden post. "This is amazing," he said, bending over for a closer inspection. "I've never seen anything like it. Do you suppose they're having a ladybug convention?"

"No, Dad."

"I'm kidding." He brushed her golden hair aside and gently kissed her cheek.

"Don't, Dad! That's *gross*!"

Her sudden rejection made his face flush. *She's definitely her mother's daughter.* Years had passed since his wife kissed him. Sadly, their daughter didn't know what a loving relationship was like. Still, he missed everyone living together as a family.

Having Kerri a few hours a week was never enough. Why did he ever agree to Amanda's terms? Two visitations a week when both parents are working is absurd. His fists were bunching. He had to force them to relax. He smiled wryly and said, "What do you say we race to—?" She was kicking up dust before he finished his sentence. "Hey, cheater, I never said go."

She laughed over her shoulder, stretching her lead. "Too bad, so sad."

He groaned and took off jogging. She loved hiding behind trees and popping out to scare him, and even though he insisted there be no hide-and-seek today, she did it anyway. He saw her in his peripheral vision and pretended not to notice. "Oh, Kerri. Where are you? Come out, come out, wherever you are."

She darted out and tagged his rear end, giggling as only a little girl can. "Boo!"

He caught her with his massive arms, tickling her until her belly ached. Her baby-blue eyes made his heart swell. "I love you, ya know."

"I love you, too, Dad."

He released her and she took off like a rabbit. Hunched over with raised hands, he cackled like a green witch. "Come back here, you little munchkin. I'll get you, my pretty!"

She shrieked and tore down the roller-coaster trail. He stopped running after a few steps. It was now seven-twenty-five AM. At this rate, they might actually reach the bench. But then that sensation returned and he grew anxious. He cupped his hands over his mouth and shouted for her to wait, but as with most six-year-olds, his words fell on deaf ears.

TWO

Randy stopped at the intersection of Eucalyptus and East Ridge trails, expecting Kerri to pop out from behind a tree. For some reason, the feeling that someone was watching had left him. "Oh, Kerri. Come out, come out, wherever you are," he playfully sang again. When she didn't appear, he knew something was wrong.

The ocean crashed through the forest. The shadows were long gone. The air smelled musty. His meeting with Wilson Industries crossed his mind. "Kerri, don't you want to see the lookout bench? We've got to hurry if we're going to get there." Rattling branches answered.

It wasn't like her to stay hidden this long, and even less likely she could keep from laughing. He noticed a deer path above East Ridge Trail that at first glance, appeared to be an extension of the intersecting Eucalyptus Trail. He followed it up the embankment until it ran into a poison oak hedge. It had only taken her one encounter to learn about that nasty plant. Her ugly rash lasted for days, oozing serum from its blisters, driving her crazy with its itch. She remembered it well, and frequently pointed out the three-leafed plant. She wouldn't be hiding in there.

Fear churned his stomach. Amanda would hunt him down if anything happened to her daughter. He wandered in circles, angry, confused, screaming Kerri's name. Was she at the East Ridge lookout bench like they'd discussed, or did she wander down Eucalyptus Trail looking for a better hiding place? The park was immense. She could be anywhere.

His brain spun out of control. Kerri loved school and was never late. Worst-case scenarios tortured him as he replayed the events. She had vanished when she rounded the bend. There were no footprints or shreds of clothing, no cries for help, no signs of a struggle. She *must* have taken Eucalyptus Trail to Phillips Loop, and then headed back to the car. That's where he always told her to go if they ever got separated. His theory made sense.

He followed Eucalyptus Trail until the overgrown shrubs narrowed its path. The sky was menacing, and the air smelled like rain. Randy cupped his hands, yelling, "Kerri, you're scaring me. Please come out."

He stopped at the intersection of Eucalyptus Trail and Phillips Loop, some fifty yards below East Ridge Trail. The lookout was to the east; his car west. East Ridge was the fastest route to the Skyline Gate parking lot, but how could he have missed her? Surely she would have called to him. Even the wind couldn't mask her screams.

He looked for dog walkers and joggers, but today there were none. Sweat chilled his nape. How could he and Kerri be the only ones in the park? Where *is* everyone?

Her strong will convinced him she was more likely to go to the Sunol overlook than the parking lot. He headed east on Phillips Loop until it merged with East Ridge Trail. It was now eight-twenty AM. School started soon. *Wilson Industries!* He cursed out loud, tugging his hair. *Where is she?* He should have stayed on East Ridge. She must be scared to death!

He lumbered back to Skyline Gate where two other cars had parked. "Is anyone here? I need help! My daughter is missing!" But no one answered. He returned to the park, arguing with his brain. *She must be at the lookout bench. But he was just there. He would have seen her. So, where is she?*

Fright followed him up East Ridge Trail where, as before, she wasn't at the bench. His chest ached and he wheezed from the frigid air. He knelt before the bench, clasping his hands as though it was an altar. "Please, God, where is my angel? What have you done with her? She's my only child. Don't take her from me."

Dust blew in his eyes and he squeezed them shut, praying she would reveal herself. When he opened them, only the empty trail lay before him.

THREE

Jessica Caruso and Jerome Damon had no problem finding a parking spot at the Skyline Gate lot. There was only one other car there; a spotless metallic-silver BMW. The black couple who routinely biked through Redwood Regional Park before work was undeterred by today's ominous weather.

In minutes they were riding up East Ridge Trail, turning right onto Phillips Loop for variety. After the half-circle trail merged with East Ridge, they continued east for several miles before turning around. On their way back, they saw a well-dressed man staggering toward Skyline Gate. Jessica noticed his pale color as she passed him. The man never looked up.

"He doesn't look so good," she said to her boyfriend.

Jerome glanced over his shoulder with indifference. "He's probably hung over. Just keep going. He's not asking for any help. For that matter, he probably wants to be alone."

He couldn't believe it when Jessica braked to a stop. She had already rescued three alley cats. Did she really want to add a middle-aged man to her collection?

"Don't look at me that way, Jerome. That man's in trouble and I'm going to see if he needs anything. Would you have kept going if that was me?"

"Of course not. You're nothing like him."

"Save it, Jerome. Do what you want, but I'm going back to check on him."

* * * * *

Randy trudged through the tranquil setting like a string-puppet. He never went anywhere without his BlackBerry, but somehow he managed to leave it at home. Until today, his worst experience in the park was getting a bad case of poison oak. It was always safe here. So what happened today? Why would anyone stalk them? Why would anyone take Kerri? Two branches collided and he wished one would fall on him. He was too consumed by guilt to notice the bicyclists pull alongside.

Jessica noted Randy's streaked cheeks, odd gate, expensive clothes. He didn't belong here. She got off her bike and walked alongside him. "I don't mean to pry, but are you okay?" When he failed to acknowledge her, she grabbed her bottle and offered it. "Water?"

Randy eagerly accepted her gift. His first sip burned like whiskey, but the second went down smoother. He downed half the bottle before passing it back. He couldn't help noticing the contrast between her warm eyes and her companion's scornful look. "My daughter's missing," he said. "I've searched everywhere." He choked and turned away.

Jessica couldn't imagine what he was going through. She loved kids, and had taught elementary school until greed lured her into the high-tech world. "He needs help," she mouthed to Jerome. She scowled when his eyes narrowed. She looked back at Randy. "Maybe we can help. What's your daughter look like?"

Randy's stomach convulsed and he hunched over. He wasn't sure the well-toned woman was for real until her firm hand rested on his shoulder. He panted several breaths before saying, "Blonde—pink coat—"

Jessica nodded. "Have you called the police?"

His head barely shook. "I don't have my phone."

She gently rubbed his back. "So, your daughter's blonde, and wearing a pink coat and jeans. Is that right?" His head bobbed. "Great. What's her name? How old is she?"

"Kerri. She's only six. Very petite, very smart." He paused to wipe his nose. "She disappeared near East Ridge and Eucalyptus. That's the last time I saw her."

"Okay, I think I got it." She then raised her voice for Jerome to hear. "She disappeared near Eucalyptus and East Ridge. By the way, I'm Jessica and that's Jerome."

"I'm Randy."

She moved in closer, gazing into his eyes. "Randy, can you tell us what happened?"

He looked up and told his story. At times he was barely coherent. Other times, he broke down. A twinge shot through her when he said that someone had been watching them. She saw nothing when she looked around, but that didn't mean they were alone. Her hands smoothed her goose bumps while struggling to comprehend his words.

Jerome was more interested in watching her than listening to a stranger ramble. Why was she always meddling in other people's affairs? That was her one quality that drove him nuts. She couldn't save every loser, but she sure as hell tried. He checked his watch, goaded by the delay. Being late for work would cost him dearly.

She ignored Jerome, and instead hovered over Randy as if he was family. His color had improved, but his body was shaking uncontrollably. She offered him water again and he downed the last of it. Her sad eyes met his. "Randy, Jerome and I just rode Phillips Loop and East Ridge Trail and we didn't see a soul. Of course, that doesn't mean much. I mean, we were pretty focused on our riding." She paused, hoping for a response, but none came. "Do you have a picture of Kerri?"

He opened his wallet and handed over his only photograph.

"Oh, she's adorable," she said, regretting leaving her cell phone in her truck. She did so because the reception out here was so poor. Jerome's was a little better, but he refused to carry it because his job never left him alone. Jerome barely glanced at the photo when she held it up to him. She moved closer to Randy and returned the photo. "I'm sorry about Jerome," she whispered. To avoid suspicion, she casually backed away. "So, Kerri is wearing a pink coat. Is she in jeans or a skirt?"

Randy closed his eyes, picturing Kerri walking down her mother's stairs, Amanda waving in the background. His eyes shot open, and suddenly he was back in the forest.

Jessica reached for his arm, concerned. "Randy, are you okay? Talk to me."

As the apparition faded, he mopped his brow and blinked several times. Jessica repeated her question and this time he heard it. "Kerri's in jeans and wearing a pink coat."

"Well, that pink coat should make her easy to find. Why don't you wait here while Jerome and I check the trails? It shouldn't take us long."

Jerome grimaced. It was freezing outside. He needed a hot shower, not another bike ride. He had already been warned about being late for work. Why jeopardize his job over some guy who can't keep track of his daughter? "Uh, Jessica? Have you noticed the time?"

Randy wiped the dirt from his hands and stood up, towering over the bicyclist. "I understand your situation, Jerome. I had an important meeting too, but it doesn't look like I'll make it. Feel free to take off. And Jessica, thanks for caring."

"Now, hold on," Jessica said. "I've taken enough kids on field trips to know how quickly they can wander off. We're not going anywhere until we've looked for your daughter. Jerome, you sweep Phillips Loop and I'll check out the parking lot."

"But—"

"Just *do* it." She climbed on her bike and feigned Randy a smile as she pushed off with her right foot. "Keep the faith, Randy. We'll be back soon."

Jerome grabbed his handlebars and jammed his toe into the pedal's harness. If Jessica hadn't driven her truck today, he would have left a long time ago. He stomped hard on the pedal and sped off.

A pang stabbed Randy when they rode off. He remembered seeing his BlackBerry on the bathroom counter. He needed the cavalry, but had no way of calling them. Instead, he found himself relying on a couple of strangers to find his daughter. How pathetic was that? How could he have been so stupid? In spite of Jessica's good intentions, he hated depending on amateurs.

* * * * *

Randy read the frustration in the bicyclists' faces when they returned. Neither was speaking. Both looked angry. He felt bad for them. "Any luck?"

Jessica shook her head. "We were hoping she was with you."

Randy kicked a pinecone into the poison oak. Leaves scattered, but nothing flew out. "Thanks, anyway." He slid his hands in his coat pockets and started heading for Skyline Gate.

"Randy, wait," Jessica said. "Just because we didn't find her doesn't mean she's not around. How long has she been missing?"

"Since seven-forty." His meeting with Wilson Industries was in an hour. Was anyone at work concerned about his absence? Had anyone called Amanda? His chest pounded, fearing she was already heading his way.

"Seven-forty," she repeated. She then handed Jerome her car keys. "Would you please get my cell phone out of the glove box?"

Jerome's middle finger started to rise, but promptly retracted with her gaze. "This is the *last* time," he mouthed before heading down the trail.

After waving him off, Jessica spotted an elderly couple walking hand-in-hand, taking in the sights. She approached them and started briefing them on the situation. They looked at Randy with horrid expressions as they listened to her tale.

Randy ignored them at first, but he soon realized that there was no harm in their helping. He stood to greet them when Jessica led them over. She introduced them as Mr. and Mrs. O'Riley.

"We're so sorry," Mrs. O'Riley said to Randy, "but we haven't seen your daughter. She sounds precious. Can we help look for her?"

"Thank you. That would be very kind."

Jessica gently patted Randy's back. "Wait here for Jerome. And feel free to call whoever you need."

"Thanks, Jessica."

Once again, Randy found himself benched. It was torture hearing these strangers shout his daughter's name. Surely, Kerri must be wondering who they were. But why not show herself? A gust forced his eyes shut. The smell told him rain was imminent. He wished he had taken her to Starbuck's instead.

FOUR

Regional Parks Ranger Terry Arandale had just completed his patrol of nearby Sibley Volcanic Park and was now heading to Skyline Gate. He took pride in his parks, and loved working outdoors. Emptying garbage cans, restocking doggie poop bags, clearing fallen trees, and cleansing bathrooms was all part of his job. He stopped his pea-green pickup in front of the fire gate at East Ridge Trail, and was keying the lock when a bicyclist was speeding toward him.

Arandale wasn't amused. The park had rules against reckless conduct, and those rules were for everyone's benefit. Posted signs warned bicyclists about fines, and this guy just earned himself one. He forgot about unlocking the gate and waved the biker down, fairly certain the man's bicycle cost more than his car.

Jerome glared at the ranger. "What's the problem, man?"

"The *problem* is you were speeding, and now I'm citing you. Do you have any ID?"

Jerome eyed the man whose dirty green uniform and scuffed up work boots seemed more suitable for a trash hauler than a park ranger. He was about to say, "Are you serious?" when he realized this guy was a godsend. With him there, Jessica had no reason to hang around. "Look, a guy up the trail lost his daughter and needs your help. My girlfriend's with him, and I'm late for work. I was just coming to grab her phone from her truck. Can you take over so we can leave?"

Arandale twirled his key chain while evaluating the biker's sincerity. At least it was an original tale. Few people went to such lengths to avoid a ticket.

Jerome scanned the parking lot, waiting on the ranger's decision, Jessica's truck keys taut in his palm. It would be easy leaving Jessica behind. Surely someone would give her a ride.

Arandale pulled out his notebook. "How old is this missing child?"

"Beats me. Go ask her father." He said that, rubbing Jessica's key fob, expecting the ranger to speak. He didn't. "Look, man, I gotta go. The dude's about a half mile up East Ridge Trail. You can't miss him."

"Okay," Arandale said, thrilled to be the first on scene. Finding the girl could improve his personnel record. Maybe it could set him up for a pay promotion. "I'll tell you what. Throw your bike in the back and show me where they are and I'll forget about the ticket."

"But I need to—"

"Don't waste my time. Get in."

Jerome tossed his bike in the truck bed and climbed in, surprised the cab's only frill was a heater. He turned up the fan and directed the heat on him while the ranger opened the fire gate. He grinned at Arandale when the ranger joined him. "I'm freezing," he said. "I hope you don't mind my turning the heat up."

"Not at all." Arandale set his truck in gear and flung dirt with his tires.

* * * * *

Randy tossed acorns while he sat. He couldn't help wondering if Jessica's boyfriend had taken off without her. In some ways, he couldn't blame him if he did. Work *is* important. Sadly, his Wilson Industries account was probably history by now. A roaring engine interrupted his thought. He spotted the pickup and stood up, surprised to see Jerome sitting in the passenger seat. Jerome climbed out, unloaded his bike, and climbed back in the cab to keep warm.

Ranger Arandale got out, straightened his ball cap, and smoothed his dark green jacket. Following a brief introduction, he reached for his notepad and prepared to write. "I hear your daughter's missing. What happened?"

Randy briefed him, adding that Jessica and the O'Rileys were still searching the area. "Are the police on the way?"

Arandale cleared his throat. "Let's see if we can find her first."

"We've tried that and now bad weather is moving in. Don't you have a helicopter?"

Arandale spotted a black woman near the top of Eucalyptus Trail. From what Jerome had told him, this must be his friend Jessica Caruso, and the O'Rileys must be the older couple behind her.

Jessica bypassed the ranger and ran over to speak to Jerome. She waited until he rolled down the window. "What are you doing in that cab? Did you get my phone?"

"Not exactly. You see, I ran into Ranger Arandale, and—"

"You don't have my phone?"

Jerome frowned, angered over being interrupted. "As I was saying, that dude over there stopped me for speeding, and when I told him about the missing girl, he ordered me to get in. The good thing is now that he's here, we can leave."

Arandale overheard them and said, "Not so fast. We're not done yet."

Jessica ignored the ranger and scowled at Jerome. "We'll talk later," she said, clenching her teeth. She then turned to Randy and said, "I'm sorry, but we didn't see any sign of her."

Randy looked at Ranger Arandale. "You see? This is why we need professional help. Kerri's been missing almost two hours and every minute counts. Is anyone else on the way?"

The ranger studied the group. Everyone was staring at him. "I'll see what I can do."

Jerome pointed to his wrist watch. "Ah, ranger? Remember what I said about being late for work?"

Randy stared at the ranger, watching his eyes shift between him and Jerome. Clearly, Arandale wasn't used to making decisions. In fact, his interference had kept Jerome from retrieving Jessica's phone. "Ranger Arandale, weren't you going to call for help?"

Arandale swiftly tucked his notepad away and zipped up his coat. "Jessica, Jerome, you can leave now. Same with you, Mr. and Mrs. O'Riley. Thank you for your assistance this morning. Randy, if you'd please hop in my cab, we have some things we need to discuss."

After thanking the others, Randy climbed in. The warm cab felt great, but his body wouldn't stop trembling. "Why don't I draw you a picture, ranger?"

"That would be great," Arandale said, handing him his notepad.

Randy drew East Ridge and Eucalyptus trails. "This is where Kerri vanished," he said, marking the intersection with an "X." "She was running as fast as she could. You know how steep Eucalyptus is. If she ran down there, she could've fallen and rolled into the shrubs and we might not ever know it."

"Perhaps," he said, knowing that kids usually stayed within fifteen feet of a trail.

Randy looked over his shoulder and noticed a rake, a shovel, a chain saw, a gas can, and a roll of trash bags in the pickup bed. He then realized that Arandale had no badge or gun. His confidence was fading faster than the ranger's jeans. "What, exactly, do park rangers do?"

Arandale cleared his throat. "Actually, that varies from park to park. For example, national park rangers are sworn law enforcement officers—"

"I don't care about national park rangers. What do *you* do?"

"As I was trying to explain, unlike national or city park rangers, East Bay Regional Park rangers maintain and patrol the parks. But I assure you, I'm qualified to handle this situation."

"Listen, ranger, either you call for assistance or let me use your radio."

"Mr. Connifer, I've been involved in ten searches, and every one turned out fine except for some doctor who committed suicide and didn't want to be found. He was our toughest case, but after two weeks of searching, we still found him."

Randy gazed at the ranger in disbelief. He leaped from the truck to calm himself. His pounding head made him desperately want to break something. He spotted a pine cone and sent it flying with his foot. He regretted not asking one of the residents near Skyline Gate to call 911 for him. *Christ!* Why did he think Arandale could help? Parks Police vehicles were white, not pea-soup green. Why didn't he remember the Park District maintained its own police force? Now the mountain peaks were obscured, and it would take a miracle for their helicopter to show.

Arandale gave Randy a moment before stepping from his truck. His physical size and emotional state made him uneasy. The ranger stood to one side, waiting for Randy to acknowledge him, and then quietly said, "I called Dispatch. The Parks Police are on the way."

"Thanks." Randy was still fuming when he said that.

The ranger rubbed his neck, checking out the deer trail across from Eucalyptus. "Did anyone look up here?"

"That's the first place I went and it dead-ends in a poison oak bush. She's not in there."

Randy's affirmation piqued his interest. It almost seemed he didn't want him to check. "You don't mind if I take a look, do you?"

"Have at it," he said, tossing his hands in the air and climbing back in the cab.

The lanky ranger climbed the five-foot bluff above East Ridge Trail and moved inward. The trail ended abruptly, just as he was told, its leafy carpet giving up no clues. But kids could be unpredictable. They had done some crazy things, even knowing they could get hurt. Frankly, it was amazing that anyone made it past adolescence. A moment later, he joined Randy in the truck. "Like you said, Randy, it's a dead end." He quickly regretted his choice of words.

"My daughter's a good kid, ranger. I could always count on her hiding two or three times on a hike, but she'd always show herself after a few seconds. Most of the time I saw her poking her head out. That's why this scares the hell out of me. Something's happened to her. She isn't hiding."

Randy's fearful tone surprised him. He was no longer playing macho man. Now, his voice was cracking. "Like I said, we'll find her." He watched the first rain drops smack the dirt.

"What's the matter?"

"I was just wondering how this road's gonna fare. Vehicles on wet dirt roads can cause serious erosion."

"I can't believe you, ranger. My daughter's missing and you're worried about a goddamn road?" Randy silently counted to ten. "What's next?"

"Well, hopefully the helicopter will sweep the area while the police do a preliminary search. If Kerri's still missing, they'll dispatch every available park employee and do a more thorough search. Of course that pretty much shuts the park down, which is one reason I hesitated to call."

"Yeah, thanks for sharing. So, why repeat the same steps? Why not do a full search now? Kerri's missing, and time's running out."

Arandale rested a hand on Randy's shoulder. "We have procedures to follow, Mr. Connifer, but I promise you, we won't stop until we find your daughter."

FIVE

Officer Hector Rodriquez of the Regional Parks Police was patrolling Redwood Road near the Upper San Leandro Reservoir when Dispatch directed him to meet Park Ranger Arandale. The ranger was a half mile east of Skyline Gate on East Ridge Trail. A child was reported missing. Rodriquez acknowledged Dispatch, curious whether it was a runaway. Most of the time, reports like this came on sunny days during weekends or summer. Why wasn't this kid in school?

Using his call sign, 1L30, Rodriquez advised Dispatch he would arrive in ten minutes. Dispatch acknowledged this and informed him that Eagle 5, the Parks Police helicopter, was now airborne. Dispatch didn't assign Rodriquez an emergency response code, so he drove at normal speed without any flashing lights or siren. His windshield wipers easily cleared the rain, but he expected it would get heavier as the day progressed.

Soon, Dispatch requested he switch to TAC 6, the Regional Park's maintenance frequency, where Ranger Arandale was expecting his call. He made the switch, but didn't bother calling the ranger because he was already pulling into Skyline Gate. He proceeded through the open gate and drove up the fire trail. Shortly after, his white Ford Crown Victoria bottomed out in a large pothole. He cursed under his breath and got out to check for damage. The car was fine, but the pothole infuriated him. They fixed it every year, and every year it washed out again. He climbed back in the car and proceeded east, spotting the ranger's pickup soon after. Arandale met him at his window.

"That was a long ten minutes," Arandale said, raising his collar to the rain.

Rodriquez shrugged, trying to place the ranger's face. It dawned on him that he was the guy who was constantly offering advice during their last search. The impression he left wasn't good. Hopefully this wouldn't be a repeat performance. "Dispatch says you have a missing child. What's going on?"

Rain streamed down Arandale's back. He considered turning his ball cap around to divert the water, but he couldn't stand the connotations associated with wearing a hat backwards. Rodriquez' tart expression confirmed he remembered him. Well, those feelings were mutual. After all, this was the officer that scolded him in front of his peers. *"Let us do the investigating,"*

Rodriquez had said. He remembered it like it was yesterday; those words still searing his brain. But so far, Rodriquez had said nothing about the past. Instead, he stared at him, waiting. Arandale shoved his resentment aside and said, "We have a missing six-year-old female. Her father's in my truck. Come on, I'll introduce you."

Rodriquez stepped out into the rain and followed.

* * * * *

Randy watched their blurry images grow, and rolled his window down when they neared.

"Mr. Connifer, I'm Officer Rodriquez. Would you mind stepping into my car?"

"Sure."

Once inside, the officer removed a notepad from his shirt pocket that was identical to Arandale's. Either these people had short memories or the Regional Parks department supplied them with the tiny books. The officer didn't notice him staring.

Rodriquez briefly looked his way. "First of all, I'm sorry about your daughter. I'm also sorry to get you muddy, but I prefer speaking in my vehicle where I can use the computer. May I see your driver's license?"

Randy fumbled through his wallet and handed it over.

"Thank you." After examining it, the officer punched the information into his computer and found Randy Connifer's Shepherd Canyon address handily close to Skyline Gate. Seeing no wants or warrants, he handed the license back. "Mr. Connifer, I know you've told Ranger Arandale your story, but I need to hear it first-hand."

"That's fine, but call me Randy."

"Very well, Randy. Please continue."

Rodriquez listened, trying not to analyze, but Randy's tale seemed full of holes. Surely he knows that you can't see Mount Diablo from East Ridge Trail, and that it hasn't snowed there since last year. And why would he let his daughter run ahead like that? For that matter, why would such a young girl be out so early? He'd reserve those questions for later. "It's hard to believe there was no one else in the park," he said.

"I know. I've never seen it so deserted."

"You didn't see any dog walkers or joggers?"

"Not a one. Kerri and I had the park to ourselves. It was bizarre."

"Was your daughter angry with you? Any reason why she'd run and hide?"

"Kerri didn't run away. Like I told Ranger Arandale, she had her heart set on getting to the lookout bench. I tried explaining to her that you can't see Mount Diablo from there, and why it wouldn't have any snow, but she refused to listen. I was moving too slow for her, and she knew it was getting late, so she ran ahead. There was no way she was going to leave without proving me wrong. I searched the area as soon as she disappeared, and again while a biker couple checked East Ridge, Eucalyptus, and Phillips Loop trails. As you already know, everyone came up empty."

Rodriquez listened, scribbling a reminder to find two bicyclists named Jessica and Jerome. But right now he needed to concentrate on the search. "Where is Kerri's mother? Does she know about this?"

"I haven't told her. Amanda and I aren't exactly on speaking terms, and I left my cell phone at home. If I had it with me, I would've called 911 myself. It's been a really bad day."

Rodriquez empathized, but also sensed there was more to this than what Randy was admitting. He reached into his pocket and gave Randy his cell phone. "Care to call your wife?"

"Not yet. I have limited visitation rights as it is, and she can be a real bitch. Trust me; I'm better off doing this alone and telling her about it afterwards."

The officer scribbled more notes. Husband and wife don't get along. Possible motive—limited visitation rights. When he finished, he looked up again. "Did Ranger Arandale mention that we've found every lost child?"

"He did, but who's to say Kerri's still here?" Suddenly, Rodriquez furrowed his brow. "Think about it, officer. She's been missing for hours, and my car is locked. If Kerri was waiting for me near the street, anyone could have picked her up. I'm not implying that she's been kidnapped; only that someone may have dropped her off at school or my house or—" He stopped talking when Rodriquez closed his notepad. "You know, I hate to be rude, but we're wasting a lot of time yakking when we should be searching."

The officer began typing on his computer keyboard. Experience had shown that making random inputs tended to keep his suspects on edge. After a few minutes, he cleared the computer screen and stared out the windshield. "Did anyone check out that deer trail?"

"Yeah, the ranger and I both looked, and it dead-ends into poison oak. Trust me—she's not there."

Rodriquez hesitated, and then opened his door. "I'll be right back." He got out and ran up the embankment, slipping twice. He stopped at the top to scan the area. Water trickled down ruts, rain splattered off leaves; something rustled in the shrubs. He looked around, and when he couldn't see anything, went back to his car for his rain gear and shotgun.

Randy grew anxious and rolled down his window. "What's going on?"

"Nothing. Stay in the car." He went back and spread the shrub with his shotgun barrel. Two dark eyes stared back. "Ranger Arandale, get up here!" He reached in and grabbed it before it got away.

Kerri! Randy got out and followed the ranger up the trail. Neither expected to see a two-foot gopher snake struggling in the officer's grip. "You bastard! You act like you found my daughter and then wave a goddamn snake in the air? What's wrong with you?"

Rodriquez calmly released his catch. "I thought I asked you to stay in the car."

Randy was burning up inside. "Why would you do that? You're sick, Rodriquez!"

The officer wanted to explain that his joke was meant to give Ranger Arandale a dose of his own stupidity. Clearly, it backfired. "I'm sorry, Randy. I didn't mean to hurt you, or have you see any of this. That's why I wanted you to stay in the car. The real reason I called for Ranger Arandale was to see if these boot prints matched the ones on his feet." He gazed at Arandale's boots and then at the ranger's face. "I don't suppose you had anything to do with these broken branches, did you, ranger?"

Arandale's face flushed. "Didn't Randy tell you we already searched this area?"

"He did," Rodriquez said, wishing the snake was a rattler so it could bite the ranger. The trampled grounds made it impossible to tell if a kid or kidnapper went in there. "Both of you wait here." Rodriquez moved deeper into the trail, forging through the shrubs. Rain dripped down his neck, soaking his khaki shirt. He flipped his hood over his head, but he was already chilled. Another twenty feet convinced him Kerri wasn't there. He turned back and reassumed the lead. "Like you said—there's nothing in there."

When he reached the bluff, he looked back at Arandale's pickup. He couldn't have parked it in a worse spot. Thanks to the ranger, the trail was scored with tire tracks and footprints. The rain was erasing whatever other evidence remained. He looked at Randy. "So your daughter was running down East Ridge Trail when she disappeared?"

"That's right."

"Did either of you see any footprints?"

"No. The ground was dry and hard when she disappeared."

The officer sighed. "Why don't you both wait in my car? There's no point in everyone getting soaked. I'll be right back."

Rodriquez back-tracked toward Skyline Gate looking for anything that would confirm the girl had gone inside Redwood Regional Park. Pine needles floated past his mud-caked shoes, but there was no sign of a child's footprints. He returned to his patrol car where Arandale sat to his right; Randy behind him. He addressed the park ranger first. "I realize you're not a professional tracker, but in the future you might want to start with looking for footprints." Having sufficiently deflated Arandale's ego, he added, "Tell you what, ranger, why don't you wait in your truck while I talk to Mr. Connifer?"

"Sure."

Rodriquez waited until the ranger was gone before addressing Randy. "Come on up front, Randy. It'll be more comfortable for both of us." Randy did as requested, scraping mud off his shoes before getting in. "Do you have a picture of your daughter?"

"I do," Randy said, digging into his wallet. He gingerly handed it over.

Rodriquez smiled genuinely. "I recognize the Tilden Park merry-go-round. My kids love that place. I see Kerri chose the zebra. My daughter loves the frog. Do you mind if I hang onto this? I promise you'll get it back."

"No problem." Randy's pulse quickened while Rodriquez re-checked his notes. Was he comparing stories? Maybe setting a trap? *Watch what you say.* "So, how long before the search party gets here?"

"Soon," he said, concerned about the close proximity of Randy Connifer's house to the park. Did his daughter go there when her father didn't show up at his car? That seemed unlikely since she lived with her mom. He deliberated on that before presenting his next question. "Why was Kerri with you so early in the morning? Doesn't she have school?"

"As I've repeatedly said, this was my time to have her. We walk here every Wednesday morning unless the weather is really ugly."

The officer looked through his rain-splattered windshield wondering what Randy's definition of "really ugly" was. Then again, it was dry earlier. "So, how often do you see your daughter?"

Randy shifted in his seat and scratched his head. *Rodriquez is fishing. Count to ten. Think before speaking.* "Same answer as before. We're together every Wednesday morning, and every other weekend," he said, and then added, "That's from my wife's court order, not by choice." He didn't mean to say that. It just came out. Blurred Monterey pines swayed. Wind buffeted the windows. Rain hammered the roof.

Rodriquez didn't comment. "Does your wife work?"

"Full time."

"Then how did you end up with such limited visitation rights?"

Randy's face tensed. "It just worked out that way."

"Did you ever hurt Kerri?"

"No, never. I love my daughter, and miss her terribly. We both love this park, so we make the most of our time together by taking walks here. This is our special place. We often come here on weekends, too, because it's so amazing. In fact, we were here last Sunday."

Rodriquez jotted that down. "How long since you separated from your wife?"

"Almost two years now."

"Wow, two years? That's a long time to be in limbo. Any chance of reconciliation?" Randy shook his head, no. "Then why haven't you gotten a divorce?"

"No offense, but that's really none of your business. Can you please call the chopper to find out where they are?"

Rodriquez glanced at the sky, wondering how a helicopter could conduct a search under such dismal conditions. He had worked several child custody cases at the Oakland Police Department before getting hired by the Parks Police. He knew that seven out of ten child abductions were committed by family members. So, was this missing child report a red herring to cover his hiding her somewhere? Did he intentionally leave his cell phone at home to make the delayed call for help seem more convincing? It seemed unlikely that a high-level executive would leave his electronic brain at home, especially when he had such an important meeting. Randy seemed tense, and at times defensive. Even so, he did seem resolved to find his daughter. Rodriquez wasn't sure what to make of him at this point. "I'm sure that you and Kerri frequented the park, but did you really come here every Wednesday morning?"

"Like clockwork. This park is like her third home. Amanda and I started bringing her here when she was just a few months old. You could say she knows this place like the back of my head."

"You mean hand."

"No, head. She was riding in my back pack, so my head's all she could see." Randy said that, expecting a smile from the officer. Instead, he got a blank stare. "For Christ's sake, Rodriquez, it was a joke."

The officer politely grinned and said, "Go on."

Randy sighed, running his fingers through his thick hair. "My point is that Kerri grew up here, and she probably knows the trails better than you. That's why I'm sure something happened to her."

The officer knew better than to pick at his hangnail, but did it anyway. He stopped when he saw Randy staring. "What about hiding places? Does Kerri have any favorites?"

Christ! "Kerri is *not* hiding! What's wrong with you people? She's never done anything like this before. She loves going to school, and now she's missing it. So where in the hell is your search party? Am I the only one interested in finding her?"

"They'll be here, Randy. Bear with me. Just a few more questions. Where does Kerri go to school?"

"Joaquin Miller Elementary. She had perfect attendance last year. Why?"

"I need it for my report. How well does she handle your family situation?"

"She hates it, but accepts it. Think about it. No one wants their parents to separate. Deep down, I'm sure she wants her mom and me to get back together, but that will never happen. What's important, though, is that she's handling it, and she knows that we both love her."

Rodriquez paused, recalling the day his father ran out on them. He still hated him, even though his mother insisted they were better off without him. Ten years later, he arrested his father in a bar fight. His answering the call was a fluke, and yet somehow he knew it was inevitable. Rodriquez shook off the memory and said, "Some kids harbor tremendous resentment after a breakup. Sometimes they'll do crazy things just to get attention. Granted, it's flawed logic, but that's the way they think. Has Kerri ever run away before?"

"I keep telling you she's not like that. She doesn't have any issues with me or her mother. Don't you get it? All she wanted to do was get to the Sunol lookout bench."

"Randy, kids younger than Kerri have hid out just to get away from their parents. They usually don't stay long—just long enough to clear their heads. And what better place to do it; especially if they know the park?"

"Why doesn't anyone believe me? Why aren't you doing something to find her? Every minute can make the difference between life and death. We were having a great time. She was full of life this morning. She played hide-and-seek, and was unrelenting in her quest to see snow. I'm begging you; please get on with the search."

Broken codes crackled over the radio. Rodriquez adjusted his squelch and volume. "Those calls concern your search. They'll be here soon." He tugged at his crotch to adjust his rain pants. It didn't help. "Don't take this wrong, Randy, but when Kerri was staying with you, did she ever call her mom asking to go home early?"

"Not that I know of, but she called me plenty of times to complain about her mother. I never gave it much thought, though, because Amanda's a good mom, and kids always complain about whoever's setting the rules. I'm sure it goes both ways."

Rodriquez grinned. "I know what you mean. Before my dad left, he spanked me for no good reason, so I got mad and took a swing at him. Then Mom got involved and all hell broke loose. To this day, I bear some scars from my daddy's belt buckle. I promised myself that when I grew up that I'd do something to prevent child abuse. As strange as it sounds, I suppose my dad was responsible for my choosing this career."

Randy nodded, but his uncaring expression suggested that Rodriquez had crossed the line by sharing his story. After all, Randy didn't come to him for a social chat. Still, everything Randy had said was suspect. "Going back to Kerri, have the two of you ever walked to the park from your house?"

"Just once. It's farther than it looks, especially for a little girl. Besides, I don't like walking along Skyline Boulevard. There's just too much traffic for a street without sidewalks."

"Yeah, I know what you mean." *Except that a few blocks doesn't seem far for a girl who walks endlessly in the park.* The officer jotted a note and closed the page. "But since you've done it and your car was locked, isn't it possible Kerri could have walked to your house?"

Randy adamantly shook his head. "She's pretty independent, but I don't believe she would willingly leave the park without me. She was supposed to be in school, remember? Besides, she was no more than two hundred feet in front of me when she disappeared. The only way she could have gotten past me was by taking Eucalyptus to Phillips Loop, and she knew that any delays would make her late for school." He scraped his shoes together and a mud clump fell on the floor mat. He casually pushed it aside.

Rodriquez sneezed into his sleeve. "Sorry about that." He dabbed his nose and tucked his kerchief away. "Two final questions. When you went to the parking lot, did you see anything unusual, like a panel van, or maybe a car with deep tinted windows?"

"No. We've been over this at least three times. The parking lot was empty when we arrived. When I went back to look for Kerri, a SUV and a car were parked near mine. I'm sure those vehicles belonged to Jessica Caruso and the O'Rileys."

"Okay. And Kerri's mother goes by Amanda Schaefer?"

"That's right," he said, and then spelled out her name to make sure the officer got it right. "You see, Amanda never officially changed her name after we married, but that's another story. Anyway, it's been two questions. Now, where's that chopper?"

SIX

The easterly wind howled. The sun was a distant memory. Swirling rain drenched the ground. The day had barely started. Rodriquez told Randy to stay put, and then went over to Arandale's truck. The ranger lowered his window. "I had my radio turned down," Rodriquez said. "Have you heard anything from Eagle 5?"

Arandale stayed away from the window to keep dry. "Dispatch reported Eagle 5 was on its way twenty minutes ago, but I doubt they'll be able to do much in this weather."

Rodriquez kept his back to the wind and keyed the mike that was anchored to his shoulder. "Dispatch, 1L30; request Eagle 5 meet me on TAC 4."

"1L30, Dispatch; roger."

Seconds later, the Parks Police helicopter's observer was radioing Rodriquez, his voice jerky from turbulence. "This is Eagle 5; what can we do for you?"

Rodriquez was amazed they were airborne. "Eagle 5, request you sweep Redwood Park from Skyline Gate. We have a missing six-year-old female, last seen near East Ridge and Eucalyptus Trails. Her name is Kerri. She's wearing a bright pink jacket."

"Eagle 5, roger. ETA, six minutes. Eagle 5, out."

The officer smiled. "Randy will be pleased. I'd better get back to him."

"I'll be here." Arandale quickly rolled his window up.

Rodriquez was still smiling when he climbed in his patrol car. "Good news, Randy. The Parks Police helicopter will be here shortly. They'll blast the area with loudspeakers asking Kerri to come out where they can see her. Their speakers are so loud that every girl named Kerri will be staring at the sky." He paused, expecting a smile, but it didn't happen. He cleared his throat and moved on. "Eagle 5 will also scan the area with their Forward Looking InfraRed equipment. FLIR creates video images from heat, so they can spot anything with a pulse."

"Finally, some good news. So why did it take so long to get help?"

Before he could answer, the silver aircraft swept overhead at treetop level, blades beating the air, blinking lights igniting the sky, its speakers so loud they could trigger an avalanche in snow country. Eagle 5 searched for twenty minutes before they needed fuel. They said they would return. Rodriquez acknowledged this and said, "How's your FLIR working today?"

"Sorry, but our FLIR is crated, waiting to be sent off for maintenance. We'll see what we can do when we get back, though. See you in a bit. Eagle 5 out."

Rodriquez sighed. Time was running out and the weather was getting worse. "I'm sorry, Randy. You have every right to be upset. We'll work through the night if we have to, but we'll find your daughter."

"I hope so. How long before the ground search begins?"

"I'm guessing ten minutes," Rodriquez said, running out of things to say. He grabbed his thermos and raised it to Randy. "Want some coffee?"

"No thanks." But the inviting fragrance hit him when Rodriquez unscrewed the cap.

The officer smiled. "Let me know if you change your mind. I've got plenty."

"Actually, it might do my throat some good." Randy accepted the cup. "Thank you."

"Any time." Rodriquez settled into his seat, enjoying his beverage. A moment later, he turned on the defroster to clear the windows. The fan was loud, so he turned it down a notch. "How much do you know about FLIR, Randy?"

"Not much."

"Well, the US Army developed it to seek out the enemy, but then they released it to the police departments. Heck, now even some television crews have it. These days there's nowhere to hide, day or night."

Randy understood that the officer was doing his best to be cordial, but he needed action, not words, to comfort him. His skin crawled when no one showed up. "Officer Rodriquez, we've already done two preliminary searches; why not call in some search-and-rescue teams?"

"You must be exhausted, Randy. Why don't you let us handle the search? I'll take you back to your car. Go home before you catch pneumonia."

"No thanks. I'm not going anywhere until we find her."

"Suit yourself, but you'll have to wait in your own car. I need to organize the search."

Randy closed his eyes and tossed his head back, feeling insignificant. "How long before you bring in search dogs?"

"Not until we complete a hasty search. You see, our dog handlers are all volunteers, so we have to be certain we need them. But don't worry. All of these people are certified in search-and-rescue operations. In fact, Alameda County is fortunate to have some of the best."

"That's great, but what if Kerri isn't here? What if someone kidnapped her and took off over the hill? Can their dogs tell that? Can they work in the rain?"

Rodriquez tilted his head, finding the notion peculiar. "You don't think Kerri's here?"

"I never said that. All I know is Kerri never showed herself to the helicopter, and no one's found a trace of her. Think of all the time we've lost. If someone kidnapped her, she could be half way to Nevada by now."

Rodriquez watched Ranger Arandale sitting in his truck. He remembered him, all right. Why is it that his decisions always cost them time? Perhaps the ranger tried too hard, or maybe had too many jobs to do. Whatever the case, he needed remedial training.

Then he measured Randy's comment. Was Randy really saying *don't* bring in the search dogs because they'd be wasting their time in Redwood Park? The radio chatter increased as the search party converged on Skyline Gate. Rodriquez put his car in gear and released the parking brake. "Well, it's time I got busy. Shall I run you back to your car, or do you prefer walking?"

"I'd appreciate a ride. And thanks again for the coffee."

Rodriquez took the empty cup and set it aside. Five minutes later he was pulling up next to the silver BMW. "Keep your cell phone handy when you get home. I'll call you when we have some news."

"Thanks for the ride." Randy pulled his coat over his head and stepped out into the rain. After sliding in his spotless car, he noticed his muddied floor mat. Oddly, it didn't matter. In fact, nothing mattered anymore. Not his ruined clothes, nor Wilson Industries. Even his flashy car couldn't arouse him. As he sat there, his life seemed as empty as his passenger seat. Kerri was out there, all right. As the temperatures continued to drop, he thought about the deer beds he pointed out to her last Sunday. He had told her that the tall grass beds insulated and hid fawns. Hopefully she remembered that and made a shelter for herself. Granted, hiding in a grass bed would make her harder to find, but at least she should be able to survive.

SEVEN

Officer Hector Rodriquez glanced at the Skyline Gate parking lot as he drove back into the park. Surprisingly, Randy's BMW was still there. Randy was cold and damp when he dropped him off. Given a similar situation, Rodriquez would be darting home to take a shower. So, what was keeping Randy there? Was he expecting a signal from someone or was it something else? Considering his suspicions, the officer determined that having Randy nearby might be beneficial. Rodriquez backed his car out of the fire trail and stepped from his car.

The Skyline Gate parking lot had become a collage of white police cars, red fire engines, and green maintenance trucks. There were so many vehicles that they spilled onto Skyline Boulevard. Randy heard someone tapping at his window and rolled it down. He wasn't expecting to see Officer Rodriquez again. "Sorry, officer, I was just leaving."

"Actually, I realized I had an extra poncho in the back of my car and thought you might want to join me." He handed it over before Randy could say no.

"Yeah. Thanks." Randy shut off his engine and slid the poncho over his head. The garment made it harder to hear, but he wasn't in the mood for conversation. He followed the officer to a red Ford Expedition where a white-haired man was studying a map under a raised tailgate.

"Randy Connifer, I'd like you to meet Fire Chief Hagley."

Randy studied the chief's face, wrinkled from years of squinting. His clear eyes suggested wisdom and experience.

The fire chief gripped Randy's hand and firmly shook it. "I'm sorry about your daughter," he said. "Would you show me where she disappeared and where you've looked?"

"Sure." Randy took the grease pencil, circled the intersection of Eucalyptus and East Ridge Trails, and pointed out the previously searched areas. He felt Rodriquez peering over his shoulder while he described his ordeal, aware the officer was listening for inconsistencies.

Chief Hagley took note, formulating ideas. He began sectioning the park before the words stopped.

"What are you doing?" said Randy.

"Assigning areas of probability so we can focus on the most likely zones. Any chance your daughter would go beyond the lookout bench on East Ridge Trail?"

"None. She knew how much time we had, and I specifically told her we couldn't go any farther. I truly expected to find her there, struggling to see Mount Diablo. She must be somewhere between Eucalyptus and the overlook."

"Then that's where we'll concentrate our search." Hagley slid the map in his truck, closed the tailgate, and turned his attention to Rodriquez. "Everyone's meeting at Ranger Arandale's truck. I'll let him know we're on the way. Mind if Randy rides with you?"

"Not at all. In fact, I was counting on it."

EIGHT

Officer Rodriquez was about to step into his car when he spotted another Parks Police officer. He looked over at Randy. "I'll be right back. Wait in the car."

"Sure thing."

Once Rodriquez left, Randy cracked his window open to hear. Rodriquez had mentioned something about Kerri, but he couldn't hear the other officer's response. He slouched in his seat, increasingly frustrated. When Rodriquez glanced his way, he waved back at him. Almost immediately, Rodriquez was returning to his patrol car.

Rodriquez got in and fastened his seat belt without sharing any information. Heavy rain hammered his squad car as they drove back up the fire trail. His meeting with the other officer took longer than expected. By the time they arrived, Fire Chief Hagley was standing atop the bluff addressing the search party.

"...The rain's supposed to continue for at least two days, and the temperature's dropping fast," Hagley said. "For the next twelve to twenty-four hours, it's expected to remain in the low thirties, so if you think you're cold, imagine how Kerri feels. While it's possible she's hiding in a makeshift den, there's an equally good chance she's unconscious.

"We'll use Eucalyptus Trail as the dividing point. Half of you search the Diablo side; the other half the bay. Limit your search to fifty feet either side of East Ridge and Eucalyptus trails. Let's meet back here when you're finished and we'll re-evaluate. If there are no questions, let's get moving."

The search party divided into two groups and marched off in opposite directions. They knew what to do. They had all done it before. Officer Rodriquez would remain the Incident Commander, or "IC", until Field Lieutenant Donovan could assume command. Rodriquez requested the Oakland Police check out Kerri's school, contact her mother if Kerri wasn't there, and, if able, search both homes. He also requested that Dispatch issue an AMBER alert on the possibility that Kerri was abducted off the street. Lacking a vehicle description wouldn't hinder the media attention given to a lost child. Nothing can be ruled out in a case like this. He glanced at Randy.

"Let's retrace your route while they conduct their search. Show me everything, and don't hold back any details."

"Let's go."

Randy's heels lifted from his shoes as he trudged through the muck. Jamming his toes forward increased the pain, but at least he kept his loafers on. He stopped at the spot where he believed they were being watched, and also where Kerri had played hide-and-seek. Rodriquez marked those areas with yellow tape.

The wind repeatedly flipped Randy's poncho up. He looked up, silently cursing God for showing no mercy. But thoughts of Kerri overrode his personal discomfort. She was out there somewhere, alone, and frightened. Compared to hers, his situation wasn't so bad. He heard grinding rotor blades and saw Eagle 5 pass overhead so low he feared it would crash. Less than one hundred feet separated the tree tops and the clouds, but still they flew. Minutes later, Eagle 5 returned for another pass. "I have to give those guys credit," he said to Rodriquez. "I really didn't expect to see them again."

"Yeah, well, they're giving it their all. Frankly, no sane pilot would fly in these conditions. I can't imagine them sticking around long."

Rodriquez' radio was breaking up. Eagle 5 was trying to reach him.

"Still—sign—th— girl," Eagle 5 said.

Rodriquez adjusted his radio and keyed his mike. "Eagle 5, 1L30; say again?"

"1L30—gle 5. No sign of the girl. Repeat. No—of the girl."

"Roger, Eagle 5; 1L30 copies no sign of the girl." He turned to Randy. "That doesn't mean they won't find her."

"I know."

"Eagle 5, any change in your FLIR status?"

"Affirmative. It's installed and functioning, but so far, no hits."

"Copy, no hits." Rodriquez looked at Randy again, explaining that FLIR favors cold temperatures because it enhances the infrared contrast. "An observer can zoom in and identify a target even from a thousand feet."

"1L30, Eagle 5; be advised we're getting bucked a—ound and the visibility's dro—ing. We'll make one more pass, and if we don't see a—thing, we're heading home."

"Roger."

NINE

Amanda Schaefer nearly spun her car on one of Skyline Boulevard's hairpin turns. She had been out running errands when she heard Kerri's AMBER Alert on the radio. She would never forget the announcer's words regarding her six-year-old in Redwood Regional Park. *"…Kerri Connifer is blonde, wearing a pink coat and jeans…"* She pictured Kerri waving at her from Randy's car and her mind went numb. Her anger recharged her when she couldn't reach him on his cell phone. Shortly after, the police called and said he was still in the park. She aimed her car at the Oakland hills, strangling the wheel.

Her steering became erratic, but somehow she stayed on the road. Driven by rage and anguish, she could barely see, much less think. *If anything happens to her…* Why didn't Randy call? Did he think he could keep this a secret? She blew through a stop sign, cursing the oncoming driver who skidded to a halt.

Images of her wedding daggered her brain. She knew marrying Randy was a mistake, but her mother kept bragging that their ceremony would be the social event of the year. *"Anyone who is anyone will be there,"* Mom kept saying. And as it turned out, she was right. Socialites from every corner of the Bay Area showed up; most of whom she had never met before. She was shaking with fear when her father gave her away. But instead of admitting her doubts and stopping the nuptials, she went through with her vows. It was wrong, she knew, but matters of the heart can stir irrational thought. The fact that she couldn't tell her mother that Kerri was missing proved that.

Since their separation, Amanda had minimized all contact with her husband. It was for the best, as Kerri had seen too much fighting over the years. It drove her insane the way that Randy always had to be right. And his business schedule was so demanding she practically needed an appointment to see him. And when they did go out, she felt like a trophy wife, suffocating under the guise of Mrs. Randy Connifer. She only used his name on social occasions.

The more she thought about the situation, the angrier she got. How could he do this to her? The flashing vehicle lights at Skyline Gate were dreadful. *Dear God! Kerri!*

She had to park two blocks away because of all the emergency equipment.

Her Lexus' windshield blurred the moment her wipers stopped. She gaped at her black pantsuit, regretting leaving her gym clothes at home. She kicked off her high heels, ran to the trunk to retrieve her trench coat and tennis shoes, and ducked back in the car. She then took the bands from her hair and slipped them around her ankles to hold her pants up. A silver helicopter roared overhead as she walked through the parking lot. Instinctively, she ducked and covered her head. When it didn't crash, she kept going.

Skyline Gate whipped her emotions. Two years had passed since she had set foot in Redwood Regional Park. For a brief moment, fond memories of them exploring the park together overrode her contempt for him. She remembered a golden retriever named Biscuit nuzzling up to Kerri's stroller and poking her nose inside. At first she had feared the dog would bite, but then Kerri giggled and pet its nose. Biscuit licked her and she giggled again. From then on, the big dog was welcome to do as she pleased. Maybe that retriever was the reason Kerri loved animals so much.

She clenched her coat as she approached an Oakland Police officer who was busy directing traffic. "It's my daughter they're looking for," she said. "Who is in charge here?"

The young man kept his head on a swivel, keeping the traffic moving. "The search party's about three-quarters of a mile in on East Ridge Trail." He paused to wave his flashlight at a gawking driver. "Come on, buddy; keep it moving." When he turned around, Amanda was gone.

Water streamed down Amanda's clothes as she jogged through the park. Rage drove her on, flinging mud with each step. Her baby belonged in her arms, not lost in a park. Her heart stopped when the helicopter went into a hover.

TEN

Eagle 5's pilot struggled to keep the helicopter steady while his observer enhanced the infrared image on his screen. The rough air made refinements difficult, but their target appeared to be that of a small child in a fetal position. "1L30, Eagle 5; your target is twenty yards west of your position, halfway down the slope."

Rodriquez acknowledged Eagle 5's call, realizing the pilot believed he was with the search party. He relayed the information to Fire Chief Hagley, who directed his group toward the reported position. Eagle 5 provided constant updates while the rescuers raced to the target.

"1L30, Eagle 5, your target is now ten yards east of your position. Recommend you form a grid and head down the slope. Watch for steep terrain. You'll need to—Jesus!" Turbulence was causing severe problems with their hover. The pilot managed to regain control only inches above the treetops. With hovering no longer an option, he circled the area to further direct the search team. "1L30, Eagle 5, your target is stationary. We've pressed our luck and are heading home. Good luck."

Rodriquez looked up just as the helicopter zoomed overhead. "1L30 copies. Thanks for the help." When he released his mike, he noticed Randy was massaging his legs. "You don't look so good. Are you gonna make it?"

"Don't worry about me. Just keep moving."

They forged ahead, praying that the deluge and strong winds would die down. A Monterey pine fell and thumped the ground hard. More giants would fall before the day was over. They joined the search party, inching forward, line abreast, but without Eagle 5's guidance, every move became a guess. "You sure we're heading in the right direction?"

Right then someone yelled, "Over here!"

Everyone ran toward the voice, slipping and sliding along the way. They spotted Fire Chief Hagley and another park employee fighting to free something.

"Kerri!" Randy screamed, fearing the worst. But then the fire chief looked up and shook his head. When he got there, Randy saw a frightened fawn pinned under a fallen branch. The rescue crew lifted the limb and the deer darted off in search of its mother.

"I'm sorry, Mr. Connifer, but that appears to have been Eagle 5's target. It was curled up just like they described. Unfortunately, FLIR can't differentiate between a fawn and a huddled child. They did the right thing directing us here."

Randy's stomach rumbled and he ducked behind a shrub. He had given all he could, and now all hope seemed lost. He bent over to relieve his nervous stomach. When it stopped, he gathered rain water to rinse his mouth. He spat and looked up, ignoring the stinging rain. "What now, God? What have you done with my daughter?"

Rodriquez overheard him and directed the search party away. He looked at the fire chief and said, "It must be tough losing your kid."

"I'm sure. Just remember—getting too close can draw myopic conclusions. Why don't you check on him while I address the search party?" Once Rodriquez walked off, the fire chief stepped in front of the group. "Obviously this is a setback, but we're not done here. I'd like everyone to return to their last position. Stay focused. Let's find the girl."

Once the groups scattered, Hagley cornered Rodriquez. "You might call Dispatch and let them know what happened. Oh, and if you don't mind, take Randy home. He's a risk I don't need."

The lines in Hagley's brow seemed deeper than Rodriquez remembered. As Incident Commander, the search was his sole responsibility, and he resented the fire chief's defiance. Still, Hagley was right, and he respected his judgment.

Dispatch acknowledged Rodriquez' report and advised him that Kerri's mother had arrived. The news wasn't welcome. Now that she was here, neither parent would leave, and he'd be stuck baby-sitting two crazy people. *Christ!* Could things get any worse?

ELEVEN

Randy sat on a tree stump thinking about Kerri when a familiar shriek penetrated the forest. He didn't have to look to know who it was. Twenty feet away, with slits for eyes, dark hair and black pant suit draping like kelp, Amanda Schaefer put every witch to shame. He didn't budge when she charged him.

"You bastard!" she said. "I trusted you! Where is Kerri? What have you done with my baby, you sonuvabitch? I hate you! I hate you!"

He accepted her pounding for a while before grabbing her wrists, applying only enough pressure to keep her from striking again. "Stop hitting me and listen." She fought a while longer, but collapsed on him when she knew it was futile.

Having told his story so often, he found that tears no longer moved him. Not even hers. He let go when she relaxed. "Amanda, I've given you plenty of reasons to hate me, but I swear I've done nothing to Kerri. We were walking up East Ridge when she took off and ran around a bend. That's the last time I saw her. We've been searching all day, but so far, we haven't found a trace."

Without warning, she resumed her thrashing. He tried catching her wrists and lost his balance, dragging her to the ground with him. The saturated earth slid out from under them and they began to slide. He clawed at the mud with her on top of him. When they stopped, she pounded some more. Fed up, he grabbed her waist, threw her on her back, and pinned her to the ground. "Damn it, Amanda, I said stop it!"

She spat in his face, but the rain washed it away. "Why should I believe you?" she sneered. "All you do is bitch about our separation agreement. So, how long have you been planning this, Randy? A month? A year? Two years? Did you really think you could take her away from me? Is this your idea of quality time?"

Her pushed her into the mud and threw his arms up. "Go to hell."

"No, *you* go to hell, you sonuvabitch!" She tried kicking his groin, but he deflected the blow.

He sat on her legs until they started to go numb. "Now, you're gonna listen to me! God knows I wanted to call you, but I left my cell phone at home. I haven't left the park since we got here this morning. I've been doing everything possible to find her. Ask anyone out here and they'll tell you the same thing. Save the blame for later. Right now, we've got to find our daughter."

Her angry eyes blinked the rain away, mascara running down her cheeks. He outweighed her by a hundred pounds. There was no way she could win. She finally relaxed and he got off her. She sat up, picking pine needles and mud from her hair.

"We *both* love her," Randy continued, "and I would never do anything to hurt either of you. It's time you faced the fact that Kerri's missing."

"She's got to be all right. I swear to God, Randy, if anything's happened to her."

"I know." He had grown used to her threats. It had been five years since they had been intimate. Early on, she was so gentle and loving; neither could keep hands off the other. How did their passion turn to contempt? He gazed at the woman he had once loved, helpless and broken, longing to hold her, but he didn't dare. "Like it or not, Amanda, we're in this together." But neither was prepared for what lay ahead.

TWELVE

Officer Rodriquez didn't expect to witness mud wrestling, but since no one was getting hurt, he stayed out of it. He started to move when they slid down the hill, but ducked out of sight once that threat ended. What surprised him was Randy's compassion for his wife. He could have tossed her fifty feet, but instead took a beating from her. When he tired of it, he threw her off and pinned her, but even then he didn't fight back. Having Amanda here might actually provide insightful. He inched closer, hoping to eavesdrop, but the rain and the wind masked their conversation.

He hid behind a fallen tree and switched to a tactical frequency to reach Parks Police Detective Dave Barnum, call sign 6L1. Rodriquez briefed Barnum on the Connifer's reunion, giving live updates as the situation warranted. "It's amazing," Rodriquez said. "First, she's hammering him with her fists and now they're sitting together, chatting like nosy neighbors. I guess she finally ran out of steam."

Detective Barnum rocked his office chair, chewing on a sandwich. Hector Rodriquez wasn't one to exaggerate, but he hadn't given him reason to get involved yet either. The detective munched another bite and chased it down with coffee. "Hector, aren't you supposed to be out looking for their kid?"

"Don't be a wise ass, Dave. I called you because this woman made a case for her husband taking her daughter. Don't you think it's worth looking into? I mean, the missing girl lives in two homes, and her father keeps telling me he never has enough time with her. Seems like a good motive for a kidnapping, don't you think? Besides, Mr. Connifer is in a lot better shape than what he's been leading me to believe. The guy's a monster. Think about it, Dave. No witnesses, not a single child's footprint or piece of fabric? For all we know, she was never even here. Granted, I'm not a detective yet, but it seems really odd."

Dispatch interrupted their conversation. "1L30, Dispatch; meet Chief Hagley at his truck."

Rodriquez acknowledged the call and continued his conversation with Dave Barnum. "Well, Dave, you heard it. I've got to meet the fire chief. We'll catch up later."

"6L1, roger."

Barnum stuffed the last of his sandwich in his mouth and leaned forward. His chair squeaked. He liked it that way.

Officer Rodriquez peered around the tree, debating whether to leave the Connifers alone. In spite of being humiliated by his wife, Connifer appeared stable, so he decided to show himself. “I take it you’re Mrs. Connifer?”

“No, I’m Amanda *Schaefer*. Trust me, there’s a big difference.”

“Sorry.” Randy had told him she went by her surname, but after seeing her fighting, he thought he’d test her reaction. “I’m Officer Rodriquez. Is everything okay?”

“No, we’re not okay.” Amanda stood tall, surprised she had an inch on him, maybe more. “Our daughter’s missing. Why aren’t you out looking for her?”

“Actually, I am. I just came by to let Randy know I have to meet with Fire Chief Hagley. You’re welcome to join us if you wish.”

“Give us a minute,” Randy said. He wasn’t sure how much Officer Rodriquez overheard, but he knew he had been there for a while. He first spotted him when he pinned his wife, but then he disappeared. What was Rodriquez up to?

THIRTEEN

Hector Rodriquez was covered in mud by the time he reached Fire Chief Hagley's truck. His pants chafed and his throat hurt. He picked a bad day to be a peace officer.

"It's about time you got here," Hagley said. "Where've you been?"

"Sorry, chief. I got caught up in something." Something he didn't need to share. "What's up?"

"I thought you might want to move your car before it got stuck."

Rodriquez glanced at his Ford sedan, its tires sinking in the muck. Getting traction would be difficult. Still, he couldn't believe Hagley called him over for this. It almost seemed the fire chief was mocking him. "The keys are in the ignition. Why didn't someone move it?"

"Everyone's busy, Hector. By the way, are you still the incident commander?"

"I am until I'm relieved. Why?"

"I'm just surprised Lt. Donovan isn't here yet."

"Apparently he's tied up with other things," Rodriquez said, studying Hagley's map. The fire chief had made marks where they had searched, and noted what they had found, but there were still miles of park they hadn't covered yet. The officer shook his head, mumbling, "I've got a bad feeling about this case."

Hagley looked up. "Pardon me?"

Rodriquez didn't intend for his comments to be heard, but Hagley kept staring at him, waiting. He had to give the chief something. "I said I wished Eagle 5 could've stuck around." Hagley wasn't buying it, but Rodriquez wasn't ready to share his view of the Connifer reunion. Not yet anyway. He left to move his car.

The fire chief pinched a wad of tobacco and tucked it under his lower lip. He liked being in the field where he could spit. He knew Rodriquez had something going on. He and Parks Police Captain Vestell were always talking, commander-to-commander. In time, he would know what Rodriquez was hiding, but for now, he had more important things to do.

Monterey pines and eucalyptus trees dueled in the gusts while muddy waterfalls flowed down the embankments. East Ridge Trail had washed out numerous times. Today's storm had the potential of doing it again.

Rodriquez shifted between forward and reverse, hoping to rock his car out of the mud, but his efforts only spun his tires. Detective Dave Barnum called just as he was giving up. They switched frequencies so they could talk freely.

Barnum keyed his mike. "Hector, I'm pulling into Skyline Gate. What's your position?"

Rodriquez raised his volume to drown out the rain. "I'm on East Ridge Trail, but don't come up here. My car's stuck in the mud. I'll meet you as soon as I can."

Static interfered with Rodriquez' radio. If Barnum responded, he never heard it. The patrol officer stepped from his car and pounded rocks and sticks under the rear tires. His efforts were rewarded by a half-spin followed by a sudden lunge backwards. Though grateful to be out of the mud, he couldn't see anything out the rear window. He didn't dare stop, though. Having no room to turn around, his only option was to back out of the park.

On his way out, he wondered how many clues the storm had washed away. Could the search dogs really pick up Kerri's scent under these conditions? His car suddenly spun sideways. He countered with brakes and turned the wheel in the opposite direction, but his car still hit the embankment. *Damn it!* His car was now forty-five degrees to the road and blocked everything coming into or out of the park. He tried rocking the car again, but the tires only dug deeper.

Barnum grew impatient. "How ya doing Hector?"

Rodriquez' face warmed as he grabbed his mike. "I'm working on it." He rocked his car again. One wheel found some traction and spun the car around. He slammed on the brakes, took a breath, and straightened the wheel. Luckily, he was now pointing toward Skyline Gate. It was his first break of the day and he keyed his mike again. "I'll be right there, Dave. Do we have any K-9 units yet?"

"None that I know of. How long ago did you request them?"

The officer didn't answer, acutely aware that he had never requested any. Lt. Donovan wouldn't be amused. "Is Lt. Donovan here yet?"

"No. I hear he's tied up somewhere, so you're still in charge, Hector."

"Roger." Rodriquez released his mike. Where in the hell is Donovan? A missing child is a big deal. Donovan should have assumed command hours ago. Rodriquez put his car in gear and inched down the road, his wipers unable to keep up. Everything was blurry. If the road washed out, he would never know until he was rolling downhill. He was hugging the upper slope when something dark crashed in front of him; its impact strong enough to bounce his car. He slammed on the brakes, gawking at the Monterey pine that now blocked his exit.

"Dave, you're not going to believe this, but a downed tree just blocked me in. How about giving Dispatch a call while I hoof it out of here?"

"Will do."

Rodriquez flipped on his emergency lights and slammed the door. He kicked the tree, cursing as he crawled over it. A few more seconds is all he needed. Then again, a few seconds later and the tree might have crushed him. His shoes sank in the mud, and his chafing was getting worse. It was turning into a really bad day.

FOURTEEN

Detective Dave Barnum sat in his car, waiting for Rodriquez to show. His large frame was better suited for a Ford Expedition than a sedan, but a sedan was all he rated. Sliding the seat all the way back made it tolerable, but it was never comfortable.

The radio reported that the storm had dumped two inches of rain in the last four hours, but that report came from the Oakland airport, and the hills always got more. He watched an armada of recycling bins float down Skyline Boulevard, thinking someone could make a bundle recovering them. He spotted Rodriquez and flashed his headlights at him. The officer waved and headed his way. Barnum handed him a towel when he got in. "Having a bad day, Hector?"

"You wouldn't believe it. We still haven't found anything that proves the girl was ever here. I can't help thinking maybe her father left her with someone before coming to the park."

Barnum's thick mustache hid his grin. "And why is that?"

Rodriquez hesitated, having been trying to make detective for two years. It seemed that Barnum did everything he could to discourage him from taking that route. Still, he respected the detective's tone that suggested he might be drawing premature conclusions. "Perhaps I should start over."

Barnum nodded and opened his notepad, ready to take notes.

"I'm seeing some serious inconsistencies, Dave. For example, Randy Connifer insists he doesn't get along with his wife, yet he refused to answer my question about why they never divorced. Then there's the child custody issue. Don't get me wrong—I'd be angry, too, if I got his deal. I mean, the guy rarely gets to see his daughter. But then after hearing his wife talk, you get the impression he's tried something before. That's why I called you. I think it's worth looking into Randy Connifer's past."

The detective scanned the parking lot. It hadn't poured this hard in years. He was glad to be sitting in his car instead of marching through the muck. "You always have interesting observations, Hector. Unfortunately, there's nothing to substantiate that the girl has even been kidnapped. Still, you may be onto something." He looked at Hector's sodden shoes, no doubt ruined after today. "Did Kerri's school call her mother when she failed to show this morning?"

"What difference does that make? Kerri's missing, and for all we know, she's left the state. We've been searching for hours and keep coming up empty. Even Eagle 5 couldn't find her. I'm pretty sure the girl's not here."

"I suppose it's possible he dropped her at a friend's or neighbor's house using some excuse, but if that were the case, you'd think they would have called the police by now. After all, Kerri's all over the news. It's got to be easier getting someone to watch her than taking her across a state line."

"I don't know, Dave. Nothing makes sense."

Barnum sighed. *You'll never make detective until you start thinking outside the box.* "You know, Hector, distraught people can do some pretty strange things. Who knows? Maybe Mr. Connifer did this to piss his wife off. You know—make her re-think their settlement agreement? It's not rational, of course, but it is possible. In any event, if the search team comes up empty, we'll ask Oakland PD for a door-to-door search. Do you know anything about Mr. Connifer's friends or relatives? Do any of them live near the park?"

Rodriquez' head dropped. "I don't know."

Menacing clouds consumed hills and stole color. Barnum licked his lips, thinking about Kerri, alone in the forest. He hated it when kids got hurt. "For now, we'll assume she's inside the park. What was your impression of Mr. Connifer before his wife showed up?"

"Actually, he seemed quite genuine. He showed me all the places where he and Kerri visited. There were times when he could barely speak because he was so choked up. More than once he stopped to puke. But all that changed when his wife showed up. Suddenly he got real cool and reserved."

"Do you think those places he showed you are red herrings?"

"Anything's possible, but like I said, Randy Connifer seemed pretty convincing."

"Well, a good search dog should confirm whether or not she was there." The windshield wipers noisily slapped rain. Barnum shut them off and reached for his door handle. "Well, I suppose it's time I got wet. You may as well stay here until Donovan arrives. Feel free to keep the heater running. By the way, you might be able to get a new pair of shoes out of this."

"Wait," Rodriquez said. Barnum looked at him curiously. "There's no point in both of us getting soaked. Pop the trunk and I'll get your rain gear."

Barnum smiled. "Thanks, Hector. You're all right."

FIFTEEN

Barnum hiked up East Ridge Trail looking for the Connifers. He passed Rodriquez' patrol car, amazed to see the tree fell only one car length away. He had barely gone past the tree when he spotted the search party marching toward him from the opposite direction. "Where's everyone going?" he said to the man in the lead.

"The conditions are too hazardous, so we're taking a break," the man replied. He noticed Barnum's badge and said, "If you're looking for the girl's parents, they're bringing up the rear."

"Thanks."

Barnum moved through the group until he spotted them. Based on Rodriquez' description, they weren't hard to find. "Excuse me, but are you Randy Connifer and Amanda Schaefer?" They acknowledged him, but didn't stop, so he informally walked with them. "I'm Detective Barnum with the Regional Parks Police. May I have a word with you?"

Randy sized up the detective like he would an opposing linemen. The guy was enormous. Randy stood six foot two, but Barnum had at least three inches on him. He glanced at the detective and said, "I don't mean to be rude, but we're tired and freezing, and I've already told Officer Rodriquez everything. You really should talk to him."

The detective grinned. "As a matter of fact, I just left him, and since they're postponing the search, I'd like you both to accompany me to the station. It's a lot more comfortable there, and I'm sure they have hot coffee."

Amanda nodded her approval, willing to do anything to warm up. "Which car is yours? I'll follow you."

Barnum's grin widened. "Actually, it would be best if you both left your cars here. But don't worry, I promise I'll bring you back."

Amanda rolled her eyes. The notion of riding in the same car as her husband was disturbing. She also resented the detective addressing Randy and not her. She angrily hugged her chest. "Why do I have to go?"

"There are always two sides to a story, and this way I'll get all the facts."

The detective looked at Amanda and she eased her way over to him. He whispered something to her and she whispered something back. Randy listened hard, convinced they were talking about him, but neither paid him any attention.

Barnum sensed Randy's discomfort and said to him, "I was just telling Amanda that the search party will keep working until they find your daughter, and when they do, you'll be immediately notified." Randy nodded, but said nothing. "Well, if everyone's ready, let's go."

When they reached Barnum's sedan, the engine was running, the heater was on, but Officer Rodriquez was gone. The detective spotted the white Ford Expedition command vehicle across the way and assumed Rodriquez was with Lt. Donovan. Barnum politely opened the front door for Amanda, but instead of getting in, she slid into the back seat. Randy took the hint and climbed in the front seat without protest. Before closing the door, Barnum poked his head inside. "I need to see the Incident Commander for a moment. I'll be right back." He closed the door and ran over to Donovan's SUV.

Lt. Donovan watched Barnum squeeze into the back seat. In contrast, Rodriquez, who was sitting in the front passenger's seat, made Donovan's SUV look cavernous. Donovan was glad to be average sized. He looked over his shoulder at Barnum and said, "I was just telling Officer Rodriquez how I got tied up with this nasty accident on Redwood Road. Sorry I took so long getting here, but I had to stay until the sheriff arrived. They were swamped with other emergencies, so it took them a while for them to respond."

"Any fatalities?"

"Yeah, the woman driver. . . Anyway, Officer Rodriquez has briefed me, and I've assumed the Incident Commander duties. We'll resume the search as soon as possible, but not until this weather eases up. I can't risk losing anyone when there's no trace of the girl. However, I did request mutual aid from the sheriff's department, so hopefully we'll get some search dogs up here."

"We could've used them hours ago," Barnum said, kneeing Rodriquez in the back. "Oops. Sorry, Hector. There's never enough leg room in these things." Rodriquez grunted and slid his seat forward. "Anyway, I'm taking Mr. Connifer and his wife to my office. Keep me posted, okay?"

"I will," Donovan said. "You do the same."

"Will do. Good luck with the search. See ya, Hector."

Barnum got out and ran back to his car. Was it his imagination or was the rain intensifying? There was a loud crack and another pine fell. At least three trees had fallen since he arrived. At this rate, it could be a while before Donovan resumed the search.

He worked his way into the driver's seat and struggled to fasten his seat belt. "Are you folks warm enough?" he said, checking his rear-view mirror for an answer. Amanda's eyes said yes. Randy's head bobbed slightly. "Good. Lt.

Donovan has assumed command responsibility, but he's not sure when they can resume the search. Some positive news though—he's requested search dogs. If your daughter's out there, they'll find her."

"*If* she's out there?" Randy said. When Barnum didn't answer, he stared into the emptiness, shivering in fear, praying for a miracle.

* * * * *

Rodriquez bunched his toes in his sodden shoes and watched Barnum drive off in his unmarked police car. The detective's windows were blurred, but he saw Randy Connifer in the front seat. He looked over at Lt. Donovan. "Something about this guy stinks, LT. I'm not sure what to believe anymore."

Donovan glanced at Dave Barnum's car just before it disappeared up the street. "I'm sure Dave can handle it, Hector. He's an excellent judge of character and a smooth interrogator. If anyone's hiding anything, Dave will figure it out."

SIXTEEN

Randy rubbed his sleeve over his window. For a moment, the view cleared, but quickly fogged over. "I can't believe this weather," he said, making conversation. "There's enough rain to float an ark. I knew a storm was coming, but I had no idea it would be like this."

"I know," Barnum said. "It always amazes me how we go from drought to monsoon." He met Amanda's eyes in the mirror, but she quickly looked away. As beautiful as they were, her eyes revealed a deep hurt, more painful than from a missing daughter. He glanced out the windshield, pretending to look around. "I'm sure Lt. Donovan will go in as soon as it's safe. Search dogs don't care about rain." Randy and Amanda sat like mannequins, their lips and eyes frozen, so Barnum added, "Did Officer Rodriquez mention that our search teams are all volunteers?" Still no reaction. *Could be a long day.* "Yup, they're all volunteers, and besides the dog teams, we have hikers, bikers, motorbikes, and mounted patrols, and all of these volunteers have spent countless hours training for situations like this. They are extremely dedicated people who take time off from work so that others may live. They're as good as they come, and we're lucky to have them."

Tiring of the detective's rambling, Randy gave him a respectful nod. The twisty road was making him nauseated. Unaccustomed to being a passenger, he definitely preferred driving.

After swallowing a vomit burp, he angled the heater vents away. He wanted to call Bob Underly to see if he had heard anything on Kerri's AMBER alert. His shop foreman must have left him a ton of messages by now. He felt naked without his BlackBerry phone.

He wanted to crack the window open, but knew his wife would complain. He squirmed in his seat, adjusted his pants, and said, "Considering how everyone keeps to themselves these days, it's hard to believe you have so many volunteers. Don't get me wrong, I'm grateful for every one of them. In fact, I'd like to know more about the program so I can contribute toward it when this is over."

Amanda leaned forward. "Why haven't we heard more about these people?"

Barnum inhaled her fragrance, an intriguing mix of perfume, sweat, and dirt. He was making progress; they were both talking now. "Volunteers aren't in this for the glory. Their reward is in the faces of those they rescue. It's not unusual for victims and rescuers to develop special bonds. Many of them stay in contact long afterwards. You can't put a price on that." He checked his mirror again. This time, Amanda didn't turn away. "Some victims even become volunteers."

"Are they on call all the time?"

"Pretty much, Amanda. Of course, they write their own schedules."

"Are most of them retired?" Randy said that more to be included in the conversation than out of interest. "I mean, where do they find the time if they have a family?"

"Everyone has reasons for volunteering. Some have lost loved ones; others just want to help out. Regardless of their motives, they know that their involvement can mean the difference between life and death. Believe me when I say these people really want to find your daughter."

"I hope so." Amanda slumped in her seat after that.

"By the way, you can take a shower at the station if you'd like. Use the naphtha soap under cool water. It can help with the poison oak."

It occurred to Randy that he had been trampling shrubs all morning and had undoubtedly contacted the poisonous plant. This shrub didn't even need leaves to spread its toxin. Brushing against a stem was enough. "Have you ever gotten poison oak, detective?"

"Are you kidding? I get it at least three or four times a year. I've had it so often I should be immune by now." A glance over his shoulder confirmed Amanda wasn't tuned in anymore. "Unfortunately, it's a hazard of the job, but it sure beats sitting in an office."

Amanda rubbed her temples, caring nothing about poison oak. A thunder crack frightened her. Thunderstorms weren't typical in the Bay Area, and the sound only reminded her of the storm's fury. She silently prayed for her daughter. When she finished, she leaned over the seat. "Detective Barnum, how many missing child reports do you get?"

"Hundreds."

"No, no, I mean how many do you get per year, not since the park opened."

"That's what I meant. We get hundreds of reports each year. Of course, most are resolved with a hasty search, but there was this doctor a few years ago—"

"The suicide?" Randy interrupted.

"Yeah. He was an interesting case."

Amanda heaved a sigh. "Can we please talk about something else?"

Randy ignored her. "What can you tell us about child abductions?"

"First, most abductions involve a family member." He paused, fishing for a reaction. He continued when neither bit. "Family abductions can be difficult because a child can be hidden anywhere. You know—grandparents, aunts, uncles, friends; whatever." He paused to let it sink in. "Of course, I'm not suggesting that's the case here; I'm merely talking generalities. On a positive note, I don't recall a single case where we haven't found the lost child. All-in-all, we've been pretty lucky."

Randy had heard those statistics before, and wondered what his wife was thinking right then. What would she tell Barnum when he questioned her? His stomach gurgled. He felt lightheaded. He cracked the window to get some air. "How much longer?"

"Ten minutes. Our station's the old Nike missile site near Lake Chabot. It's not much to look at, but it's functional."

"Your station was a Cold War nuke site? I thought they tore all that out years ago."

"Obviously, the missiles are long gone, but we do occupy the former Army barracks and missile maintenance building. It's interesting working in an old Cold War relic."

Randy's mind flashed back to the 1960s when the world was at the brink of nuclear annihilation. Nike missiles were designed to take out bombers that might attack the Bay Area's military might. Today, those bases are gone, but nuclear fear lingers from a new invisible enemy. Today's foes strike randomly with no regard for human life. Perhaps the Cold War was a lesser evil. Hitting a pothole jarred him back.

"Sorry about that," Barnum said. "Unfortunately, that's nothing compared to the mud flow in front of us." He pulled off the road and turned on his emergency flashers. "Looks like we'll have to take a detour." The detective reached for his mike and held it to his lips. "Dispatch, 6L1, Skyline Boulevard is blocked by a mud slide. We need to close the road." There was no response. "Dispatch, 6L1, how copy?" After several failed attempts, his rueful eyes found them. "Don't worry. The radio reception is always a problem down here. I'll be right back."

Randy watched him light a flare; its red flame bright against the gray background. He leaned over the seat while Barnum readied another. "Amanda, did you say anything that implied I took Kerri?"

"When have I had any time alone with him? Besides, is there something I should know? Level with me, Randy. Do you know where she is?"

"No. I just don't want our differences tainting this investigation."

"Our *differences*? Name something we have in common."

"Kerri."

"You bastard! I knew you'd say that." She looked at her drenched clothes and muddy shoes, wondering how it came to this. "We agreed to be civil when we separated, and until now, we've done a pretty good job of that. I haven't said anything negative about you because I'm completely over you. If only I'd gone through with the annulment right after we were married, none of this would have happened."

"So we're back to that, are we? As always, everything's my fault."

"I never said that."

"Then don't. I don't need you giving any negative impressions of me."

"I don't think you need *my* help in that department."

"Damn it, Amanda, knock it off. You know I'd never hurt Kerri."

She heard the trunk close and leaned back in her seat. "Don't worry. I haven't said anything to him. At least not yet."

SEVENTEEN

Barnum had done all he could to warn drivers about the mudslide. He took one last look and climbed into his car. "Man, it's cold!" he said, holding his meaty hands against the heater vents. "You folks doing okay?"

"We're fine," said Amanda.

"Good." The detective checked his mirror as he turned his car turned around. Mud had already swallowed two of his flares, and it was likely the others would be snuffed, too. But he had done everything he could. Hopefully, drivers would see the danger and avoid it.

Static crackled over his radio until they exited the canyon. Soon after, he turned onto a narrow road that twisted up a grassy slope. Near the top, an off-white cinderblock building bore the name "Regional Parks Police Headquarters." Barnum navigated around several flooded potholes and pulled into a parking space a few feet from the entrance.

"Well, this is it. As you can see, the Army didn't waste any money on esthetics. Sadly, the Parks District is maintaining that tradition." He had tried for a laugh, but failed to get one. "You see, with budget cutbacks and such—" His voice trailed off. "Anyway, we're here."

He escorted them to the entrance and tugged on the weathered door. "I can't figure out why they won't fix this door. The darned thing sticks every time it rains."

The receptionist saw him struggling and opened the door from the inside. Barnum ducked through the entry and waved the others in. "Thanks, Doreen," said the detective. "By the way, these are the missing girl's parents. I don't suppose we have some spare sweats lying around, do we? I'm sure they'd like to get cleaned up."

"I'll see what I can find."

"Thanks."

Barnum turned to them after the receptionist left. "Doreen's the greatest. She'll get you fixed up." He punched the code into the cipher lock and held the second door open. "After you." Once they were inside, he tugged on the door to make sure it was secure. "Amanda, help yourself to some coffee in the break room. Randy, follow me and I'll show you to the shower."

Amanda found the break room and poured herself a cup. One sip confirmed it was police brew. There was no way anyone could fall asleep drinking this stuff. She added water, sugar, creamer, and more water, but nothing made it palatable. She sat at the table, letting the cup warm her hands.

Barnum returned a few minutes later and handed her a couple of towels. "We have plenty, so use them to wipe the mud off. I'll get you more if you want to shower, but right now, let's go to my office and talk." She followed him, toweling her hair.

The detective peeled off his rain gear and draped it over a chair. He shared the tiny office with four other detectives. Thankfully, none were around. It was embarrassing having to maneuver around stacks of papers, boxes, a fax machine, and several file cabinets to get to his desk, but that's how it was. "Pardon the mess," he said, "but with the exception of my wife and some fellow officers, no one ever comes in here."

"It's okay." Amanda's eyes traveled from Barnum's citation to the photo of a young boy on his desk.

Barnum's eyes followed hers. "You seem to be nursing that brew. It must be the oil slick version. How about I make us a fresh pot?"

"That would be great."

When he left, Amanda moved to her only link to the outside world and watched the wind whip the forest. On her way back to his desk, she noticed a document marked "Confidential" sitting atop the fax machine. Above it was a color-coded map of the East Bay Area posted on the wall. She was studying it when Barnum walked in.

The detective noticed the confidential file and dropped some papers over it. He handed her a fresh cup of coffee and seated himself behind his desk. "So, how are you holding up?"

"As well as can be expected. What's this map for?"

He got up and moved next to her. "It defines our jurisdiction. As you can see, the Parks Police covers a lot of ground, which is why it took Eagle 5 so long to arrive on scene. We're responsible for the former Alameda Naval Air Station as well as the uninhabited areas south of Livermore. Not all of it is East Bay Regional Parks District property, though. East Bay Municipal Utilities District, or East Bay MUD as we call them, hires us to patrol some of their watershed areas, too. We couldn't function without our helicopters."

She nodded, stoically sipping her coffee. "This is much better, thanks. So, how much detective work does the Parks Police do? No offense, but how much criminal activity can there be in a regional park?"

"Oh, you'd be surprised," he said, returning to his chair. The beat-up seat sagged under his weight. "Anyway, Randy will be back soon, so we'd best get started."

"Please do." She seated herself in the hardwood chair across from him. She watched him flip open a notepad and prepare to write. "You don't use a computer?"

He shook his head. "I write faster than I type."

"Really? How so?"

"Shorthand. I only write enough to jog my memory."

"I see," she said, wondering how that stood up in court.

He set his pencil down and folded his hands. "Does my shorthand bother you?"

"Ah, no. I'm just surprised, that's all. I mean, even Kerri types on the computer. Shorthand seems unimaginable these days."

"Well, it works for me." He leaned back and his chair squeaked. She was bold, liked being in control, and wasn't intimidated by him. But it was her lack of compassion that made him wonder if she was part of her daughter's disappearance. The JonBenét Ramsey murder came to mind. "Amanda, in order to understand this case, I need to ask you some pointed questions." She hiked her shoulders and downed another sip. "Tell me about your marriage."

"I never *had* a marriage; only a marriage license."

"I see." He squeaked his chair again. "Care to elaborate?"

"Not really." She draped her towel over her neck like a scarf, and twisted her long black hair, awaiting his next question.

Barnum smiled. She may have a model's looks, but not even her full lips could distract a seasoned interrogator like him. "Humor me, Amanda. Tell me about your relationship with Randy."

In an elegant move, she set her coffee cup on his desk and crossed her legs. She preferred burying the past. Mistakes were part of life, but that didn't mean she had to share them with anyone. His impatient eyes waited so she feigned a tear worthy of a president.

"I thought I knew him. Things were great while we dated. He made time for me, brought me flowers, we went out to the theater—but once we were married, it was clear I was his mistress, and he was married to his work. At first I spent hours preparing nice dinners, but I tired of him coming home late. I'd make plans to do something and he'd say he didn't have the time. Ironically, he'd get upset when I invited friends over, claiming that we never spent any time alone. I was losing my identity, all sense of who I was. It didn't take long before we drifted apart."

"Then why aren't you divorced?"

She knew that question would come up. It always did. She dragged her fingers through her hair, and then downed the last of her coffee. The light in her blue eyes faded. "It's not a money issue, if that's what you mean."

"I wasn't implying anything."

She grimaced when his chair squeaked again. "I guess it's the finality of divorce that bothers me the most. I mean, neither of us accepts failure." She paused to explain that, but decided to let it go. "What does this have to do with Kerri?"

"Maybe nothing, but the more I know, the easier it is to solve a case."

She crumpled her cup and tossed it in the trash. "Okay. I'll answer your questions, so long as they're concise and relevant. Just remember, you're not a shrink."

He grinned, twirling his pencil, studying his notes. Making people uncomfortable was part of his job. It kept them on edge; made them speak before thinking. He kept twirling as he looked up at her. "So, you're legally separated and have no intention of getting back together. Is that right?" Her cold stare confirmed that was the case. "Do either you or your husband harbor any resentment about your marriage or breakup?"

She belted a laugh. "Of course! Why else would we have separated? We get along best by not speaking to each other. The less contact, the better."

He jotted down "resentment" and looked up at her. "And how does Kerri feel about that?"

"She's dealing with it, and no, she didn't run away."

"Amanda, please don't get angry with me. I'm just trying to find a motive. Sometimes kids run away. We have to explore every possibility."

"I agree."

Barnum rubbed his forehead, glancing over his notes. "Sorry to be so blunt, but do you believe your husband is capable of kidnapping his own daughter?"

Amanda hesitated. She had promised Randy she wouldn't implicate him, but Barnum clearly shared her concerns. However, Kerri dearly loves her dad, and he loves her. She drew in a breath and bent forward. "My husband can be a cold-hearted sonuvabitch, but I don't believe he'd stoop to this level to get back at me."

"Back at you?"

"Yes, back at me."

Barnum cocked his head, begging for an explanation.

"You see, *I'm* the one who filed for divorce. I've wanted it since the day we married, but he keeps stalling." She smiled thinly, removed her lipstick from her pocketbook, and smoothed some on. After checking her mirror, she stowed the items, folded her hands over her nicely crossed legs, and waited for his next question.

Barnum stared at her, confused. Why would a woman who harbored such contempt for her husband have a child with him? And she dared call *him* cold-hearted? The image stirred new possibilities. A rhythmic squeak erupted from his chair while rain from the overflowing gutters pelted the window. He glanced at the ceiling, half-expecting a leak. He moved on after making a note to revisit the divorce issue. "Do you have a picture of Kerri?"

"Of course." She dug through her wallet and handed him her daughter's school photo.

"She's very pretty. I don't suppose you have her student ID with you?"

"Student ID? Kerri's in first grade, for Christ's sake."

Barnum discretely scribbled, "Check on student ID. Father has one—mother knows nothing about it," and looked up. "Amanda, student ID's aren't limited to upper level schools. They not only help with security issues, but they can assist police in identifying missing children. At a minimum, most contain the child's thumbprint, photo, and physical description."

"Well, as far as I know, they don't have IDs like that at her school."

He desperately wanted to show her the one Randy gave Officer Rodriquez, but instead said, "Would Randy ever do anything to hurt Kerri?"

"No way. He loves her. He'd give his life for her."

"Maybe. But earlier you implied he wanted to get even with you for filing for divorce, and Officer Rodriquez saw you two fighting in the park. I also know your husband strongly resents his current visitation schedule, perhaps even enough to do something irrational, so with this in mind, can you think of any place where he might have taken her? Maybe to a friend's house? A relative's?"

She shook her head. "Randy's done a lot of crazy things, but he wouldn't dare take her from me. I'd ki—" Her thoughts scared her. She took a moment to compose herself before adding, "Randy's a very driven man. Back in college, he knew he was going to be hit hard, but he was in a position to score the winning touchdown so he went for it. The resulting injury ruined his football career, but his winning attitude made him a successful businessman. Nothing ever gets in his way." She bent over, burying her face in her hands.

Barnum stopped rocking to study her face. "Are you okay?"

She smoothed her cheeks and accepted his tissue. "I'll be all right. Just drop the divorce issue, okay?"

"No problem."

Kerri's photo showed her mom's features. It didn't appear that she received any of her father's genes. "Do you mind if we distribute this photo?"

Amanda crumbled her tissue in her fist. "Of course not. You've got to find her. I can't take much more of this."

He nodded, sensing she was hiding something. Why did she physically attack her husband and then claim he could never hurt his daughter. Did they know Rodriquez was watching them in the park? Was their fight just for show? He jotted down "insurance scam" and set his pencil aside. "Let's go back to the visitation issue. How often does Randy get to see Kerri?"

She smelled a rat. "I already told you, he has her on Wednesday mornings and every other weekend. Last weekend was his turn to have her and, as always, they went to Redwood Park. I'm afraid he doesn't have much imagination."

Barnum raised a brow. *No imagination?* "Isn't he an advertising executive?"

"Yes. Why?"

"Forget it." He made a note, wishing he could hear Kerri's point of view. What was it like having two parents that worked full time? Who was raising her? After chewing on his lower lip for a moment, he said, "Who picks Kerri up after school?"

"If I can't do it, her nanny does."

"What's the nanny's name?"

"Elvia Romeros."

He jotted the name down; extortion on his mind. He waited for more, but she offered nothing. "And how long has Ms. Romeros worked for you?"

She sprang to her feet, her emotions unraveling. "What's wrong with you? Kerri's lost and you're trying to convict her nanny?"

"Please sit down." She defiantly looked back. He allowed her a moment, and said, "I don't mean to upset you, but as I said, I have to explore every possibility, and that means learning about everyone who has had recent contact with your daughter." He paused again. She had every right to feel anguished. He would feel the same if his son was missing. "Amanda, I'm not trying to convict anyone. I only want the truth."

She felt faint. A failed marriage, a missing daughter, and tales of kidnapping were too much to bear. But what if Kerri *was* running? Every time her father dropped her off, Kerri reminded her how much she hated living in two homes. Admittedly, anything was possible.

She noticed the smeared mascara on her finger and laughed. "I must look hideous," she said, grabbing another tissue. She wiped her cheeks and looked at the detective. "Elvia is a wonderful nanny. She's worked for me for a year. I hired her on a friend's recommendation, but I'm not sure she has a green card. I know she sends money to her family in Mexico. I beg you; don't involve her in this."

He suspected she was illegal. He allowed her time to finish her thought, uninterrupted.

"Our marital problems have nothing to do with Kerri. We both love her very much. I may have chosen the wrong husband, but that doesn't make him a criminal. He's always provided for us, and he's successful in so many other ways. I believe he's telling the truth, and I pray they find Kerri soon."

"Me, too."

Barnum sought the squeak in his chair that had proven to irritate so many people. Most broke after the fifth squeak, but she was stronger than that. Normally, he would have been finished by now, but he still couldn't read her. "Where do you work?"

She closed her eyes to relax, but it was no use. These loose-ended scenarios had given her a walloping headache. "I work for Chevron Oil at Point Richmond," she said, while groping through her purse for some Advil. "You know, you really should oil that chair." She downed her pills dry.

"How about I take care of that right now?" Barnum made a point of opening his bottom drawer, taking out a can of 3-IN-ONE, and oiling every accessible part. He hated losing the squeak, but he thought he might get something in return. He located Point Richmond on the wall map. The Bay Shore freeway crawled during rush hour. How did she get Kerri to school and still make it to work on time? Then he remembered she had a nanny. "Must be a tough commute."

"Name someplace where it's easy."

He smiled again. "I'm curious. Why didn't you find a house closer to where you work after you separated? I mean, with such limited contact with Randy, why put up with a long commute? Surely there are suitable places in El Cerrito or San Pablo. Admittedly this has no bearing on this investigation, but I don't know anyone who can stand driving in gridlock."

"You're right. My commute is a royal pain, but I tolerate it because everything isn't about me. We live in the Oakland hills because we love the area and the schools. Randy grew up there and wanted Kerri to have the same experience. Why change that just because we went our separate ways?"

"That makes sense. Now, here's another thing that puzzles me. You both work full time and yet you end up with sole custody. You live within a couple of miles of each other and you say this isn't about you, so why wouldn't you agree to joint custody so your daughter can divide her time equally? I'm no expert, but it seems that would alleviate some of her anxiety."

"Kerri's custody has nothing to do with your finding her, and I'd appreciate it if you didn't tell me how to raise my child. As for our settlement agreement, it's legal and binding, so please keep your thoughts to yourself."

Barnum tapped his pencil, fascinated. He needed to look into their separation agreement. There was no need to pry further since their concurrence was a matter of record. Charlie's picture caught his eye again. He prayed his son would never end up in a situation like this.

"Here's my problem, Amanda. You claim Randy's a good father, yet you don't believe he should share custody of his daughter. Maybe it's because I'm a father, but I'd be pretty upset if I had that kind of arrangement."

"That's nice. Now, here's *my* problem. You obviously haven't heard a word I've said. I don't give a damn what you think, our custody agreement is between me and Randy. Got it?"

"Got it."

"Good. Now, here's a question for you. Do you think Randy kidnapped my daughter?"

Barnum locked his hands behind his head. "I'm not prepared to make such judgments."

She felt queasy. He was getting to her and knew it. Eyes never lied. She gracefully re-crossed her legs. "Let me rephrase that. In your opinion, do you believe he kidnapped Kerri?"

The detective stared back at her. Interrogations were like chess games, and she was a worthy opponent. "Opinions have no place in police work," he said. "As I already told you, I'm gathering facts. Nothing more, nothing less."

Her face softened. "Are you married, detective?"

"Almost eight years now."

She studied the boy's picture on his desk that looked to be about Kerri's age. She was surprised by Barnum's lack of compassion. "Who disciplines your son, detective? You or your wife?"

"When I'm gone, she does. When I'm home, we both do. Why?"

"You see? That's the difference. I've had to do everything because Randy was never around. In fact, he never has to be the bad guy around her. It's always play time when they get together. He spoils her rotten." She shook her head, massaging the finger that once wore his ring. "I quit work when Kerri was born and spent four years watching her do her 'firsts' while her father was at the office. He may as well have been a sperm donor, considering the extent to which he raised her. Kerri is everything to me, and that's why I have custody. I only went back to work so I could remain in the Oakland hills."

Her words speared the detective. He did whatever he could to help raise his son, but there were times when his job took priority. Today would be one of those days. He needed to talk to his wife to see if she harbored similar resentments. He dusted Charlie's framed photo and returned it to its spot. "So you're saying this custody issue isn't about jealousy?"

"What's there to be jealous of? Randy doesn't have time for us, so Kerri lives with me. He'd be the first to admit that his business would suffer if Kerri lived with him during the week. But don't take my word for it. Ask him."

I will." He twirled his pencil some more. "Where is his business located?"

"Emeryville, near Pixar Studios. It's called Bay View Advertising Agency. Like I said, he's hardly original. I suggested a different name, but of course, he ignored me." She settled back in her seat, surprised at how nasty that sounded.

Barnum studied the map. Her commute was twice that of his, and Amanda's living arrangements made as much sense as her skewed opinion of her husband. From what he saw, Randy Connifer was a dedicated father who craved time with his daughter. And if his business really meant that much to him, why risk it with a kidnapping? "Amanda, we both know your commute stinks, so how much time do you really have to spend with your daughter?"

"Look, I'll never be crowned Mother-of-the-Year, but I do the best I can. I work an early shift so I can pick her up after school. Elvia gets her there in the morning. She always helps with dinner, we watch TV together, and we *always* read before bed. In fact, thanks to me, she's already reading at the third grade level."

"That's terrific," Barnum said, still stuck on the custody issue. Charlie smiled at him from inside his picture frame. His son was growing up too fast. "Well, it sounds like Kerri gets plenty of attention. My apologies if I insulted you." She indifferently waved him off. "Now, let's revisit your tiff in the park where you attacked your husband. If you don't care for him, then why the anger, the passion?"

Her jaw dropped. *Passion?* The thought never occurred to her. Is it possible she still had feelings for him? Is that why she hadn't finalized their divorce? Is that why he still drove her nuts? *Impossible! He's just baiting you.* She swallowed softly and said, "My daughter disappeared in her father's custody. I reacted as any mother would. Now, unless you have some questions that deal specifically with Kerri, I'd like to take that shower you offered."

"Actually, I do have some questions about her. Does Kerri have any relatives in the Bay Area?"

"Sure. Randy's mother lives in Danville and my sister's in San Jose."

"What about his father? Is he—?"

"Dead? Yes, and if it matters, Randy's an only child."

"What about your folks? Are they still around?"

She stared at the rain pounding the window. "When Dad retired, they moved to Florida to get away from this miserable weather." Her life would have been so different had she moved there with them. She coyly looked up at him. "Detective, do you consider me a suspect?"

Barnum's hands went up. "As of now, no crime's been committed."

She clasped her hands together and leaned forward. "I still don't understand why they postponed the search. My daughter's out there alone and possibly dying. Would you sit around if *your* son was missing?"

He leaned back, pondering her comment. The phone's ring startled him. He grabbed it before it rang again. "Detective Barnum," he said, watching her while he listened. "Okay, keep me posted." He replaced the receiver and smiled at her. "That was Lt. Donovan. He said there's been a lot of press interest, and he'll handle them. He also said some dog teams are arriving, but that it's still too dangerous to let them in the park. For now, all we can do now is wait."

She bowed her head in defeat. "I understand."

"Would you mind telling me a little about your job?"

She shrugged to hide her concern. She was running errands this morning and didn't get to work until ten. Less than an hour later, she was out running more errands with no one to corroborate her story. She tugged at her damp clothes and met his gaze. "I'm a quality control technician. Basically, I test fuels for octane and contaminants. It's not rocket science, but I enjoy it."

He smiled genuinely. "How did you get into that field?"

"Chemistry. I found it fascinating, so I majored in it at UC Berkeley. I was working at Chevron when I got pregnant with Kerri. At first I was content staying at home, but when my marriage went sour, I went back to work. Fortunately, I had no problem getting my old job back, and I've recently been promoted to senior technician." She paused to read Barnum's citation that recognized him for arresting a robbery suspect without ever drawing his weapon. Nice to know brute force is good for something besides football. "Anyway, I'm back on track for a management position," she continued. "I've been very fortunate."

"I'd say so," he said, scanning his notes. "Do you currently receive any child support? Alimony?"

She grimaced and crossed her arms. "Of course. My salary's a pittance compared to Randy's. Surely, as an officer of the law, you know he has financial obligations to his child."

"I do, but alimony is separate from child support, and since you're not divorced, how can you be drawing it?"

Her eyes hardened. "You have no clue what it's like to be a single mother.

Never mind that my expenses more than doubled when I moved out. But you're right; I could manage without his money. The truth is I'm not willing to let him off that easy. You see, money has always been his first priority. He's so tight his wallet squeaks worse than your chair, so it's only right that Kerri and I get some of it. Besides, most of that money goes into her college fund."

Barnum scribbled more notes and looked up. "Okay, one last question, and this one's easy. Do you have anything of Kerri's with you? Lt. Donovan said the search dogs need a scent."

She rummaged through her purse and shook her head.

"Anything in your car?"

"No. I just had it cleaned."

He sighed. How could she not have a toy or stuffed animal with her? "I'll tell you what—let's stop by your house on the way back and find something she loves. If she's been traumatized, it will help having something personal."

There was a discreet tap at the door followed by an officer poking his head inside. The detective met him at the door. "Mr. Connifer has been waiting a long time," the intruder said. "How much longer?"

"Just a couple more minutes. How about giving him a tour of Dispatch while we finish up?"

"I'll do that." The officer then pulled the door shut.

EIGHTEEN

Randy's escort led him inside the Dispatch Operations Center. The dimly lit room was packed with computers and glowing operators' faces. Radios buzzed, but not from anything that concerned Kerri's search. His teeth began to chatter. "Have they resumed the search yet?"

"I don't know," the escort said. "Let's ask a dispatcher."

They waited for an opportune time, but the woman stayed busy answering non-stop calls. Randy couldn't stop shivering. "This is all very interesting, but I'm freezing."

"That's because our computers don't like heat. You want more coffee?"

"Do you have any decaf?"

"We may have some instant. Let's take a look." Randy's escort officer continued his discussion while searching the break room cabinets. "Sorry we couldn't get an update from Dispatch, but the last I heard, the Red Cross was setting up a shelter, and some dog teams had arrived. They're prepared for an extensive search, but this storm is really kicking their butts."

"Tell me about it," said Randy, warming his hands under some hot water. He leaned against the sink, drying them, facing the officer. "Any idea what's taking them so long? I mean, my wife's been in there long enough to have an affair."

The officer chuckled, still rummaging for the decaf. He had rearranged the entire cabinet before finding the Folgers jar. He dusted it off and handed it over. "I knew we had some, but as you can see, no one drinks it."

"I guess not," he said, taking the jar. He unscrewed the lid and sniffed its contents. Everything looked okay, so he spooned some of the crystals into an empty cup. The aroma came to life when he added hot water. Powdered creamer added some froth. He raised it to his lips, took a tentative sip, and licked his coffee mustache. "It's not too bad. Thanks."

He set it aside, concerned about his wife's lengthy meeting with Detective Barnum. She could seriously damage his reputation in that amount of time. Was their marriage really that bad? They were so happy when Kerri was born. But then Amanda changed. At first, he wondered if it was post-partum depression, but things never improved. Eventually he realized that their marriage was over and it was pointless living together.

Randy's escort informed him that Detective Barnum was now ready for him. Following the policeman down the narrow hall made him feel like a convict. Walking in borrowed orange sweats completed the image. The officer knocked, opened Barnum's door, and the giant behind the desk waved him in. Randy entered and closed the door.

"Have a seat," Barnum said, allowing Randy a moment to get comfortable. He wouldn't, of course, but it was fun watching him try. "So, what do you think of our dispatch facility?"

"I think your dispatchers are freezing."

"Yeah, it is a bit chilly in there." The detective leaned back in his seat, locking his hands behind his head like he always does. "So, how are you holding up?"

"Okay. By the way, thanks for the shower and sweats. I get the impression they're holding my clothes hostage until I give these back."

"I wouldn't be surprised."

Randy's eyes roamed the room while the detective reviewed his notes. Barnum's office resembled a recycling dump. How could he possibly find anything in this mess? He avoided the detective's silent intimidation ploy by playing dumb. "So, where's Amanda?"

"You're shivering. Are you warm enough?"

"I've been warmer." Another moment passed. "I was asking about my wife."

"Oh, she's showering. Hopefully, the naphtha soap will help prevent a rash."

"Any soap that smells that bad ought to do something good."

Barnum chuckled. "I hear you. Anyway, your wife and I had an interesting chat. She said you were the one who filed for divorce. Is that true?"

"Our marriage wasn't working. It was a mutual filing."

The detective twirled his pencil between his lips. "You surprise me, Randy. Usually people filing for divorce can't say anything good about their spouse, but you've been remarkably polite."

He hiked his shoulders, slouching to let the space heater warm his feet. "I have nothing against her. We just weren't a good match."

"You want me to move that heater for you?"

"No, I'm fine."

"Good," Barnum said, flipping through his notebook. "Randy, has your wife ever denied you visitation rights?"

"Detective, we may still be legally married, but it's been years since she was my wife, so please refer to her as Amanda."

Barnum nodded, tapping his fingertips together. “We were discussing visitation rights.”

Randy reached down to massage his legs, then leaned back to rub his neck. “Kerri is always ready when I come to get her. In that regard, things have worked out well.”

“Glad to hear it. So, how do you two handle holidays, birthdays?”

“We alternate, of course. Kerri understands. In fact, I think she kind of likes celebrating multiple Christmases. More presents, you know.”

Somehow he doubted Kerri understood how Santa filled stockings at both houses. The Easter Bunny posed similar problems. He felt sorry for kids of divorce. Too many grew up blaming themselves for the breakup. He moved on. “So you say that Kerri’s dealing with it; what about you? Does it bother you when you can’t see her on her birthday or Christmas?”

“Of course, but it’s ludicrous to think we should celebrate these events as a family. For starters, Amanda’s mother hates me, and neither she nor her husband acknowledge me. Their last visit was on Kerri’s birthday, and she made a point of *un*-inviting me. Of course, it hurt, but I figured as long as Kerri was handling it, I could too.”

Barnum noted the time. His shift would end soon. All this talk about divorce and missing children was depressing. He yearned to hug his son and tell him how much he loved him. He needed to spend more time with Charlie.

“I don’t get it, Randy. Why would you agree to such a restrictive visitation schedule when you could have sued for joint custody? After all, you both work, have nice homes, and love your daughter. I would think any reasonable judge would support you.”

He adamantly shook his head. “Amanda threatened to move to Florida and I couldn’t let that happen. By the way, her parents were the ones encouraging the move.” He rose from his chair, pacing the room. “Have you ever been to divorce court, detective?” Barnum shook his head. “Judges always take the woman’s side in custody battles; especially if it’s a female judge like ours was. Women judges empathize with stay-at-home moms, which Amanda was at the time. Of course, now that she’s working again, I could probably take her back to court, but that would make Kerri a pawn, and I’d never do that to her.”

“I see.” He underlined “check custody documents” in his notes as a reminder.

It occurred to Randy that he was saying things he had never told his marriage counselor. If he had, maybe they would still be together. He dragged a finger across a computer monitor, leaving a dusty trail. “As I said, Amanda’s a fine mom. It was a big sacrifice, quitting her job to raise Kerri. I've always wondered if Kerri resented me for making her mom go back to work. She's never mentioned it, but I wouldn't be surprised if it came up."

"What did your lawyer think about this settlement agreement?"

"Actually, he recommended I go along with it, saying I had little chance winning against a full-time mother. I stupidly accepted his advice, believing a set schedule, meager as it was, is better than nothing."

"Have you dated anyone since you separated?"

"Do I *look* like I enjoy pain? Besides, technically I'm still married, remember?" He clasped his hands together and squeezed until his knuckles turned white. "What does this have to do with Kerri?"

"Just answer the question, please."

"No, I haven't dated anyone, nor do I have any desire to."

Barnum gave a silent nod as he pondered more inconsistencies. *Randy wants to spend more time with his daughter, yet his wife claims he doesn't have the time. Amanda loves her job and tolerates a long commute to keep Kerri in the Oakland hills, yet threatens to move to Florida.* Will she move to Florida once her divorce is final? Similar threats have provoked kidnappings. "Randy, I've only heard bits and pieces of what happened this morning, so how about starting from the beginning, and don't spare any details."

He settled into his chair, pleased to finally field a question about his daughter. He closed his eyes, picturing her smile when he picked her up this morning. He bragged about her school work, and how she always helped around the house. He reminisced about how the leaves made ocean waves, and how she always giggled before running ahead. He tried to mimic her sound, but it came out more like a trumpeting elk. His eyes opened and a muddle of cold and fear shot through him as he described being stalked. "Kerri disappeared soon after that."

Barnum set his pencil down. Everything Randy said matched what Rodriquez had told him, except that this was the first time he had ever heard about a stalker. If Randy Connifer was acting, he deserved an Oscar. He may want Kerri for himself, but who would agree to her kidnapping? More importantly, why didn't she scream if she was being carried away? Surely someone would have heard her. Until proven otherwise, he had to believe that Kerri Connifer had vanished without a trace.

NINETEEN

The phone rang again and Detective Barnum answered, eyeing Randy as he listened. "He can't call back later?…Fine—put him through." The detective cupped his hand over the phone. "I'm sorry, Randy, but I have to take this call. Would you mind waiting outside? It shouldn't take long."

"No problem."

Randy stepped into the hall and closed the door, curious who was on the phone. Did it concern the search or was it something else? He looked for Amanda, but she was nowhere in sight. He figured he had a few minutes to kill before he would be recalled.

* * * * *

Parks Police Officer Hector Rodriquez waited for Barnum to say something. He hated interrupting an interview, but this couldn't wait. He was calling from Skyline Gate, huddled under a large tent where Lt. Donovan was addressing the search party. The canvas sagged under the water weight. A gust rattled the fabric, flinging pooled water to the pavement. The resulting splash doused him, and added to his misery.

Barnum tried his best to interpret Rodriquez' phone conversation. Wind and rain made him difficult to understand. From what he gathered, Lt. Donovan was now letting the dog handlers in, but they still needed Kerri's scent before they could begin. "I'll get you your scent, Hector, but I expected your interruption had more content than this."

"Say again, Dave? I can't hear you." People turned around, staring at him. Rodriquez lowered his voice and cupped his hand over the mouthpiece. "I've got to go. Get here as soon as possible. Everyone's waiting on you—"

The detective slid his notepad into his desk drawer and went to the door half-expecting to find Randy leaning against it. Instead, the hall was empty. He was supposed to be off duty in ten minutes. Why did Rodriquez have to call him?

Barnum located Randy in the break room where he seemed to be comparing notes with Amanda. "That was Officer Rodriquez," he said to them. "Grab your belongings. We're taking a ride."

They piled into the detective's car, this time with Amanda in the front seat so she could give directions to her house. The visibility had improved slightly, but the rain remained heavy. Barnum found Randy in the mirror. "No offense, but I figure Kerri's mother would have a fresher scent."

"That's fine, but can you swing by my place so I can change clothes?"

"Sure, right after we stop by the park. And just so you know, we're not finished talking." He slowed the car for another detour. "Looks like more downed power lines."

"At least the work crews are here," Amanda said, gawking at them as they inched by.

Barnum waved to the crew. "Let's hope your house has power."

They arrived at Amanda's home soon after. Randy tucked his hands under his pits to warm himself. "If it's okay with you, I'll wait in the car."

"Fine with me," Barnum said, and followed Amanda to her door. After she kicked off her shoes, he stepped forward to go inside, but she blocked the entry, staring at his feet. He took the hint and removed his shoes, embarrassed by the hole in his sock. When she wasn't looking, he adjusted it so the hole wasn't as obvious.

He entered and soon realized why she insisted he go shoeless. Her house was spotless with light tones and bay windows that made it feel spacious. Potpourri refreshed the air. A potted palm stood in the corner. "Nice place," he said, looking around.

"Thanks. It's perfect for the two of us. Kerri's room is down the hall. Why don't you pick something out while I change?" She disappeared upstairs before he could answer.

Kerri's bedroom was typical for a young girl of her parents' stature. Her white bed frame and lace curtains complimented the light-blue walls. Disney pictures were neatly hung. Stuffed animals lay everywhere. There were photos of her mother, but none of her father. He was sorting through the stuffed animals when Amanda came in wearing skin tight blue jeans, hiking boots, and a fleece top. The detective grabbed the first two animals he came to and held them up. "Which one's her favorite?"

She pointed to the pear-shaped yellow fuzz ball whose orange bill and feet gave minimal clues as to its identity. "You have to use your imagination, but it's a duck. Kerri loves that thing. Come on, let's go."

He was about to stuff the toy under his coat when he noticed the white formal dress hanging in the closet was draped in plastic. He removed the dress cover and started wrapping the worn-out duck in it to minimize contamination. "Does Kerri sleep with this thing?"

"Every night. His name is Taco, and the park and school are the only places she won't take him. It's as much a part of her as her smile."

Barnum contemplated that while following her to the exit. He handed Taco to her while he tied his shoes. She was locking the front door when another thought came to him. "Sorry I didn't ask sooner, but do you have a photo of Kerri that we can release to the press?"

"Of course."

He followed her into the living room where she handed him the studio portrait from the mantle. It was the first photo he noticed, and though beautiful, he had hoped for something more natural. He thanked her and slipped his shoes on for what he hoped was the last time today.

* * * * *

Barnum glanced over his shoulder to apologize. "Sorry we took so long, but we had to get a picture. You live on Shepherd Canyon, right?"

"That's right. A couple of blocks below Skyline."

"That's what I thought. We'll drop the duck and photo off at the park, and then head to your house."

"Would you mind dropping me off at my car?" Amanda said.

He abruptly shook his head. "We need to stick together. Who knows what we might miss if we don't?"

His comment jabbed Randy. What did he think? That he had stashed Kerri somewhere in his house? Randy grabbed his legs, but they wouldn't stop shaking.

Amanda was not happy. Her former home was the last place she wanted to go. When she moved out, she had vowed never to set foot in there again. Whenever her husband invited her in, she always declined, just as he did at her place.

Barnum double-parked on Skyline Boulevard, then explained to the traffic cop what he was doing. He grabbed Taco, dashed to the tent, and returned shortly after; smiling as he buckled his seat belt. "Good news, everyone. The winds have died down so they're going back in. Lt. Donovan said he'd give Taco to the dog team coordinator. He promised they'd take good car of him."

Randy sighed, thinking about Kerri. "I hope so."

TWENTY

Amanda's heart hammered her when they pulled up to Randy's house. His one-story stucco was nicely framed by tall pines and a narrow grass strip. Sadly, it still felt like home. The only thing missing was their daughter. She hoped that no one recognized her sitting in the car.

Barnum looked over at her. "Okay, let's go."

"That's all right; I'll stay here."

"Actually, that wasn't a request, Amanda. I'd like everyone inside."

"*Fine.*"

She got out and sprinted to the entry, dreading going through the door.

Randy squeezed past her to unlock it. He left it open and headed straight to the bedroom. "Feel free to look around."

The detective ignored Randy and glanced at Amanda. "How about showing me around? It'll save us some time."

Her pulse quickened, standing in front of the entry. "Why are we going inside? You already gave Taco to the Incident Commander. What do you expect to find here?"

"If I knew that, I would've found it by now."

She stood her ground, wondering why the detective was being so elusive. He was like a different person from the one she spoke to earlier. *What did Randy say to change him?*

Barnum slid past her and invited her to join him. "Humor me, Amanda. Detectives are naturally curious. My job is like that box of chocolates Forrest Gump talks about. You know—the one about never knowing what you got until you bite into it?" She gave a sneering look, so he added, "Relax. I'm not setting a trap. It's just that the more I know about your daughter's environment, the easier it is to find her. That's why I need your cooperation."

Reluctantly, she led the way.

The detective was amazed at what he saw. Unlike Amanda's house, this place looked lived in. There were pictures of the three of them as though time stood still. Kerri's room reflected the same love and devotion as in her mother's house, with stuffed animals cluttering her white four-poster bed. A matching desk with a half-completed rainbow painting awaited Kerri's return. A children's book lay open, upside down on the nightstand. Her kindergarten graduation certificate hung centered above the kid-and-dog-on-toboggan sculpture on her desk. Fake snowflakes and rainbows adorned her windowsill.

"Can we leave, now?"

Barnum called down the hall. "Randy, are you about ready?"

"Yup." He emerged from his room wearing bright yellow rain gear.

"Wow. You're quite the man of the sea," the detective said with a grin.

"Remnants from my single days," he said. "I used to crew on a friend's sailboat and always knew these would come in handy. I just never imagined it would be like this."

"Well, no one will mistake you for a deer, that's for sure. Let's go."

Amanda knew his seafaring comment was directed at her. It was filled with resentment when he said it. When they first met, he kept inviting her to go sailing, but she preferred watching from the shore. After several declines, he never asked or even mentioned sailing again. No doubt he missed being part of that crew, though. She headed for the door, dismayed.

Randy felt bad for saying that. Amanda's hurt was not an act. He yearned to hold her, tell her everything would be all right. Instead his arms hung limp at his side. He caught up to her and met her eyes. "I'm sorry he made you come here. I know it's hard on you."

"As always, you give yourself too much credit." She darted off, solo.

He locked his front door and ran to join them in the car. All conversation ceased after he got in. He wondered what they were thinking as they chugged uphill to reach Skyline Boulevard. Two minutes later they were at Skyline Gate.

Panel vans with raised antennas were parked across the street, ready to transmit. Tragedy always made great news, but this storm sensationalized the missing child story. A reporter spotted the unmarked police car and ran over, microphone in hand. Before Barnum could turn the ignition off, a throng of reporters and videographers converged on them like piranha. "Are you Kerri's parents?" one asked. A woman toward the rear shouted, "How are you feeling right now?"

The detective saw Amanda slouch in her seat, trying to hide. "Reporters can be a pain in the ass," he explained, "but in this case I recommend you exploit them. The more people see of Kerri, the better off we are."

She gave a cool nod while fixing her hair.

Barnum's comment caught Randy's attention. He was right; they needed to exploit the press. He climbed out of the car and someone fed him a microphone. He ignored someone's remark about his sailor suit and blurted out, "I'm Kerri's father." To his surprise, his wife nudged his side. "And this is—"

"Her mother?" a reporter said, hoping to edge out her competition. Her videographer zoomed in for a close-up. "Do you think Kerri's been kidnapped?"

Randy shielded his eyes, straining to recognize the woman. Her microphone identified her as being with Channel 4. Her aggressive nature just might play into his hand. He searched for some eluding words. "The Regional Parks Police are handling this case," he calmly said. "I suggest you talk to them."

"We already have," the woman threw back. "They said you were the last one to see her. Can you tell us what happened?"

Randy trembled. The reporter was right. He was the last one to see Kerri. But as for what happened, his mind spun like a kaleidoscope. He saw that Amanda was overcome by the swarming hive of microphones. He detested reporters who baited people and then distorted what they said. It happened every day on the evening news. He cleared his throat and confidently said, "I wish I knew what happened. One minute Kerri and I were having fun and the next she was gone. She ran ahead of me, rounded a blind corner, and vanished. No one's seen her since."

"But you're her father. How could you let her run ahead like that?"

He bit his tongue. He had been asking the same question all morning and still didn't have an answer. He wanted to say he didn't believe in putting kids on a leash, but he saw no benefit in raising that issue. "It could've happened to anyone."

"Lt. Donovan said someone was stalking you. Is that true?"

"Actually, what I said was it felt like we were being watched. I never saw anyone, and I have no way of knowing if anyone was ever there." His neck throbbed. He pictured himself floating above the crowd, calling Kerri's name. He imagined her popping out from behind a tree and saying, "Boo", but the spotlights burst the image. The reporter prompted him to continue, but he couldn't. Not now.

"Do you accept responsibility for your daughter's disappearance?"

"I let her get too far ahead. In that regard, I accept the blame."

The cameras found Amanda who gave them a baffled look to buy some time. Randy had perfected that technique in business meetings, stalling while his associates checked out his competition. She pictured today's *Live-at-Five* lead-in: *"Advertising mogul accepts blame in daughter's disappearance."* She couldn't let that happen. He didn't deserve more ridicule. She took his hand, staring into the lights. "It wasn't my husband's fault. We'll see this through together."

Detective Barnum had stepped out of his car just as Amanda made her statement. Her unlikely shift in support reminded him of siblings that form alliances against outsiders. He could cut the reporters off at any time, but so far, neither parent was asking for his help. *They opened Pandora's Box, and now they have to deal with it.*

The reporter pressed Amanda for more. "So, to clarify, are you implying that our regional parks aren't safe, or that some parents can't properly watch over their children?"

Amanda's narrow eyes pierced the reporter. "Every parent knows that six-year-olds are curious and full of energy. Kerri was no exception." She stopped herself, and the crowd grew silent. Everyone knew she had something more to say. The rain bounced off the pavement. Spotlights lit up her face. Finally, Amanda's expression softened and her eyes welled. "Kerri ran ahead, and now she's gone," she tenderly said. "If anyone has my baby, I beg you to drop her at a hospital, police station, fire station, wherever. We love her and desperately want her back."

Barnum stepped forward, flashing his badge, wanting to end this before any accusations were made. "That's all for now. Lt. Donovan will provide you with updates."

"Hey, wait a minute," someone said. "You can't end an interview like that."

"I can and I did. Now, either keep your distance, or prepare to be arrested for interfering in a police investigation. Do I make myself clear?"

Channel 4's TV reporter glanced at her videographer who assured her they had plenty of footage for her story. Kerri's parents were walking away with the detective when the reporter yelled out, "We'll be here if either of you care to talk." Neither turned around. Perhaps it was for the best, as she had to rush to get her story on the evening news.

Barnum led Randy and Amanda to the assembly tent and seated them in a corner table. "Wait here. I need to speak with Lt. Donovan."

"No sweat."

Emergency personnel spent their time talking amongst themselves, but occasionally glanced over their shoulders at Amanda. Randy knew they were admiring his wife. Even under a rain hat, she looked as beautiful as the day he met her. He fumbled with his hands, wanting to hold hers. He avoided her eyes and said, "Thanks for bailing me out."

"You would've done the same for me."

"Even so, I appreciate your support."

She looked at him and then back at the forest, her heart full of resentment.

His eyes were worrisome. She pitied him as she would a lost child. Still, they were in this together and she managed a smile. "So, you finally needed me, eh?"

"I do, and always have. I'm just not very good at saying it."

She glanced his way, but he still avoided her. His emotional display confused her and complicated things. She watched the rain pound the asphalt. She thought about the TV reporters hounding them. Hopefully, Barnum's intuition was right about them exploiting the media. With luck, whoever had Kerri would see their pleas on TV. But as of yet, no one had responded to Kerri's AMBER Alert. Surely, someone would have picked Kerri up if she was wandering the streets. Her chin quivered as she leaned her head against her husband's shoulder. "I'm sorry I attacked you, Randy. I should've given you a chance to explain. I can't blame you for what happened. I just pray someone finds her." She nudged Randy when she noticed Barnum leading a uniformed police officer and a woman with her search dog over to them.

Barnum smiled at them. "Randy, Amanda, I'd like you to meet Lt. Donovan and Stacey Webster. Lt. Donovan is the Incident Commander; Stacey is one of our rescue dog handlers. That's her dog, Tracker."

Randy stood to exchange handshakes with them. Donovan's grip was firm compared to Webster's. From her face, Webster looked to be in her early thirties. Her insulated orange pantsuit and white helmet concealed her physical features. She held her German shepherd's lead taut, so Randy resisted the urge to pet him. "Thanks for helping," he said to them.

"You're welcome," Webster replied. "I only wish we were meeting under more pleasant circumstances." She smiled at her dog. "Tracker, shake." Tracker stuck out his massive paw, but pulled it away as soon as Randy bent down to shake it. To spare any awkwardness, he stayed down, pretending to admire the dog's backpack that bore a white cross.

"I'm sorry," Webster said, "but Tracker's all business whenever he wears his backpack." She watched her dog sniff the air. "He's pretty frustrated, so we're taking a break. Lt. Donovan pointed you out, so I wanted to come over and say hi."

"We're glad you did. You say your dog's frustrated?"

"It's complicated. You see, several dogs have found Kerri's scent, but so far there's no sign of her. Of course, we haven't been at it very long." Her words faded into the forest where flashlights darted like fireflies and commands were occasionally shouted. She turned back to Kerri's parents. "Tracker and I walked East Ridge Trail, and then Eucalyptus to Stream Trail. We came back after he got burned out."

"Burned out?" Amanda said. "What does that mean? You just said you haven't been at it long."

Webster kneeled, stroking her dog's neck, hoping they could see the determination in his eyes. If they knew anything about animals, they could see that he was frustrated. "Tracking can be exhausting," she said, searching for a suitable analogy. "Have you ever smelled cinnamon rolls and then sniffed the air until you located the source?" She assumed Randy's shrug meant "yes" so she continued her explanation. "In a sense, that smell is like a scent cone, and like pastry, every person's is unique. The problem is dogs inhale all kinds of scents so they have to sort the one they're seeking. That, in itself, is tasking enough, but Tracker's feet were caked with muck, so every step is the equivalent of five or six on dry dirt. While every dog has a heightened sense of smell, German shepherds and bloodhounds are particularly well-suited for search and rescue. When they sniff, they inhale huge volumes of air. The result is like us hyperventilating, and eventually it tires them.

"The good news is Tracker has found Kerri's sent several times and he's working hard to narrow the search, but for some reason, her scent keeps breaking up. It's strong in some areas; weak in others." She looked at Randy. "I was told you and Kerri were on East Ridge Trail near Eucalyptus when she disappeared. Is that right?"

"Yes, but we were also here last Sunday. But doesn't the rain wipe the forest clean?"

"Surprisingly, no. Search dogs have located victims under several feet of water, so this rain shouldn't make much difference."

"How is that possible?" Amanda said that while admiring the dog.

"Well, scents come from the skin cells we constantly shed, which are why everyone's scent is distinctive. Now, imagine these cells dispersing in a cone like blowing powder from a nozzle. The farther from the source, the more dissipated the spray, but the powder is still there." She continued after her audience bobbed their heads. "Dogs zigzag while searching for a scent cone. Once they find it, they home in on it like a beacon. Unfortunately, old scents can also distract them. These gusty winds haven't helped matters."

The ground thumped and everyone searched the forest for the tree that must have fallen. Soon after, a radio call came in saying a member of the search team has a large splinter in his leg. Someone requested a four-wheeler to get him out.

Lt. Donovan stepped aside to handle the request and then re-joined them. "Sorry for the interruption, but I'm afraid it's not safe to continue. It could be morning before we resume operations. I'm sorry."

"Morning?" Amanda said. "But it's barely dinner time."

Stacey Webster skimmed the rain off her dog's fur. "Amanda, I'm not happy about this either, but the delay is actually good for Tracker and the other dogs. They'll perform better once they get some rest."

Amanda pleaded with Donovan. "So that's it? Everyone's leaving?"

"Under the circumstances, it's for the best," he said.

"Every handler knows their dog's limitations," Webster added. "Tracker and I have an incredible bond, so I can usually tell what he's thinking." She ruffled his thick fur and then stroked it smooth. "You see the way he's sitting? He may look relaxed, but I know he's still searching for her scent. To him, this is a game, and he hates losing. Trust me, he knows where we left off, and he desperately wants to finish this."

Randy got up. "So, what happens if the weather doesn't clear by morning? Do you keep postponing until all your volunteers quit? Don't you understand? We've got to find her before she dies of exposure." When Donovan didn't answer, he turned to Stacey. "If Tracker's as good as you say, then let me lead him into the woods. It's worth the risk. I have nothing to lose."

Webster sighed. "While I appreciate your concern, you're not hearing what I said. Tracker knows she's in there. This isn't a question of wanting to go back into the woods or about my dog's abilities. In fact Tracker's been credited with over twenty saves, most of which came from the attack on the World Trade Center. He's one of the best search dogs I've trained, but I agree that it's not safe to continue right now. Believe me, there are no egos in play here. It doesn't matter who finds your daughter. We'll all share the joy when she's found."

TWENTY-ONE

Randy watched the water flow under his feet. The asphalt shimmered like seal skin; its ripples giving it life. His mind went numb once Stacey said she was quitting. He sat there, mentally retracing every step that he and Kerri took during their last three visits to Redwood Park. Scenes kept playing in his head like an endless video loop. Last Sunday they walked Stream Trail. Eucalyptus connected Stream with East Ridge and Phillips Loop. The park was a labyrinth with endless possibilities. No wonder Tracker was confused. Finally, he looked at Webster. "Stacey, I'm sorry. I didn't mean to be rude. Thanks for trying."

"It's okay; I'd feel the same way." She tugged at Tracker's leash and led him to her car.

Randy watched her leave. "Well, lieutenant, how can we find Kerri if the dogs can't?"

"Miracles happen, Randy. Keep the faith." He checked his watch. Late again. He thought about Amanda's criticism of her husband. He needed to get home fast. "Well, I'm outta here. I suggest you folks get some rest. Randy, we'll talk another time."

"I'm sure."

When the detective left, Randy looked at his wife, her eyes echoing his fear. The lot emptied as quickly as it filled. Soon, only two cars remained. *Theirs*. "I don't know about you, but I can't just sit here," he said. "I'm going back in."

"Oh, that's real smart. The police won't risk it, but you will? You've combed the area, and so did the dogs. Either Kerri's not there, or she's—"

"Don't say it. Don't even think it." He walked to his Beemer and grabbed a couple of flashlights from the trunk. He didn't expect her to follow him.

"You're not the only one who cares," she said, grabbing a light. "So, tell me hero, what's your plan?"

"To keep from falling. If anything breaks loose, I'll be taking a long slide."

"I've got news for you. If *I* fall, I'm taking you with me."

He cautiously led her into the park where the ground sucked at their feet like giant tentacles. Her hiking boots must have weighed twice what they did before, but she didn't complain. When they paused to catch their breath, a distant street light shaped her silhouette. *Still beautiful.* "Thanks for coming."

"I didn't do it for you."

He watched her turn away, her sharp words blindsiding him. He stepped back and suddenly the ground gave way. For the second time today, he was riding a mudslide, only this time he was falling head-first on his back. He spread his legs and arms, and dug a heel into the dirt. His action flipped him around, but did nothing to slow him. He guarded his neck and eyes with one hand and clung to his flashlight with the other. He crossed his legs, bracing for impact as the ferns, redwood needles, and his rain suit accelerated his fall. When the shrubs tore into his rain gear, his brain went into the survival mode and made him twist to the right. He stuck the butt end of his flashlight in the mud, but this action caused him to roll. Now sideways and out of control, he kicked his feet to straighten himself, but this put him on his belly, feet first. He grabbed some ferns, dug in his toes, and finally came to rest. Miraculously, he was fine except for minor lacerations. Amanda was frantically calling to him from above. "I'm okay," he yelled back. "Stay where you are and wave your flashlight so I can see you."

She shone her beam into the abyss, horrified when he didn't answer. Figuring he must be hurt, she sat down and started easing her way down the slope. "I'm coming, Randy."

"No, Amanda! Stay where you are! I'm okay. Just wave your flashlight."

This time she heard him and waved her flashlight like she would a July 4th sparkler. She moved to her left and felt her foot slip. Without warning, the saturated ground let go, and she found herself riding a mud avalanche. "Randy!"

He was climbing toward the light beam fifty yards above him when it suddenly disappeared. He heard a murky rumble and instantly knew what it was. His light found a suitable tree that he could hide behind just before the slide reached him.

His flashlight dug into his fingers as he clung to the trunk while the oozing mud grabbed at his feet. Thankfully, he and the tree both stood their ground.

Once the slide passed, he found some solid ground and checked himself over. His hands were raw, mud seeped from his yellow slickers, but at least he was alive. He sat down, thinking about Kerri. What if she had fallen like this? What if she lay face-down in the stream bed? It would be a raging river by now, eroding slopes, and uprooting trees. Under these conditions, she would drown for sure.

His mind wove appalling scenarios until he remembered she was missing before the rain, the mud slides, the raging river. Besides, Jerome and Jessica had searched the stream bed. Later, Stacey Webster and her dog had done the same. His wife's shrieks brought him back. He looked up the slope for her light, but only saw black. "Amanda! Where are you? Are you okay?"

She lay on her back, struggling to catch her breath. She was thirty feet from the summit and her body hurt like hell. She was lucky a small pine stopped her, but her ribs felt like they'd been knifed. She slowly rolled over and discovered her flashlight digging into her chest. The pain went away as soon as she removed it. She forced herself to sit up to clean the mud off the lens, and to aim her beam down the slope. Randy's light signaled back and started moving toward her again. *Thank God.*

It took thirty minutes for Randy to reach her. Without thinking, they embraced; grateful they had both survived their foolish stunt.

Amanda smiled, patting his chest before awkwardly stepping away. "Well, that was interesting."

"Yes it was," he said, quickly adding, "The last thing Kerri needs is to lose both her parents through an act of stupidity." Amanda seemed relieved by his comment.

Randy aimed his light, guiding the way for Amanda's climb. When she reached the end of his beam, she sat down and cast her light back at him. They leapfrogged light beams until reaching the summit, then sat there, breathing hard, contemplating their predicament.

She was the first to break their silence. "You know, Kerri's the best thing that ever happened to us. I can't imagine our lives without her."

"I know." He ached to hold her again, but held back. Maybe things would be different some day, but the thought soon left him. He struggled to his feet, aimed his light down the trail, and offered his arm for support. "Let's go home."

She accepted his gesture and limped along with him. "Randy, I've always known that you adore Kerri, but I never realized how much until I stepped inside your house. Why all the pictures of the three of us? Of me?"

"Why not?"

She didn't answer. Instead, she maneuvered him around a puddle, thankful he never toured her house. She had worked so hard to rid herself of him, and yet for some reason, he never let go. What did that say about her? That she was still struggling with her demons? He was right about one thing; no matter what, they will always be connected through Kerri. She finally said, "I'm glad you kept the pictures."

He smiled warmly and walked with her.

TWENTY-TWO

Arriving at Skyline Gate ended their tender mood. The empty parking lot drove home the reality that their daughter was missing. They went their separate ways with barely a good-bye.

Randy pulled into his driveway and set the parking brake, stretching his back before getting out. How many messages did he miss concerning Wilson Industries? His gossamer-thin concern soon vanished. Wilson Industries no longer mattered. In fact, nothing mattered any more.

He stripped off his rain gear and lumbered into the bathroom. Following a quick shower, he went into the living room and plopped on the sofa, intent on watching the news. But before his finger could hit the remote, his body succumbed to slumber. Soon, Kerri was taunting him from another realm. "*Why did you abandon me, Daddy? Was it something I said? I only wanted to get you and Mommy back together.*"

Kerri's image was jarringly clear. Gale force winds messed her hair and shred her clothes. She reached out to squeeze his throat and he screamed, pushing her away. The phone rang and Kerri was gone. He sat up, soaked in sweat, rancid with the smell of fear. He finally answered. It was Amanda.

"Did I wake you?"

"No." He lied, swallowing to soothe his raw throat. What a nightmare! He needed a drink. Anything non-alcoholic would do. Then again, maybe a shot wouldn't hurt. "I take it you couldn't sleep either?"

Her voice cracked. "I'm sitting in Kerri's room, going through her pictures. My God, Randy, I can't believe she's gone."

"Don't torture yourself, Amanda. We've been over this. She's alive; they just haven't found her yet." His body trembled in the darkness; Kerri's hand at his throat again. Then he realized it was his own.

"Randy? Are you there?"

"Yeah. Sorry." He was holding the phone over his chest when she started whimpering. He was on the verge of losing it himself. It took a while for the lump in his throat to go away so he could speak. "Listen, Amanda, since neither of us can sleep, why don't we get together and brainstorm over what we can do to find her? I can't leave this up to Lt. Donovan, and I suspect you feel the same." She maintained her silence. "Amanda? Would you mind coming over?"

His invitation made her tense. In fact, going back to his house scared the hell out of her, but not as much as losing Kerri. "Put on some coffee and I'll be over—and make it strong."

After turning on a lamp, he noticed a spider web in the corner. A drywall nail was working its way out. The ceiling fan was covered in dust. How in the world did she keep her house so immaculate?

His brain conjured interchanging images of his wife and daughter. He had once overheard Kerri praying for them to reconcile, but he refused to believe that she would run away. Besides, Kerri would never ever leave Taco behind. He walked into the kitchen and slid a coffee pouch into the machine.

While the coffee dripped, he went to take a bath, hoping it would sooth his itching skin. He first noticed his poison oak rash when he slipped off his pajamas. Barnum warned him to use cool water, but his body ached too much for that. His lacerations stung as he sank into the tub. He closed his eyes and his breathing slowed. He fought to stay awake. The banging at the front door dragged him back to the real world.

The bath water was cool now; his skin wrinkled. He shivered and grabbed his robe as the banging continued. "I'm coming," he yelled, hobbling to the door. A sour face greeted him when he opened it. "I'm really sorry, Amanda. Please, come in and pour yourself some coffee while I get dressed."

He disappeared into the bathroom and spread Calamine lotion on his rash. He emerged with the pink stuff all over his face and arms. He held up the bottle. "You need any?"

"No, thanks." She wore no makeup; her hair was tangled, dark bags hung from her eyes. Surprisingly, she didn't care.

Randy refilled her mug and sat down next to her. "Do your folks know?"

She shook her head. "Mom would go ballistic. You know how she is. It's always easier explaining things after the fact. For now, I'm not telling anyone."

"But doesn't Karen still live in the Bay Area? I mean, how can you keep it from your sister when it's all over the news? And if by some chance she didn't see it on TV, she'll certainly read about it in the morning paper."

She casually gulped her drink. "Even if Karen knew, she'd never call Mom without talking to me first, and since neither has called, I'll assume they don't know."

He went to add sweetener to his coffee, but instead opened the freezer door. "You want something to eat?"

She rubbed her head, hoping the Advil would kick in soon. "No thanks.

The thought of food is enough to make me sick." She heard the freezer door close. "Look, Randy, I appreciate your hospitality, but I thought you wanted to talk about Kerri."

"I do. I've been thinking about her all night and I keep asking myself how I'd handle this from a business standpoint." Her eyes sharpened. "No, wait—hear me out. What I'm saying is we have to promote her like we would a product. Remember what Detective Barnum said? The more people that see her, the better chance we have of finding her."

She took another sip, giving him the opportunity to explain.

"Now, I doubt that our press interview came off very well," he began, "so if we want more sympathy, we'll need to change our tactics. No one's found any sign of her, so it's time we assumed Kerri's not in the park." He paused for a moment. He had thought everything out, but it was so hard speaking his words. After a few breaths, he said, "What I'm trying to say is if by some chance she's been abducted, then I think we should make a formal appeal to her captor."

Amanda wrapped her hands around her coffee mug, angered that Randy would turn this into a business solution. But once she analyzed it, she realized he was right. "What did you have in mind?"

He paced the kitchen, gaining momentum with each step. "I've heard that kidnappers get their kicks from destroying other peoples' lives. I'd be willing to bet that whoever's responsible for her disappearance is watching it play out on TV, so it's essential that we appear united." He paused, and she gestured for him to continue. At least she was listening. "Right now, Kerri is just another missing child, but we're going to change that. Before the day is over, every major television station across the country will be airing the news of her disappearance. She could be anywhere, and the only way we'll keep her story alive is by making noise."

"And how do you propose to do this?"

"For starters, we'll make posters and get people to tape them to casino walls, post offices, bus stops, malls, parks, train stations, airports—any place people hang out. Sooner or later, someone will recognize her. We'll offer a reward and set up a toll-free number. Greed always generates interest. Then we'll—"

"How much reward money are we talking about?"

"Ten thousand dollars."

"Ten thousand dollars? I didn't think you had that kind of change."

"I don't." Her comment stirred bitter thoughts. Why is money always at the forefront of their disagreements? Even in a good year there was never enough, and without Wilson Industries, his budget will get tighter. "I'm hoping for donations, but I'll refinance my house if I have to. Don't worry about the reward. One way or another, I'll get it. Money talks, Amanda. Right or wrong, it talks."

She walked to the rain-splattered window, staring past her image. "The news said the cold front stalled, and it's supposed to rain for another three days." She grabbed a tissue from the counter and dabbed her nose. "Randy, neither of us has much money, so why would anyone kidnap Kerri? Besides, no one's contacted the police with a ransom demand." She wadded her tissue and tossed it in the trash. "God damn it! Why Kerri? It doesn't make any sense!"

"I know." A thought came to him from a book he read long ago. He sat down across from her. "Do you remember John Walsh; the host of America's Most Wanted?"

"What about him?"

"When his son was kidnapped, he made Adam's disappearance a national media event. His actions paved the way for victims like Kerri. It's been a long time since I've read his book, but I remember his biggest recommendation was to pressure the media to keep the story alive. As long as she's in the news, the police will have to stay on the case."

"And how did his story end?" He avoided her gaze. "Damn it, Randy, what happened to Adam Walsh? Did they ever find him?"

"Two weeks later they found his head, and as best I recall, that's all they ever recovered."

She doubled over, repeating "Oh, my god." After a few minutes, she steadied herself and added, "I'm not sure anyone who does such things gives a damn about money or pleas."

"I know," he said, falling into her nightmare. He sat there, stirring his coffee. She seemed annoyed, so he set his spoon aside. The heater kicked in and blew the curtains. Rain beat the roof. He clung to his mug, absorbing the last of its heat. Truth be known, he felt lost outside of his business world. Then a loving memory resurfaced and he chuckled. "Do you remember when Kerri and I painted her bedroom? Man, could she fling a paintbrush. It's a good thing she was wearing old clothes. She was so—"

"Happy?" Amanda smiled, remembering it well. But that was so long ago. She sat up in her seat and straightened her blouse. "So, when can we get started on her poster?"

"How about now?"

TWENTY-THREE

Dog handler Stacey Webster arrived at Skyline Gate at half past six AM. The winds had eased up, but the scud clouds had kept Eagle 5 grounded. As it was still raining, she wasn't sure if she and Tracker could resume their search. Thankfully, Lt. Donovan gave them the go-ahead.

She waved Taco the stuffed duck in front of Tracker's nose, unhooked his lead, and gave the search command. He darted up East Ridge Trail, nose and tail high, sniffing the air for Kerri's invisible scent cloud. She kept her distance as he went from tree to tree, smelling everything Kerri had touched. She kept hoping he would return with a stick, which was his signal that he found his target. Strange as it sounds, that stick is also his reward. Though he appeared confident, his constant zigzagging showed he still hadn't centered on her scent.

After passing the downed tree near the abandoned patrol car, she found another pine had fallen across the deer trail near Eucalyptus. Soon after, she learned about a large washout on Phillips Loop. Not only were clues vanishing, but with all vehicle access blocked, any medical response would be significantly hampered.

Despite the unfavorable conditions, she remained confident her dog could find Kerri. Last night, something near that deer trail raised his hackles, but today he sniffed there undaunted. At one point, he sat down, nose twitching; seemingly lost. She took Taco out and waved it again. "Come on, boy. You can do it. Seek." But Tracker didn't budge.

She surveyed the area to hide her aggravation. Her dog had been onto something, but Kerri's scent was in too many places. They had been searching for over an hour, yet they were no better off than they were last night. An odd sensation came over her and then Tracker's ears perked up. She spun around, ready to defend herself, when a police officer suddenly appeared. "Hector, don't ever do that again!"

"Sorry, Stacey." But Officer Hector Rodriquez couldn't hide his delight from his stealthy approach. He kneeled down to pet her dog. "I love dogs. Did you know I have one just like him?"

"Is that right?" Tracker was ignoring them, sniffing the air.

"Did you know that's my patrol car that's stuck on the trail?"

"No, I didn't. Bummer," she said, wishing he would leave. She never liked his flirting, yet he seemed to do it every time their paths crossed. He'd always be adjusting his gun belt and winking at her. Even though she had never encouraged him, and he stood three inches shorter than her, he still figured he had his game on. *A legend in his own mind.* He may be a fine police officer, but she had no use for him.

Rodriquez tugged at his Sam Brown belt and winked at her. "So, Randy Connifer and I walked this area before it rained. I marked every place that Kerri visited, or at least where Randy said she had visited. Is there any way to confirm Kerri Connifer was ever here?"

Webster looked down on the officer. "Oh, there's no question that Kerri was here, but I can't say whether it was yesterday or five days ago. Tracker's having problems because her scent is everywhere. As you know, scents can last for days." She said that because of his pungent after-shave, but she doubted he'd take the hint.

The officer nodded, watching her dog. He desperately wanting to believe her, but they had yet to find a single footprint, or shred of Kerri's clothing. "Could Tracker find her scent if someone carried her away?"

"Sure. It doesn't make any difference whether she was carried, dragged, or walked out, her scent is still here. I can tell that by the way Tracker's sniffing."

As if on cue, Tracker's body tensed and he focused on the deer trail. Webster expected him to dart off, but instead he stayed put. Then Rodriquez had an incoming radio call, but for some reason, chose to ignore it. She had worked with Rodriquez several times, and still couldn't read him. "How many people are currently searching this area?"

"I'm not sure," he said. "Lt. Donovan says it's too hazardous for horses, but he has dirt bikes and ATVs searching the outlying trails, and foot searches closer in. The numbers keep increasing. We must have thirty people out here now."

Tracker relaxed and she sighed. "It's hard to believe that with all these rescue dogs and search parties, no one's found anything."

"I agree. Unfortunately, until there's a reason to search elsewhere, we have to assume she's still in the park. What bothers me is how badly this area's been trampled. Between the storm damage and foot traffic, we're bound to have lost some clues."

"True, but Tracker's also found people buried under piles of rubble. No one could see or hear them, but he knew they were there."

"Well, let's hope he can work some of that magic today."

Tracker's body stiffened again. He hunched over, practically driving his nose into the mud. "What's the matter?" said Stacey. "What do you smell, boy?"

Her dog started down Eucalyptus Trail, but stopped fifty feet in. Webster and Rodriquez caught up, waiting for his next move. He sniffed the air again. "I sure wish he could talk. Something's really bothering him." A moment later, Tracker ran uphill like a fox chasing a mouse.

Rodriquez shook his head and rested his hands on his gun belt. "You do realize this is the area where Kerri was last seen?"

"Yeah, and it's also where Tracker's had the most trouble. I think we should do a full grid search here. Tracker wouldn't keep coming back if there wasn't a reason."

"But we've searched this area three times."

"Then I suggest we make it four."

TWENTY-FOUR

Randy and Amanda sat at the kitchen table, exchanging ideas. Both agreed to the poster concept, but there had to be more they could do. Randy remembered that John Walsh's *Tears of Rage* had some excellent ideas; if only he could find his copy. "Come into the living room," he said. "I'd like to show you something."

She followed him there and sat on the love seat, slightly amused by the irony.

Randy grabbed the VCR remote, settled into his recliner, and pressed the rewind button. "I set the timer on the bedroom TV to record the evening news while you and Detective Barnum were in Kerri's room."

"I'm surprised you had the presence of mind to do that."

The VCR stopped and readied itself. He pushed the play button and a perky blonde appeared on screen.

Amanda pointed to the TV. "Say, isn't that the same reporter who kept sticking her microphone in our faces?"

"Yeah. Sandy Blake."

"She looks so different."

"I know. Like she just came from the beauty salon. Makeup artists are amazing."

"Shhhh!" said Amanda, drawn to the screen.

The video panned the Skyline Gate entrance to Redwood Regional Park. Then Eyewitness News reporter Sandy Blake's voice-over began. *"A tragedy continues to unfold in the Oakland hills where six-year-old Kerri Connifer is still missing."* The camera scanned the plethora of emergency vehicles and zoomed in on the wind-whipped forest. *"Kerri disappeared early this morning while walking with her father in Redwood Regional Park. Incident Commander, Parks Police Lieutenant Bill Donovan said Kerri vanished after running around a blind corner on East Ridge Trail. Eagle 5, the Parks Police helicopter, used its infrared imaging to scan the area, and directed a team of parks employees to what they hoped was the missing girl. Sadly, their target turned out to be a trapped fawn. The deer was freed unharmed.*

"By mid-afternoon, the Regional Parks Police summoned the Alameda

County Sheriff's Department for assistance under their mutual aid agreement. Shortly after the search commenced, a felled tree injured would-be rescuer Dan Devolski. Mr. Devolski was treated and released with minor injuries.

"Lt. Donovan immediately aborted the search, saying he couldn't risk any further injuries. The incident commander offered no prediction as to when the search might resume. So far, no suspects have been named in Kerri's disappearance, but we understand a criminal investigation is currently underway.

"Kerri's mother, Amanda Schaefer, joined the search after learning her child was missing..."

"I look awful."

"That's not a bad thing, Amanda. It might gain us some sympathy."

"Yeah, maybe." She went back to the TV.

"...I spoke with Kerri's parents as they prepared to join the search. Ms. Schaefer, who appeared to be in shock, asked that we pray for Kerri's safe return."

"Hey, I don't remember saying that."

"Shhh! Listen, learn."

The camera panned away from Barnum's police car to show the near-horizontal rain sheeting a streetlight. The dark background highlighted the treacherous conditions. *"When the storm hit, temperature plummeted into the thirties. However, officials are dismissing concerns of hypothermia, saying that Kerri was dressed for the weather and should be fine if she managed to find shelter."*

"How can they say that?" Randy said. "They've already searched every shelter, picnic area, and rest room, and came up empty."

"Quiet!"

"No!" Randy said, launching from his chair. "This is a recording, remember?"

Amanda crossed her arms, pouting.

"I'm sorry, Amanda, but my point is they're putting out lies. Besides, we can review the tape as often as we want. I can't understand why Lt. Donovan won't admit she's not there so they can start looking for kidnapping suspects." He paused, realizing he was getting loud again. He sat down again and calmly finished his thought. "Do you remember that Florida girl who was held captive for three days across the street from her own house?"

"Yeah. Jessica Lunsford. I only remember her because it was so sad."

"That it was, and I can't help thinking that if the police had done a more thorough search, Jessica might be alive today." He paused, thinking about his daughter's situation. "Amanda, there are tons of homes surrounding Skyline

Gate and Kerri could be in any one of them. All I want is for the police to do a thorough search of the area."

Amanda anxiously said, "Would you please hit the play button?" He did, and Lt. Donovan appeared on screen; his name and title in bold captions near the bottom. *"If Kerri manages to stay dry, she could last for days."*

Randy shook his head again. "Who's Donovan kidding? If she's outside, she's drenched like everyone else."

Channel 4 reporter Sandy Blake reappeared on screen, this time, live; seated next to the anchor. *"With no hint of the weather breaking, Kerri is losing precious body heat with each passing moment. The petite blond-haired, blue-eyed, first-grader was wearing a pink overcoat, white shirt, blue jeans, and white tennis shoes. Anyone with information on this case should dial 911 or contact the Regional Parks Police at (510) 555-1245. Sandy Blake, Eyewitness News."*

Randy paused the tape when they showed Kerri's photo. Surprisingly, Sandy Blake's clip never once showed his face. Apparently, he wasn't sensational enough for her tastes. Well, the next time he would have to do a better job of playing to the camera. Amanda kept staring at him, expecting him to say something. "Well, it's not much of a report," he admitted, "but at least they showed Kerri's picture and gave a phone number. I doubt she'll get much more coverage unless we force the issue. Unless there's something new to report, Kerri will be yesterday's news by five."

"Then what are we waiting for?"

TWENTY-FIVE

The phone rang and Randy answered. Hysterical over the news, Karen Schaefer was oblivious to the late hour. "Randy, what the hell's going on? I just heard Kerri's missing and I can't reach Amanda. Where is she?"

"Calm down, Karen. Amanda's right here."

After passing the phone, Randy reminisced over his sister-in-law. She was the nicest of the Schaefer clan, and used to drop by all the time. After their split, he only heard about her through Kerri. He left the room to allow his wife some privacy.

Amanda had hoped to avoid talking to her sister, but there was no way to do that now. It took both hands to hold the phone steady. Her headache was back. "Karen?"

"What's going on, Amanda? Kerri's picture is all over the news. I can't believe you haven't called me. I can be there in forty-five minutes. I can help, you know."

"Slow down, Karen. I know you want to help, but things are unraveling faster than anyone can imagine. Yes, Kerri is missing, and everyone is doing all they can to find her. You didn't call Mom did you?"

"Of course not. She'd totally freak. Listen, I can meet you at the park and we can search for her. Kerri won't hide from me. I know how she thinks."

"No, Karen. Randy and I already did that and nearly died." *And I know my daughter better than you.* "The police are handling the search, so Randy and I are taking a different direction. I really appreciate your wanting to help, and there may be a time for that later, but right now I need you to stay home. I promise I'll call as soon as we know something. I'm sorry, but I have to go." Amanda heard a click and the line went dead.

TWENTY-SIX

Amanda's mind was as foggy as the road she had driven. She had gone home to clean up, knowing Randy would be by soon to pick her up. It was hard to believe that nearly a day had passed since she waved good-bye to her daughter.

* * * * *

Randy drove them to his office and then slipped in through the side door. Bay View Advertising Agency shop manager Bob Underly spotted him and came over. "Hi Bob. I'm sorry I missed the big meeting."

"Yeah," said Underly. "I couldn't believe it, but then I heard Kerri had disappeared." His face froze when saw Amanda.

Her drowsy eyes found him. "Hello, Bob."

"Ah, hi, Amanda."

Randy stepped between them. "Bob, we're here to make a poster for Kerri. I'll need your help in a while."

"Just say the word. I'll be in the shop whenever you need me." He headed for the door, pushed it open, and disappeared.

Amanda's eyes traveled from the door to the picture on her husband's desk. It was his favorite photo of her with Kerri at Redwood Regional Park.

"I hope you don't mind," Randy said, "but that picture's too good to put away." He turned on his computer and took his seat, waiting for the machine to boot up.

"Why would I mind? It's a nice picture." She rubbed her hands together, uncomfortable being there. The computer's hard whined. A truck drove by. "So, Bob looks the same."

"He does, doesn't he? Not that bald people change much." Randy paused, thinking how the years had flown by. "I never imagined I'd have an employee stick around for eighteen years, but Bob's been here since the beginning. He knows every aspect of the business. I'm glad he's still here."

She nodded, lost in her own thoughts.

He sat there, thinking about how Bob supported him when things were going downhill at home. Executive assistant Jerry Meshner was a superb manager, but lacked Bob's compassion. His shop foreman was always there for him. He never offered advice; only listened. But having only heard Randy's side of the story corrupted him, and it was evident that Bob still blamed Amanda for their breakup. Looking back, Randy realized that Amanda had her own version. One that he never shared with Bob. There was no time to repair the damage, but perhaps he could smooth things over. He got up and looked at Amanda. "I'll be right back," he said.

He went to the shop and waved his foreman over. "Bob, I'm sorry I blindsided you like that, but there was no way to warn you that Amanda was here." When Underly gave him a confused look, the moment seemed even more awkward. He rested a hand on Bob's shoulder and gave him a friendly pat. "All I'm saying is, please give Amanda a break."

Underly shrugged. "I don't have any problems with her being here."

Printers spit out paper. Forklifts moved pallets. At best, hearing was challenging inside the industrial shop. Randy moved closer to Underly so he wouldn't have to shout. "Moving on," he said, "We might need to delay some of our lower priority jobs to get these posters out. Work overtime if you have to, but Kerri's posters are the top priority. Let Jerry handle any deadline issues."

"Like I said, whatever you need, we'll get it done." Underly started to walk away, but then turned around. "Hey, Randy—did you know you could probably get a free website for this?"

"Really? How?"

"I'm not sure. I just remember seeing one from that missing girl in Florida. You could print posters right off her web site. I'm sure any missing child organization can steer you in the right direction. Oh, one more thing—I'd check out some corporate sponsors for the reward money. It's happened in the past."

"Thanks Bob. Do me a favor and have Jerry look into those things. I still want those posters, though."

"They'll be ready."

* * * * *

Amanda couldn't believe all the dust on the wood-paneling. The air was musty. The fern she gave him was still there. Nothing had changed. She sat at Randy's desk staring at Kerri's photo, recalling the moment it was taken. It was good to remember their happy times together. She didn't notice Randy looking over her shoulder until he breathed on her.

"Too bad we can't turn the clocks back," he said.

"Ah, yeah—too bad."

She didn't mean for her words to sound so harsh. She got up from his chair and went over to the fern, soft to the touch. The plant was happy there. Thriving, in fact. She had given it to him when he first moved into this office. He set it in that very spot and then kissed her passionately. Things got heated and they made love on his desk. She grinned, reliving the moment. She was glad the plant was still alive.

She looked at her husband who had taken over the chair. "Randy, is Bob okay with me being here? I mean, he seems really uptight around me."

"Don't worry about Bob. I kind of dropped a bomb on him with this poster thing and he's worried about the business." He offered her an empty Styrofoam cup. "Help yourself to some coffee."

"No thanks, but I will take some Advil if you have any. I ran out."

He opened his desk drawer. "Is Extra Strength Excedrin okay?"

She rubbed her temples. "Anything to stop the pounding."

He handed her the medicine. "There's some water and soda in the fridge. Grab whatever you life."

She took a bottled water, downed three pills, and went to the window. Kerri's photo was a sad reminder of how much things had changed. She yearned for happiness, but it seemed she'd forgotten how to obtain it.

Randy began searching the Internet for ideas. "Amanda, would you mind handing me two Excedrin and some water? My head's throbbing, too."

"Sure." She set the items on his desk and stood behind him. He downed the drugs and hammered the keyboard, oblivious to her being there. She suddenly felt invisible, just like in the old days. "Randy, are you sure you want me here?"

"Hell yes." He typed "missing child organizations" into the search engine and waited for a response. Ten pages came up. "We're in this together and I value your input. You've always had great ideas."

"Thanks." Feeling better about herself, Amanda leaned over his shoulder, staring at the monitor. "I had no idea there were so many organizations for missing and abused children. These kids must go through hell." Then she gasped, "What if Kerri's on her way to Mexico?"

Randy thought it better to ignore that one, and casually said, "Bob mentioned we might be able to get a free web site for Kerri." He called up the next Internet page. "Hey, check this out. There's a web site for the National Center for Missing and Exploited Children, and another for National Missing Children's Locate Center." He paused to read an article. "Jesus! Did you know over a million children are reported missing each year?"

She read the article and collapsed in the other chair like a rag doll. "Two kids have been missing ten years? How can a parent or child cope that long? Kerri will be driving by then."

He rested his hand on her shoulder, surprised when she didn't pull back. "I think we're getting a little ahead of ourselves. Once we finish this poster, we'll check into a web site. With luck, they'll find Kerri soon, and all of this will have been a giant waste of time."

She rolled her head toward him. "We can only hope." She straightened herself and slid in closer to see the screen. "So, what do you have in mind for this poster?"

He browsed through his on-line photos and made one of them full screen. "I've always liked this one of Kerri and Taco." Kerri was three when she latched onto that stuffed toy duck. He ended up purchasing it for her on a whim. She was beaming when they left the toy store. Randy slid out of the way so his wife could view the picture.

"It's a beautiful shot all right. She adores that silly duck."

"That she does."

He copied and pasted the photo onto a blank document, expanding and centering it until he was satisfied. "I like it because it shows her personality. People will empathize and call 911 if they know anything. No one can resist this cutie."

"That's the problem. Kerri may be too cute for her own good."

Randy reflected on that, but rather than say anything, he went back to his project.

Amanda admired how he effortlessly worked the keyboard. It was thrilling seeing Kerri's poster come to life. Her husband truly was the genius behind Bay View's success.

Satisfied with the template, Randy glanced at her over his shoulder. "What do you want it say?"

"That's easy. Our daughter is missing."

He typed her words in bold and leaned back. *Our* daughter. It was nice to hear. Her message was simple, yet effective. He experimented with different fonts and colors, refining the document. Polar white over a blood-red background dramatically framed her photo. Adding black around the white lettering made it even more eye-catching. "There. No one can miss the reward."

"I don't know. No offense, but it sort of looks like she has a bounty on her head. Can you soften the reward a bit?"

He studied the poster, moved the reward to the bottom of the page, and reduced its font. He leaned back again and realized he had forgotten to include a phone number. "Would you mind calling the phone company to see if we can get a toll-free number while I work on the finishing touches? See if they have anything that spells 'Kerri'."

"I'll see what I can do."

Amanda sat at Jerry's desk, pleading with the phone company. Getting a toll-free number proved more difficult than she would have thought. The conversation stalled and she was getting frustrated. A few minutes later she hung up.

"Well?"

She grinned and proudly set her note in front of him. "I wasn't getting anywhere with the first person, but her supervisor couldn't have been nicer. She said it will be set up to ring into my house by four PM with a special phone that handles multiple incoming calls. The toll free number spells HLP-KERI."

"Wow, that's great. Thank you."

"Don't mention it." She sat next to him and watched him enter the phone number on the poster. "It's perfect," she said. "Don't do anything else."

Randy saved the document, printed a copy, and walked it back to Bob Underly. "Here you go, Bob. It's ready to print." The phone rang and Randy ran back to his office. He was grateful that Amanda resisted the temptation to answer.

"Where have you been?" Evelyn Connifer said to her son. "I've been calling your house and cell phone all morning. What's this about Kerri being missing?"

Amanda knew it was her mother-in-law before Randy ever said a word. Her voice was loud; she sounded upset. He had turned away from her, but she could still hear his words. "Yes, Mom, Kerri's missing. Everyone's looking for her. Amanda and I designed a poster. Yes, I'm offering a ten thousand dollar reward. Hopefully someone will take the bait."

"My God, Randy. Tell me I'll see Kerri again. I haven't seen her in months."

Randy felt the phone slipping from his hand. "I know, Mom. The police are doing all they can. I'm hoping someone took her because they think I'm rich. At this point, I'd actually welcome her being held for ransom over some of the other possibilities." He rubbed his eyes and looked for his wife. She had moved to the window, staring outside. "Mom, this isn't a good time. Can I call you later?"

"No! I hate being put off like that. You're not the only one affected by this, Randy. How's Amanda holding up?"

He lowered his voice. "As well as can be expected." He paused to review Kerri's poster, her shiny blue eyes staring back at him. "Listen, Mom, we're pretty busy right now. I'll call you when I know something, okay? I love you, and thanks for calling. I promise I'll call you later." He quickly cradled the phone, torn between all the women in his life.

Amanda turned and leaned against the wall. "Your mother?"

He nodded. "She never said it, but I suspect she's heading this way. I don't have a clue what I'll do if she comes. Hell, I'm not sure about anything anymore."

"I know what you mean. Where can we find John Walsh's book?"

"The library I suppose, but I probably oversimplified things when I dropped his name." He thought about Charles Lindberg's baby. That kidnapping became the first high-profile case in the United States. That's when the FBI got involved in missing child cases.

Amanda shook her head, concerned about Randy. They both needed to stay focused and remain confident. She smiled thinly. "Try not to worry about your mom. You did a great job with the poster, but we still have work to do."

Nice role reversal, Amanda. He wanted to add that they made a good team, but felt that might be pushing things. Right now, finding their daughter was all that mattered. His mother would have to wait.

He picked up the phone, preparing to dial. "Amanda, would you ask Bob to come in while I call Lt. Donovan? And if you haven't already done so, please call your folks. They need to hear about this from you, not your sister."

TWENTY-SEVEN

For the third time, dog handler Stacey Webster and Police Officer Hector Rodriquez followed Tracker back to the intersection of Eucalyptus and East Ridge trails. The search dog's actions backed up Randy Connifer's story about his daughter disappearing there. But now the fallen pine kept them from ruling out the deer trail as a possible escape route, and there was no easy way to clear it.

The rain had slowed to a drizzle, but the fog dropped the visibility to one hundred feet. The odds of seeing the sun any time soon were as likely as Tracker finding Kerri.

Webster leaned against a tree, scrutinizing her dog's behavior. At her request, Lt. Donovan had expanded this grid sector by a half mile without yielding any results. She was getting the distinct impression that she and her dog were the only ones who still believed Kerri was nearby.

"It doesn't make sense," she finally said. "If Kerri knows this park as well as her father says, then why didn't she go back to Skyline Gate? If she fell down a slope but was still mobile, then why didn't she go to Girls Camp off Stream Trail, or maybe one of the other staging areas? I can't believe we haven't found her yet."

Rodriquez scraped mud from his shoe, listening.

She watched him, adding, "I'm worried Lt. Donovan might scale back the search."

"That's a real possibility, especially when we keep coming up empty."

"But don't you see? Tracker *knows* she's here! Lt. Donovan might be ready to throw in the towel, but my dog and I refuse to give up."

"No one's giving up, Stacey, but don't you think someone would've heard something from Kerri if she was here? I've never known a runaway to hide this long. In fact, I don't know of any kid who would take this miserable weather over a warm bed. Hell, I'm freezing and I'm reasonably dry."

"There are a lot of reasons why kids can't scream, Hector. Sometimes it's because they've been crying so long their vocal chords are shot. Or maybe her jaw is hurt and she can't form words. In any case, her lack of communicating doesn't prove she's not here; it only makes our job more challenging."

She unfolded her laminated trail map and oriented herself. "How many people have searched the other side of this hill?"

"Beats me."

It seemed everyone was second-guessing him these days. Lt. Donovan had the big picture, though, and Webster was only seeing her part. "I do know that we've conducted at least two ground searches in that area, and Eagle 5 scanned it with FLIR. Since then, it's been identified as an area of low probability so we've been concentrating on other areas. Besides, the only way to get there is through a gate that's a half-mile down the road toward Diablo. That means Kerri would've had to run down a wide trail unseen, find the gate that she may or may not know is there, and then disappear over the hill. Since no one's found any of her footprints, and her father searched this area minutes after she vanished, that seems a bit of a stretch. No offense, but neither you nor Tracker has given Lt. Donovan any reason to overturn his decision."

Webster studied her trail map while Rodriquez babbled. The officer may have a valid point, but nothing he had said changed her mind. "Has anyone reviewed the FLIR tapes?"

"The crew went over every detail trying to explain how they mistook a fawn for a girl. Their mistake cost valuable time, and may have even directed the search away from Kerri, but we can't change that any more than we can the weather. Please don't outguess Lt. Donovan, Stacey. Unlike you, he can't base his decisions on gut feelings. That being said, if you have any new theories, I'm all ears."

She lowered her map, shaking her head at her dog. "I wish I did. Unfortunately, Tracker's nose is my only proof that Kerri was here." Her dog's eyes met hers, understanding her tone. "Damn it, Hector, Tracker knows what he's doing. I only wish he could have swept that deer trail before that tree fell over it. What are the odds?"

"I know, and I'm sorry. I also wish my patrol car hadn't been blocked, but shit happens, right?" He scratched his tingling nose. "Does this eucalyptus scent affect your dog like it does me?"

"Not at all. It may seem overpowering to you, but it's just another scent to him. He's memorized Kerri's scent and he disregards everything else, sort of like the way that you rule out suspects based on physical appearance."

Suddenly Tracker's body stiffened. He let out a yelp and froze with his nose pointing toward the embankment. "Okay, Tracker, lead the way." But her dog wouldn't budge. She climbed up and the small ridge, poked a stick into the brush, and inched forward, her heart in her throat.

Rodriquez unsnapped his pistol guard and followed her. "What's going on?"

Webster angrily gestured for silence. He unhappily complied with her request, staying close. After three steps, her dog darted past her and blocked her path, hackles raised, and growling fiercely. “Don’t move,” she whispered to Rodriquez. “He senses danger.”

Fog drifted through the forest. Rain poured from the leaves. Her pulse raced as her dog’s threatening posture kept her spellbound. “I think it’s best we retreat.”

“I’m right behind you.”

Tracker followed them, glancing over his shoulder several times. When they reached East Ridge Trail, his nose was high and his tail relaxed as though nothing had happened. Webster frowned at Rodriquez. “You’re not going to report this, are you?”

“Let’s just say I’m not about to give Lt. Donovan a reason to think your dog’s a nutcase.”

“Thanks,” she said, stroking Tracker’s head. “I’m guessing there’s a bobcat in there. He encountered one as a pup, so now he’s scared of them. Bobcats are rare, but we know they’re in here. Kind of funny, don’t you think? My big dog being afraid of a cat?”

The officer shrugged, blowing warm air into his hands. “It looks like Tracker needs another time out. What do you say we get some coffee? This damp air cuts right through me.”

TWENTY-EIGHT

Karen Schaefer couldn't help herself. How could she not call her mother with news like this? Relieved to hear Sharon's voice, she said, "Have you heard from Amanda?"

"No, dear. You sound a bit off. Have you been drinking?"

"No, Mother. Swear you won't tell Amanda I called."

Sharon wavered. "And why would I do that?"

"Just—ah—don't." She blurted that out, not knowing what else to say. "You see, Amanda didn't want my help, so I spent all night making yellow ribbons. I'm going to hang them all along Skyline Boulevard to remind people what happened. It can't hurt, right?"

"Karen, I have no idea what you're talking about. Are you sure you haven't been drinking?"

Amanda's sister was starting to get angry until she realized her mother knew nothing about what happened. Karen gulped some more wine and said, "You'd better sit down, Mom. Kerri's missing."

* * * * *

Amanda did as Randy requested and asked Bob Underly to step back in the office. After doing that, she stepped outside to call her parents. After three failed attempts saying she had no service, she finally got through. Her battery was low, but she couldn't handle a lengthy conversation anyway. It was hard enough discussing this with Randy, but breaking the news to her parents would be unbearable. She could barely speak when her mother answered.

"Amanda? Is that really you? You sound strange. I've been worried sick ever since Karen called. Have they found Kerri? Is she okay?"

Amanda stood there, befuddled. First Karen promised she wouldn't call them, and now her mother's frenzied questions were driving her insane. Randy peeked outside to check on her and she angrily waved him off. "Mom, this is so hard. The helicopter can't fly and the search dogs can't find her—"

Sharon clutched the phone, knowing her daughter would never let Kerri out of her sight like that. How could her son-in-law do such a thing? Her contempt for him contaminated her thoughts. "Where is Randy now? Do you think he's involved? After all, he's always complaining about your having custody."

Goosebumps dotted her creamy skin. Amanda turned her back to the wind and tightened her coat. "Randy's inside printing Kerri's posters, so in that sense, he's definitely involved."

At first, Sharon resented her daughter's tone, but then she decoded her message and realized Randy was near so she couldn't speak freely. As tempted as she was to hang up, fright and curiosity kept her on the line. "You're a better person than me, Amanda. I don't think I could be that close to the man who lost my child."

"You know Mom, we'd get along a whole lot better if you would listen to reason rather than set blame." While waiting for her mother's response, it occurred to her that she had repeatedly done the same thing to her husband. It was a bad trait to inherit. No wonder she offended him so. She scratched her scalp, tormented by her past, angered by the present. "I'm sorry, Mom. I don't mean to take this out on you. It's just that Randy and I are both sick over what's happened, and neither of us has slept much. You should know that Randy's the one who wanted me to call you to warn you that we're going nationwide with Kerri's story. We have to assume she could be anywhere. Say hi to Dad."

"Hold on, Amanda. Taking this story nationwide is actually a great idea. Do you have a web site yet?"

"Randy's working on that, too."

"Well, tell him to forget about the posters and start working on a web site. Nearly every child that's made national news has had one."

"I'll pass that on. Mom, my battery's dying so I'd better go. I love you." She hung up before her mother could add anything. Feeling drained, she went inside, sat at Jerry's desk, and rested her head on her arms.

Randy looked up when she came inside. Her depression was evident so he gave up his seat. Rather than say anything, he stood behind her and gently massaged her shoulders. It was a fallacy, thinking he could fix this. A leaky faucet perhaps, but finding his daughter? Nothing prepared him for this. He stood there, thinking that maybe his pompous attitude is what destroyed his marriage. It seemed that whenever Amanda wanted to vent, he immediately began offering solutions rather than listen to her. Funny how he never saw how his problem-solving ways were driving her insane. But this time he would keep quiet. She would speak if she wanted to.

Amanda closed her eyes and slowly twisted her head. His massage was unexpected, but very welcome. His hands always communicated better than his words. His warmth reminded her of how close they once were. As her tension eased, she finally spoke. "Karen broke her promise and called my mother. Of course, Mom's frantic now."

Randy kept massaging. Sharon's contempt for him grew as their separation neared. She verbally attacked him like a soccer mom after a bad call. It was a godsend when she and Donald moved to Florida. Having two thousand miles between them didn't end her scorn for him, but it sure made it easier to handle. And to Kerri's credit, she never once said an angry word about her grandmother. At least not to him. Poor Kerri was always caught in the middle.

Amanda looked over her shoulder at him. "Why are you so quiet?"

He whispered in her ear, "I'm just listening."

A pleasant tingle shot through her body. Had the circumstances been different, she would have pulled him to her lips. *What happened to Mr. Fix-it?* Maybe he learned something since they separated. Then again, she had learned a few things herself.

Bob Underly rushed through the door waving a poster. "Hey Randy, I've got your proof ready." He stopped mid-sentence, shocked to see Randy massaging Amanda. "I'm sorry. I didn't mean to interrupt." He started to back away.

Randy smiled. "It's okay, Bob. I'm just working out some knots. Let's see that proof."

Amanda sat up, rubbing her neck while Randy reviewed the print. She didn't expect him to show it to her and ask for her opinion. She looked it over and handed it back. "Like I said, it's perfect."

"I think so, too." Randy passed it back to Underly. "Let's start with five hundred."

Amanda sat on the desk, looking at Randy. She waited until Underly left and said, "Five hundred seems like a lot, especially if they find her before we ever get them up."

Randy smiled back at her. "Nothing would make me happier than for Kerri to give her unused posters away. Anyway, Bob can handle it from here. I need to see Lt. Donovan. Would you like to come with me, or should I take you home?"

"I'll go with you," she said, easing her coat on, her ribs still sore from her flashlight.

Randy peeked in the shop door to wave at Underly. "I'll check back with you later, Bob. My cell phone's on if you need to reach me."

"Will do."

* * * * *

Amanda's eyes popped open when they reached Skyline Boulevard. "Look at all these yellow ribbons," she enthusiastically said. "I wonder where they came from."

Randy noticed them, too. How could he miss them? They were everywhere; on trees, mail boxes, telephone poles. "I'm sure whoever put them up meant well, but ribbons can't replace Kerri."

"Maybe not, but to me, they mean hope. Yellow ribbons pull communities together. I just wish I knew who is responsible so I could thank them." She noticed the detail as they drove by. "They look homemade, don't they?"

Randy slowed the car. "They do. By the way, I'm sorry I mouthed off. It really is a nice gesture."

Just after he said that, the advertising mogul realized there was another waiting opportunity.

TWENTY-NINE

Red Cross volunteers busily served meals and beverages to Kerri's search party. Pleasant smells drifted through the Skyline Gate tent where Lt. Donovan was sipping coffee. His official shift ended hours ago, but time becomes irrelevant in situations like this. He saluted Kerry's parents with his steamy cup as they headed his way. "Good morning. I didn't expect to see here you so early."

"You know you can't keep us away. What about you? Don't you ever sleep?"

"Too many things on my mind, Randy. You look hungry. They have tuna sandwiches and fresh—" Amanda covered her mouth and ran to the port-o-potty. "Is she okay?"

"Shattered nerves. Actually, neither of us can eat."

That's understandable." Following an awkward pause, Donovan said, "You do realize I would've called if we'd found anything."

"I know, but it's hard staying away."

"I understand that, but nothing's changed. Every police department in the state has Kerri's picture."

"In the state? Hell, for all we know, Kerri's in Mexico. We need police with national jurisdiction. Have you talked to the FBI?"

Randy's comment reminded Donovan of celebrity murder suspects who, in the face of damning evidence, vow to find the culprit. Of course, no one is ever caught so their murders go unsolved. The thought drained him like his coffee. "It's a little early for the FBI, Randy. Kerri's only been missing for a day and we just resumed our search. The feds have bigger issues to deal with, like national security."

"Yeah, right, except that if Kerri was a celebrity's daughter, they'd be all over this by now. What's wrong with you people? Why is it so hard get help? Have you at least sent bulletins to Nevada, Oregon, Arizona?"

Donovan shook his head. "I'm not willing to cry wolf and disgrace this department." He watched Amanda emerge from the port-a-potty and rinse her hands and mouth at the nearby faucet. Before she came over, he said, "Randy, you're both exhausted. Go home and let us do our jobs. If you really want to do something helpful, then take your wife home."

"I will, but remember, finding missing children is part of the FBI's mission."

"Like I said, we're doing all we can. Eagle 5 will return as soon as the weather breaks. We have seventy people searching the area, and we've turned hordes of amateurs away. We also—"

"Say what? You're turning away free help? Why?"

Donovan rubbed his hands over his face. Sleep would do him more good than a thousand untrained volunteers. Amanda joined them, dragging toilet paper across her lips.

Randy smiled at her. "Are you feeling better?"

"A little."

Donovan looked her way. "Amanda, I was just explaining to Randy why we're turning away volunteers. First, I'm responsible for everyone's safety, and so far, we've sustained an injury, trapped a patrol car, and lost valuable evidence because people aren't paying attention. Second, even with the best intentions, inexperienced people can complicate matters. The bottom line is I don't have the manpower to rescue a novice who gets into trouble. I'm sure you can appreciate that."

"Actually, I can't. A thousand volunteers could turn every stone. Two thousand would be better. I don't care if they obliterate every shrub and fern, so long as they find our daughter."

"I don't have time to debate you, Randy, but I will say that experience counts more than numbers." Donovan paused and looked across the way. "Those white vans across the street are press vehicles. I've asked them to leave you two alone, and frankly, the fact they haven't mobbed you yet makes me wonder if they're even awake. In any case, the reporters come to me every hour or so for an update and I give them the same response I just gave you. By now, they're probably bored out of their gourds, so if you want to give them a story, be my guest."

Amanda glared at the IC. "Are you nuts? I wouldn't give those blood thirsty bastards the time of day. They don't give a damn about Kerri or us. All they want is some bleeding heart story, and I refuse to do that."

Randy's face contorted in thought. "Amanda, I share your contempt for the press, but they might come in handy. Let's go talk to them."

"Have at it," said Donovan. "Just remember how it turned out the last time. Before you go, help yourself to some food and coffee from the Red Cross van. Even better, go home and get some rest. Like I said, I'll call if anything changes."

THIRTY

Randy was drawn to the coffee's scent. He grabbed two cups and handed one to his wife. They went into the staging tent, recognizing some of the search party members from the day before. The empathy in their faces was sincere. Randy walked to the center to address the group. "As you probably know, we're Kerri's parents. Amanda and I would like to thank you for all of your time and effort. We're hopeful you will find our daughter alive and well. Thanks again for your help."

Some applauded while others came up to offer their sympathy. Amanda felt weak and sat down at a table. Randy excused himself and sat next to her. "Are you okay?" he said.

"Not really. It feels like my head's in a vice."

"Then let's get out of here."

Amanda nodded and got up.

Randy dumped his coffee in the trash and escorted her back to his car. He didn't see any cameras, but he knew they were around. Hopefully, their exit would make a good photo. He held the door open for her, admiring a saggy yellow ribbon, its meaning dying faster than its color. "We really need to get those posters up. Lt. Donovan may be turning volunteers away, but we still need them to walk streets and answer phones. When did they say that toll free number would be ready?"

"By four this afternoon."

"That's great. Thanks again for arranging that."

He closed her door and ran to the other side. It was barely ten AM, but it felt like midnight. He got in and started the car, feeling more awake than before. "It's a bit early to worry about staffing so I'll take you home. Get some rest. I have a feeling it'll be another long day."

Amanda closed her eyes and was drifting off, but Randy was fired up now. He would call the radio stations, newspapers, and TV stations to plead for volunteers. If all went well, the help line phone would be ringing off the hook by five.

* * * * *

The car jerked and woke Amanda. Randy's knuckles were white. He was leaning over the wheel, sweating, staring straight ahead. "Are you okay?"

The car jerked again. "Ah, yeah. Sorry about that. My mind's full of ideas."

"Do you want me to drive? I mean, you seem rather distracted."

"It's okay. We're almost there."

She watched the white line, suddenly wide awake. "Listen, Randy, when we get to my place, why don't you come inside and we'll discuss your ideas?"

"Sure."

He relaxed his grip and his driving smoothed out. When he pulled into her driveway, Amanda's neighbor Beth was running toward them in her bathrobe and slippers. Amanda quickly tossed her keys to Randy. "Go on inside, but take your shoes off first. Feel free to make some coffee. I won't be long." She then hugged her friend and darted off.

As upset as Amanda was right then, he was amazed she got that many words out. He watched Beth lead her inside, the key to her house uncomfortable in his palm. Did he really want to go in without her? He hesitated for a moment, but realized it would be idiotic standing on the porch or waiting in the car. He waited until they disappeared before slipping her key into the door. Someone called his name as he reached for the handle. He turned around and saw a short man at the bottom of the stairs who appeared to be in his mid-thirties; his cheap tie and white shirt having "press" written all over them. The white van across the street looked like one he'd seen at Skyline Gate. *So, Cheap Tie followed him here.* That wasn't part of his plan. "Who are you?"

The man climbed a step. "Sam Razini, *Oakland Tribune*. I'd like a minute of your time."

Randy scanned the street both ways before looking at Razini. "Where are the rest of the reporters?" He was hoping for something more than the Oakland newspaper.

Razini climbed the next step, dodging the question. "I tailed you from the park. Is this your second home?"

"Not exactly." Randy was relieved to see Amanda hurrying over. It wasn't his place to invite a stranger into her home.

Amanda ducked her head into the rain and ran right past Cheap Tie. She grabbed her keys from Randy, opened the door, and said, "Why didn't you go inside?"

Randy shifted his eyes toward the street. "We have company."

She turned and looked; surprised she didn't run over the short man. "Who is he?"

Randy motioned for Cheap Tie to join them. "This is Sam Razini from the *Oakland Tribune*. Sam, meet my wife, Amanda Schaefer."

Amanda kept her hands in her pockets. "What can we do for you, Mr. Razini?"

Razini licked his lips, recognizing her from the TV report. Randy's reluctance to go in confirmed this was her house, not his. He was lucky that no one else followed. Very lucky. "First, I'm sorry about your daughter. I have a three-year old, and I'm always worried that something like this might happen to her."

"Is that so," Randy said, blocking the entry after Amanda went inside.

Razini smirked, undeterred. "Look, Mr. Connifer, I'll be blunt. Every businessman recognizes an opportunity. I can help you, but clearly, you don't know how to play the game."

So far, Cheap Tie wasn't scoring any points with him. "Thanks for sharing. Now, please excuse us; we have things to do."

Razini pushed on the door. "Look, Lt. Donovan hasn't given us much to work with, so if I don't get something from you, Kerri's story will die. So, what'll it be? Death or headlines?"

Amanda rushed to the door. "We're listening, Mr. Razini."

Cheap Tie smiled. *They're hooked—now reel 'em in.* "It's like this. If you want to hold a reader's interest, you have to give them a scoop. You know—something they can relate to. Face it, folks. We need each other. Agree to make this my story and the *Tribune* will carry it so long as it remains exclusive. Of course, if you talk to others—"

Randy glowered. "I don't like being blackmailed, Razini. Like I said, we have work to do."

Razini stuck his foot in the door as it started to close. "What if I say you can do press conferences, but I get all your personal interviews?" He waited for an answer. "Either that or I'm outta here." His smirk left him when there was no response. "Look around, folks. Do you see any competition? Make your decision. It's now or never."

"Give us a minute." Randy closed the door and whispered, "This guy's an ass, but he seems to be the only game in town. I've seen his name on some of their major stories. What do you think?"

"But what about the radio stations? Don't we need their help? Are you sure you want to limit us to this devious gnome?"

"I think we have to risk it." Randy peered through the peep hole and saw Razini fidgeting, staring at the street. "Speak up if you don't like it."

Amanda covered her mouth and yawned. "I think we should give him a chance."

"Very well." Randy eased the door open and saw Cheap Tie smiling like a snake oil salesman. As much as he wanted to slam the door shut, he felt he had to go through with his plan. "So, here's the deal, Mr. Razini; you can take notes on anything we do. Call it an exclusive interview if you like, but we've got to be able to talk to radio stations and anyone else who can help spread the news. It's that or nothing."

Still hooked, but far from shore. Razini rubbed his chin to hide his delight. "So you're saying I can hang around and take notes on whatever you do?"

"That's up to Amanda. After all, it's her house."

Amanda fired a gaze, sizing up Cheap Tie. "Randy's right about the note taking and it being my house, so if I let you in, I expect you to keep quiet while we work."

"Agreed."

She looked at him sternly. "And don't you dare cross me, Mr. Razini."

Cheap Tie raised his hand with three fingers extended. "Scout's honor."

"Then leave your shoes by the door and come in. The carpets were just cleaned. Now, if you'll excuse me, I'm going upstairs to change."

Razini slipped off his shoes, ecstatic over netting them both. He stopped to admire the family photos in the hallway. "These are some great shots."

"That they are," Randy said, equally intrigued. Like Razini, he was seeing some of them for the first time. In the center was his favorite picture he had taken of Kerri in Redwood Park, her long golden hair waving, a single strand splitting her forehead. Kerri gave it to her for Mother's Day. He never heard anything from Amanda, so he assumed she must have stashed it in a drawer.

Amanda gracefully walked down the stairs wearing fresh makeup and combed-out hair. It must have pained her to be unkempt for so long.

"Randy, don't you have some calls to make?"

"I sure do. Which phone should I use?"

"The one in my office. I'll make some coffee."

Randy searched the hall for her office. The second room that he came to had a desk, a computer, books, and certificates on the wall. He went inside and closed the door.

Razini watched her in the kitchen, still amazed he was invited inside. Not only did he have an exclusive story, but he'd soon be sipping coffee with a beautiful woman. He raised his digital camera. "Mind if I snap a few photos?"

"Of what? Me making coffee? I don't think so."

"But photos are the heart of every story and entice people into reading it. Trust me, with photos, people will read my articles whether you're making coffee or talking on the phone. Without them, Kerri's story will be glossed over and dropped in a couple of days. In three, they'll barely remember her name."

Amanda looked down the hall feeling the urge to consult her husband, but then her pride took over. "Fine. Take your pictures, Mr. Razini, but you'd better not take any that give away my location. I don't want any gawkers in front of my house."

"No sweat." Razini settled into a chair and snapped her photo.

"I'll be right back." She headed for her office.

Randy cupped his hand over the phone when she came in. She looked like she needed to talk. He mouthed "give me a second" to her and told his caller, "Can you hang on for a second? Thanks." He punched the hold button. "What's up?"

"Are you sure having Razini here is a good idea?"

"I think so. Why? What's he doing?"

"He says he needs pictures to keep the readership and then snaps a picture of my ass. I made him promise not to take any of my house, and I'm sure he won't, but only a sleaze would take a picture like that. I'm not sure I trust him."

Randy contemplated it and then looked at her. "We've got to do whatever it takes to keep Kerri in the news, so if it means having a few photos snapped, so be it. If it's anything inappropriate, then we can seek legal action. I think Razini's right about the reporters, though. Without him, we could be dead in the water."

"Maybe, but I still don't like having strangers in my house."

"Can we discuss this later? I really need to finish this call."

"Sure." She pulled the door shut, brooding over Randy's decision on her way back to the kitchen. Until yesterday, her house was her sanctuary. It would never be the same after this. Was it pride or stubbornness that brought the toll-free number to her house? Soon, more strangers would be coming. Maybe curiosity seekers would follow. She agreed to do whatever it takes to keep the story alive, but she never anticipated it would lead to this. *Damn whoever took Kerri! Damn him to Hell!*

Randy finished his phone call and joined them in the kitchen. Cheap Tie was sitting at the table, his camera at the ready. Amanda had raised some legitimate concerns about Razini. Did they do the right thing by granting him full access?

Amanda looked his way, troubled. "Did you finish your calls?"

"I thought I'd use the kitchen phone so Mr. Razini could listen in. After all, no secrets, right Razini?"

"That's right, and call me Sam." He held his camera up. "Mind if I snap a few?"

"Do as you will." Randy dialed the speaker phone and identified himself to the KFRC telephone operator. Surprisingly, he was immediately connected with Dusty Rhodes, the radio station's disk jockey. "My daughter's missing and—"

"Hang on, Randy," said Rhodes.

Randy turned to them and said, "He put me on hold." Rhodes quickly came back.

"Sorry about that, Randy. Give me a second." Dusty Rhodes flipped a switch so they were live on the air. "I'm on the line with Randy Connifer, whose daughter has been missing since yesterday morning. Randy, can you fill us in on the details?"

Randy ignored Sam's clicking camera. "Sure. My six-year-old daughter, Kerri, disappeared yesterday morning while we were walking in Redwood Regional Park." Following an abbreviated account of his story, he said, "Several searches have been conducted, but nothing has turned up. My wife and I believe Kerri's been kidnapped."

"I'm sorry, Randy, but can you repeat your last? Your voice was fading."

Click, click. Randy ignored Razini. "I said we believe Kerri has been kidnapped. She is everything to us and we desperately want her back. We're offering a ten-thousand dollar reward for information leading to her recovery. Our toll-free number is HLP-KERI. That number should be in service later this afternoon. We desperately need volunteers to help distribute posters as well as staff the help line. With enough people, I'm sure we'll find her."

"Man, that's powerful stuff. I'm really sorry. My heart goes out to you and your wife. So how about it, listeners? If you have any information on Kerri's whereabouts or have some free time to volunteer, please call Randy toll free at HLP-KERI."

"Thanks, Dusty. Oh, one more thing. Please be patient if we can't answer right away."

"Got it, listeners? Please be patient. Randy, is there a song we can dedicate to Kerri?"

He closed his eyes and only one song came to mind. "She always loved, *Baby Baby.*"

"Okay, we'll dust off Amy Grant's oldie, *Baby Baby* for Kerri Connifer—"

Randy's hands were shaking when he hung up. "That's the hardest interview I've ever done. I don't know if I can call any more stations right now."

"But you must. You've set things in motion and it's a good plan. There's no turning back."

He ran his fingers through his hair. "You're right." *Click.* Razini must have taken twenty pictures already. Just then, the doorbell rang.

"I'll get it," said Amanda, eager to get away from Razini.

He recognized his mother's voice, but why was she here? And how did

Evelyn Connifer even know where Amanda lived? Randy certainly never told her. Even more baffling was the warm reception she received from Amanda. Clearly, Evelyn had been here before, but why? Randy joined them in the hallway and gave his mother a hug, whispering, "Hi, Mom. What a surprise." He turned around and the camera clicked again. "Razini, either put that away or I'll smash it!"

"But—" Randy's look made Cheap Tie flee.

Evelyn scrutinized her son's tattered appearance. Blistered skin, dark eyes, slacks hanging from his waist. Stress takes a toll, but that didn't explain his cuts and bruises. She would ask him about that later. "Who's the guy with the camera?"

"Sam Razini. He's with the *Oakland Tribune*." With that, his mother raised a brow. "We thought we needed his help, but now we're not so sure. Giving him free rein was like making a deal with the devil. Make sure he's not around if you want to talk."

"Don't worry. You're forgetting I'm part of the 'loose lips sink ships' generation. If I could handle the Nazis and the Japanese, I can certainly handle Sam Razini."

Randy chuckled. "I've always admired your sense of humor, Mom." Razini's proximity ended their chat. "Amanda, would you excuse us for a moment?" Randy escorted his mother into the office; his smile vanishing as soon as the door closed. "Why didn't you tell me that you and Amanda see each other?"

Evelyn calmly seated herself and crossed her ankles. "Randy, you're my son and I love you, but I love Amanda, too." She let that sink in for a moment before saying, "Now here's one for you. Why didn't you tell me you were here? After all, Kerri's my only granddaughter. Surely you knew I'd come whether you wanted me here or not. I drove by your house, but it looked like a half-dozen reporters were waiting to pounce on whoever approached the front door. When they finally gave up, I drove here, taking the chance that you were with Amanda. So, the way I see it, you're the one who has some explaining to do."

Randy noticed a fresh carpet stain. Even worse, he hated losing arguments. He met his mother's hazel eyes. "You're right," he said. "I should've called you, but I wasn't trying to exclude you. It's just that we've been rather busy with all that's going on."

"I'm sure. Anyway, I'm here, so what can I do to help?"

"Well, we're supposed to get a toll-free number this afternoon, so if you want to answer the phone, that would be great."

"I'd be happy to, but don't patronize me. You're internalizing everything just like when you two broke up. Unless you want another ulcer, I suggest you let me in."

The ulcer. The stabbing pain that wouldn't go away. He had to gulp that chalky liquid six times a day, and even then his stomach ache lingered. *Right again, Mom. It's coming back.* He smiled politely to end their conversation. "Thanks for coming. I'd better check on Sam."

Evelyn watched him leave, feeling like a hypocrite. She had always kept her heartaches to herself, and now she was scolding him for doing the same. Still, it was never too late to change. She caught up with him and pulled him aside. "I'm sorry, Randy. I probably should've told you that Amanda and I stayed in touch, but I didn't want to hurt you. Why should my friendship with her end just because you two went your separate ways? I hope you understand."

"It's okay, Mom. No hard feelings."

He started to walk off and she grabbed his arm. "Now hold on, son. Can't you see it's important for me to be here? I need to be involved just as much as you do."

Feeling her pain, Randy wrapped his arms around his mother and rested his head on her shoulder. "I'm sorry, Mom. I don't mean to take this out on you. If I'd taken Kerri out to breakfast or cocoa instead of going to the park, none of this would have happened."

"Stop blaming yourself, Randy. What's done is done. Besides, it does no good to wallow in pity. You look dreadful. I bet you haven't eaten or slept since yesterday." His head bobbed pitifully. "Then go home and get some rest."

He pouted like a kid, and then thought about his wife. If this is how he treated her, it's no wonder she wanted out. It was a struggle remaining calm. "Mom, you have no idea what I've been through, so please don't lecture me; especially when I'm this tired."

She paused for a moment. "Really? Don't you remember the time you got lost at the flea market?" When he grimaced, she said, "Oh, never mind. I've told you that story too many times. Anyway, why don't we forget about us and concentrate on Kerri?" She stuck her hand out. "Truce?"

He smiled, accepting it. "Truce."

THIRTY-ONE

Swirling clouds had completely engulfed the Oakland hills. Rain peppered Amanda's bay window. Randy stood there, reflecting on how he had treated people over the years. Truth be known, he was spoiled growing up. He never had to share anything, and most of the time he got his way. It was time he changed.

The furnace kicked in and a draft hit him. He sat atop the floor vent, contemplating his lesson. *Okay, God, I get it. I messed up, and I'll do my best to change. Now please bring Kerri back.*

He caught his mother's likeness in the glass pane. Her hands soon found his broad shoulders. Neither moved when the phone rang. Amanda would yell if it concerned him. He was lost in thought as her fingers dug into his back. "I never realized there were so many shades of gray."

Evelyn kneaded her son's shoulders like they were pizza dough. Physical contact brought people closer together. Her husband's touch always made her feel wanted. She missed him dearly. She looked out the window as she worked the kinks out of Randy's neck. "Those clouds are relentless, aren't they?"

"That they are." Her massage warmed his heart as much as his skin.

"How's Amanda holding up?"

"She's terrified, of course, just like us."

"Does she blame you for what happened?"

Randy didn't answer. His mind kept drifting like the clouds.

Evelyn dropped her hands and sat down next to him. Seeing him there took her back thirty years when he sat on the floor vent at their house. He was tiny then, but just as determined. "I don't mean to pry, but has she ever forgiven you for ending your marriage?"

"Why in God's name would you bring up our marriage? All we talk about is Kerri, and right now, that's all that matters."

"You're right." She paused again. "You know, regardless of the circumstances, it's good seeing you two together. I think the last time that happened was—"

"Two years ago in Montclair," he quickly said. "We were celebrating Kerri's fourth birthday together because Amanda's parents were moving to

Florida. I never imagined that would be our last family reunion." He rested his arm on his mother, soaking in the memories, a smile spreading across his face like a morning shadow. "Do you remember Kerri hamming it up at her music recital?"

"You mean when she flashed the audience, lifting her dress?"

He laughed. "Yeah. That was hilarious. She was so intent on remembering the lyrics that she never even knew she did it." His smile dulled, saddened by how everything changed. Soon after, Kerri found herself living in two homes, and half her grandparents had deserted her. The telephone rang and a stranger answered it. "God, this is horrendous."

Evelyn tenderly patted him. "Randy, I never stop thinking about your father. After he died, I never wanted to see another sunrise, but that was five years ago and I'm doing fine. Trust me, son. You never forget those you love, but life goes on with or without them. Once Kerri gets back, we'll do our best to put this behind us, but right now you need to think positive."

"I'm trying, but what if she never comes back? What if she's dead?"

"I won't listen to that kind of talk. Besides, what if that reporter is listening? How will it help Kerri or Amanda—speaking of which, I need to check on her. Who knows what Ratman, or whatever his name is, is up to?"

"His name's Razini, Mom. Sam Razini. But now that you mention it, I should check on him. He could have her in tears by now. I shouldn't have left her alone with him."

He led his mother to the kitchen, astounded to see Cheap Tie eating cake while his wife cleaned the counter. Randy cleared his throat, and Amanda and the reporter looked at him like *he* was the intruder. "I, ah—who was that on the phone?"

"Bob Underly," said Amanda. "He said the posters are on the way."

"Great." Randy reached for his BlackBerry, punched in Kerri's help number, but discovered his phone had no service. *Goddamn hills*. He tucked it away, frustrated. "Any update on when they're connecting that help line? Surely people are calling by now."

Cheap Tie's camera followed Randy as he dialed KFRC. "Hi. This is Randy Connifer again. I spoke to Dusty Rhodes about my missing daughter and wondered if he could pass on another phone number?"

"Oh, yes, Mr. Connifer," the station operator said. "I'm glad you called back. We've had several calls from people asking how to get in touch with you." After taking down Randy's information, she said, "I'll have Dusty pass this number on right away. I hope they find your daughter soon."

"Me, too." Randy hung up and searched the Yellow Pages for more radio stations. He needed a sympathetic audience and several stations didn't qualify. He picked up the phone and heard someone on the other end.

"Hello? Is anyone there? Are you the people asking for volunteers?"

"Yes!" Randy smiled at the others. "Can you hold, please? I have another call." He hit the flash button, put the second caller on hold, and went back to the first. He minimized his time, giving them both the same information. He had a third caller before he could hang up. "This is insane." *Click, click, click.*

Evelyn shook her head. "Randy, you need to take them one at a time. They'll call back."

As always, she was right, and he did as she suggested. His voice was shot after twenty minutes of non-stop talking. "Amanda, can I please have some water? I'm dying here."

She rushed him a glass, which he sipped while taking the next call. Razini's camera no longer bothered him. A few minutes later he waved his mother over. "Can you take over? I need to make some calls on my cell phone."

"Sure." Evelyn handled the pace like the receptionist she once was.

Randy discovered his cell phone worked okay in the office. The phone company explained the help line delay was due to storm damage, but they expected to have everything working within an hour or two. Satisfied, he resumed his calls to the radio stations. As with KFRC, most stations provided some air time for his appeal.

The doorbell rang and Amanda answered. She expected to greet their first volunteers, but instead, two men in dark overcoats were flashing their FBI badges at her. "Hello. I'm Special Agent Essex and this is Special Agent Andredi. Are you Amanda Schaefer?"

"I am," she said, troubled over Essex' robotic quality and the rain water pooling at their feet. Andredi, the shorter of the two, was peering down the hallway. Unsure of his intentions, Amanda shifted her body to block his view.

Razini raised his camera when he heard Amanda yell for Randy. Through his lens, he saw an unhappy agent shaking his head.

"It's not wise taking photos of federal agents," Andredi said to Cheap Tie.

"Hey, whatever happened to freedom of the press?"

"Have it your way, but if you snap any photos of us, I'll confiscate your camera."

Cheap Tie lowered his lens, but didn't leave.

Randy sensed something was wrong and hurried to the door. It didn't take much imagination to finger the trench coats for government agents. "Welcome," he said, extending his hand. "I'm Randy Connifer and this is my wife Amanda. We were hoping to see you." The agents nodded; their handshakes as cold as their faces. Randy stuck his hands in his pocket, glancing at his wife before looking back at the agents. "So, what's the status? Do you have a profile of the kidnapper yet? Any ransom calls?"

Essex casually dried his glasses. "Actually, Mr. Connifer, we're here to get the facts."

"The facts?" Randy grew uncomfortable with the way Essex kept looking at him. The agent had yet to say a word about Kerri. This wasn't the reception he was expecting. "We've already gone over everything with the Parks Police and the Sheriff's Department," he said. "What other facts could you need?"

"Mr. Connifer, police statements are a good starting point, but experience has shown that many critical details are often omitted. Your cooperation is in everyone's best interests."

"Very well. Come in, but please take off your shoes first."

"And I'll take your coats," Amanda said. She took their coats into the bathroom to dry.

Randy waited until the agents had slipped off their shoes and set them with the others. "We desperately want our daughter back," he said. "We'll do whatever it takes to find her."

"I'm sure," Essex said, "but under the circumstances, it's best we interview you and your wife separately. Is there some place private where we can talk?"

Amanda came back in time to hear that remark and anxiously said, "Randy, why don't you take Kerri's room and I'll use my office?"

"Sounds good to me."

Agent Essex followed Randy into Kerri's room. The federal agent observed his suspect check out his daughter's surroundings as though he'd never seen them before. Randy Connifer's eyes didn't match his calm exterior, either. He kept scratching his nape and picking at his filthy fingernails. But this was neither the time nor place to look for inconsistencies. Essex moved closer and leaned against one of the bed's corner posts.

"Mr. Connifer, we're here because the Parks Police asked for our assistance. Now, every investigation begins with the parties involved, so please relax and don't make any assumptions." He removed a small tape player from his pocket, set it in front of them, and began recording. "Standard procedure," he lied. "Now, according to the Incident Commander's log, it appears the Park's Police followed their protocol once they got involved. Our problem is there is still nothing that confirms your daughter ever went beyond the Skyline Gate parking lot. Mind you, no one doubts your word. I'm just informing you that no one has been able to support your claim."

Randy pondered that for a moment and said, "You say no one's doubting me, and yet it's the first thing you bring up. I assure you that Kerri went into the park with me. I have no reason to make up such a tale. Somehow I get the feeling you're not here to ask me about Kerri."

The agent glanced out the window and then back at Randy. "You seem tense, Mr. Connifer. Why is that?"

Randy stood next to him and crossed his arms. They were nearly the same height, but Randy outweighed him by forty pounds. Essex' tuna breath sickened him, but he stood his ground to prove he wasn't afraid. "I'm confused, Agent Essex. It seems you're treating me as if I kidnapped my own daughter, and yet Lt. Donovan can confirm I'm the one who requested your involvement.

"Amanda and I are going through a rough time. Our nerves are shot and our eyes barely focus, yet somehow we keep going because people we've never met want to help us. So if I seem uptight, it's because I've spent far too many hours talking to authorities when I should have been organizing my daughter's campaign. With that in mind, do you have any specific questions I can answer about Kerri, or should I get back to what I was doing?"

Essex smiled at one of Kerri's photos. "You have a very pretty daughter," he said, "and I'm sorry. I should be more sensitive in her bedroom. So, assuming she disappeared as you described, is it possible she might have gone to a friend's house when she couldn't find you?"

Randy sat on the bed, staring out the window. "No. There's no way Kerri could have snuck past me. I've maintained that from the beginning, but it seems no one believes me. Why is that? Why can't you accept the truth?" He flexed his toes and adjusted his socks to avoid looking at the agent.

"But you said you lost sight of her, so theoretically, it's possible she could have taken Eucalyptus Trail to Phillips Loop and returned to Skyline Gate without your knowledge. If that were the case, she would have been free to go anywhere."

"True. Or she could have been kidnapped on Skyline Boulevard. But that didn't happen either because Kerri was too intent on going to the lookout bench."

"To see snow on Mount Diablo."

"Exactly."

"Even though the overlook bench you're referring to faces Sunol and not Mount Diablo."

"That's right. I reminded her of that, but as I told the police, she refused to listen to me."

"But you also said she knew every trail in the park."

"No, what I said was Kerri and I have walked every trail in the park.

Some trails offer spectacular views of Diablo, but for the most part, the forest canopy blocks it. My daughter's in first grade, for Christ's sake. She was thinking of the bench on West Ridge Trail where you can clearly see Mount Diablo." Randy paused, expecting another attack. When that didn't happen, he said, "Agent Essex, I'm happy to cooperate with you in any capacity, and I hope you're here with the same intention. But to avoid duplicating our efforts, would you mind telling me what the FBI is doing to find her? Have you located any witnesses? Talked to any neighbors? Have the police conducted a door-to-door search? Where, exactly, do we stand?"

Essex stretched his stiff neck and arched his back. He spent far too many hours sitting, and not enough exercising. "Agent Andredi and I are here because we want to solve this case and find your daughter. Now, the sooner you answer my questions, the sooner I can be out of here. Do you have any relatives in the Bay Area?"

"Of course. My mother's in the kitchen answering phones." Essex didn't smile at his joke. "Okay, Mom lives in Danville and my sister-in-law Karen lives in San Jose. That's everyone, and there's no way Kerri could have gone to either."

Randy went back to the window to watch the dancing forest. "Look outside, Essex. People die from hypothermia in weather like this. It would almost be a blessing if Kerri was kidnapped. At least that way, she'd probably be sheltered."

Essex nodded. Randy's logic made sense, but the fact is child abductions don't just happen. Officer Rodriquez had given him plenty of reasons to believe that Randy was involved in this. The agent brushed the lint from his pants and tie. It was odd conducting business wearing socks. He joined Randy at the window and casually said, "Just so you know, there are some sick pedophiles in the Bay Area, and they do despicable things to little girls like yours. Nothing pleases me more than meeting those criminals face to face."

"That's great, but I think you missed my point. All I was saying was I'd rather see her with a kidnapper than have her die from exposure."

"Fair enough." Essex locked his fingers together and cracked his knuckles. Things weren't going as well as he had hoped. He needed to start over. He leaned against the wall, staring at Randy. "Mr. Connifer, I realize you've been through this several times already, but tell me about yesterday morning. Feel free to bore me with the details."

Randy scanned his daughter's room, lost in memories, fighting to stay focused. His eyes welled as he recounted that morning. He nearly broke down before he finished. "I'm afraid that's all I can do right now."

"I understand. Perhaps the next time we can discuss this downtown."

Randy looked up. "Is that a threat?"

"Not at all. I was just thinking that you might be more comfortable there than here in your daughter's bedroom."

Randy nodded. "You have no idea how hard this is. Kerri's all I have and I miss her terribly. Whenever the phone rings, I pray it's Lt. Donovan saying they found her. It never happens, of course, but I keep praying."

The agent held his silence. Randy overheard his mother speaking on the phone. The doorbell rang and he looked toward the exit. "I assure you I have nothing to hide," he said. "Call me anytime if you need anything else. I'll even submit to a lie detector test if you want, but right now I need to organize our volunteers."

Essex rubbed his chin. "I understand. Thanks for your time."

Randy got up and opened the bedroom door. "I hope you'll enter Kerri's name in the national database for missing children so that every police agency in the country can be watching for her. We really do need your help."

The agent smiled, wondering if his partner's interview went any better. Randy Connifer was challenging; even entertaining at times, but hardly enlightening. Determining guilt was a difficult process. One that required time. For now, Randy Connifer was free to do as he wished. "Go organize your volunteers, Randy. I'll be in touch."

THIRTY-TWO

Having ditched his federal agent, Randy went to the kitchen where a surprising number of volunteers sat. Sam Razini was at the table chatting with them. Amanda was missing, presumably still talking to her fed. Evelyn was busy talking on the phone. Randy moved closer to his mother, but he didn't interrupt.

Agent Essex poked his head in the kitchen. "Anyone seen Agent Andredi?"

Evelyn shook her head while her son headed for the bathroom. After promptly ending her conversation, she followed him in and locked the door behind her. "Randy, you're white as a ghost. Go lie down. We'll handle this." Then the phone rang. She was going to get it, but overheard Razini answer. She smiled at him assuredly. "I never expected it, but Sam's actually been quite helpful."

"Glad to hear it." Then came a second ring with a different tone. Randy's face lit up. "That must be Kerri's help line." He darted from the bathroom, stared at the new phone, and punched a button. "Hello? Are you trying to help Kerri?"

"Yes," the caller said. "I can't believe I finally got through."

Randy felt revived. "I certainly thank you for your patience," he said. When he finished his call, he returned to the kitchen where his mother was finishing her call on Amanda's home phone line. The new phone automatically put callers on hold. He took a moment to address his volunteers. "May I have your attention, please?" Everyone stopped talking and looked his way. "Thank you all for coming. Pardon the chaos, but it's been this way ever since Kerri disappeared. We have missing child posters on the way. As soon as they arrive, I'd like you to hang them everywhere within a five mile radius of Redwood Regional Park. While you're doing that, please talk to whoever you see and ask about Kerri. If anyone reports anything suspicious, call 911 immediately." The help line rang in the living room and Evelyn left to answer. "As you can see, we also need help answering the phones. There is plenty of work, so jump in and do whatever suits you. Oh, one more thing. Please leave your name and phone number in the logbook on the table so we can properly thank you. Are there any questions?"

"Yes," a teen in bib-top coveralls said. "What's happening with the search?"

"The last I heard, it was still postponed due to falling trees, but hopefully that's changed." He looked around the room and noticed Agent Essex was gone. "Are there any other questions?" No one said anything. "Okay, well, thank you again for coming."

The doorbell rang and he went to answer. He peered through the peep hole, pleased to see his shop foreman. "Good timing, Bob. Come on in."

"No thanks. I'm double-parked. Can you give me a hand with these posters?"

"Sure, hang on." He went back into the kitchen. "Can I get a couple of people to help unload some boxes?" Two people jumped up and followed them outside. Underly left as soon as the posters were unloaded.

Randy carried one of the boxes inside and set it on the kitchen counter. "Put the rest on the floor so we don't break anything." The volunteers did as he requested and began opening the boxes. Amanda walked in just as the last volunteer was leaving with a bag full of posters. "Well?" he said to her. "How'd your interview go?"

"Okay." She saw Evelyn talking in the living room. A stranger was talking on the kitchen phone. She was relieved the help line was now operational. "Where is everyone?"

"They left to hang the posters Bob dropped off. I haven't seen either of the federal agents lately."

"They left a few minutes ago," Amanda said, staring at the stains and pine needles in her carpet. Dirty glasses and coffee mugs filled her sink. The house smelled like smoke. Her haven was spoiled. Why did she do this to herself? "Randy, don't you think we have enough help right now? If others call, we can take their names and phone numbers and call them back if we need them. There's no point in bringing them here if we don't have any jobs for them."

"I agree."

THIRTY-THREE

Kerri's poster hung from nearly every telephone pole, street light, and bus stop along Skyline Boulevard. No one could miss her yellow ribbons. Now, no one could miss her face. Still, there were no calls about her whereabouts, and canvassing homes near Redwood Regional Park yielded no leads. It seemed Kerri was nowhere to be found.

Amanda collapsed in her living room chair, overwhelmed by it all. Randy moved behind her, massaging her shoulders as he did at the office. "You're beat. Please take a nap."

She glanced over her shoulder at him. "I think I will. You should, too. Don't worry; I'll stay on my side of the bed."

Randy was stunned. Though his wife's invitation didn't extend beyond a nap, it still came as a shock. They hadn't shared a bed in years. Even with a phone to her ear, Evelyn overheard Amanda and encouraged Randy to go. Thankfully, Cheap Tie was in the kitchen.

Randy seemed reluctant, so Amanda grabbed his hand and led him toward the bedroom. She laid him on top of the covers and grabbed a blanket from the closet. When she joined him, two kids and a large dog could fit between them.

She lay on her side, staring at him. The real reason she wanted him in the bedroom was so they could have some privacy. Evelyn would make sure no one bothered them in here. "Level with me, Randy. What are the chances of finding Kerri alive?"

His eyes glossed over. "I wish I knew. I keep praying she's okay. I haven't prayed this hard in years. I'll never give up on her, though. Never."

"I know. Nor will I." She stared at the ceiling; boring white, as her carpet used to be. "So, what was your interview like?"

"It was pretty straight forward, though hardly what I expected. I answered all his questions, and even told him I'd take a polygraph if he wanted. I offered that because I got the feeling he thinks I masterminded her disappearance. Of course, nothing could be further from the truth. Anyway, before he left, I asked him to list Kerri in the national data base. I plan to do the same with the missing child organizations. There's so much to do and not enough time."

"I know." She looked his way, glad to have him there. She couldn't cope without him. "Do you really think Kerri was abducted?"

"I don't know what happened to her, but I do know we have to think positive and also need rest." He turned toward her and gently brushed the hair from her forehead. He couldn't help seeing Kerri's face in her; the contours of her mouth, high cheek bones, perfect teeth. "Somehow we'll get through this. Thank you for your support."

She pressed her finger to his lips to silence him. "Close your eyes."

Her slurred words trailed off.

THIRTY-FOUR

Randy tried to sleep, but his brain refused to shut down. After fifteen minutes, he slid off the bed and gently tucked in his wife's blanket. She called to him before he reached the door, asking where he was going. "I can't sleep, so I'm going back to the park. Get some rest, okay? Mom's here if you need anything. I'll call if anything changes."

She pulled the covers up to her neck. Her breathing slowed. Darkness consumed her before he was out the door.

* * * * *

Lt. Donovan watched Randy pull into Skyline Gate. He wasn't happy to see him again. "Randy, you look worse every time I see you. If you keep this up, you'll end up in the hospital."

"Yeah, I know, but fortunately I feel better than I look."

"Well, I wish I could say that something's changed. We've been combing the park all day, but all we've found is a cold-case skeleton."

Randy's brow furrowed. "A cold-case skeleton?"

"Yeah. Sometimes people use our parks as dumping grounds. The coroner's office is searching for a match, but don't worry, it's definitely not Kerri. By the way, her posters look great. It looks like you've got some good help."

"Yeah, thanks to the radio stations," he said, wondering if the skeleton Donovan mentioned was the missing doctor. Then Randy realized that the police had already found that body, and suddenly his nightmare worsened. Until now, he had always felt safe in Redwood Regional Park. He never imagined the park could become a dumping ground for bodies. Still, the skeleton wasn't Kerri's, so he shoved the thought aside. "So, now you're convinced Kerri's not in the park?"

"It's beginning to look that way. I'm expanding the search area, but statistics show that children don't wander far from where they got separated. I hate to say it, but if Kerri's out there, the odds of us finding her alive are rapidly diminishing."

Randy gave a sad nod.

Donovan resisted saying anything else. It's never easy discussing the truth, but parents still needed to hear it. "Randy, not long ago they found a child's body about Kerri's age in a North Bay park. The person responsible for her murder turned out to be a serial rapist who was recently released from prison. The FBI has checked out all the released sex offenders in the area, but so far there are no connections to parolees, and there is nothing that suggests Kerri has fallen victim to a sick-o. I just wanted to keep you in the loop."

Randy held his handkerchief to his nose, knowing that thousands of released sex offenders prowled the metroplex. Was one of them here yesterday? He empathized with the North Bay family who lost their child, wondering how they coped.

The officer read Randy's mind. He hoped the truth would make things easier, but now regretted sharing his story. But Randy was also like a statue, impervious to the elements. He had more stamina than an Arabian horse in the desert. Lt. Donovan finally walked him back to his BMW. "You know, there are several Bay Area organizations that offer crisis counseling. You might want to contact them. Support groups can help with grief."

Randy slid into his car, agonizing over the prospect of a child molester torturing his daughter. He wouldn't share this with his wife. She was already on the verge. Waiting for the outcome would be less stressful. He waved at Donovan and turned his key. Numb from the experience, he drove back to Amanda's house for some much needed rest.

* * * * *

Randy awoke in his wife's arms, buzzed and disoriented. His damp clothes convinced him he wasn't dreaming about being at the park. Everything was dark; his wife was in a deep sleep. He slipped free, walked to the master bath, and saw a ghastly image in the mirror. But his oozing poison oak rash was the least of his concerns. He couldn't stop thinking about the North Bay murder. Was Kerri still alive? Would her face be one of those on the Internet twenty years from now? If she was recovered in Mexico in ten years, would she still remember them? Ten years was a lifetime. How would they survive that?

Guilt became Randy's Albatross. He'd be telling Kerri's story for eternity, just like the ancient mariner. He peeked into the bedroom, thankful his wife was still asleep. He slipped out and walked to the kitchen, surprised to see his mother was still there. Everyone else was gone. "Hi, Mom."

"Hi, Randy. Did you get any rest?"

"A little." He poured himself some coffee and added milk. "What time is it?"

She looked at the microwave. "Ten after nine, as in nine PM."

He shook his head, baffled. *Where did the day go?* Vague memories of Bob Underly delivering the posters, and meeting Agent Essex and Lt. Donovan stumbled through his brain. But that was this morning. What happened since? He seated himself across from his mother, troubled.

"Why don't you stay with me tonight, Mom? It's a lot closer than Danville."

"Actually, driving clears my head." A pleasant thought came over her as she sipped her coffee. "By the way, the most wonderful thing happened this afternoon. A bunch of volunteers held a prayer vigil at Skyline Gate. Apparently, someone tipped off the media so it made the evening news. In fact, there was even a brief CNN clip on it. Anyway, from the looks of it, there must've been a couple hundred people there. They even zoomed in for a close-up of Kerri's poster. It was a great story."

"A prayer vigil? Really?" He contemplated that as he drank. He was still angry at God, but he'd take all the help he could get. He hugged her and then kissed her cheek. "Thanks for being here. You should go home and get some rest."

"Is that right? And what makes you think I can sleep any better than you?"

He smiled. "Well, if we're gonna stay up, I'd better make more coffee."

THIRTY-FIVE

The phones stopped ringing, the kitchen was clean, the dishwasher hummed. Outside, the deluge continued. Randy turned on the ten o'clock news and sat next to his mother, hoping to see the prayer vigil. Amanda wandered in, rubbing her eyes. Evelyn patted the seat next to her and said, "Come join us. How are you feeling?"

"This is it!" Randy said, cutting them off. He turned up the volume and leaned forward, wide-eyed, shedding all vestiges of sleep once Kerri's picture appeared.

"This afternoon, neighbors and well-wishers banded together in a prayer vigil for missing six-year-old, Kerri Connifer," the reporter said. *"Kerri disappeared in Redwood Regional Park early yesterday morning, and despite a massive search effort, has not been found. A volunteer group organized by her parents, Randy Connifer and Amanda Schaefer of Oakland, have spent the day hanging posters while police searched neighborhoods door-to-door. Today's candlelight vigil was held at the Skyline Gate entrance to the park where Kerri was last seen. Kerri's parents were unable to attend as they were busy staffing her help line. A twenty thousand dollar reward had been posted for information leading to Kerri's safe return. Anyone having information as to her whereabouts should dial 911, or toll free HLP-KERI. In other news, the Bay Bridge—"*

Randy stopped the video recorder and rewound the tape. "I hope I didn't record over anything important. The first tape I came to said Disney cartoons. Sorry."

"Who cares? Did they say the reward was twenty thousand dollars? Play it again."

He moved closer to the television and replayed the segment, pausing it as the camera panned the attendees. "Do either of you recognize any of these people, because I sure don't."

Amanda and Evelyn studied the faces, shaking their heads.

Randy replayed it again. "Do you realize that we could be staring at her kidnapper and not even know it?"

"Oh, my God!" Amanda said. "That's Karen!"

Randy froze the image and moved closer to the TV. "It sure looks like her. You should give her a call."

"Not now," Amanda said. "What were you saying about the kidnapper?"

"All I know is arsonists have been caught because they hung around their own crime scenes, so why is this any different? I mean, what's the point in committing a crime if you can't see it on the news?"

He picked up the phone and dialed; an FBI clerk promptly answered. Beeps in the background indicated his conversation was being recorded. "This is Randy Connifer. I need to speak to Special Agent Essex. I have a possible lead on a case."

"One moment while I connect you."

Randy fidgeted and sipped his coffee while waiting.

"This is Special Agent Oromo," said a woman with an unfamiliar accent. "Special Agent Essex is out right now. May I help you?"

He enlightened her with his theory about the candlelight vigil broadcast, adding, "We've been soliciting volunteers all day. What if the kidnapper was among our group? He could've been here and no one would have known. For that matter, we might be playing right into his hands, feeding him information."

"That's a bit of a stretch, Mr. Connifer. First of all, most abductors don't leave their victims alone, and second, their appearing on television is highly unlikely."

"But what if he didn't mean to be on TV? Maybe he just liked being part of the group. Won't you at least look into it? Maybe screen the group for registered sex offenders? This is a solid lead."

"I'll bring this to Agent Essex' attention. Are you at home?"

"No, I'm at my wife's house, but he can always reach me on my cell phone."

"Mr. Connifer, I have Kerri's file in front of me, and it says you were reluctant to discuss the case with Agent Essex. What happened to change your mind?"

"What are you talking about? I told Agent Essex everything I knew and that I had nothing to hide. I called you because I wanted to pass on an aspect that you may not have considered. If it's not too much trouble, how about watching the evening news broadcast? You might find it interesting."

"Like I said, I'll pass this on. Is there anything else?"

"Nope, that's it. Have Agent Essex call me if wants." Randy cradled the phone, looking glum.

"What's the matter?" Evelyn said.

"The FBI doesn't seem too interested in my theory."

"Well, maybe they think you're trying to do their job," Amanda said.

"I don't care," he said, trudging over to the sofa. "I just want Kerri back."

Evelyn folded her hands in her lap. It pained her seeing him like this. "Randy, you're not looking at this from their point of view. To us, Kerri's the most important thing in the world, but to the FBI, she's just another case. You need to let them handle it. The best thing you can do is to get some rest."

"I know. It's just that it seems the FBI is more interested in pinning this on me than they are in finding Kerri."

Randy picked up the remote and replayed the tape again. Something caught his eye and he reviewed it three more times. He froze the frame with several women on screen. "So, we know that Karen wasn't in this house today, but about these ladies?"

Amanda leaned forward. "I recognize three of them from my neighborhood. That's Beth in the back."

Evelyn slid on her reading glasses and moved closer to the TV. Her back was to the volunteers most of the day, but it was worth a look. She let her glasses hang from their strap and moved back to the sofa. "Sorry, but Karen and Beth are the only ones I recognize. Of course, people were coming and going all day. For all I know, Smokey the Bear could have been here drinking coffee with Oscar the Grouch." Amanda chuckled. Randy didn't. Another thought came to her. "Say, maybe Sam Razini could help."

"Yeah, that's all we need," said Randy. "A front-page story full of innuendos. I think I'll pass." The doorbell rang and they all looked at each other. "Who would be coming over at this time of night?"

No one moved. The bell rang again. When they started banging, Randy hustled to the door. He peeked through the view port and then opened the door.

Sharon Schaefer stared at him in shock. "What are *you* doing here?"

Upon hearing her mother's voice, Amanda came running. "Mom?"

"Your father's getting the luggage. Have they found Kerri yet?"

Amanda was too bewildered to prevent her mother's arms from shrouding her.

Sharon stroked her daughter's hair as if she was five. "It'll be okay, sweetheart."

Amanda broke her unwanted embrace and coolly stepped back. "Thanks for coming, Mom, but we're handling it."

"You're handling it? Is that why *he's* here?"

Randy retreated to the living room to avoid an argument. "Let's go, Mom. Amanda has company." He grabbed his coat and headed for the door.

Evelyn followed him, sliding past Sharon to hug her daughter-in-law. "I'll see you tomorrow, Amanda." She slipped on her shoes and coat and prepared to unfold her umbrella. "Nice to see you again, Sharon."

Sharon flung a wave at Evelyn, thankful she was leaving with her son.

Randy stopped half way down the stairs and turned around. "Amanda, thanks for your help. Call me if anything comes up."

"Excuse me."

Randy turned in the direction of the voice and nearly bumped into his father-in-law. He tried helping Donald with his bags, but the old man shook him off. Rather than say anything, Randy quietly escorted his mother down the steps.

Amanda closed the door, glaring at her parents. "I can't believe you. How can you be so rude? They've been working here all day and you come barging in like you own the place. I never asked for your help. Why did you come?"

"Because Kerri's our granddaughter," Sharon said. "We flew out as soon as we heard, and we're not leaving until she's home." Her eyes moved from her daughter's head to her feet. "My goodness, Amanda, you're skinny as a rail. Don't you ever eat?"

Donald sensed a fight was looming and escaped to the living room. Disgusted, Sharon stormed off after him, leaving their daughter alone with her thoughts.

Amanda was speechless. What good could come from them being here? Then again, how could she turn them away? She took a moment to compose herself before joining them. "So—coffee anyone?"

THIRTY-SIX

Randy opened the car door for his mother, noting how she was moving slower than he remembered. Until today, she seemed ageless. He didn't need another reality check from God. She leaned on her door, easing herself into the driver's seat. "I'd really appreciate it if you'd come home with me," he said. "I could really use some company."

Her eyes smiled at him, pleased that he had asked again. "All right, I'll stay with you, but only if you leave your car here and ride with me. I don't want you falling asleep at the wheel."

"Mom, I'm fine. I had a nap, remember?"

"Well, you don't look like it." She got out, grabbed her purse, and locked her car.

He stood there, flabbergasted. "What are you doing? I thought we were leaving."

"We are, but you obviously don't want to leave your Beemer here, so we'll take it and leave mine. By the way, if you still want me to come, I'm driving."

"Fine." Randy punched his key fob and the car's interior lights came on. He watched her slide into the driver's seat and fumble with its electric adjustments. No one had ever driven this car but him.

"Stop staring and get in." She started the engine and waited for him to climb in. "I can't believe Sharon treated us that way. It's really inexcusable."

"Don't worry about it. Actually, I should be honored. That's the most she's spoken to me in years."

Evelyn laughed and set the car in motion.

* * * * *

Driving inside a cloud was bad, but driving in rain clouds was worse. Evelyn crawled down Skyline Boulevard, hoping a deer wouldn't cross their path. The reflection from her headlights was so bad, she considered turning them off. At this rate, it would take fifteen minutes to go three miles.

But Randy's problem was with his mother-in-law, not the windy road. How could he get anything done with her being here? And why was Sharon so bitter, anyway? Didn't Amanda explain to her that their split was mutual? Sharon treated him like a leper, for Christ's sake. And Donald was too meek to intervene. Thirty-five years of marriage had trained him to cower whenever Sharon raised her voice. Hopefully, Amanda was strong enough to ignore her mother's cruelty.

Evelyn glanced at her son, still worried about him. Sharon's appearance tonight was like salting an open wound. She caught a glimpse of the Skyline Gate sign before it vanished in the fog. The familiar landmark was a welcome sight. In a few more minutes, they would be at his house. "Randy, promise me you'll eat something when we get home."

Considering how much effort it took him to drink water, the thought of eating repulsed him. Randy slumped in his seat when she turned into his neighborhood. "Don't stop, Mom. Drive around the block." Except for some deer munching flowers, the street was deserted.

"This is ridiculous," she said. She completed one loop and then pulled into the garage.

As soon as the car stopped, Randy jumped out, closed the garage door, and opened her car door.

"Why, thank you, Randy. You're such a gentleman."

"Thanks." He went inside, but left the lights off.

Evelyn thought that was odd, but followed his lead. She wasn't amused about tripping on the step. "What's going on, Randy? Did you forget to pay your electric bill?" He didn't answer. She felt her way to the sofa and sat across from him, wondering why she came. "Would you mind telling me why we're sitting in the dark?"

"I'm conserving electricity."

"I see," she said, wondering how she could help him if he wouldn't let her in. Ten minutes passed, and no one had said a word. She yawned, sleep tugging at her eyes. "Are you going to stay out here?" She gave up when he didn't respond. "I need to use the rest room. Mind if I turn on a light?"

"Go ahead, just use my bathroom, okay?"

Evelyn stopped and stood in front of him. She remembered his bathroom didn't have a window, and for some reason he wanted it dark. "Okay, Randy, what's going on? Who are you hiding from? Did you rob a bank and forget to tell me?"

Her attempt at levity wasn't working this time. "No, Mom. No banks this week. I just figured that if anyone sees my lights on, they might come over, and frankly, I can't face anyone right now."

"Sorry, I'm not buying it."

He crossed his ankles and started twitching his foot. His mother was one smart lady, all right. She also wasn't going to move until he leveled with her.

"Okay, fine. It's Sharon, but you probably suspected that. I was doing okay until she showed up. You know how it is. Ever since Amanda and I split, she's made me feel like shit."

Evelyn returned to the sofa and gently rubbed his back. "You're a good man, Randy. Why do you let her get to you?"

"Because we used to get along, and now we don't. I mean, Amanda and I used to go to the theater with them. Afterwards, we'd laugh and share good times over a cocktail. I really liked her. And do you remember how you and Sharon tapped at the nursery glass when Kerri was born? I thought they were going to kick you both out. And after Kerri's baptism, you and Sharon proudly posed with your new granddaughter. We had plenty of great moments together, but everything changed once she learned our marriage was spiraling. Amanda must have said some pretty ugly things to turn her mother against me like that." He settled into his chair with his hands on his head. "Mom, the thing I admire most about you is how you never pass judgment on Amanda or me. You've always been there for me, willing to listen. Thanks for everything that you and Dad ever did for me. I'm sorry I'm such a pain in the ass."

"Oh, please; I assure you I'm no Mother Teresa. Your father and I had plenty of problems, but marriages only fail when both people give up. Yes, you two have some serious issues to work through, and your future's uncertain, but there's no reason to give up on your wife. Especially now."

The heater clicked on. He shifted uneasily in his seat. "Mom, I think Sharon believes I kidnapped Kerri."

"You can't be serious."

"But I am. Eyes don't lie. I've known her too long."

"Come on, Randy. Sharon may resent you, but I doubt she'd condemn you."

"It's true, Mom. Sharon is irrepressible, and she'll do whatever it takes to convince Amanda that I'm guilty. God, why did she have to show up?"

White lights pierced the blinds and stabbed the walls. A moment later, they recoiled and the room was dark again. Randy went to the window and saw a white sedan head up the street. It was too small to be a police car. Wrong model, too. He returned to his seat and slouched.

Evelyn watched his silhouette; his features sharpening as her eyes adjusted to the dark. "Randy, by now you should realize that parents are always protective of their children, even when they're grown. It always hurts watching your child suffer. Sharon and Donald came for the same reason I did. They're protecting their daughter just like you're protecting Kerri. We're all stressed and hurting, but none of us will get anywhere by dwelling on the past. As much as I'd love to blame God for not watching over my granddaughter, it would only cause more pain. I can't predict the future, but I know He has a plan. Perhaps it's time you put some faith in Him."

He looked away, shaking his head. "Frankly, I don't understand how you can preach to me about faith and God when the last time you went to church was at Kerri's baptism."

Evelyn listened. It was good that he vented. Maybe now he could rest. It appeared he was finished, so she quietly said, "You don't need a church to believe in God, and regardless of what name He goes by, most people believe He created us in His image. When you were young, we took you to church every Sunday, knowing that you could draw from that experience as you grew older. It doesn't matter what religion you practice, the principals of respect are the same. We stopped attending church once you lost interest, but that doesn't make us hypocrites or heathens. Your father and I felt you were old enough to find your own direction, so find it in your heart to pray. No one has all the answers, Randy. He's there to help you get through this. All you need is faith." Having said that, she got up, went to the guest room, and closed the door.

Randy shook his head in the dark. He didn't believe her. God would never take Kerri from him. It had to be the work of a madman. Tired and emotionally drained, he staggered to his bedroom and promptly fell asleep.

THIRTY-SEVEN

Randy awoke, chilled from sweat. He swung his legs over the bed and slowly got to his feet. Feeling faint, his fingers traced the bathroom walls where a red-eyed, scabby-faced man mimicked his every move. He started to turn away, but knew Kerri deserved better. He washed the dried serum from his whiskers and lathered his face with shaving cream. The razor's sting was nothing compared to the aftershave he applied afterwards. He gently smoothed some lotion on his cheeks and looked in the mirror. "Well, this is as good as it gets." He turned out the light and went to the kitchen.

He thought oatmeal might ease his stomach, but he gagged on the first bite. He didn't notice how badly his hands were shaking until he reached for a glass. No doubt he was destined for the hospital if something didn't change.

Evelyn heard the noise, threw on a robe, and hurried to the kitchen. "Are you okay?"

"No. I'm going to fix some peanut butter toast. I'm hoping that might stay down. You want some?"

"Sure, I'll have a piece."

She sat at the table, watching him totter like a dope addict. He nearly dropped the peanut butter jar as he moved to the counter. She knew better than to help, though.

"Mom, I'm not sure I can go back to Amanda's. I can't think clearly around Sharon."

"Then I suggest you go to your office and work there. Amanda and I can handle the phones."

Randy looked up, weighing her suggestion. "Actually, that's not a bad idea. Bob and Jerry are probably going nuts about now. I can only hope Jerry has smoothed things over with my clients. I haven't talked to either one since Bob delivered the posters. I should get down there."

"What's the hurry? You've only been gone two days, and no one's going to be there at five in the morning. Why don't you lie down and get some more sleep?"

He shook his head. "I'm not tired anymore." He pushed himself away from the counter and looked at her. "You want to go with me?"

"Give me ten minutes."

THIRTY-EIGHT

Kerri's posters plastered the walls of Bay View Advertising Agency. Randy smiled at his mother and said, "I imagine everyone knows Kerri's face by now."

"We can only hope."

He pulled into his parking space, surprised to see so many cars. "So much for no one being here," he said, concerned about the overtime. But then he remembered telling Bob to do whatever it takes to get the posters out. Bob wouldn't have them there unless they were needed.

Randy unlocked the side door and led his mother to his chair. "Why don't you wait here while I find Bob?" He returned a few minutes later. "As expected, he has everything under control." He began rummaging through the papers on his desk, angrily shoving them aside. "You know, Mom, no matter how sympathetic my clients may appear, they can always find someone else to meet their needs."

"Aren't you the one that always says deadlines are deadlines?"

He nodded. That is what he promised his clients, and his reputation depended on meeting them. "Bay View Advertising Agency has never made excuses and it won't start now," he said, rubbing his eyes. Apparently he wasn't as well rested as he thought. He had planned on designing the web site, but that would have to wait. "You know, Mom, Jerry's been my executive assistant for three years; it's time I treated him like one and let him handle the business."

"Now you're thinking like a CEO."

He picked up the phone and placed the call. Jerry sounded groggy when he answered. "Sorry to wake you, but I need you here as soon as possible. Everyone else is already here, including me." He cradled the phone and divided the stack of mail; half went to his mother at Jerry's desk, he kept the other half. "Would you mind sorting through this pile? Toss the junk and save the bills."

"Hand me a wastebasket. I can't believe this is only two day's worth of mail. Why hasn't Jerry opened it?"

"Good question." Randy picked up a manila envelope and sliced it open. He then reached inside and pulled out the contents, but found he couldn't read a thing. The harder he tried to focus, the more blurred it got. Soon, everything went gray. His head jerked and his eyes opened like a student dozing in class. "This is ridiculous. I can't see a thing. How can I talk business if I don't have a clue about what's going on?"

"Shouldn't Jerry be briefing you?"

He sighed. *Right again, Mom.* And all this time he thought he got his business savvy from his father. He set the mail aside and cleared some space on his desk. "I'm just gonna rest my eyes until Jerry gets here. Sorry I dragged you down here, Mom. Feel free to take my car and go home. I'm sure you need the rest as much as I do."

"Somehow I doubt that. Go ahead and nap. I can sort the mail."

She waited until he laid his head on his desk. He was dozing within seconds. There was no reason for him to be here. Jerry and Bob kept the business afloat whenever he vacationed. Why was this any different? She suspected he was having similar thoughts, but got angry when Jerry wasn't here with the others. Without supervision, mistakes happen, clients switch agencies. Hopefully, Jerry would take his time getting here so Randy could nap. Somehow, she doubted that would happen.

Thirty minutes later, Jerry Meshner dashed in wearing a green suit, and looking like a six foot red-bearded leprechaun. "Jesus, Randy, you look awful!"

Randy barely lifted his head. "Thanks, Jerry. Honesty has always been one of your most admirable traits." He sat up, pawing his eyes.

Meshner smiled at Evelyn, surprised to see her asleep at his desk. "I take it things aren't going well with the search."

Randy hiked his shoulders and raised his palms. "I have no idea how it's going."

Evelyn lifted her head and yawned. "Hi, Jerry."

"Hi, Evelyn. Sorry to wake you, but it's nice to see you."

"Thanks. Nice to see you, too." She promptly gave up her seat.

Randy got up to greet Meshner. "Jerry, I noticed we have a lot of mail to sort through. Mom and I started, but I'm really not in the mood to deal with it now. If you haven't already done so, please call our clients and let them know why we're behind. Use your charm. Maybe it will buy us some time."

Jerry looked at the papers scattered across his desk. He had a system. Everything had already been sorted. But there was no point in explaining that now. Eventually, he'd get everything back in order. "Randy, our clients already know about Kerri. In fact, nearly all of them have called or sent e-mails expressing their condolences. I've kept them all for you to see," he said, handing him the folder. "As for not being here, I didn't leave until after midnight because I was working on Kerri's web site. Bob told me you'd planned to start one, but didn't get to it. Anyway, it's up and running now. I hope you don't mind my doing that for you. Oh, by the way, the Oakland Athletics matched your reward money. Of course, Kerri's posters won't reflect that because you wanted them so fast, but the media did announce the change." Meshner then smiled at Randy and rested his arm on his shoulder. "Randy, let me handle the business until this is over. Bob and I have been doing fine without you. Even Wilson Industries is giving us another chance."

Evelyn looked at her son. "Listen to him, Randy."

Randy's head hung. "You're right, Jerry. And thanks for all you've done. You always do a great job." When the phone rang, Randy couldn't resist answering. He didn't expect it to be his wife. He turned his back to Jerry and his mother and spoke softly. "Hi, Amanda. You sound upset. Is everything all right?"

"I don't know. The FBI came here looking for you. You need to call Special Agent Essex right away."

"What's so bad about that? Maybe he has some news about that vigil group."

"I don't think so. Not at this time of day. Besides, there was something about his tone that bothered me. I found it very odd he wouldn't tell me anything."

Randy waved assuredly at his mother and Jerry. "Well, I'm glad that's all it is," he said. "Thanks for the heads-up, Amanda. I'll call Essex and see what's up."

After ending his call, he casually removed the agent's business card from his wallet. Essex answered right away. After exchanging a few words, Randy cradled the phone.

Evelyn raised her brow. "Well? What's going on?"

"Agent Essex wants me in his office. He wouldn't discuss any specifics over the phone other than they still haven't found Kerri. He wants me there in thirty minutes."

"Well, maybe he's identified some suspects and wants to see if you recognize anyone."

"That's not it, Mom. Judging from his tone, I'm sure he considers me a suspect. Amanda sensed it, and so did I. Pick any child kidnapping case and they always go after the father first." He turned his wrist to check the time. The morning commute was just beginning. He'd have to take the back roads to get there within the allotted time. "Jerry, I need to go. Would you mind taking Mom home? I have no idea when I'll be done."

Evelyn stood up. "That's okay, Jerry. I'll drive him. Randy has enough on his mind."

Randy knew better than to challenge his mother. Once again, he tossed her his keys and they headed for the door. "See ya, Jerry. And thanks again for all your help."

"That's what I'm here for."

Once outside, Evelyn looked at the sky. "I'm so glad it stopped raining."

"You're right," Randy said, seeing the hills for the first time since Wednesday. "I can't believe it. Eagle 5 is probably doing another sweep. The search teams must be in the park by now. If Kerri's in the park, I imagine they'll find her today."

"Let's hope so." But Randy's tone was disconcerting to his mother. It had a frenzied quality to it. They both knew the chances of finding Kerri alive were slim, and she feared Randy was heading for a breakdown. This wasn't a good time for him to be talking to the FBI. She parked across from the Federal Building and glared at him. "Why is it so important for you to do this now?"

"Mom, I was ordered here, and I need to hear what Essex has to say. Do you want to wait here or come inside?"

She yawned, and stretched her back. "I'll be waiting right here. Good luck, Randy."

"Thanks, Mom."

After passing through the door, Randy emptied his pockets, walked through the metal detector, and approached the security desk. The rotund clerk who checked his driver's license and copied down his personal information never once looked up. He leaned over slightly and saw his image in the video monitor that was sitting on her desk. He wanted to say, "For an organization that uses security cameras for protection, why wouldn't they want to review the prayer vigil tapes?" But clearly, this woman wasn't the person to ask.

"Make sure this badge is visible at all times," the clerk warned, handing it to him.

"Sure thing. Where can I find Agent Essex?"

"Take the elevator to the second floor and make a left. The third office on the left is his. I'll let him know you're on the way."

"Thanks."

When the elevator doors parted, Randy expected to find Essex waiting for him, but the hall was empty. He found Essex' door ajar and tapped once. He was told to come in, and in a classic power play, the agent remained seated behind his desk.

On occasion, Randy had found this tactic useful, but that was during business meetings where there were others to impress or intimidate. So, why would Essex do that when it was just the two of them? This was an informal meeting. He was only here because he was invited. His stomach groaned.

Perhaps he should have eaten a second piece of toast. "Good morning," he said to the agent. "Did you notice it stopped raining?"

The agent glanced out the window. "Oh, yeah; how about that?" He removed his glasses, cleaned them, and then slipped them back on. "Have a seat, Mr. Connifer."

"Actually, I still go by Randy."

"Oh, sorry, Randy. I'll try to remember that. Please, have a seat," Essex said, gesturing toward the hardwood chair across from his desk.

Randy's eyes roamed Essex' office, which was larger than Detective Barnum's at the Parks Police Headquarters. The Wanted posters looked the same, though. He sat down, and slid forward as soon as he crossed his leg. He chuckled to himself, having heard of such ploys. Shortening the front legs was supposed to keep its occupant uncomfortable, but rather than get upset, he decided to make a joke of it. "So, what's with this chair? You'd think with all the government pork, the FBI would have something decent."

"Yeah. Sorry about that." Essex calmly touched his fingers together and sat up straight. "I'll be frank, Randy. We took your suggestion and reviewed the raw footage of that candlelight vigil and found a pedophile that matched the kidnapper's profile. Unfortunately, the suspect that we came up with is still in prison, so we looked into his family history. It turns out the suspect's kid is a dead-ringer for his dad, and he's the one who was at the vigil."

"So, crime runs in the family? Is that what you're saying?"

Essex shook his head. "Apparently, this guy was so humiliated by his father, he became a child protection advocate. Once he learned about Kerri's disappearance, he was one of the first to volunteer his time. He said he saw you at Amanda's house."

"You could have told me this over the phone. What's really on your mind?"

"Okay, I'll get right to the point. Since you were the last one to see Kerri, and there is no evidence to suggest otherwise, you are our prime suspect."

Randy shook his head. "Just like I told my mother. Guilty until proven innocent."

"That's not true. The FBI doesn't work that way."

"Oh, really? Not only am I the one who requested the FBI get involved, I'm also the one who asked you to look into the vigil tapes." He sneezed into his handkerchief and then wiped his hands. "Pardon me." Essex nodded his sympathy. "Anyway, all I've done is to try and keep this investigation moving. How can you even think I'd be lying about Kerri?" His mouth went dry. He slid his tongue around, but no juices flowed. He sneezed again.

The agent handed Randy a water bottle from his desk drawer and waited while he drank. Essex resumed their talk once Randy set it aside. "The last time we met, you said you'd be willing to submit to a polygraph. I'd like to act on that request today. Do you wish to speak with your lawyer first?"

Randy's brain died. He wasn't ready for this. And even if he agreed to go through with it, what was he supposed to do with his mother? He couldn't just leave her in the car. Then there were Amanda's parents to consider. How would this look to them? And as far as a lawyer goes, who would he contact? A sharp pain stabbed his gut. *Damn it!* Finally, he looked up and said, "I meant what I said. I have nothing to hide. How long will this take? My mother's waiting in the car."

Essex scratched his chin. "I hope she's prepared to wait. It could take an hour just to establish your baseline. Are you rested?"

Randy laughed. "Don't the bags under my eyes give you a clue? I've barely slept since Kerri disappeared."

"Would you rather come back this afternoon?"

"That's all right. Let's get it over with."

"Very well. I'll have someone tell your mother what's going on. Where is she parked? What kind of car?"

"The silver BMW across the street."

Essex split the blinds again. "700 series, eh? Nice car. Would your mother like to wait in our break room?"

Randy shook his head, glancing at the *Gun Digest* on the desk. "She said she'd wait in the car, and I don't think anything's going to change that. She'll probably take a nap."

"Then we'll leave her alone." Essex then slid a paper in front of Randy. "You'll need to sign this consent form stating this polygraph is voluntary before we can begin."

Randy looked it over, but the type was too small for him to read. He spun the document around. "Would you mind reading it to me? My eyes won't focus."

"No problem." Essex read it out loud and placed his finger where Randy should sign. Once Randy made his mark, the agent countersigned as a witness. "Okay, follow me."

Randy tailed him, having second thoughts about not calling a lawyer. For all he knew, he just signed over all of Bay View Advertising's accounts.

He was taken to a small room where a technician was waiting. The intense overhead illumination highlighted the dingy walls. Electronic gadgetry near the suspect's chair resembled a seismograph. A large mirror covered much of one wall. As intimidating as it was, Randy refused to appear weak. "Hidden cameras, I presume?"

"Trust me, you're not being filmed."

The technician connected all the color-coded leads and raised a thumb, signaling the machine was ready. Essex seated himself across from Randy. "Okay, it looks like we're all set. I'll be asking you a series of questions. Some may seem stupid or redundant, but please answer all of them as best you can. Remember, this establishes your baseline and it's not a timed test. Are you ready?"

The blinding lights shrunk the room. Strange images came and went. Sweat trickled down Randy's spine. He closed his eyes, unsure whether the polygraph would free him or convict him. A voice inside told him to relax, but he couldn't tell who was speaking. His mother always said, "Be true to yourself." Right now, her advice was all he had going for him.

THIRTY-NINE

Outside the Federal Building, horns honked, sirens blared, gulls squawked, long shadows stretched across downtown Oakland. Essex probed Randy's world with no mention of Kerri. His script reworded the same questions numerous times. Initially, Randy remained calm, but as Essex dug deeper, he became increasingly agitated. At one point, the agent nearly aborted the test, but the technician urged him to continue. When Randy's answers became slurred, Essex gave the cut signal.

"That's enough for now, Randy. Your mother's still in the car. Go home and get some rest. Be back at four and we'll finish up."

Randy felt dizzy. "Four," he said. "Yeah, sure. Be back at four." He rose from the chair forward and nearly fainted. Someone grabbed his arm to steady him and he pulled it free. "I'm fine," he said, bending over to let the blood fill his brain. Once he felt he could move, he staggered down the hall.

Reaching the first floor, he handed his visitor's pass to the receptionist. When he went outside, the sun nearly blinded him. As expected, his mother was asleep in the back seat, so he gently tapped at the window so as not to alarm her.

Evelyn lifted her head and reached for the door lock. She didn't notice the time until she climbed into the driver's seat. "Is it really nine-thirty?"

"I'm afraid so. Did you get any rest?"

"I did." After saying that, she noticed there was a note under the windshield wiper. "Can you grab that note, please?"

"Sure." Randy snatched it, smiling as he read it. He found Essex' window and waved his thanks before climbing in the car. He didn't see anyone wave back.

His mother read the note out loud, "FBI – DO NOT TICKET."

"It must have come from Agent Essex," said Randy. "He knew you were out here."

"Well, that was nice of him. We got here so early I never gave the meters a thought." She turned the defrost on to clear the windows. "So, how did it go?"

"Beats me," he said, leaning his neck to one side. When it popped, he did the same in the opposite direction. "I'm supposed to be back at four this afternoon. For some reason, Essex didn't think I was ready to continue."

"Imagine that. Now, let's get you home so you can rest."

Randy shook his head. "I can't lie down until I see Lt. Donovan. I need to know that their chopper is airborne and they've resumed the search."

Evelyn wasn't going to argue. She started the car and merged into the traffic.

Randy relaxed once his car pulled away from the curb. The next thing he remembered was being at Skyline Gate. The parking lot was nearly full, but there were only a handful of emergency vehicles. The Red Cross van was gone, as was the white assembly tent. "This isn't good," he said. "That white Ford Expedition must be Donovan's." He threw his door open and headed toward the SUV. Evelyn had to run to catch up with him.

Lt. Grimes sipped his coffee in his Expedition, watching them approach. He recognized Randy from the newspapers and assumed the woman was his mother. Lt. Donovan had warned him he might drop by. He climbed out of his truck to greet them. "Hello. I'm Lieutenant Grimes. I've assumed command of the search. Lt. Donovan has the day off.

Randy wasn't smiling. "Where is everyone? What's going on?"

"The search was scaled back after Eagle 5 failed to find anything. They made two complete grid searches early this morning and didn't find any new FLIR targets. We still have twenty people walking the park, though. We're not giving up."

"Glad to hear it. Neither am I."

"I hear the FBI's talking to a kidnapping suspect."

"I've heard that, too." Randy wondered if the lieutenant knew that he was the one being questioned. He quickly changed the subject. "Why are there only twenty people searching? Twenty people can't possibly cover a park this size."

"Among them are four dog teams. Unfortunately, they haven't found any sign of her either. I hate to say it, but it doesn't appear your daughter's here."

Randy's skin felt like it was on fire. No wonder Essex didn't believe him. He checked his watch. *Be back at four*. The thought repulsed him. No doubt this time he'd be asked about Kerri's disappearance. He really wished he had some answers. Suddenly his knees buckled and everything went dark.

Grimes used his body to break his fall as Evelyn rushed over. "I'll call an ambulance."

"No, wait," Evelyn said, sliding his head on her lap. She put her palm to his face. "He's warm, but not clammy. This happened once before when he got dehydrated and he didn't eat anything. Give him a minute and let's see what happens. He can't help anyone if he's confined to a hospital bed."

Grimes tensed. It had been a tough shift already, but lord help him if anything happens to this guy. "It's going against my better judgment, but I'll give him a couple of minutes before making the call. I'll get some water from my truck."

"I'd appreciate that."

When Grimes returned, Evelyn dripped some water into her palm and patted her son's forehead. "Come on, Randy, talk to me. It's Mom. I'm here." She pressed her fingers to his jugular vein. His pulse was fast, but steady. She looked up at the lieutenant who was hovering over her. "I don't suppose you have any smelling salts, do you?"

"I might." Grimes fetched the First Aid kit from his truck, regretting not calling an ambulance. That was standard police procedure. Someone goes down, you call it in. There wasn't any room for interpretation, and yet he made an exception for a mother and her son. He handed Evelyn two gauze-wrapped ammonia capsules. She broke one and waved it under his nose. Randy's head jerked a couple of times and then his eyelids opened. His eyes darted wildly until he fully regained consciousness.

Randy looked around, dazed. Why was his mother upside down? And why was a police officer looking over her shoulder? For that matter, why was he on his back? As his eyes focused, he recognized the Skyline Gate parking lot and remembered meeting Lt. Grimes. "What happened?"

"You fainted," Grimes said, his heartbeat gradually slowing. "It's a good thing your mom's here or you'd be on your way to the hospital right now."

"He's right," Evelyn said, unconcerned with the onlookers.

Randy sat up and grabbed his ankles, squinting at his mother. Surely it was a coincidence, but her sun-halo made her appear angelic. He felt humiliated. Real men don't faint. After nodding his thanks to Grimes, he said, "I'm glad you were here, Mom. I can't be stuck in a hospital." When his head cleared, he slowly struggled to his feet. It took some time to regain his balance, but with his mother's help they started walking. "Come on, Mom. Let's go home."

After helping him in the car, she tugged on his shoulder harness to make sure he was strapped in. "You had me worried back there. Are you sure you're okay?"

"Of course not. You heard what Grimes said. Kerri's gone, Mom. It's hopeless."

Her chin quivered. Hopeless or not, someone had to remain optimistic. She got in the car, glaring at her son. "Before we go anywhere, you should know that I'm always here for you, but I won't put up with your pity party. I don't give a damn what the police or anyone else say, I'm not giving up on Kerri."

Randy tenderly clasped her hand. "How do you do it, Mom? How can you be so strong and me so weak?"

Evelyn smiled lovingly. "Randy, nature gives mothers the strength to protect their offspring. Physical size isn't important. Don't *ever* cross a protective mother." She let it sink in before patting his hand. "So when we get home, you're going to eat some soup and go to bed. No arguments."

FORTY

Evelyn left her son in the living room and searched his kitchen cabinets. She found two cans of chicken soup hiding behind an open bag of enriched flour. Everything was covered with dust. She washed the cans and checked the dates. Not surprisingly, they were the same ones she bought when she took Kerri shopping two years ago. She slapped the can against her palm. The return slap meant there were no air leaks and its contents were still good. Satisfied, she opened the can and added some water, wondering if he ever ate a meal at home. As she set the bowl in the microwave, the answering machine's blinking light caught her eye. "Randy, you have some messages. You want me to play them?" She heard the toilet flush. He came into the kitchen, buckling his belt. "I hope you washed your hands."

"Yes, *Mother*." He grabbed a pen and paper from the drawer, preparing to take the messages, but something held him back. "What if it's a ransom demand?"

"Then you save the message and call the police. Just play them."

Randy's fat finger pounded the play button. "*You have three messages. First message, Wednesday, nine P.M. Hi Randy, it's me—*" He skipped his mother's message. "*Second message, Thursday, three P.M. Hi Randy, it's Lt. Donovan. I just wanted to let you know we have seventy people and four dog teams searching the park and hope to find Kerri soon. I'll keep you posted.*" "Nice of Donovan to call," he told his mother. "*Third message. Friday, eight AM. Hi Randy, it's Amanda. I'm really sorry about my mother. She had no right talking to you that way. She's hurting like we are and doesn't know how to handle it. We had a long talk and I don't think it will happen again. Things are crazy over here. Call when you can. Bye.*" He immediately dialed, but her line was busy. So was Kerri's help line number. He gave up after several tries. "I can't get through and I don't know her cell phone number. I'm going over there."

"You're not going anywhere until you eat this soup and take a nap! You can't think straight, nevertheless drive. I had a good nap in the car. Once you're asleep, I'll go over and see what's going on. She has plenty of support. I'm sure she's fine."

He snarled. How in the hell could she be fine? He grabbed a soupspoon, pouting at the table. "There's a reason those cans are still around, you know. I've never liked canned chicken noodle soup."

"Just eat. And don't spit it in the toilet like you did when you were a kid."

He looked up, surprised. "You knew about that?"

"Like I said, never underestimate a mother."

She sat across from him, watching him spoon his soup. When he finished, he lay down on the sofa. Once she was convinced he was asleep, she slipped out the door. As she approached Skyline Gate, the Parks Police helicopter swooped low overhead. She pulled off the road, praying for a miracle. When the helicopter returned from the opposite direction, she knew nothing had changed. She stepped on the gas and continued up Skyline Boulevard.

Amanda's house was adorned with yellow ribbons. Why weren't there any at his place? Did his neighbors even know Kerri was his daughter?

She got out and looked at the sky, letting the sun warm her skin. Kerri loved going for walks on days like this. A sapphire sky, emerald hills, ruby red wildflowers, dew diamonds. With luck, Kerri's reunion would share nature's renewal. Sharon Schaefer met her at the door and Evelyn smiled politely. "Hello, Sharon."

"Hi, Evelyn. I'm sorry about last night. There's no excuse for it, and I want to apologize to Randy the next time I see him. I'm really not as bad as you think. I only want what's best for my daughter. Surely, you understand."

"Sharon, you and I have had our differences, but we're in this one together. As for your manners, I never thought you were a bad person, but I'm curious why you insist on treating Randy so badly? What's he ever done to you?"

Sharon's head dropped. "I don't know. I guess it's because I hate seeing Amanda hurt. Well, that and I've always been overprotective of her."

"But Randy's hurting, too. Besides, whatever goes on between our children is their business, and we should have enough sense to butt out. Of course, Kerri's ordeal is an extraordinary event, and it's no one's fault." The phone rang and Evelyn left to answer it.

A moment later, Sharon went over to Evelyn, unaware she was talking on the phone. "I'm sorry," she said, interrupting her. "I meant to say that I'm glad you're such a good friend to Amanda."

Evelyn covered the phone and said, "You're forgetting, Amanda's my daughter, too."

Amanda overheard their conversation and went over to hug Evelyn. She whispered "thank you" as she held her close.

Evelyn whispered back, "I meant every word." She then said, "So, how's it going with the phones?" She wanted Amanda's mother to hear that, but Sharon had already left the room. Evelyn shrugged and smiled at her daughter-in-law. "Are they ringing like they were yesterday?"

"Not at all. We've had a few calls from volunteers, but still no leads on Kerri. Sam Razini's here, but he's mostly been working on other stories. Where's Randy?"

"Hopefully, asleep on his sofa. He can't leave his house because I have his car. Frankly, I don't know how he keeps going. He spent three hours with the FBI this morning and he's supposed to be back at four. I say screw 'em. He needs to rest. If they really want him, they can get a warrant and pick him up."

Amanda rubbed her chin. "I don't know," she said tensely. "Do you really think it's smart blowing off the FBI?"

"Let's not worry about that now." Evelyn kept thinking how a ringing phone would provide her with a graceful exit. Sadly, the phone remained silent. "By the way, I saw the Parks Police helicopter is still scanning the park. It's good to know they're not giving up."

Amanda gazed out the window, trapped in her thoughts. "I'm as worried about Randy as I am Kerri. His blood pressure can go through the roof when he gets stressed. This polygraph could—"

"He'll be all right," Evelyn said, choosing not to share his latest incident.

Amanda reached for her coffee mug and accidentally tipped it over. "Damn it!"

"It's just a little spill." Evelyn grabbed a washcloth, wiped up the mess, and tossed the dirty rag in the sink. "Any word from the police?"

Amanda leaned against the counter. "Let's see; someone from the Oakland Police came by and bugged my phones in case there's a ransom demand, and Detective Barnum of the Parks Police called to say they were sharing information with the FBI. So far, nothing's come from any help-line tips, but Detective Barnum assured me that they would investigate every lead that comes in. It doesn't exactly inspire you, does it?"

Evelyn rinsed the soiled washcloth, listening. Wringing that rag released some of her tension. It was something she desperately needed to do. "I hope they hang whoever took her."

Amanda refilled her coffee mug and headed for her office. "If you don't mind, I'm going to review Kerri's web site."

"Good idea," Evelyn said. "We can handle the phones."

* * * * *

Reporter Sam Razini overheard their conversation and jotted some notes. He hurried to his van to write the story, picturing "FBI Questions Suspect Dad" in the *Oakland Tribune* headlines. His laptop's last keystroke transmitted his story to his editor. He wouldn't blame Amanda if she threw him out, but this story was worth it.

FORTY-ONE

Parks Police Detective Dave Barnum spoke to Lt. Grimes from his office phone. He concurred with the Incident Commander's decision to re-open Redwood Regional Park this morning. The Parks Police Air Division commander reported that Eagle 5 had just completed its final scan and was returning to Hayward Airport. Unless their FLIR tapes showed some new infrared returns while the helicopter was being refueled, Eagle 5 would resume its routine patrols.

Barnum felt duped. Every recently released child molester and sex offender in the Bay Area had been accounted for. Sadly, Kerri Connifer was either dead or had been kidnapped, and lacking any ransom calls, the odds of the latter being the case weren't good.

He had to give Randy credit, though. Thanks to his campaign, Kerri's case had become national news. While that was good for her, it was an embarrassment to his police department, and something had to be done about that, pronto. Barnum poked his head into the dispatcher's room and caught someone's attention. "Is Officer Rodriquez working today?"

"Affirmative," an overweight lady in a black sweater replied.

"Would you have him call me, please?"

"Yes, sir."

By the time Barnum got to his desk, his phone was ringing. He answered, knowing it had to be Rodriquez. "Hi, Hector. Can you swing by the office? I'd like to go over a few things."

"Sure, so long as nothing else happens along the way. I'm on Redwood Road near Pinehurst. We've got a lot of downed trees and power lines out here. Fortunately, East Bay MUD's already on site."

"That's great. Get here when you can."

Rodriquez tucked his cell phone away, curious why Barnum wanted to see him. It stung being removed from the Kerri Connifer case. He suspected Stacey Webster had something to do with it, but it wasn't worth pursuing. He radioed Lt. Grimes to see whether Barnum's request or his patrol took priority. Not surprisingly, Barnum won, again.

The Parks Police patrol officer arrived at the headquarters building twenty minutes later. He hoped his meeting would be short. Barnum was in the break room, pouring coffee when he walked in.

"Hi, Hector. Care for some coffee?"

"No time. I need to get back on the road. We're pretty busy right now."

"Okay, then let's go in my office and talk." Rodriquez followed him in and took a seat. "Hector, this Kerri Connifer case is getting cold. Since you were the first officer on scene, I wanted to go over everything one more time."

Rodriquez sighed, wishing he had stayed home that day. No doubt this case would shadow him for the rest of his career. He repeated his previous statements, including his regrets over delaying the hasty search, and then twiddled his thumbs.

Barnum nodded and spread the park map over his desk. "I still don't get it, Hector. We've searched in and around the park using every available resource and we keep coming up empty. Kerri was within a half-mile of the Skyline Gate parking lot when she disappeared. Where in the heck could she have gone?"

"You're assuming that she disappeared where Randy said."

"Precisely. That's another reason why I called you in. I don't know what it is, but there's something about Randy that bugs me. What was he like when you first met him?"

Images came to mind. "Well, he was frantic when I arrived on scene. I found him on East Ridge Trail yelling his daughter's name, randomly searching behind trees and shrubs. From what I saw, his behavior seemed pretty normal for someone who had just lost their kid."

Barnum tapped his pencil against his teeth, flinching when he found a cavity. His dentist warned him about it, and he meant to get it fixed, if only he could find the time. He jotted a reminder to do that and tapped his pencil on the other side of his mouth. "It appears Mr. Connifer is a regular Boy Scout. He's never had parking ticket or speeding violation, no sign of any financial troubles, and his daughter's life insurance policy is barely enough to cover a decent burial, so if he's responsible, what's his motive?"

"Well for one thing, he hates his wife."

"A lot of people hate their wives, Hector, but they don't go around kidnapping their kids. Besides, Randy and Amanda have been working surprisingly well together. On TV, they even appear to be in concert, so they must have a working relationship."

"Are you forgetting how she wanted to rip his head off when she first saw him?"

"I'd probably feel the same way, Hector. That's called emotion. She was quite rational when we spoke in my office." Then Barnum recalled her contempt for her husband and concern for her daughter. Perhaps he should re-think things. "Anyway, getting back to the park, let's assume this elusive stalker Randy sensed took Kerri. What would his most likely escape route be? Bear in mind, Connifer maintains Skyline Gate's parking lot was empty when he arrived."

"Well, if I was to kidnap someone near Eucalyptus and East Ridge, I'd take Eucalyptus down to Stream Trail and then follow it to my getaway car at the Canyon Meadow Staging Area. It's pretty deserted down there, especially first thing in the morning. I doubt anyone would notice. That's my input, anyway."

Barnum traced the route with his finger. "That's plausible, but this park's a haven for hikers, bikers, and dog walkers. It's nearly impossible to walk the trails without being spotted. I still don't understand why the park was so deserted that day."

"It's a dense forest, Dave. If someone really wanted to, they could hide in there for weeks unless Eagle 5 happened to spot them with their FLIR. Still, the trails can get pretty steep, so it would be a tough hike with a kid slung over your shoulder. Then again, it's possible someone was waiting with a horse."

"Maybe, but if that's the case, where are the tracks?"

Rodriquez hiked his shoulders.

Barnum tapped his pencil, thinking that he should have been a drummer instead of a cop. He was pretty good in his younger days. Being a drummer would have less stress and better pay. Then again, maybe not. "Assuming whoever masterminded this thing had accomplices, that still doesn't explain how they nabbed her without being seen."

"I agree, but Eucalyptus Trail does have a steep drop-off. Still, I'd have thought the search dogs would've found her by now."

Barnum leaned back, missing the squeak in his chair, vowing never to oil it again. The map called to him. "Even the rescuers are losing hope of finding Kerri alive. About all we can do now is hope the rain runoffs might unearth a grave."

Rodriquez lit up. "That reminds me, Stacey Webster was adamant about searching the East Bay MUD property just north of the park. I kept reminding her that Eagle 5 had covered that area, but she insisted her dog sensed something there. I never thought about the shallow grave notion until now, but it makes sense. Did we search that area on foot?"

"Actually, they searched it this morning and found nothing. Not a single child's footprint on either side of the gate, and no FLIR hits. That property has steep terrain with few places to hide. I can't imagine anyone using it as an escape route."

"It was just a thought." Barnum's ticking wall clock reminded Rodriquez of the time. "Dave, I have to get back to work. You need anything else?"

"No, but thanks for stopping by, Hector. Oh— you never told me what you thought about Randy. Just give me your gut feeling—strictly off the record."

After making sure the hall was empty, Rodriquez closed the door and leaned over the desk. "Okay, Dave; you really want my opinion? Yes, I think Randy could have pulled it off, and Ranger Arandale's bungling and the nasty weather only worked to his advantage. Randy Connifer had the motive, opportunity, and gave a grand performance at the park, but whether he's guilty or not isn't for me to decide. Mind you, I'm not accusing him of anything, I'm only saying he could have done it." With that, Rodriquez hurried to the door. "See you around campus, Dave." He made a quick exit, Kerri Connifer on his mind.

Detective Barnum dialed Special Agent Essex' number, eager to share Rodriquez' insight. While the phone rang, it occurred to him that Hector might actually make a good detective one day. When Essex came on the phone, Barnum introduced himself and said, "I was wondering if you had anything new on the missing girl."

"Nothing new here." Apparently, the Parks Police was just as baffled by the Kerri Connifer case. The longer it took to find her, the more likely Kerri was dead. Death came with the job, Essex mused, but it was different when it involved a little girl. He outlines Kerri's features on her poster as he spoke. "What's happening on your end?"

"It's hard to say. I just had a discussion with the patrol officer who was the first on scene and he thinks Randy Connifer could've kidnapped her. How did his polygraph go?"

"It never happened," said Essex. "He blew me off."

"Say what? Are you gonna arrest him?"

"For what? Missing a voluntary test? I have nothing on him."

Barnum rubbed his eyebrows. "Somehow, I'm not surprised."

"Still, I find it interesting there are so few suspects. Usually, there are at least a couple of parolees who have gotten themselves in trouble, but for some reason none can be tied to this case. I'll say one thing about Randy; he looks like shit and can barely speak, but he keeps going like the Energizer Bunny. Then again, maybe his ragtag appearance plays well to the cameras."

Barnum toyed with his pencil, wondering if Randy looked that way because he was stressed over Kerri, or a ploy to throw them off. He didn't share his thoughts. "If by some miracle Randy comes in for the polygraph, would you mind if I sat in? I realize that's not how you operate, but I probably have a better feel for this case than you do, and I might be an asset." When

Essex didn't reply, he added, "I know the park well, and I can talk specifics if need be. Come on, Essex. I'll leave if I get out of line, but I'd really like to be there. I promise I won't say anything unless you ask me. How about it?"

Essex closed his eyes, contemplating his options. "I'll tell you what. If Randy Connifer shows up, I'll give you a call, but don't mention this to anyone. He's a smart businessman and knows his best defense is a good offense. If word gets out about this, you're history."

"I understand."

FORTY-TWO

It was a little past sunrise when Evelyn walked into Randy's study. She awoke to his typing in the middle of the night, but promised herself she wouldn't pry until now. "Good morning, Randy."

"Hi, Mom." He kept typing because his thoughts were still flowing. "Did you get any sleep?"

"A little. What are you working on so diligently?"

"I'm documenting everything that's happened. Agent Essex mentioned how easy it is to omit things, and if I end up doing this polygraph, I want to make sure my memory is right." He felt his mother peering over his shoulder and minimized his computer document so she couldn't see it. "Frankly, I'm surprised the FBI never called. I definitely got the impression they would."

"No one's called, but you should know I wouldn't have awakened you even if they had. You really needed the sleep."

He gazed at her after that one. "Did you know they called off the search?"

"I did. Lt. Donovan said they're treating this as a kidnapping now, but he also assured me that they would resume the search if any new evidence turned up."

Randy nodded. "What really concerns me is there's still no ransom demand. When you were answering the help line, did anyone call from an airport or bus stop asking about the reward money?"

His mother shook her head. "I would've noticed it in the background. In fact, not one caller has ever mentioned money. All anyone's wanted to do is help."

Randy leaned back in his chair, dreading another FBI session. "No ransom calls still leaves me their prime suspect. You do realize Essex is trying to pin this on me? Hell, he's so desperate, I wouldn't be surprised if he was planting evidence."

"There you go again. I can handle your lack of appreciation and your being stressed, but I'll be damned if I'll listen to your false accusations. The police and the FBI are doing their jobs. We both know it's normal to check out the parents in a kidnapping case, so either you straighten up or I'm leaving." She stormed out, slamming the study door.

She was right. What happened to his fighting spirit? Where was the corporate executive who formed a million dollar enterprise? Gone? Hardly. But for the first time in his life, he was truly afraid. Afraid that this polygraph might reveal things that should be kept buried. Afraid Essex would probe into his marriage. He went back to his typing to get his facts right. *Think! Type! Practice!*

A few minutes later, Evelyn found herself tapping at his door. She poked her head inside and he invited her in. She quietly slid a chair next to him and sat down. "I'm sorry, Randy. That was a bit harsh. I'm angry, tired, and worried sick about you. Why would you do another polygraph when there's no reason to? Why take the chance?"

"Because I'm innocent."

She nodded, got up, and headed for the door. "I'm going to take a shower. I'll be around if you need me." This time, she left his door open.

Randy went back to his typing, weighing her concerns. Maybe his lawyer should accompany him this time. But the posters, overtime, and reward money had drained his bank account. Then again, he didn't know any trial lawyers, and what does a corporate lawyer know about criminal defense?

Re-reading his story convinced him that a polygraph was still the best way to clear his name. *Believe what you write. Believe in yourself.* The pre-test had taught him that his answers needed to be consistent and concise. Any needle spikes would require explanation, and a prolonged exam could bring about an uncertain outcome. He re-read his notes five more times before backing away from the computer. He moved his document to an obscure file where no one could ever find it. Satisfied, he shut his computer down.

FORTY-THREE

Clouds drifted, birds chirped, newspapers skidded up driveways, Randy's polygraph neared. Nearly forty-eight hours had passed since he picked his daughter up at her mother's house. She vanished an hour later, and no amount of preparation could change those facts. He put some water on to boil and went outside to retrieve the morning paper. He waved at his next-door neighbor and she darted inside wearing an uglier face than usual. "Yeah, have a nice day," he muttered under his breath. It was no loss; they never spoke anyway.

He scanned the *Tribune*'s front page on his way in. **FATHER QUESTIONED BY FBI IN MISSING GIRL CASE, by Sam Razini.** He slapped the paper against his thigh. "That back-stabbing sonuvabitch! I'll kill him!" He quickly looked around, hoping no one overheard that. He went inside and kicked the waste basket across the kitchen floor. Thankfully his mother was still in the shower.

Razini's headline was like a death sentence. He wanted to strangle Cheap Tie until his eyes bulged and his face exploded. Amanda had opened her house to him. They both trusted him. How could he cross them like this? A libel suit came to mind. Thanks to Razini, taking the second polygraph was now a requirement. Randy moved his coffee and newspaper to the kitchen table and started reading.

> "...Unable to find any sign of six-year-old Kerri Connifer, the FBI continues to question her father...Randy Connifer maintains that his daughter disappeared on their Wednesday morning walk through Redwood Regional Park...The advertising mogul has been separated from his wife for..."

The pain in his gut worsened and he had nothing to help calm it. He was very disappointed in the *Tribune* writer. While technically correct, Sam Razini's insinuations were deplorable. Then again, some of this could have been the editor's doing. He grabbed the phone and dialed Amanda's number. Her calm voice was reassuring.

"Of course I read the article, Randy. I'm not happy about it either, but don't go ballistic over it. Are you still taking that polygraph?"

"I have to, now. Everyone thinks I'm guilty. You should've seen my neighbor's face when I went to get the paper."

"From what I remember, she didn't smile much anyway."

Randy chuckled. "You have a point."

She giggled with him, but then came an awkward silence. "Are you still there?"

"Yeah, I'm here. You believe I'm innocent, don't you? Tell me you believe me."

"Of course I do." She had to say that. Anything else would destroy them both.

Randy clung to the phone, unable to speak, yet unwilling to hang up. It sounded like she was breathing harder than he was. What was she thinking right now? "Amanda, has anyone asked you to come in for more questioning?"

"No, and as far as I know, no one's issued a warrant for you. You do realize you wouldn't be in this predicament if you hadn't volunteered for that polygraph. If they don't have a warrant, why on earth would you go back?"

He sighed, tired of having to explain himself. "Coach Hutchison always said you can't win a football game without a good offense. I need to clear my name so the authorities will look for the real criminal."

Her mind drifted as he spoke. She couldn't explain why, but the more he talked about clearing his name, the more she wondered if she was too close to see the truth. But she also feared the FBI was feeding Randy the rope that would eventually tie his noose. Torn and confused, and having no idea of what he just said, she offered no response.

Randy stared at the wall, her silence making him wonder if she and Razini had reached some sort of accord. He didn't want to believe that, but where else could Cheap Tie have obtained such personal information? He pressed his back to the wall and let himself slide to the floor, watching his world slip away. Regardless of his polygraph's outcome, his reputation would be tarnished, and companies like Wilson Industries would never sign with him again. But then Coach Hutchison taught him better than that. Down to their last plays, Hutch told them, *"When you're behind, you fight harder because you have nothing to lose."* His speech inspired Randy to score the winning touchdown, and that's how he'd get through this polygraph. A smile found his face. "I'll be all right, Amanda. Don't worry. I'll call you when it's over."

FORTY-FOUR

Randy sat in his kitchen, aggravated by the cheery birds chirping outside his window. Any other day and their singing would have brought him joy. But not today. Not when he had to go downtown. He called his lawyer at seven AM and was lucky to catch him as he was already out the door.

Paul Cohen listened to Randy's concerns as he strapped into his car. While backing out of his driveway, he said, "Only agree to the polygraph if you can quit at your will." He stopped the car, changed gears, and hit the gas. "Listen, Randy, I've got another call. Good luck."

When the line went dead, Randy called Agent Essex to brief him on the terms. Essex agreed, saying to come in at his convenience. Randy ended the call after that. Neither had time to chat.

At nine AM, he straightened his tie for the third time and reached for the doorknob. *This is it.* He twisted the knob and looked for his mother. "Bye, Mom. Wish me luck."

Evelyn went to hug him. "Are you sure you don't want me to go with you?"

He smiled assuredly. "There's no way I'd have you sitting in the car for another three hours. Are you going to Amanda's today? She probably needs you."

"I'm sure she does." Evelyn backed off to smooth his coat and straighten his tie. "Good luck, Randy. I'll be thinking about you."

"Thanks, Mom."

On his way out, Randy noticed a yellow ribbon on his mailbox with Kerri's name on it. Was it there when he picked up his newspaper? How could he have missed it? Maybe his mom put it there. She cared so much for him and Amanda. Even through their roughest times, her love remained resolute. He waved at her as he backed out the driveway, wishing he had taken a Motrin.

* * * * *

This time, Special Agent Essex met Randy at the security desk and handed him his visitor's pass. He had wagered two other agents that he could break Randy Connifer in thirty minutes, and was eager to proceed. Randy's fashionable coat and tie didn't change a thing. When the elevator doors closed, Essex said, "I see you made the news again. Those headlines don't paint a very good picture, do they?"

Randy gazed at Essex, thinking Essex may have fed Razini the story. But then the agent's stern face confirmed that was an absurd notion. After all, the FBI never shared anything. Especially with reporters like Cheap Tie. "Come on, Essex, you know that story's garbage."

"Maybe. But I must admit that *Tribune* article came as a complete surprise. I have no idea where Sam Razini gets his information, but whoever his source is seems pretty enlightened. Unfortunately, there's not much you can do about it."

Randy yawned and scratched his head as if he was bored. "You're probably right. Do you suppose we can get on with this?"

"Sure. Follow me."

On his way down the hall, Randy kept wondering who might sell him out. Only Sharon Schaefer came to mind. She and Razini were at Amanda's yesterday. It *had* to be her.

Essex stopped in front of the now-familiar room. "Here we are."

Randy emptied his thoughts, reminding himself that he controlled the outcome. Even so, Sharon had dogged him with years of criticism. He was never good enough for her. He felt like he was being judged at every family get-together. He didn't hear Essex speak. Someone grabbed his arm and sat him in the chair. He closed his eyes, terrified. *Fourth down. One yard to go. Ten seconds on the clock. The pass, the catch, the pain.* It was the last ball he ever caught, but he made it, and he'd make this one, too. He opened his eyes and saw Detective Barnum. "What's he doing here?"

Essex glanced at Barnum and back at Randy. "Sitting in."

"You never said anything about him being here."

"What difference does it make? You're innocent, right?"

Randy suspiciously eyed both of them. *Of course I'm innocent! Isn't that why I'm here?* If only it was as simple as saying those words. But Essex had a valid point. It shouldn't make any difference who was there, so long as he spoke the truth. His mother had taught him patience by having him count to ten before speaking. Her childhood advice still rang true. He ignored Barnum and said, "Let's get on with it."

Essex looked at the detective. "Just so you know, Randy and I agreed that he could stop the test at any time. This is a fact-finding interview, not an interrogation."

"With no video cameras," Randy added.

"I assure you the only thing that's being recorded is the polygraph results.

I'll even give you a copy. Now close your eyes and relax while we verify everything is in order. Try putting your mind at ease. Imagine yourself at a beach, a park…"

His eyes widened. "A *park*? Is that supposed to be funny?"

"I'm sorry—really. Forget the park; go back to the beach." Essex gave Randy a moment to relax before continuing. "Listen to the waves, the gulls. Smell the sea air. Take in long soothing breaths and slowly let them out.

The technician indicated the machine was still working properly. Essex nodded, and the technician left the room.

"Okay Randy, it looks like we're ready to begin. We'll start with some of the same questions from yesterday to compare your responses. Are you ready?"

"Ready."

"Good. Now, state your full name."

Randy did that, and his electronic response signaled no deviations.

"And Kerri Connifer is your daughter, right?" Again, no deviations. "All right, moving on, were you the last one to see Kerri after you picked her up at her mother's house on Wednesday, October 12th?"

Randy counted to ten. *Don't let him lead you.* "I have no way of knowing that," he calmly said. "The Skyline Gate parking lot was empty when we arrived and we didn't see anyone on the trail, but that doesn't mean someone else wasn't there."

"Oh, right. You thought someone was watching you."

"Trust me; we weren't alone, and whoever was out there took Kerri."

"But you never saw anyone."

"That's correct."

Essex studied the polygraph tape for any spikes. There were still no deviations. "What time did you arrive at Skyline Gate?"

"Approximately seven A.M."

"Seven AM? Really? That's when I wake up."

Randy opened his eyes. Barnum was smacking his gum and Essex was staring at him. Neither was talking. Randy shut his eyes again and slowly breathed through his nose. *Relax. Don't let him bait you.* He folded his hands in his lap and said, "We're always there by seven AM because of my job and her school. It works out well because her mother leaves right after I pick Kerri up." An eternity passed without a follow-on question. Finally, Randy opened his eyes again. "Agent Essex, my time is quite valuable, so if you have a question, please spit it out. Otherwise, take these wires off me."

Essex grinned. "Okay, Randy. Did you kidnap Kerri?"

"No."

"Did you hire or otherwise arrange someone else to take her?"

"No."

"Do you have any idea where your daughter is now?"

"No I don't, *do you*?"

"I'll ask the questions," Essex said, his tone sharpening. Barnum's grin wasn't helping matters. "Did Kerri want to go to the park?"

"Absolutely. She was smiling and eager to go when I drove up. She loves me, and loves going to the park."

"I'm sure she did—I mean, does."

Detective Barnum crossed his arms, leery of the federal agent's tactics. His last comment was below the belt. He wanted to leave, but after all he went through to sit in, he felt committed to stay.

Essex stood in front of Barnum so Randy would focus on him and not the detective. "For the record, please describe the route that you and Kerri took the day she disappeared."

Randy closed his eyes and Kerri's image became as clear as her photo in his wallet. He felt her presence in the room; calming, not alarming. "As I said, we went to Redwood Regional Park on Sunday as well as Wednesday, which is probably what's confusing the search dogs. Last Sunday, we headed down Stream Trail and checked out Girl's Camp. We stopped to check out some ladybugs, and then headed to the old mill site. Kerri got tired, so I put her on my back and we climbed Eucalyptus to East Ridge. I set her down before we got to Phillip's Loop. We spent five hours in the park that day because it was so beautiful."

Barnum leaned forward and said, "Why did you go to Girl's Camp?"

Randy's eyes opened, surprised to hear Barnum's voice.

Essex silenced his police guest with a look. "You don't have to answer that, Randy."

"It's okay, I don't mind. Kerri knew that's one of the places where ladybugs hibernate and she wanted to see them. There weren't as many as last year, but she spotted another bunch a little further down the trail. Then on Wednesday, we saw more on East Ridge Trail. We've never seen them there before, and she was so happy to see them buzzing around. They kept landing on her clothes, her hair. We were both giggling before it was over."

"We get the idea," Essex said, "but we're getting sidetracked. Now, go back to Wednesday the 12th. How long were you and Kerri in the park before she disappeared?"

"I'd guess a half-hour. She's interested in everything, so we don't move very fast. We must have spent at least three minutes staring at those ladybugs."

"But then she ran so fast that you couldn't keep up."

"That's correct."

Essex grew edgy. His time was about up and he had never lost a bet before. "So Kerri ran ahead and disappeared near Eucalyptus?"

"Yes."

Detective Barnum inspected the polygraph tape. He wasn't a trained expert like Essex, but from he could see, there were still no deviations. He stood up, towering over Essex, and said, "How can it take a half-hour to reach Eucalyptus Trail? I can crawl it in twenty."

Essex spun around and Barnum sat back down. The agent refocused on Randy. "Detective Barnum has a point. Why did it take so long to cover such a short distance?"

"Like I said, Kerri loves exploring the park, hiding behind trees, kicking pinecones. She'll sniff a wildflower and then dart ahead until she finds something new. She's a child, for Christ's sake. Didn't you ever listen to birds sing or the wind whip the leaves when you were growing up? Haven't you ever stopped to watch a bug cross your path or stare down a lizard? If not, then I feel sorry for you, but if you did, then you've obviously forgotten what it's like seeing the world through a child's eyes. I look forward to the day when Kerri and I can go back to the park. She loves nature."

"Right." Essex found it interesting that Randy never once referred to his daughter in the past tense. But questions remained about how she disappeared and where she may have gone. Why hadn't the search dogs or Eagle 5's infrared imaging found her? Barnum passed Essex a note. Essex glanced at it and then tucked it in his pocket. "Okay, let's wrap this up. What did you do when Kerri first disappeared?"

"I called her name expecting her to come out from behind a tree like she always did. When that didn't happen—" Randy stopped abruptly, firmly gripping his arm rests. "I'm sorry, but I can't do this anymore. It hurts too much. Everything's in my statement. The mountain bikers, Ranger Arandale, Officer Rodriquez—everything. As far as I'm concerned, this interview's over."

Essex sighed and pressed a button to signal the technician. "Well, Randy, I appreciate your coming in. Machines don't lie, and clearly, neither do you. Once your leads are disconnected, I'd like your opinion on something—off the record, of course. Please think it through before answering." Eyes shifted while the technician worked. Once he finished and left the room, Essex said, "Do you think the Parks Police Department properly handled this case?"

Detective Barnum was stunned, but didn't raise any objection.

Randy cleared his throat twice before giving his answer. "I don't have any problem with the Parks Police Department, but I'll never understand why Ranger Arandale was so reluctant to call for help."

"If it's any consolation, Ranger Arandale has been reprimanded," said Barnum.

Essex rolled his eyes, making a mental note never to let someone else sit in. He looked back at Randy. "So you're saying that the problems stemmed from Ranger Arandale, not you."

Randy stood up and buttoned his sleeves. "I never said that, Agent Essex. I never even implied it. I've always accepted responsibility for Kerri's disappearance, but I've also maintained that whoever has her, stalked her first. There's no doubt in my mind that Kerri was ambushed after she rounded that blind corner. This wasn't a random act. If I had listened to my instinct, this never would've happened, but I was too preoccupied with allowing her to go to the bench. I've hurt so many people because of my negligence. Regardless of the outcome, I'll never be able to forgive myself for what happened. Now here's a question for Detective Barnum. Why did they abandon the search so soon?"

Barnum shrugged. "I can't answer that, Randy. I wasn't involved in that decision."

"Somehow, I figured you'd say that. Would you please call your headquarters and let them know I'll be looking for Lt. Donovan? Oh, and Agent Essex, please mail me a copy of the polygraph results."

With that, Randy slipped his coat on, headed for the door, and left with a clean slate. He was glad this ordeal was over, but he couldn't help wondering why Detective Barnum was there to observe his polygraph. Thoughts about Amanda and that idiot newspaper reporter Razini caused him another stir. Surely his own wife wouldn't betray him. Or would she? He climbed in his car and started it, unsure what to believe.

FORTY-FIVE

The polygraph was tucked away, wires coiled, needles still. An AC Transit bus hissed before it roared and sped off. A pigeon landed at the window sill, peeked inside, and flew off. Special Agent Essex stared at his Parks Police guest in disgust. "Detective Barnum, you agreed to be a silent observer. Why did you go back on your word?"

"Instinct, I guess. I'm sorry."

"You said you'd be an asset, not an ass. What the hell were you thinking, spouting off like that?"

"It just came out." Essex kept scowling at him, so Barnum went to the window. Randy had just exited the federal building and was walking toward his car, never once looking back. "I was prying for a reaction," Barnum continued. "Once it was clear that Randy was passing his polygraph, I figured I'd throw in my two cents to test his reaction. Like you said, we have nothing without a confession."

"Well, next time stick to your word. Anyway, it's a moot point. Randy Connifer didn't have a single significant deviation, and everything he said matches his previous statements." Essex joined the detective at the window. He watched Randy's BMW pull away from the curb and smiled. Actually, I'm glad he's no longer a suspect in this case. I don't know of any father who has worked so hard to find his missing daughter. The only down side is his innocence brings us back to square one."

* * * * *

Randy contemplated his polygraph results during his drive to the Parks Police Headquarters. The time he had invested in going over the facts was worth the effort. Thinking before speaking helped, too. But having gotten some solid sleep was the real key.

He parked in the headquarters lot and presented his driver's license to the woman behind the bulletproof glass. He was shocked when she denied him entry, stating only that Lt. Donovan was in the field.

"But this is urgent," Randy said. "May I please speak to whoever's in charge?"

The woman watched him and lifted her phone. Following a brief conversation, she pressed her microphone button. "Pull on the door when it beeps and I'll meet you on the other side." Randy did, and she opened the second door after the first one closed.

"Follow me," she said, and led him down a corridor. "Please wait here." She tapped on the door and went inside. She came out a moment later. "Captain Vestell will see you now."

Randy gave a quick tap and poked his head inside. Captain Vestell was of medium height and build, and clearly in shape. His uniform was neatly pressed, his captain's bars shiny, his sullen face and thinning hair suggesting many years of experience. Randy was surprised to see one of Kerri's posters was on his desk. "Sir?"

"Come in, Mr. Connifer. What can I do for you?"

"I was hoping to see Lt. Donovan, but I understand he's in the field."

"Well, that's what we pay him to do." Vestell slipped on his reading glasses and reviewed some notes. Detective Barnum had warned him Randy might drop by, and he had a pretty good idea why he was there. "Just so you know, we haven't called off the search, but we did scale it back. We—"

"Have no reason to believe Kerri's there." Vestell's look told him he shouldn't have finished his sentence. "I'm sorry captain, but I keep hearing that same line."

Vestell looked sternly over his rims. "I'll forgive your rudeness once, but don't do it again." Randy nodded his apology and Vestell relaxed. "What I was going to say is we received some disturbing news and Lt. Donovan's on his way to the scene."

The scene? Randy blood drained from his head. "Did they find Kerri?"

"No, but one of the searchers found a large paw print that appears to belong to a cougar. We've hired an expert to confirm it."

"And you think this cougar took Kerri?"

"I never said that. First of all, the chances of encountering one are extremely remote, and one attacking a human is even less likely. Besides, the paw print was found near Stream Trail, not Eucalyptus or East Ridge, so the animal probably stopped to drink while passing through the park. Don't get me wrong, it's always a concern when cougars are spotted in public parks, but there's no reason to panic. They've been sighted near Mount Diablo and Sunol, but there's only been one report in Redwood Regional Park, and nothing came of it. Still, the possibilities are worth considering, which is why I wanted to personally break the news."

He shuddered, remembering the missing dog poster at Skyline Gate.

"Are you okay?" Vestell said. "You don't look so good."

“I was just thinking about a poster I saw at Skyline Gate about a missing Chow dog near Lake Chabot. I remember it because of its name. Purina, of all things. What if Purina became cougar chow?”

Vestell shook his head. “Our parks always have missing dogs. I’ll mention it to the wildlife management folks, though. I’m no animal expert, but to the best of my knowledge, cougars still eat deer.”

Vestell didn’t mention how the local deer populations now favored urban gardens to the forest. The most fearless cougars stalk their prey in broad daylight. The ramifications were disturbing.

“How fresh is this paw print?” Randy said that wondering why no one noticed it before. If they missed a cougar print, what else did they miss?

Vestell eyed his park map. “It’s hard to say. We’ll know more once the expert shows up. Dog prints have been mistaken for cougars before. Try not to worry about it.”

“Yeah, right. Dog prints have nails, cats don’t.” He thought for a moment and looked up. “Can Eagle 5’s infrared imagery distinguish a cougar?”

“Yes and no. First of all, most cougars sleep during the day, so if it’s hiding between rocks or in a den, it would be difficult to detect. Second, even if one’s roaming the park, it may not have any connection with Kerri’s disappearance. I will say this, though. If our expert determines there’s a cougar out there, his dogs will track it down.”

“Good. Maybe he’ll find Kerri while he’s at it.”

Vestell’s look warned him that he was wearing out his welcome. He should have counted to ten before saying that. “I’m sorry again,” said Randy. “Just promise me that if this tracker finds a cougar, he’ll tranquilize it, and not kill it.”

The captain leaned back in his seat. “I suppose that’s up to the cat.”

“Captain Vestell, you know as well as I do that fear causes people to react before thinking. Countless animals have died needlessly because they roamed residential areas. I donate a lot of money to protect these animals and don’t want anything to happen to this one. For that matter, neither would Kerri. She’d be mortified if an animal was killed in open space. After all, isn’t that why we set the land aside?”

Vestell scraped one of his polished boots on his desk as he shifted in his seat. He looked at it, frowned, and then looked back at Randy. “Son, there’s a fine line between saving human lives and protecting carnivores. My job is to protect and serve the public, and I will do so at all costs. Still, I share your concerns about protecting wildlife, which is why I chose a career with the Parks Police. I understand what you’re saying, and if there’s a cougar, I’ll do my best to save it.”

"That's all I ask. Thanks for seeing me, and please give my regards to Lt. Donovan. He's done an excellent job."

"Thank you. I'll be sure to pass that on."

Randy mulled over his meeting while waiting for the receptionist to let him out. He heard the buzzer and waved his thanks to the woman behind the bullet-proof glass. Once outside, the mud reminded him that the ground was dry when he and Kerri were walking together, so the paw print must have come afterwards. He breathed easier knowing the rogue animal couldn't be connected to her disappearance.

FORTY-SIX

Randy decided to take Redwood Road to Amanda's house as it was a more scenic drive. He had to detour two times, but it was worth it to see the sun filtering through the redwood forest.

His eyes grew heavy as his body relaxed. It was only one o'clock, but he was exhausted. He was pleased he had the sense to turn his business matters over to Jerry Meshner.

An unpleasant sensation came over him as he pulled into Amanda's driveway. It was quiet. Too quiet. The streets were nearly deserted. Had their volunteers lost interest already? Was she even home? He hurried to her door, the paw print on his mind. Why would Lt. Donovan be wasting his time if they believed the animal had moved on? He rang the doorbell, relieved to hear footsteps.

Amanda looked through the eyepiece and opened the door, greeting him warmly. "I was hoping it was you. How'd it go?"

"Fine," he said, cautiously peering down the hall. "Are your parents still here?"

Amanda nodded. "They're in the living room. What's going on? Did they find Kerri?"

"No." Randy gently eased her outside and shut the door, aching to hold her, stroke her hair, do something, anything, to assure her all was well. Razini's van was nowhere in sight. The only thing holding him back was his conscience. "Why don't you grab a coat and we'll take a walk."

"Okay." She opened a closet and slipped a coat on. "Mom, Dad, I'm going out for a while. I'll be back shortly." She zipped her coat, hurrying to meet Randy on the street. "You're scaring me, Randy. What's going on?"

"Well, for starters, Detective Barnum attended my polygraph exam. I guess since he doesn't have any other suspects, he wanted to see how I'd fare. In his defense, I'm sure he's getting a lot of pressure from his supervisor. Hell, I'd probably do the same if the roles were reversed. Anyway, I was a serious disappointment to him and Essex."

Her eyes widened. "So you passed?"

"Was there any doubt?"

"No," she lied. "None at all."

"Anyway, after the polygraph, I went to the Parks Police Headquarters to ask about the search. Lt. Donovan wasn't there, but I spoke to his superior, Captain Vestell, and he assured me the search was still ongoing. He also said they found a large paw print that might be from a cougar."

"A cougar? Here? Dear God, do they think it got Kerri?"

"I didn't get that feeling. After all, the print is near Stream Trail and we never went there on Wednesday. Besides, it couldn't have come until after Kerri disappeared because dry ground won't leave paw prints. The only reason Captain Vestell mentioned it is because they don't have any other leads. Personally, I think this is someone's idea of a sick joke. You know—mount a fake paw on the end of a stick and leave an impression? I mean, how else can you explain a single paw print?"

Amanda looked pale. The thought of a cougar in Redwood Park was dreadful, and as much as Randy had tried to dismiss it, she could see the fear in his eyes. "Only one print, huh?"

"Yeah, just one. But on a positive note, Captain Vestell called in a tracker. I asked them to tranquilize the animal, not shoot it. Vestell seemed agreeable."

"Randy, I know you're an animal right's activist, but would you still feel that way if a cougar got Kerri?"

"Amanda, I refuse to believe that Kerri is dead or got mauled by a cougar. Someone took her, and the police aren't doing enough to find her. I'm only passing on what I know. Now, what do you say we go back to your house so we can concentrate on getting her back? At some point, whoever has her is going to slip up or maybe seek the reward money, and when he does, the police will put an end to this nightmare. That's all that's keeping me going, and until there's proof to the contrary, that's what I'll believe."

"Me, too." But squeezing his hand didn't shed her doubts. Nearly all of their volunteers had lost interest. All were willing to donate their time until Lt. Donovan snubbed them. Now, the phone barely rang. "I'll never stop searching for her, you know."

"Nor will I."

Randy clutched her hand and let her warmth flow through him. He walked a few steps and said, "Did Sam Razini ever apologize for his article?"

"Not yet."

Randy nodded. "I was thinking about telling Sam about the paw print."

Amanda jerked her hand free, glaring at him. "Are you nuts? He violated our trust and publicly condemned you before you had the chance to prove your innocence. He's also the reason no one's here. I never want to see Cheap Tie again!"

"Believe me, I feel the same, but I walked out of that FBI office a free man and I need him to print that. I figured I'd leak the paw print story while I was at it. Imagine how much publicity we can milk out of that."

"Publicity or panic?" she fired back.

"Look, it's only been two days and the interest in Kerri has already dropped off. This is a big break, Amanda." She turned and started walking away from him. "Wait, Amanda. Don't you remember how Razini used us to get his name on the front page? Don't you think turnaround's fair play?"

She turned and studied Randy's face. He was never good at lying, and it was clear he was telling the truth. "Why would you share this with him after what he did to you?"

"For the exposure. Cougar stories always get great coverage. Think about it; they've attacked horses near Stanford, zoo animals in Oakland, and roam Palo Alto neighborhoods. I'm betting that once people learn there's a big cat in the park, their outrage will force the police into stepping up their efforts to find Kerri."

She listened, scraping her muddy shoe on a rock.

"Oh, come on, Amanda. You don't honestly believe that a one-legged cat got Kerri, do you? Do you know anyone who's actually seen a cougar in Redwood Regional Park?"

"I seem to recall there was a sighting on East Ridge Trail in 2004."

"Maybe, but who knows what that old lady really saw? My point is, why not take advantage of the free publicity so we can get our volunteers back? They reopened the park this morning so we can legally do our own search. Come on, Amanda. What do we have to lose?"

"Nothing, I guess." She peeled a breath mint and tucked it in her mouth.

"Once Razini's jumped on this, I'll leak the story to the radio stations. Better yet, we'll get the TV stations involved so they can flash Kerri's help line number again. Our search will prove that she's not in the park, and the police will have no choice but to rule it a kidnapping."

Sadly, Amanda didn't share his enthusiasm. Her cougar fears had a funny way of stealing her courage. Not even Randy could deny that Kerri was petite enough for a large animal to carry off. "You do realize that Razini will imply Kerri's dead. That's his style. Sensationalize it, just like he did your polygraph story. Besides, what makes you think he'll cooperate?"

"Because of what he did to me." Randy felt his skin warming and counted to ten. He calmed himself and said, "I need to know what was stalking us that day. Human or beast, I'd give my life to protect Kerri."

Amanda shivered under her long coat. "Mom's at the front window spying on us. I swear she should head the neighborhood watch."

Randy looked up and waved. Sharon disappeared as if Scotty had beamed her up.

Amanda looked at him sternly. "I want to listen in when you call Sam, and I don't want my folks around when you do it, so can you wait in your car while I send them to the market?"

"No problem." They parted ways and he waited until he saw Sharon and Donald drive off. Once they were out of sight, he went inside to place his call.

* * * * *

Sam Razini arrived at Amanda's house a short time later. He was expecting a fiery reception, but instead, Amanda welcomed him inside. Razini's eyes glistened as Randy shared his polygraph results with him. His cougar story was like icing on a cake.

Randy straightened himself and looked squarely at Cheap Tie. "So, here's the deal, Sam. No one's called since your damning article on me came out, so I need you to fix that by clearing my name in this new report. Anything less and I'll slap you with a law suit."

"Is that right?" Razini said, used to such threats.

Amanda looked at the men. "Come on, guys. Forget about law suits. We need our volunteers back so we can do a complete foot search of the park. The more people the better. What do you say, Sam? Can you help us?"

Razini smiled at her. "I'll see what I can do." He closed his notepad and got to his feet. "I'm curious, Randy. How will you cope if a cougar got your daughter?"

Randy's eyes narrowed. "Don't go there, Sam. Kerri was kidnapped, and this search will prove it. I'm also a staunch supporter of protecting wildlife, and have made it clear they should relocate animals, not kill them. You can quote me on that if you like."

Razini nodded respectfully. Cougar stories were nothing new to the Bay Area. The only thing interesting about this one was the possibility that the animal took the girl. "You do realize this won't come out until tomorrow morning?"

"That's fine. It's too late to organize a search, anyway."

Cheap Tie looked at Amanda, feeling a pang of guilt. "Give me until six AM before talking to the TV stations. Then maybe you can get some TV spots on the morning news. With any luck, your phones will be ringing off the hook by ten."

Amanda smiled cordially. "Thank you, Sam." After letting him out, she and Randy went to the window to make sure the reporter really left. She looked at her husband. “You did the right thing calling him. It’s probably the only way we’ll get more help.”

Randy saw that Razini had parked in the same spot where he picked Kerri up on Wednesday morning. The memory stabbed his gut. “God, I miss her.”

Amanda leaned on his shoulder. “I know,” she said, holding back her tears. “I pray every day that we’ll see her again.”

He tenderly wrapped his arms around her.

FORTY-SEVEN

Stacey Webster wasn't surprised when Lt. Donovan invited her and Tracker back for another search. She always kept her search-and-rescue gear in her truck, just in case. A cougar in the park might explain her dog's odd behavior while she was with Officer Rodriquez. A quick twist of her key had them heading back to Redwood Regional Park.

The morning commute moved better than expected, so it only took her forty minutes to reach Skyline Gate. Lt. Donovan was busy talking to Amanda and Randy, so Webster waited in her truck. When they looked over at her, she got out, gave a polite nod, and said, "So, where's this mountain man you hired, lieutenant?"

Donovan casually scanned the area. "He hasn't arrived yet. He's coming from Carmel, so it could be a while before he gets here."

"Well, Tracker and I are ready to get started. Do you still have the duck?"

Donovan shook his head. "I thought it was in my truck, but apparently I left it at the office."

Amanda immediately fished through her purse and offered a pair of filthy pink socks. "I just found these this morning. Kerri wore them on Tuesday. Will they do?"

"They're perfect," Webster said. "I'll get Tracker."

"Wait, Stacey," Donovan said. He grabbed a portable radio and handed it to her. "Keep this with you. Your call sign is 1501."

"1501; got it. Anything else?" The lieutenant shook his head.

Webster let Tracker out and waved Kerri's socks under his nose. "Take a good whiff, boy." His body stiffened, tail shot out. "Go on, boy. Search."

Randy watched the dog take off and looked at Webster. "Mind if I tag along?"

Webster noticed the scabs on his face. Poison oak, most likely. She was immune, but if he got another dose, he could be in serious trouble. "Actually, Tracker works best alone." It wasn't the first time she had used her dog as an excuse.

"I understand. Good luck."

Randy watched Webster head up East Ridge Trail, wondering if anything good would come from her search.

FORTY-EIGHT

Freelance animal tracker Mathew Bodine pulled his pickup into the Skyline Gate lot, parking in a remote spot so his dogs wouldn't bother anyone. He had been tracking a habituated cougar in the Carmel hills when he was informed that this case took priority. He stepped from his cab, stretched his body, and approached Lt. Donovan. He assumed the missing child's parents were the ones with him.

Randy watched the scraggly man approach. At five-nine and one-hundred-fifty-pounds, Bodine was hardly the mountain man he imagined. Sporting three-day-old stubble, a baseball cap, faded jeans, and worn cowboy boots, the tracker looked old, but up close, Bodine's smooth skin and light brown hair matched his youthful age of thirty-one.

Bodine greeted them as Donovan gave the introductions. After receiving his instructions from the lieutenant, Bodine headed back to his truck. He sensed he was being tailed, but didn't bother to look back. He retrieved his nickel-plated Colt .45 from under the seat and holstered it to his waist. The gesture alerted his three bloodhounds that they were about to go hunting, and caused them to yelp in their crates. "Easy, boys. We'll be going soon enough."

Randy was curious about the black box Bodine took from his cab and moved in for a better look. "What's that?" he said.

The tracker eagerly showed him the apparatus. "Let's just say that thanks to technology, there's no guessing anymore. You see, all my dogs wear collars that close an electrical circuit when they stand on their hind legs. That sends me a signal that they've treed a cat, so all I have to do is track 'em with this azimuth receiver."

"And what do you do after you tree them?"

"Well, I sure as hell don't put leashes on 'em and parade 'em through town."

Randy raised a brow. "Captain Vestell agreed to tranquilize and relocate this animal."

"Well, he told me the cougar's outcome depends on its actions. These hills are full of people, so if the animal poses a threat—well, let's worry about that later."

"Like I said; tranquilize it, don't kill it."

"Mr. Bodine, if anything happens to that cougar, I'll have every animal rights activist in the Bay Area up here protesting. Animals have rights, too."

Bodine chuckled. *Animals have rights*. What a joke. It was getting late and his dogs were eager to hunt. He went over to Donovan for a decision. "Lieutenant, what do you really want me to do if I find this cougar?"

Donovan knew that Randy could get media attention, and the Parks Police didn't need any more negative publicity. He thought up a plan. Bodine was his backup in case his plan failed. "Let me know if you find a cougar and I'll get someone with a dart gun. Got it, Bodine? Don't shoot the cougar."

"Yeah, I got it."

Mathew Bodine spat and looked over Donovan's trail map, a tobacco leaf clinging to his chin. He wiped his sleeve across his face to get rid of the leaf.

Donovan pointed at the map. "This is where they found the paw print. Your first job is to confirm it's from a cougar. We'll go from there once we know what we're dealing with."

"No sweat."

Bodine tucked the map in his pocket and went to release his dogs. The first dog leaped out, flinging slobber as he shook. The second made a beeline for a tree. The third stood by his master, wagging his tail. The tracker slung his Remington 30-06 deer rifle over his shoulder and whistled at his dogs. "C'mon boys; let's go huntin'."

Donovan watched until they disappeared down Stream Trail, aware of how quickly situations like this change. "I'm not sure what to hope for, Randy."

Randy sensed there was more going on than analyzing a mysterious paw print. "Why did Bodine and Webster head in opposite directions?"

"Separate goals. Stacey Webster's convinced that she knows where Kerri is, and Matt Bodine's looking for a cougar. They're both experts in their respective fields, the weather is good, and we still have a few hours of daylight. I expect something will turn up."

"We'll be waiting in my car."

FORTY-NINE

Stacey Webster followed Tracker up East Ridge Trail. He showed surprisingly little interest in the areas he had searched before. When they reached Eucalyptus Trail, he sat and sniffed the air again. She sat next to him, scratching his neck. "I don't get it, Tracker. Kerri's out here somewhere." Her dog licked her face.

She thought about her cousin who was buried alive in the 1989 Loma Prieta earthquake. It took rescuers a week to find her, but they were too late. Her autopsy revealed she had lived at least five days before expiring. *Five days!* Stacey swore an oath that she would give someone else the gift of life by learning search and rescue. Her banking job allowed her to work from her home so she could always respond. Tracker was her third and most experienced search dog. Nothing was more important to them than finding a missing person, and neither gave up, even when things weren't going well.

But Kerri's case was unique and Webster was beginning to share the police department's opinion that the girl wasn't in the park. She pressed the radio to her lips and keyed the mike, reporting to Donovan, "There's nothing on East Ridge. "We're heading down Eucalyptus to Stream Trail."

"Roger, Stacey. Avoid lower Stream Trail. Our tracker's got bloodhounds working in that area."

Webster was speechless. She only knew one tracker who used bloodhounds, and he was more trophy hunter than government tracker. She detested anyone who killed animals for their heads. She keyed her mike, praying it wasn't him. "What's this tracker's name?"

"Mathew Bodine."

She lowered her radio. "Shit," she said to her dog. "Why isn't he in Arizona where he belongs?" Tracker cowered over to her. "It's okay, boy. I'm not mad at you, I'm mad at me."

Then Donovan broadcast another warning to her. "Stacey, be advised Mr. Bodine is armed and doesn't have a radio. Confirm you will avoid lower Stream Trail?"

"Affirmative; will avoid lower Stream Trail." *At all costs.* "We'll check out Phillips Loop instead." She got up and brushed herself off, keen on avoiding Matt Bodine.

* * * * *

Randy overheard Donovan's conversation and decided to stick around. "She sounds pissed," he said to the lieutenant. "Why would Stacey change her mind like that when no one's found anything on Phillips Loop? What's going on?"

"Beats me. Maybe her dog picked up a new scent."

"Yeah." But Randy didn't believe it.

He walked back to his car where Amanda was inside, staying warm. She seemed unusually quiet when he got in. He waited for her to say something, and when she didn't, he said, "I think something's going on between Stacey Webster and this animal tracker, Bodine."

"And why is that?"

"Well, first she reports she's taking Eucalyptus to Stream Trail, then changes her mind as soon as she hears Bodine's name. She covered herself by saying she was taking Phillips Loop instead, but she sounded like she knew him."

"Then maybe you should confront her when she comes out. At least that way you'll know what's going on."

"I don't know. She could be in there quite a while. You want to go home?"

"No, I want to be here when they find Kerri. My folks can answer the phones."

He noticed her shivering. "You want some heat?"

"That would be great, thanks."

He started the engine and turned on the defrost. His windshield fogged over before it began to clear. He wiped it with his handkerchief, but saw no sign of Stacey Webster or her dog. He caught a glimpse of himself in the rear-view mirror as he watched a fire engine speed down Skyline Boulevard. He quickly pushed the mirror away. "I look like a fiend."

"It's not that bad," she said. "Besides, no one cares what you look like."

"Thank God for that." But his canted mirror now reflected her perfect complexion. "How did you manage to avoid the poison oak?"

She shrugged, moved the air select knob from defrost to floor heat, and jammed her toes against the vent. She then reclined her seat, folded her arms over her chest, and closed her eyes.

Randy stared at her. "So, what do you think's going on between Bodine and Webster?"

"Jesus, Randy, give it a rest. Who says they even know each other?"

"You're right." He reclined his seat and closed his eyes, too.

* * * * *

Someone was banging at Randy's window. Everything around him was dark except for a spotlight over his shoulder. It sounded like someone was telling him to open a window, but the ghostly voice was muffled. When he turned away, the banging resumed, and the voice grew louder.

Lt. Donovan tapped the glass again. "Randy, open the window or I'll break it!"

Randy's head jerked and he squinted into the light. Where was he? And why was he in his car? Why were his fingernails dark and Amanda's lips purple? Adrenaline forced him awake and he pressed all four power window buttons. A wave of cool air rushed in, breaking their spell. "Amanda, wake up!" He shook her shoulders and she began hacking. Soon after, her color began returning.

Lt. Donovan flung Amanda's door open and helped her outside. "I can't believe you'd leave the windows up with the engine running," he said to Randy. "Are you two okay?"

Randy struggled to interpret Donovan's words as he fumbled for his door handle. He released the catch and lost his balance as he pushed the door open. Someone caught him; his nametag read, "Davis." "What's going on? Are we under arrest?"

"Just breathe," Officer Davis said. "You're hypoxic from carbon monoxide poisoning. You could've died."

Nausea smacked Randy like a breaking swell. He hunched over, trying to recognize the officer who was holding him. He didn't recall seeing him before. Then slowly, things started to make sense. "Where's Amanda?"

"Lt. Donovan's walking her around. She'll be okay."

Randy's head hung. "What about Stacey Webster?"

"Ms. Webster left hours ago after she and Matt Bodine came up empty. She wasn't in a very good mood, so it's probably best you didn't catch her."

The officer waved his light in front of Randy's eyes again. They were still dilated and weren't responding. "Are you okay, Mr. Connifer? Do you need any oxygen?"

"No, I'm fine."

"Well, you'd better get your heater checked out. You must have a leak somewhere."

"I'm sure you're right. What about that paw print?"

"Mr. Bodine says it's a cougar print all right, but he believes the animal moved on. He says the grass fires we had near Sunol probably drove it this way."

"That makes sense." Randy rubbed his throbbing head while his wife leaned against his car. He draped his trench coat over her, which she gratefully accepted.

Donovan observed them, amazed at how cozy they had become. They looked nothing like how Officer Rodriquez had described their first reunion. Admittedly, it was far-fetched to think that they collaborated on their daughter's disappearance, but finding no other clues, he still believed anything was possible. He joined them and said, "I need to get back to work. Are you sure you don't need to go to the hospital?"

"No thanks," said Randy, "but could you please take Amanda home?"

"I'd be happy to. Officer Davis will follow you to make sure you get home okay. You're lucky I spotted you while I was driving by. You'll probably have a bad hang-over."

Randy nodded. No doubt Lt. Donovan and Officer Davis saved their lives. He thought about the search and called to Lt. Donovan who was escorting Amanda to his vehicle. "Hey, lieutenant—when are Bodine and Webster coming back?"

Donovan stopped and turned. "I'm not sure about Stacey, but I imagine Mr. Bodine will be here pretty early."

After his sluggish brain caught up, Randy said, "One more question. Why would Stacey be so upset about Mathew. Bodine being here?"

"I'm guessing it's some kind of grudge match. Both are talented trackers and think their dogs are invincible, but the truth is their dogs are trained for different missions. I have to admit, Stacey has never packed up and left like this, but who knows? Maybe they have a history together. In any event, that's none of my business."

Randy picked at a scab on his hand. "I don't suppose you have her phone number? I'd like to thank her for her efforts."

"Hang on; I think I have her card in my truck." Donovan made sure Amanda was strapped in and returned a few minutes later. "Here you go. I have her number in my e-book so feel free to keep her card. That way no one can accuse me of giving out her personal information."

"Thanks," Randy said, reviewing her business card. It showed her dog with his backpack. At the bottom, it read, "*That others may live*"; a motto common to rescue organizations. "It seems Stacey lives for search-and-rescue."

"That she does. In fact, I wouldn't be surprised if she sleeps in her jumpsuit. She's always been the first to volunteer."

"Don't you find it odd that someone who lives and breathes search and rescue would quit just because an animal tracker showed up?"

"Like I said, why Stacey quit is none of my business. You sure you're okay?"

Randy nodded. "I'll be fine once I get over this headache."

Amanda threw her door open to give Randy his coat. "Here, you'll need this. Thanks for sharing."

"You're welcome. I'll call you later."

She nodded and pulled her door shut. Soon after, Donovan drove off.

Randy ogled his three-year-old BMW that nearly became his coffin. He would get the heater fixed all right. After that, he'd buy a new car.

FIFTY

Evelyn heard Randy's garage door open and rushed to greet her son. Unable to reach him on his cell phone, she had been pacing the living room for hours. She wrapped her arms around him, hugging him tight. "Thank God you're safe. Sharon kept calling to see where Amanda was and I didn't know what to tell her. Is she okay?"

"Yeah. We've been at the park all afternoon. What's the problem?"

"You tell me. Sharon said the police took Amanda home and she refused to talk about anything. What's going on, Randy? Did they find Kerri?"

"No, nothing's changed, and Lt. Donovan was doing me a favor by driving Amanda home. Honestly, it was no big deal. I've got a splitting headache and need to make a phone call. I appreciate your concern, though."

Evelyn backed out of the way, wounded by his neglect. She had hoped to take him out to dinner, but clearly he'd rather be alone. She sat on the sofa and turned on the TV.

Randy went to the bathroom and downed three Motrin. He bowed to the porcelain god when his empty stomach rejected the pills. Whether his vomiting was caused by carbon monoxide poisoning or personal devastation was irrelevant. Either way, this time, he felt as bad as he looked.

He washed his face and toweled it dry, pained over how he had treated his mother. Still, she didn't need to know about his car problems or the feuding dog handlers.

Evelyn overheard his retching and started to get up. She quickly sat down, realizing he didn't need or want her help. She grieved for her son as much as for her granddaughter, wondering if their lives would ever be normal again. An annoying attorney appeared on TV. *"If you've been hurt in an accident, call The Strong Arm—"* She flipped the channel before he spoke another word.

Randy rinsed his mouth and held a damp washcloth to his face, revolted by what he saw in the mirror. Maybe he should grow a beard. Then again, changing his appearance might renew suspicion. He applied rubbing alcohol to his rash, surprised when it didn't burn. He sat on his bed, staring at the phone, thinking he should call someone, but realized the only person he wanted to talk to right then was sitting in the other room. He went to the sofa and hugged his mother. “I’m sorry I haven’t been much company, but I’m glad you’re here. Please don’t leave.”

Evelyn smiled, returning his hug. “You can’t get rid of me that easy. I’m not going anywhere.”

Relieved, he sat down and leaned his head on her shoulder, feeling her love, confident they would be okay. After a few minutes, he staggered back to his room and lay on his bed. The room spun like it was attached to a helicopter blade. He took a couple Tylenol PM to help him sleep. Soon after, darkness cloaked him.

FIFTY-ONE

Randy awoke to squawking jays, and squirrels scampering over his roof. He stumbled out of bed and went to the kitchen to brew some coffee. He added some extra coffee grounds before hitting the start button. Once it began to drip, he went to retrieve the morning *Oakland Tribune*, grateful his neighbor wasn't out.

The headlines read, **OAKLAND HILLS COUGAR MAY EXPLAIN GIRL'S DISAPPEARANCE**. The bold caption was expected, but Sam Razini's implications were still hard to accept. He kept reading as he walked inside.

> "...Rescuers found a large paw print in the vicinity of lower Stream Trail. Professional animal tracker Mathew Bodine confirmed the print was that of an adult male cougar with an estimated weight of one-hundred-thirty pounds. Cougars, also known as mountain lions, pumas, catamounts, and panthers, roam nearly all of California's wilderness. While normally reclusive, this is the second animal to have been confirmed in Redwood Regional Park in recent years.
>
> "Offering no explanation as to why there was only one paw print, Mr. Bodine believes the animal was exploring new habitat after brush fires ravaged the open space in the Sunol hills above Fremont. While attacks on humans are extremely rare, Bodine warns that cougars are unpredictable, and have been known to attack livestock and pets. Although his radio-collared bloodhounds were unable to locate the animal, he plans to resume the hunt today. The cougar's fate, should it be found, remains undetermined.
>
> "In a statement to the press, Lt. Bill Donovan of the East Bay Regional Parks Police said, 'the possibility exists that Kerri Connifer may have fallen victim to this animal.' Kerri, the six-year-old daughter of Oakland residents Randy

> and Amanda Connifer, has been missing since Wednesday morning. Over seventy rescuers and a police helicopter armed with infrared imaging have combed the park, but have yet to find any sign of her.
>
> "Although Redwood Park has reopened to the public, park visitors are encouraged not to hike or jog alone, and avoid the hours between dawn and dusk. People encountering a cougar should stand tall and wave their arms to make themselves appear as menacing as possible. Slowly back away so the animal can retreat. If it appears aggressive, screaming and throwing rocks may deter it as they are not accustomed to defending themselves. Never lie down in a cougar encounter. Should the animal attack, try gouging its eyes.
>
> "By nature, cougars are reclusive and normally sleep by day. An adult cougar is over six feet long, has sandy brown fur, and a long tail. Anyone seeing this cat should immediately call 911."

Randy poured himself some coffee, curious why Razini didn't use Amanda's real name. He ignored the error and skimmed the rest of the paper. On the bottom right-hand side of page four, a smaller article caught his eye.

Father Ruled Out as Kidnapping Suspect Seeks Volunteers
By Sam Razini
Oakland Tribune Staff Writer

> "The FBI has officially cleared Randy Connifer of any involvement in his daughter's disappearance. Grateful, yet desperate, Mr. Connifer and wife Amanda are once again soliciting volunteers for help. 'We need closure,' said Connifer in an exclusive interview. 'Kerri disappeared without a trace, but I'm convinced there is evidence out there that will lead to her recovery. Now that the park has reopened, I am asking the community to come together for a massive sweep of the area. With enough people, I'm sure we can find her.' Interested parties should call toll free HLP-KERI, or simply show up at the Skyline Gate entrance to Redwood Regional Park at one o'clock this afternoon."

He had barely finished reading the article when Amanda called to say her phones were ringing off the hook with volunteers asking how to get to the park. "That's great," he said. "Razini really came through this time. I've got to call the TV stations to see if they'll add to the story. I'll talk to you later."

As he hung up, he spotted Stacey Webster's business card on the counter. He had planned to call her last night, but forgot. After calling the local television stations, he dialed her number, but hung up before it went through. *She'd offer her services if she really wanted to help.*

As a courtesy, he notified the Oakland Police Department, Regional Parks Police, and East Bay Municipal Utilities District, otherwise known as East Bay MUD, of his intent to have volunteers sweep the park. The Oakland Police agreed to provide a traffic detail while the Parks Police made Eagle 5 available from one to four P.M. Not to be left out, East Bay MUD promised to send supervisors to guide them through their neighboring watershed property. Randy cradled the phone, ready to get to work. Even his stinging razor didn't faze him. With the help of some eye drops, pressed slacks, a polo shirt, and his mother's makeup, he emerged from the bathroom looking respectable again.

Evelyn was sipping coffee when he entered the kitchen. "Wow! You look great!" She stretched on her tiptoes to kiss his cheek. "I'm proud of you, son. Good luck today."

FIFTY-TWO

Amanda barely recognized her husband when she pulled into the Skyline Gate lot. He looked radiant, confident, prepared for battle. Kerri would be pleased. But where were the volunteers, news vans, and utility trucks? Randy would be devastated if no one showed. She pulled alongside and rolled down her window. “Hey, handsome, where is everyone?”

“Beats me. How’s your head?”

“I’ll live. My folks are answering the phones. By the way, Mom’s really sorry.”

Her words were like a sucker punch. After years of treating him like dirt, Sharon sends her daughter to apologize? He spotted movement out the corner of his eye and saw a brown truck heading his way. “All right! East Bay MUD’s here.” He ignored Amanda and waved to the driver. “I’d better go talk to them. I’ll catch up with you later.” He didn’t hear a response.

East Bay MUD team leader Robert Sutton parked his truck and scanned the scene. An Oakland police officer stood ready to direct traffic. A pair of bikers tailgated a Toyota 4X4 down Skyline Boulevard. A yellow Volvo wagon drove up the hill from the opposite direction. Seconds later, a black Mercedes drove by. Sutton thought he might have to park three blocks away, but instead he pulled right up to the fire gate. He scratched his head, and then donned his helmet while watching Randy approach. “Are we early?”

“Nope; you’re right on time,” Randy said, sliding his fingers into his back pockets to steady them. “Don’t worry, they’ll be here.”

Sutton wasn’t convinced. “What, exactly, do you want me to do?”

“Lead the search through your property north of East Ridge Trail near Eucalyptus. One of the search dogs kept getting hits there.”

The supervisor frowned. “That area’s had a lot of storm damage. We don’t need any more mudslides.”

“I understand, and that’s why I’m only asking for one pass.”

Sutton pulled a round tin from his shirt pocket and removed the lid. He scanned the park while he tucked a pinch of tobacco under his lip. Many of his crews were busy making repairs from the last storm. Being there seemed a waste of time, but he had his orders.

"Mr. Connifer, I'm here to assist you, so let me know when you're ready."

Randy nodded, feeling like the village idiot. Amanda waved her encouragement and he waved back. He stood there for ten minutes without a single vehicle entering the parking lot. Then a loud rumble preceded a motorcade that came up the hill. The Oakland Police officer leaped from his car to direct the unexpected traffic. Vehicles crammed the streets for ten minutes. He was told more were on the way.

One of the first to arrive came over. "My hat's off to you, son," the older gent said. "Our citizen action group carpooled from the Mormon Temple because we knew there wasn't much space up here. Sorry we're late. I was afraid everyone would leave before we got here."

"You're not late at all, and thanks for coming. We'll give it a few minutes, and then get started. This is the miracle I was hoping for."

Amanda ran over and hugged her husband. "Isn't this great? Can you believe it?"

"I have to admit I was ready to give up."

She felt the same.

By a quarter past one, every side-street within a half-mile of Skyline Gate was packed with cars. Two live-feed television vans had received permission to double-park. Eagle 5 buzzed overhead on its first pass. Everything was falling into place.

Randy took Sutton's megaphone and stood on the truck's bumper. "Can everyone please gather around?" As people closed in, he saw Detective Barnum and Lt. Donovan standing near the front. Stacey Webster and her dog stood to the side. Randy gestured for Amanda to join him, but she shook him off.

"First, Amanda and I would like to thank you for coming. This is an extraordinary turnout. To maximize our time, I'd like you to divide into four groups. The first group will go with Mr. Sutton from East Bay MUD to search the watershed area, the second will cover East Ridge Trail, the third will sweep Stream Trail, and the fourth will take West Ridge Trail. Please remain line-abreast walking a pace that will ensure nothing is overlooked. If everyone works together, we should be done in a couple of hours.

"Bear in mind that every clue is significant. Immediately bring anything such as footprints, paw prints, torn clothing, broken branches, makeshift shelters, McDonald's wrappers, or cigarette butts to your team leader's attention, but please do not pick anything up. Also, tread lightly as the ground is still saturated.

"As you can see, the Parks Police helicopter is patrolling the area. If you need help fast, try waving them down.

"I can personally attest that poison oak is abundant here, so wear protective clothing, and wash them separately once you get home. If able, cover your car seats before you sit down to keep the poison from spreading." Someone started tapping a cigarette pack. "Oh, one more thing. Absolutely no smoking." That person quickly tucked the pack away. "Finally, as most of you are aware, it's possible we have a cougar in the park. No one has seen it so it's probably moved on, but if you should spot it, remain calm and give it a chance to leave. Once again, thanks for coming. Mr. Sutton, do you have anything to add?"

Sutton took his megaphone back. "Thank you, Randy. As most of you know, the property that borders the north side of this park is normally restricted because it's part of our watershed. As Randy said, the ground is quite soft, so we only want one sweep. Take your time, stay together, and be thorough. Are there any questions?"

Lt. Donovan raised his hand, took the megaphone, and introduced himself. "I'd like to add that each group will have a Parks Police officer along to assist with communications. Rather than call 911 on your cell phones, please notify your assigned officer if you should find anything.

"This is an impressive gathering, and you should be commended for your spirit and actions. Thank you for your help. Let's go find Kerri."

Randy took the megaphone back. "Thanks, lieutenant. Now, if you would divide into four groups, we'll get started."

Amanda ignored the press and kissed Randy on the cheek. "You've always had a knack for organizing," she said. "I'm glad this worked out. By the way, which group are we going with?"

"I'm staying behind, but don't let that stop you."

She looked at him, puzzled. "You're staying behind? Really?"

"Yeah. I figure one of us should be here in case the press wants an interview."

"Then I'm staying, too."

She noticed a young woman in a business suit approach, her videographer shadowing three feet behind.

"Susan Landers, KRON TV," the suit said. "I'm sorry for your tragedy. I'm sure this is a very difficult time."

Randy and Amanda exchanged glances, perplexed by what seemed obvious to everyone except the reporter.

"This is an impressive turnout," Landers continued, "but why are you doing this after the official search failed to find your daughter?"

Randy's jaw tightened. "Do you have any children, Ms. Landers?" She shook her head, grateful they weren't broadcasting live. "Well, perhaps when you have children of your own you'll understand that parents do whatever it takes to protect them. I don't blame the police for scaling back, but we feel Kerri deserves a more thorough search. People walking elbow-to-elbow should ensure nothing's been missed. Each of these volunteers has their own reasons for being here, but they all want to find our daughter. With luck, they'll find something that will prove a stalker was waiting as she rounded that bend. There must be a clue that will help find her. People don't just vanish."

Landers discretely motioned for her assistant to keep taping while she held Randy's attention. "So, do you believe that someone has Kerri rather than her being in the park?"

Randy faced the lens. "This search should prove she isn't here. We hope her abductor is watching and will make arrangements for her safe return."

"I see," Landers said, turning her attention to Amanda. "Ms. Schaefer, do you have any idea who would take your daughter and why?"

Amanda's glossy eyes pleaded for Randy to step in. He understood and said, "Ms. Landers, the expansive green belt that encircles the Bay Area is a perfect haven for pedophiles, rapists, and child abusers. Frankly, we don't care who has Kerri or why, so long as she gets home safely."

Landers' camera zoomed in on the father, half-expecting him to wave the American flag. What he said was perfect for an election campaign, but it did nothing for her missing child story. People want to see tears, distraught parents. Things were going fine until Randy interfered. She felt robbed.

She separated them, holding the microphone to Amanda's face. "Ms. Schaefer, I still haven't heard from you. What do you think the chances are of finding your daughter alive?"

Amanda's eyes started to well, but then she thought about the kidnapper and her face hardened. "I need Kerri in my arms again. She is everything to me. To us," she said, glancing at her husband. "I beg you, if you have her, or know where Kerri is, please call her help line now." She turned to Landers. "That's all I have to say."

Landers passed the cut signal and pulled her videographer aside. "Did you get that?"

"I have all the footage we need."

"Good. We'll stick around for an hour, but without a body, there is no story."

* * * * *

Randy feared he had hurt Amanda again, setting her up like that. Reporters like Landers will always go for the throat. He should have done a better job of protecting his wife. Then it dawned on him that he was being "Mr. Fix-it" again. Amanda chose to speak, and she handled herself just fine. It would have been wrong for him to protect her further. He put his arm around her and escorted her to her car. He grinned and said, “Is your heater working?”

“Better than yours. Come on, get in.”

He slid into the passenger seat, warming his hands. “Did you happen to notice that Stacey Webster is here with her dog?”

“I did. She went with the group searching the East Bay MUD area.”

“That doesn’t surprise me.”

FIFTY-THREE

Trapped by thoughts of Matt Bodine, Stacey Webster lagged behind her group. Tracker wasn't showing much interest, so there wasn't any need for them to be in front. She had met Matt at a dog competition two years ago, and never expected to fall for someone like him. But somehow, their mutual love for dogs pulled them together. It wasn't until she visited him in Arizona that she discovered their opposing views on wildlife. Only then did she learn about his trophy-hunting business.

Still, Matt's charm and wit held her interest throughout their countless debates on wildlife management. On the morning before she was supposed to fly home, he brought her a road-kill and sawed through the deer's leg as if it were a wooden dowel. He said the lack of bone marrow meant the deer was starving and whoever was driving the pickup did it a favor. *That's why we must hunt wildlife*, she remembered him saying. *Some day you'll understand there's a fine line between wildlife protection and wildlife management.*

His words left as big an impression as the doe's permanent gaze. She had given Matt the opportunity to make his point, but it still wasn't enough for her to accept his trade. In their final debate, he bragged about how his dogs kept a cougar treed until his wealthy out-of-state clients arrived. She left immediately, and never spoke to him again.

To her, there was no doubt that Matt Bodine would kill this cougar just to plug his business and see his name in print.

* * * * *

Mathew Bodine never forgot his first cougar encounter. He was a young kid in a small town whose main street consisted of a gas station and a general store. He was panning for gold in the stream less than one hundred yards from his parents' house when he spotted a sandy brown feline stalking him. Her golden eyes kept him frozen as she hunched over, ready to pounce.

His father always said to stand tall and scream if he ever encountered one. Screaming wasn't a problem at that point. When the cat failed to retreat, he picked up some rocks and pelted her. She hissed and walked away, annoyed, but unafraid. Memories of her gaze and bared teeth still burned his brain. He swore he would kill her if he ever saw her again. Ironically, it was fear, not bravery, that led to his becoming a tracker. Years later, and after countless cougars to his credit, he still couldn't shake his fear.

Bodine made his way up Stream Trail, searching for a place to position the road-kill bait the Parks Police was delivering. The deer became the victim of a one-car accident on Redwood Road. The car and deer were both totaled, but at least the carcass would be put to good use. The driver was pleased to know that.

The giant redwoods offer a unique reverence. Where a lumber mill once stood, sunlight and time had cleansed the damage done to this wonderland. The stream rippled, ferns were plentiful, yet there was little evidence of deer. After scouting the perfect spot, Bodine headed back to his truck to await its arrival. He polished his sidearm to pass the time, aware the cougar could be watching his every move.

The canyon floor was mostly dry now, and the only new tracks were from deer. When the carcass finally arrived, Bodine dragged it near the lone cougar print, and then left to grab some breakfast. If the doe was missing when he came back, he'd know the cougar was still here.

He returned two hours later and found the deer carcass untouched. The rising sun decreased the odds that it would take the bait. He headed toward town to keep his dogs away and pulled off at the hill's summit where he could see the Mormon Temple's golden spires reaching to Heaven. The early light reflected the bridges and skyscrapers in the bejeweled bay. But as spectacular as this view is, Mathew Bodine knew he didn't belong in a place where his barking dogs were drowned out by city noise. Today was his tenth day on the road and he still had to finish the other job. He couldn't wait to return to the desert.

He went back to Redwood Park at half past noon and leashed his dogs together. His bloodhounds tugged at their leads as he guided them to the baited area. This time, cougar tracks had replaced the carcass. He smiled and gave each dog a pat as he unhooked its lead. "Looks like the plan worked, boys. Go find him."

The bloodhounds bolted in the direction of the tracks, howling in anticipation. With his dogs gone, he compared his plaster casting to the fresh tracks and found the right front paw was a perfect match. He returned to his truck to retrieve his casting material to document his latest find. Once they dried, he would mark and date them like he did the original. If nothing else, the castings made great paperweights.

He had just finished pouring the last of his plaster when his receiver indicated a cat was treed. The cat wasn't going anywhere so he called the

California Fish and Game warden on his cell phone per Donovan's instructions. His phone's service was minimal, but thankfully he was able to complete the connection.

"I've got a cougar treed in Redwood Regional Park," he said to Game Warden Ben Hollinger. "Are you coming with a dart gun, or should I take care of the problem myself?"

Game Warden Hollinger resented Bodine's involvement. He remembered him from an earlier hunt and feared for the cougar. *"I'll meet you in the Canyon Meadows staging area,"* he said, and promptly hung up.

Bodine tucked his phone away and sniffed the air. The best part of his job was being outside. The worst was listening to clients talk while hunting. He returned to his pickup to await the warden.

From his tailgate, he imagined what this place must have been like when elk, deer, grizzly bear, and cougars roamed free. That all changed when sawmills started slicing up redwoods into mining timbers and railroad ties. The rush for gold ravaged hillsides, beasts, and Native Americans without remorse. The thought churned his stomach.

Stacey Webster's disdain for his hunting business denied him the opportunity to prove how pro-environment he really was. He knew that when habitats were destroyed, its inhabitants weren't far behind. At the current rate of development, he estimated he had another twenty years before human encroachment put him out of business. Then again, trapping habituated wildlife could create a whole new industry.

FIFTY-FOUR

Lt. Donovan dialed Randy's cell phone, eager to relay the latest. He answered on the first ring. "I just heard from the game warden. Matt Bodine treed a cat and the warden's on his way to tranquilize it."

"Thanks for the update, lieutenant."

Randy ended the call, pondering the possibilities. Any connection between the cougar, the missing Chow dog, and Kerri, could only be determined through a necropsy, and that meant the cougar would have to die, too. When Amanda awoke, he shared Donovan's latest, but nothing else.

Five minutes later, his phone rang again. This time Lt. Donovan was energized. Randy listened to him, speechless. Someone had found a child's shoe in a poison oak bush at the end of the deer trail. He dropped the phone in his lap. *Kerri!*

* * * * *

Matt Bodine spotted Game Warden Hollinger's truck heading his way. To him, wardens were nothing more than paper pushers who had no clue about managing wildlife. Hunters were the true guardians of the forest. They thinned herds so the majority could survive. He would be civil to Hollinger, but he didn't have to like him.

Hollinger stepped from his pickup and tugged his coat over his belly. "Hi, Matt. It's been a long time."

"Not long enough," he said, picking at his teeth.

Hollinger grinned. "You did a good job, Matt. I didn't anticipate such prompt results."

Bodine pictured the pudgy man sitting in his office, feet propped up, waiting for his call. "You know me, warden. I aim to please." He eyed the steel cage in Hollinger's truck bed, doubting it would be necessary. "My dogs treed a cat about a mile in. You're better off killing it, you know. Cougars have great memories. It'll be back."

"I doubt it. I plan to tag it and release it in the Sierras. If somehow it manages to find its way back, then we've got a problem. So, tell me Matt, how many cubs have died from your trophy hunting business?"

"I fail to see how that has any bearing on my services here."

"You're right, it doesn't. I was just making the point that I'm paid to protect animals while you're paid to kill 'em. Well, sometimes I have to kill them, too, but unlike you, I never get pleasure from it. What I'm trying to say is this animal deserves a chance to live. That's why I'm here."

"Yeah, well, thanks for the speech, reverend, but I don't need your crap. We both know I run a legitimate business, so I suggest you drop it and gather your stuff so I can get to my next job."

Hollinger huffed, slung a large-barreled rifle over this shoulder, jammed a cushion under his arm, and grabbed his tackle box.

Bodine chuckled, shaking his head. "Need a hand, warden?"

"Yeah. How about getting the other cushion from the cab?"

"What the hell do you need cushions for? You plan on taking a nap?"

"Hardly. They're to break the cat's fall after it's been tranquilized. Like I said, I don't want it hurt, and that includes getting it out of the tree."

Bodine grabbed the pad and let his azimuth tracker guide him. He and Hollinger were opposites all right. *Padding for a cougar. Christ!* It was hard putting up with the game warden, but his connections in Arizona could impact his business. He had no choice but to comply with his given instructions, no matter how ludicrous they might be. Thankfully, this job would be over soon.

The strong radio signals made navigating easy. Bodine's business required him to have the latest equipment. He glided through the woods hoping to lose the warden, but somehow Hollinger was matching him step for step. Even worse, Hollinger kept jabbering at him like a bad client.

"So, how'd you end up in the tracking business, Matt?"

"Call it destiny. I learned to track as a kid, and hunting wild game is big business. Trophy hunting's been a pastime of royalty since the first kings. Many of our presidents were avid hunters, too. In fact, Teddy Roosevelt was as passionate about hunting as he was the environment, so don't get down on me because I happen to enjoy what I do."

"I wasn't criticizing—just making conversation."

Hollinger knew that Bodine had picked up the pace to try and ditch him. The warden figured if he pestered the tracker long enough, Bodine would stop and glare at him. Soon, Bodine did just that. The warden smiled, drew in a few welcome breaths, and said, "Matt, I've always been confused about the term, sport hunting. I mean, where's the sport if the animals can't shoot back?"

Bodine's expression hardened. "What's the matter?" Hollinger said. "Did I hurt your feelings?"

"You know, Matt, I've always been confused about the title, 'sport hunting.' I mean, where's the sport if the animals can't shoot back?" The tracker predictably stopped and glared. "What's the problem, Matt? Did I hurt you feelings?"

"Don't flatter yourself, warden. I only stopped because we should be hearing my dogs by now."

Bodine chambered a round in his rifle and double-checked his sidearm. *Treed cats can't fight, so why is it so quiet?* A gust provided the answer. They were upwind of his dogs! How could he miss such an obvious detail? He scowled at the warden. "Can we cut the conversation? Distractions can prove fatal."

Hollinger hiked his shoulders and Bodine took off again. He stopped at the bait site and pointed to the ground. "Nice prints, eh, warden? You can't get any fresher."

"Wow. That's a pretty big cat. Probably a tom looking for new turf."

"Yeah, that was my guess, too. Come on, let's keep going."

Bodine moved swiftly and deliberately. Why would anyone be opposed to killing a cougar that hunted by day, especially one that could end up roaming urban streets in search of garden-munching deer. Human encounters were likely any time a fearless beast was on the loose, yet somehow, Hollinger and the others seemed oblivious to this fact.

He checked his direction finder again. *Two hundred yards, dead ahead.* But fallen trees and steep terrain made straight-line navigation impossible. They had walked a mile and still hadn't found his dogs. Bodine recycled the power switch on his radio receiver. A green light confirmed it was still functioning. Twenty yards later, he heard barking, but the canyon walls masked his dogs' position.

"Hey, Matt, how should we get this cat—"

Bodine tilted his head, finding it odd that the warden never finished his sentence. He turned around just in time to watch Hollinger disappear down the hill.

Hollinger tossed his gear aside and rolled over onto his belly. He dug his rifle butt and toes into the dirt and came to rest soon after. Bodine was laughing while he brushed the dirt from his uniform. The warden calmly picked up his gear and started uphill. "I'm glad I can be so entertaining."

"Oh, believe me, warden, you are. You need a hand?"

"No thanks, I'm fine."

The helicopter swooped low overhead. Bodine couldn't see it through the trees, but from the sound, knew it was near. He focused on his radio receiver. "We've got seventy-five yards to go, warden. You gonna make it?"

"Don't worry about me. I'm right behind you."

Their progress was slow, but they could hear the dogs' bellowing. Bodine grinned when he saw a bouncing floppy-eared head. "They love chasing cats. Treeing them is their reward."

"Some reward," said the warden.

When Hollinger got his first glimpse of the prey, it was his turn to laugh. "So *that's* your cougar, eh Matt? I hate to say it, but maybe you should get a wildlife handbook so you'll know what they look like. Let's see, a twenty-five pound bobcat versus a one-hundred-plus cougar. A bobcat stands fourteen inches tall compared to several feet. Bobcats have short tails, cougars long ones. One targets rabbits, the other deer. Shall I go on?"

"Piss off, Hollinger."

Bodine's dogs were too preoccupied with the hissing bobcat to notice his approach. "*Heel!*" he shouted, slapping their leads in his palm. One cowered over and the other two followed. The bobcat fled as soon as he tethered them.

"Okay," he said to Hollinger. "Now we're even, but you've seen the cougar tracks, and you know the carcass was dragged off. We definitely have a cougar in the park, and I'm gonna find it."

"Relax, Matt. I never doubted there was a cougar, but even you have to admit that was funny. Thanks for finding the only bobcat in the park. It's nice to know it's still here. I'll be in my truck. Call me when you find the real cat."

Bodine snarled at his dogs. "Congratulations, you mangy mutts. You just made me the laughing stock of the Fish and Game Department!" He yanked at their leads, unwilling to forgive them. Hanging onto three bloodhounds made the trek impossible, but if he set them free, they would probably go after the bobcat again. How in the hell could this happen? Surely they knew the difference between a bobcat and a cougar. All he could figure was the bobcat must have crossed their path and piqued their interest.

Still fuming, Bodine backtracked through the forest figuring if he found the deer carcass, he would probably find the cougar. Carnivores don't stray far from their cache. But his guide dogs were now a hindrance, and having them near would keep the elusive cat at bay. Not only could it smell them, but it could spot them a hundred yards away. He tethered his dogs to a tree near the stream and shed everything except his sidearm and rifle. He would retrieve them once he located the deer.

Dried blood and chunks of gray fur stained the bait area. He followed the drag marks until they vanished in dry dirt. Even if the cougar ate a substantial portion, the carcass would still be difficult to drag. It had to be near, but where?

The sun ducked behind some clouds and made everything look the same. It seemed he was traveling in circles. The cache could be anywhere. The cougar could be stalking him with the same goal; to kill.

His yelping dogs ignited his heart. There could only be one explanation and he didn't like it. He charged toward the sound, scaling downed trees, sliding on his rear when necessary. Running at full speed, he stumbled, and his rifle fired. He sprang to his feet, bolted another round, and kept running without missing a beat.

FIFTY-FIVE

Officer Hector Rodriquez led his volunteers down Stream Trail to the Canyon Meadows Staging Area. They had meticulously combed the sloping trail and stream bed, but unlike the group near Eucalyptus Trail, found nothing unusual. He spotted Game Warden Hollinger standing near his truck in the staging area's parking lot and went over to join him.

"Hey, Hector," the warden said. "What are you up to?"

"Just leading a group on a nature hike. What are you doing here?"

"Waiting for Matt Bodine." Rodriquez seemed bothered by that. "Hector, you *do* know Bodine's out looking for the cougar, don't you?" Anger rode him when the Parks Police officer hesitated. "Jesus, Hector, don't you guys talk? I can't believe Lt. Donovan would let you parade all of these people through the park while this trophy hunter's out there with a loaded gun."

Just then a shot cracked through the forest. Birds flushed, women screamed, and men scanned the woods for the shooter.

"Shit!" Hollinger said, leaping from his truck. "That had to be Bodine! Tell Donovan what's going on. I have to go." He grabbed his gear and took off running.

Rodriquez immediately addressed his group. "Folks, we have a situation in the park, so I need you all to wait here until I get back."

The cop tried raising Donovan on his radio while running after Hollinger, but the static confirmed the canyon was in a dead zone. Not surprisingly, his cell phone had no service, either.

* * * * *

Matt Bodine spotted his dogs and ran toward them. His favorite was lying on its side, bleeding, while the other two viciously gnawed at their leads. Bodine freed them and they ran off with blood lust.

He stripped off his tee shirt and wrapped it around his injured dog; revenge driving him as his shirt soaked up blood. His dogs knew where that cat was and wanted it dead as much as he did. He searched the forest, suspecting the cougar was stalking him the whole time. The cat had waited for him to tie his dogs up and then leave before making its attack. But why didn't it go for his dog's throat? Did it just claw it to taunt him, or was it scared off by his bullet? He never should have left his dogs behind.

He calculated his options while dressing his dog's wounds. If he told Hollinger the truth, he might not get another contract. On the other hand, who would question his firing a round at an attacking animal? *That's it!* He'd kill the beast and claim he was protecting his dogs. *Justice will be served!*

Bodine tied a stick to the loose ends of his shirt/bandage and twisted it to slow the dog's blood loss. Having done all he could for the animal, he went to gather his equipment. He found his radio receiver covered in dirt, several yards away, probably kicked aside during the fracas. Luckily, it still worked. He went back to comfort his injured pet.

FIFTY-SIX

Officer Rodriquez reached Lt. Donovan via Eagle 5's radio relay. Communications were difficult in the ensuing chaos. He finally managed to say, "Clear the park and have Eagle 5 find Bodine."

Eagle 5 relayed that was already in work. "They closed the park when they heard the gunshot. Two patrol cars are enroute to the Canyon Meadows Staging Area. Say your status?"

"Everyone's okay and waiting at Canyon Meadows. I've got to go." Rodriquez leaped over a log to catch up with the game warden.

Hollinger located the injured dog though its cries. It was in serious trouble, but Bodine's bandage was keeping it alive. No doubt, Bodine was now out for revenge. Somehow he had to reach the cat before the tracker did, and Bodine had a head start.

He removed a syringe from his tackle box, filled the front portion with anesthetic, and then slipped a plastic sleeve over the needle. Next, he charged the back portion with compressed air to shoot the fluid into the animal. If all went well, the sleeve would slide back so the medicine would inject and the animal would fall asleep. He prepared a spare dart and loaded one in his rifle. Officer Rodriquez caught up to him just as he was closing his tackle box.

"Where's Bodine?" Rodriquez said.

"I'm not sure, but his dogs are going nuts. I hope I can get there in time."

The officer looked up as Eagle 5 flew overhead. "They're looking for Bodine, too. If their FLIR is working, it shouldn't take long to find him." After several passes, the helicopter went into a nearby hover, and Rodriquez' radio came alive.

"1L30, Eagle 5; how copy?"

Rodriquez adjusted his volume and keyed his mike. "Eagle 5, 1L30; go ahead."

"IL30, Eagle 5; it appears two dogs have treed a cat, but there's no sign of Bodine. We'll circle the area so we don't cause a downdraft, and stick around until you move in. I have you on FLIR. Take Stream Trail to the first bend, then head up the western slope; how copy?"

"Eagle 5, 1L30, copy five-by. We're heading up Stream Trail now."

The warden looked at Rodriquez. “Hector, hand me the mike.” Rodriquez passed it over and Hollinger said, “Eagle 5, can you confirm the dogs have treed a cougar and not a bobcat?”

“All I can say is it’s a big cat.”

“Eagle 5, this is the game warden speaking. Can you pick me up so I can get a clear shot?”

“Unable. We only have the animal on FLIR; negative visual contact.” Following a short pause, the helicopter observer said, “Be advised we have a new contact. Someone with a rifle is closing in on the cat. It must be Bodine.”

Rodriquez took his mike back from Hollinger. “Roger, Eagle 5, 1L30’s on the way.”

Hollinger took off running, fearing a bullet could be headed his way. Rodriquez wore a protective vest. All he had was a cotton jacket. The helicopter noise made it difficult to home in on the yelping dogs. He was tempted to send the chopper away, but without Eagle 5’s guidance, he knew he would never reach the cougar in time.

FIFTY-SEVEN

Bodine searched for the helicopter, but the forest blocked it from view. Hollinger would be coming, but he'd be too late. The tracker raised his rifle in triumph. "To the victors belong the spoils, warden." Andrew Jackson's quote was never more fitting.

He traversed the slope, hoping the rough terrain would work in his favor. There was no time to double back to erase his tracks. His dogs' vigor assured him it was the cougar this time. They wanted it dead as much as he did. But when he spotted those golden eyes framed in sandy brown fur, he suddenly found himself back at the river, panning for gold. Panic shot through him, but only for a moment. He moved closer and drew a bead on the cougar's chest. He drew in a breath, slowly exhaled, and started to squeeze the trigger.

"Freeze, Bodine! Drop the gun!"

Bodine ignored Hollinger and steadied his aim. The golden eyes found him and the cat exposed its fangs. A loud *pop* followed and the gun fell from Bodine's hands. His body tingled and started to go numb. "You bastard!" A bed of redwood needles cushioned his fall.

Hollinger reloaded, moved closer, and fired his second dart. It was a perfect shot, hitting the cougar mid-thigh. The cat hissed and licked the dart, then clung to a branch for support. Rodriquez was hovering over Bodine so the warden said, "Forget about him. Get the dogs before the cat falls or they'll rip it apart."

Rodriquez quickly grabbed one of the dogs. Hollinger got the other one and cuffed their collars together just before the cat fell from the tree. The warden removed his belt and tied the two dogs to a log before checking on the cougar.

Two Parks Police officers showed up just as Hollinger was sliding a plastic tie strap over the cougar's jaws. The cat's glassy eyes seemed to follow them.

Officer Rodriquez saw the dart sticking out of Bodine's torso and looked at Hollinger. "What's with this?"

Hollinger went over, casually removed the dart, and dropped it in his tackle box. "He left me no choice, Hector. If I didn't shoot him, he would've killed the cat. In time, they'll both be okay. I just wish he'd just dropped his gun."

"I'll let Eagle 5 know what happened," Rodriquez said before addressing the other officers. "Take Bodine's dogs back to his truck. There's another one near the stream that needs prompt medical attention."

Officer Davis looked at Rodriquez. "What about Bodine and the cougar?"

"We'll figure something out when we get more help. In the meantime, get these dogs out of here. I can't hear my radio with all their yelping."

Davis and the other officer led the dogs away.

Rodriquez watched the warden strap the cat's feet together while Bodine lay comatose nearby. "So, how do you expect us to get these two out?"

Hollinger glanced his way. "Unfortunately, we'll have to carry the cat out the old fashioned way. You know, by slipping a branch between his legs and carrying it."

"And what about Bodine?"

"Well, as much as he deserves to be treated the same way, we should probably have Eagle 5 fly him out."

Before Rodriquez could key his mike, Eagle 5 was advising them that two other police units were closing in, and that they would be landing near the Canyon Meadows Staging Area to evacuate Bodine.

Hollinger overheard and said, "You see, Hector? Everything's under control."

Rodriquez squinted at the warden, unsure about that. "How long will Bodine be unconscious? I sure don't want to be around when he wakes up. I hear he's got quite a temper."

"Don't worry. He'll be out for a while."

Rodriquez shook his head and went to find a suitable limb.

Three more officers arrived on scene and Hollinger explained everything. The officers looked at each other and then back at Hollinger before carrying Bodine to the landing site. Granted, it was an anomalous situation, but Hollinger felt no remorse over what he had done.

Rodriquez returned with a large eucalyptus branch. "How's this, warden?"

"Perfect. Now slide it between his legs." Surprisingly, the branch barely accommodated the animal. "Okay, ready? Lift!" They did, and the cougar's head and tail hung. "Wait, Hector. Set it down, real easy." The warden stripped off his coat and fashioned a sling for the cat's head, then lashed its tail with another tie strap. "Okay, let's try it again."

This time they were successful. Rodriquez took the lead so the warden could monitor the cat. At the staging area, they carefully set it down, Hollinger cut the straps, and they tossed the log aside. Two of the officers stood over them, firearms drawn, but the cat never twitched. Officer Davis kept the volunteers a safe distance away.

Hollinger rubbed the cat's head affectionately. "Sorry it had to come to this, old boy. Take it easy while we get you in the cage."

He cut the muzzle strap and the cougar's jaw flung open. One of the officers nearly fired his weapon. "Put that away!" Hollinger said. "It's a reflex. Now come over here and take a look. You'll probably never see another animal like this outside the zoo."

FIFTY-EIGHT

Oakland Tribune reporter Sam Razini heard the reports on his police scanner and rushed to Canyon Meadows to see the cougar. Readers cared far more about the beast than a kid's shoe. He arrived just as Hollinger was securing the cage. His editor loved this story and craved pictures for the sequel. "So this is the cat that got Kerri Connifer."

Hollinger cautiously eyed Razini. "Actually, this is the animal that strayed into Redwood Regional Park, and until proven otherwise, hasn't done anything wrong. I plan to tag it and take it back to the high country. End of story."

Razini snapped a few photos and grinned at the warden. "I wouldn't be so sure about that."

* * * * *

Lt. Donovan paced the Skyline Gate parking lot, feeling his career slip away. First, his search parties failed to find the shoe, and then he had somehow forgotten about Bodine being in the park when he agreed to the civilian search. He should have closed the park for as long as the tracker was in there. Thankfully, no one was struck by Bodine's bullet. Hopefully, Captain Vestell would take that into consideration at his review board.

He reopened the park as soon as the cougar was subdued. By then, half of the volunteers had left, but those who remained were committed to completing their task. Stacey Webster and her dog Tracker were among those that stayed.

In the final hours before sunset, Randy addressed everyone near East Ridge Trail's fire gate. "Thank you for your patience," he began. "As you know, the cougar is now in custody, but there is no evidence that suggests it had anything to do with Kerri's disappearance. Please return to the site where you left off. Move as quickly as possible, but don't overlook anything. Good luck."

The volunteers immediately dispersed.

* * * * *

Eagle 5 returned to the park after airlifting Bodine to the hospital. The search parties were showing up on its FLIR, but like before, they saw no new targets. They had enough fuel to remain on station until the foot search was complete. Hopefully they would get lucky this time.

* * * * *

Randy watched the helicopter make another pass over the parking lot. Finding a shoe offered a ray of hope. It was no longer a struggle to stay awake. Suddenly the tone changed and his eyes widened. He and Amanda both searched the sky, but the chopper was nowhere in sight. He leaped from the car when the noise didn't fade. From all he could gather, it was hovering on the north side of the park near the East Bay MUD property. He feared Stacey Webster may be right.

Amanda latched onto his arm, fearful of what lay ahead. "What's going on?"

"I don't know, but I think we should ask Lt. Donovan." Randy looked around for him, but suddenly all of the Parks Police officers were gone. "Wait here."

Randy sprinted toward the Oakland Police officer and said, "Do you know why the helicopter is hovering? Did they find something?"

Unaware of whom he was addressing, the police officer kept waving his hands as if he had no way of stopping them. "I'm sorry, sir, but I'm only here to direct traffic."

Randy overheard a radio call mention something about a coroner. He turned to look for Amanda, and she fainted in his arms. A cameraman caught the action while the officer stopped traffic. He hurried everyone off the street, but that didn't prevent the ensuing mayhem.

When Amanda opened her eyes, she was lying in the back of Lt. Donovan's Expedition, his glum expression confirming her fear. She squeezed her eyes shut, shaking her head from side to side. "No! Not Kerri! It can't be!"

"We don't know for sure," Donovan softly said, "but they found some human remains buried under dirt and leaves. The officer on scene reported the body appears to be that of a small child with blonde hair. The shoe they found in the poison oak matches the one on the victim's foot."

When Donovan presented the shoe, Amanda knew it was Kerri's. She screamed hysterically, banging her head against the seat while news cameras frenzied to feed on her misery.

Randy blocked the cameras with his body. "Please give us some space," he said to the mob.

Amanda barely heard his words, as her heart was empty. She buried her face in her hands, praying he'd say nothing else. "Randy—please take me home."

Randy walked her to the car and crawled into the driver's seat. The engine made a horrible noise when he turned the key. Only then did he realize the engine was already running. His gushing eyes forced him to hit the brake and stop the car. "God, Amanda, I'm sorry! I'm so, so sorry!"

For a brief moment they clung to each other, but then they silently drifted apart. He dried his eyes and started up the road again, knowing this was the end of the line.

* * * * *

Sharon Schaefer came running when she saw her daughter's car pull into the driveway. Randy helped his wife from her seat and turned her over to her mother. He tucked her keys in her coat pocket and walked away, grief haunting him as Amanda climbed her stairs.

* * * * *

The sky was dotted with stars by the time Randy reached Skyline Gate. Any other night and it would have been a beautiful walk, but tonight it only reminded him of his loss. The fire gate had been open so the police and coroner could finish their business. He got into his car and wept over his empty life. When he finally headed home, he wasn't sure he would ever return to this special place.

Evelyn met him at the door wearing a ghastly look. Kerri's fate had been all over the news. "Oh, Randy—"

They held each other sorrowfully. When they parted, she sat him on the sofa. Several minutes passed before he broke his silence.

"I can't believe how I wasted my life building a business when I should have been with my family. Owning the Bay Area's most successful advertising agency means nothing without Kerri." He sniffled and dried his eyes. "I kept praying that God would give me another chance and bring her back to me. I promised I'd be a better father and husband if He did." He unfolded his wallet, staring at Kerri's picture. "So tell me God, what did Kerri do to deserve this? Why not take me instead?" He paused again, too choked up to continue.

When he was able, he looked at his mother and said, "When I first heard about the cougar, I prayed Kerri wasn't in the park. I can't fathom never seeing my baby again."

Evelyn took his hands in hers, wishing his faith was stronger. They sat there, quietly clinging to each other. The phone rang and Randy didn't move.

She ran to answer before the machine picked up. She handed the phone to him, despondent. "It's Lt. Donovan."

He reluctantly took the phone. "It's Kerri, isn't it?"

"I'm afraid so," said Donovan. "I've already informed Amanda. The coroner confirmed she was mauled by a cougar. A forensics technician from the Department of Fish and Game is working with the coroner. If it's any consolation, they say she didn't suffer."

"She didn't *suffer*? How in the hell don't you suffer when you're being mauled?"

"What I meant was she never knew what hit her. Randy, her neck was broken and her spinal cord severed." He spared him the details of how her face was also ripped off, her innards eaten, and her ribs gnawed like dog treats. "I don't recommend you see her."

The lieutenant was still talking when Randy dropped the phone. Evelyn tried taking him in her arms, but he headed for the garage. "I've got to see Amanda."

"I understand, but I'm driving."

Evelyn hung up the phone and grabbed his keys, not looking forward to their reception.

FIFTY-NINE

Amanda watched for Randy's car from the same window where she saw Kerri for the last time. He was on his way over, she knew. She reflexively backed away when he drove up. She thought she could handle seeing him, but she was wrong. She ran to her bedroom and locked the door.

* * * * *

Randy and Evelyn started to get out, but he stopped his mother from opening her door. He waited, staring at the window. Five minutes later, nothing had changed. "I can't do this, Mom. Amanda was at the window and now she's gone. I know she saw me. If she wanted me here, she would have opened the door by now. Let's go home."

He was about to start the car when the front door opened. Amanda was waiting on the porch, staring at him.

Evelyn patted Randy's thigh. "I think we should go inside."

Randy swallowed the lump in his throat. "Yeah, we should."

He slowly led his mother up the steps, the lump in his throat larger now. He met his wife's eyes when he reached the porch. "Amanda, I—"

She shook her head and motioned them inside. She wanted to hold him, tell him it wasn't his fault, but all she could see was him whisking her daughter away in his fancy car, her golden hair flowing as she waved back at her.

Once inside, Randy embraced his wife, sharing her pain. "I'm so sorry," he whispered. Evelyn slid past them so as not to be in the way.

He held her close, thinking of ways to ease her pain. He could disconnect the help line, handle the press; do whatever it took to make things easier. Thankfully, he silenced Mr. Fix-it before uttering a word. Silence is golden, he reminded himself.

She gently pushed herself free. "Let's join the others."

Randy followed her to the living room. On his way, he couldn't help noticing the dirty dishes in the sink, the soiled carpet, and that everyone had their shoes on. Evelyn, Sharon, and Donald were embracing one another. On the mantle, a lighted candle sat between Kerri's Mother's Day picture and one of him in his college football jersey. His eyes beckoned Amanda's for an explanation.

Amanda smiled fondly. "I found your old football photo when I was rummaging through Kerri's desk. She loved you, Randy. You were a good father."

His chin quivered, holding her words close.

"By the way, Karen finally admitted she made all those ribbons. She's also the one who organized the vigil."

Randy looked her way and Karen shrugged. "I had to do something."

"Thank you, Karen. You couldn't have done anything nicer to boost our spirits."

Karen dried her eyes with a tissue. "You're welcome."

Amanda opened a box and spread more pictures on the coffee table. Everyone shared memories as they looked them over. Today there were no accusations; only remembrances of happy times. It was two in the morning when Amanda finally walked them to the door. "Thank you for coming over."

"Thanks for having us," Randy said. "The photos really helped."

"Let's think of this as a beginning, not an end." She closed the door, letting the thought sink in.

SIXTY

The human remains were transferred to the Alameda County Coroner's Office where Coroner Edmund Pokno confirmed Kerri's identity. News of her death flashed across the nation before Pokno could report his findings to Game Warden Hollinger.

Hollinger listened, disturbed at how this young girl's life had been reduced to DNA samples and lab reports. Animal attacks required interaction with numerous government agencies, all of which were under pressure to find answers. But cougars weren't as predictable as government bureaucrats. Cougars know no boundaries, and encroachment has forced them to seek other food sources. One cat developed a taste for pig while another favored dogs. Although there is no evidence to confirm this, it seems logical that once a cat tastes human flesh, the chances for another attack increase.

"It's a sad day for everyone," the warden said. "After comparing the cougar's paw to the casting from Bodine's truck, I had no doubt it was the same animal that visited the park earlier."

"I concur. What's the status of the cat?"

Hollinger heaved a sigh. "Once the news hit, I had no choice but to put him down. The Public Health Department determined it was healthy so they passed on doing a rabies exam. Someone from the forensics lab is coming to collect samples. I'll be taking the animal to Sacramento for evaluation."

"Actually, forensics specialist James Mason is already here taking bite mark measurements and collecting animal hair samples from the body," Pokno said. "When he's finished, he plans to drop by your place to take custody of the cougar."

"That's fine. I'll be here."

Hollinger set his phone down and stared at the cougar's lifeless body from his window. Two lives were lost in this terrible tragedy. It wasn't a good day.

* * * * *

James Mason arrived an hour later. Hollinger took him out back where the cougar lay on a tarp. Mason immediately examined its right foot pad, compared it to Bodine's casting, and then pried its mouth open. "Mind holding it open for me while I measure its teeth?

Hollinger did as requested.

"Okay, you can let go."

Hollinger did and the mouth snapped shut.

Next, Mason measured the claws and compared them to his notes. When he was done, he looked at the warden and said, "It definitely appears to be the same cat."

The warden already knew that. "I hate destroying animals," he said. "The problem is there are just too many people."

"Or too many cats."

Hollinger frowned, preferring to defend the animal. "The girl's father said she was running and laughing when she disappeared. The cougar probably mistook her for prey. If those damned deer would live in the forest instead of the suburbs, this probably wouldn't have happened."

"I'm not so sure. Animals kill to survive, and such attacks will continue so long as we encroach into their space. Sadly, I don't see either side changing, nor do I have a solution. Can you give me a hand loading it in my truck?"

"Sure, but do me a favor and save the body for me. I'm an amateur taxidermist, and I'm sure some museum would love having this magnificent creature on display. Of course, I'd never tell them he killed anyone."

"No problem. We'll call you when we're through."

SIXTY-ONE

Two hours later, James Mason arrived at the Fish and Game's Wildlife Forensics Laboratory in Rancho Cordova. He grabbed a gurney and slid the cougar onto it. Dr. Burgess Cutler from the Wildlife Investigations Lab saw him wheeling it in and came over to inspect it. Peering over his half-rim glasses, he stroked his gray beard and said, "That's a beautiful cat, James. Clearly it wasn't starving like some we've seen. It's a shame he ended up here."

"Yeah, I know, but he sure made life tragic for a little girl and her family. I should be done late today, then he's all yours. Oh, the game warden requested you save what you can. For some reason, he wants to stuff it."

"I'll see what I can do."

Mason wheeled the cat into the exam room and gathered his tools. Claw and teeth scrapings, and hair and tissue samples would prove whether this was really the human killer. Once this was done, he would turn it over to Dr. Cutler who would determine whether anything was medically wrong with the animal that might have provoked the attack. Lacking any sign of disease, they would then take the environmental factors into account. It was a lengthy process.

As a minimum, DNA results took 24 hours, and then Dr. Cutler would need another day to complete his analysis. Hopefully, their public affairs office could appease the press until they could release their results.

Mason's first task was to slit the cougar's belly and peel the skin. Using oversized pruning sheers, he snapped ribs and pulled them apart to remove the organs. He opened the stomach and carefully washed its contents. Patches of fine blond hair and course brown hair were separated from the tissue. DNA tests would confirm their identity.

Twenty-five hours later, Mason confirmed this was the killer cougar and turned the remains over to Dr. Cutler for a necropsy. Dr. Cutler immediately began his examination, dictating while he worked. "Muscle tissue appears healthy. No sign of disease." He slit the cougar's scalp and sliced through the bone to remove part of the brain. "Brain tissue appears healthy." He set the parts aside for further analysis.

* * * * *

Game Warden Hollinger kept going over the cougar's attack on Kerri. Mason was right about shrinking habitats and human encroachment. These days, wildlife interaction with people was commonplace. The cougar was one of many species that had made a startling comeback after hunting restrictions were imposed. As such, it was only a matter of time before another human was mauled. Perhaps he should have let Matt Bodine kill it. After all, the end result was the same, and it would have saved Bodine a trip to the hospital. He decided to visit the tracker to smooth things over.

* * * * *

Matt Bodine surveyed his cinderblock ward room, wondering why he had an IV stuck in his arm and a curtain drawn around his bed. A woman in white said something about him being shot while trying to kill a cougar, yet he was wearing no bullet holes or bandages. He vaguely remembered cursing before everything went dark, but that could have been in a dream—or maybe a beer brawl at the Last Chance Saloon in Apache Junction. Or was it that Mexican restaurant in Tucson, not that it matters. Blurry eyed and exhausted, he tried focusing on the uniformed police officer who was staring back at him. "Who in the hell are you?" he said. "Why are you here?"

"Hi Matt. Lt. Donovan, Regional Parks Police. You were tracking a cougar in Redwood Park for us?"

Things were coming back. *A cougar in Redwood Park.* He scratched the spot where the dart hit him and jerked so hard he nearly ripped out his IV. He grimaced as Warden Hollinger's face crossed his mind. "Why am I here?"

"You were going to kill the cougar so the game warden decided you needed the dart more than the cat. The doctors say you'll be fine. How do you feel?"

"Hung over," he said, taking a moment to realize what Donovan said. "Did you say that sonuvabitch shot me with a dart?"

"Well, it's not exactly standard procedure, but I have to support the warden in this case."

"Then you're an ass, too," Bodine said, bunching his sheets with his fists. For some reason, this seemed to amuse Donovan. "If you think that's funny, how about if I sue your ass?"

"You know, Matt, your bad attitude precedes you, and you haven't disappointed anyone." Donovan checked his watch and patted Bodine's shoulder. "Glad to see you're okay. I should get back to work. Thanks for helping us out. I'll make sure you get your check."

"Wait," Bodine said, grabbing Donovan's arm. He quickly let go to press his palms against his throbbing temples. His pain was endless. Visions of the redwood forest kept flashing before his eyes, nagging at him as though he had unfinished business. A dog barked a block away. *That's it!* "Where are my dogs?"

"At the vet's. The one that got scraped is doing fine, by the way. He took a bunch of stitches, but he should be out in a couple of days. The other two are being boarded until you can pick them up. Of course, we'll cover their expenses, too."

Bodine settled down; his eyes clearing. He remembered tying his dogs up. Things were falling into place. "I appreciate that. What about the cougar?"

"Sadly, Warden Hollinger had to put him down. I wish I could say that all's well that ends well, but—"

"Jesus. So it really got the kid, huh?"

Donovan was surprised by his concern. He postponed his departure in case the tracker wanted to discuss it further.

Matt's brain took him back to the river where he nearly met the same fate. He always knew a cougar attack was a possibility, but the police led him to believe the Connifer girl had been kidnapped. "Her parents must be devastated."

"Of course they are. I hope to attend Kerri's memorial service."

Bodine thought for a moment. He couldn't leave town until his dog had recovered. He mournfully looked at the lieutenant. "If they don't mind, I'd like to come, too."

"I'll let you know. Anyway, I need to go. Take care, Matt."

* * * * *

Donovan waited for the elevator doors to open. When they did, Game Warden Hollinger stepped out. "Well, this is a surprise," he said. "Are you here to see Matt?"

"Yeah. I feel bad about shooting him. How's he doing?"

"He was pretty ticked off when I told him what happened; especially when I said I supported your actions. He called me an ass and you a son of a bitch."

Hollinger chuckled. "Maybe I am, but then I'm not the one recovering in a hospital bed, am I?" Donovan grinned. "So, did you tell him about the cougar?"

"Yeah. I said you had to put him down. I expected him to blow up, but he actually seemed pretty shook up when I told him it got Kerri. Like everyone else, he didn't expect it would turn out this way."

"Well, what do you know? Maybe Bodine's human after all. By the way, I plan to stuff that cougar."

"Why would you do that?"

"Because people need to see what they look like and I hated putting him down. His necropsy showed he was in perfect health." He noticed a blond hair on Donovan's coat and wondered if it was one of Kerri's. Out of respect, he didn't mention it.

"It's sad all the way around, warden. Incidentally, would you be interested in attending her memorial service?"

"Absolutely."

"Okay, I'll call you when I know the details." He glanced at the clock above the nurse's station. He had stayed longer than planned, but he had one more thought to share. "Be prepared for an ass-chewing from Bodine. Maybe if he blows off enough steam, he won't sue you."

"I'll keep that in mind," Hollinger said, and then headed down the hall.

* * * * *

The game warden stood in front of Bodine's room, hesitating to go in. He straightened his uniform, breathed deep, and went inside. "Hey, Matt. How are you?"

Fury burned through the tracker when he realized who it was. "What is this? Visit the invalid week?"

Hollinger stayed near the door, prepared for a quick exit.

"So, tell me warden; why in the hell did you shoot me if you were gonna kill the cat?"

"Matt, the last thing I wanted to do was destroy that animal. I had every intention of releasing it until I heard the news. The lab reports confirmed it was the same cougar. You have no idea how hard it was for me to take its life, but I did it because one human kill could lead to more."

Bodine nodded and pressed the call button next to his bed. When the nurse came in, he said, "Any idea when can I get out of here?"

"I believe the doctor plans to release you once he finishes his rounds."

"Thanks."

The nurse left and he stared at the warden. "If you have a moment, I'd like to know more about the girl."

"Very well." Hollinger seated himself in the vinyl chair across from Bodine's bed and shared all he knew, which he admitted, wasn't much. The tracker listened, genuinely moved by the story. The warden folded his hands together, leaned forward, and then looked up at Bodine. "That cougar killed a dog, too," he said, confirming that it was a problem animal. "It appears to be the same dog that was missing near Lake Chabot. I'm glad we got this cat before it attacked someone else. We both know it's inevitable."

Bodine turned away.

"Well, I'd better be going," Hollinger said. "By the way, I really am sorry about the dart, but I didn't see I had a choice."

"Don't worry about it."

* * * * *

Hollinger's visit stirred Bodine's mind. He relived every detail of what it was like being a child numbed by terror. He had just dozed off when the phone rang. He knocked the phone off the hook, cursing as he reeled it in. "What!"

"Hi, Matt; it's Stacey Webster. I heard you were in the hospital. Are you okay?"

Her soothing voice brought pleasant memories, but also brought heartache. She was the first woman he truly loved. How could two people with so much in common drift so far apart? He had done his best to make her a memory, and suddenly she was back. Pain shot through him as he pushed himself up on his bed. Webster repeated her query. "Oh, sure," he said. "I've felt worse after a night on the town. Who told you I was here?"

"Lt. Donovan."

"Wow. He's a busy man. I wonder where he finds the time for such details."

"He was concerned about you, Matt. Don't be an ass."

Bodine laughed. "I'm sure I deserved that." She wasn't laughing, but she hadn't hung up, either. "It's been a long time, Stacey. How are you? How's Tracker?"

"We're both fine, and thanks for asking. Did Lt. Donovan tell you that Tracker's the one that found her remains?"

"No, but I'm not surprised. He's a fine search dog."

"Actually, I wish we hadn't gone. Kerri's body was a mess. People were puking. I've relived the scene a hundred times since then. It's the worst I've ever seen."

"I'm sorry." A painful silence followed. He didn't want the call to end. Her voice put him at ease like no one else's could, and it had been a long time since he felt this way. "So, how did Tracker find her?"

"It was more of a fluke than anything. Tracker didn't have a clue, and then he went over to this bush. I figured he needed to relieve himself, but then he refused to come back. I bent over to grab him and spotted something covered with dirt and leaves. It's the first time either of us truly smelled death."

Bodine stared at the curtain. Everything she said made sense. Each tracking dog has its own specialty. Some track over ground; others over water. Tracker sought the living, not the dead. That's probably why he didn't find her earlier. "Do you have nightmares?"

"I'll let you know, should I ever get to sleep." She paused for a moment, unsure where their conversation was heading. She finally said, "It's good to hear your voice, Matt. You were pretty good company until you put on that macho hunter act. I don't want to inflate your ego more than it already is, but Game Warden Hollinger kept talking about your superb tracking abilities. Have you ever thought about applying for a full-time government job?"

"You know that's not my style." She didn't respond to that. He needed to change the subject or he'd lose her. "Are you going to Kerri's memorial service?"

"I'm planning to. Will I see you there?"

"You bet." He paused again, clinging to the phone. "Stacey? You still there?"

"I'm here."

"It's good to hear your voice too."

SIXTY-TWO

Randy was driving to his office when Lt. Donovan reached him on his cell phone. He pulled off the road so he could listen to the autopsy and necropsy reports without posing a hazard to anyone. Donovan's apology was sincere, but it did nothing to ease Randy's pain. "So, the cougar's dead, too," he said, pinching his eyes.

"There was no choice," Donovan said. "Game Warden Hollinger did everything by the book. Nothing was done until he was sure it was the right animal. We can't have a cat like that running free. I know how much you respect nature, but it's our job to protect lives. Surely, you understand."

Randy choked. Following a long pause, he said, "Lieutenant, Kerri would have wanted the cougar to live. There is no way I'd want it released, but I was hoping it could go to a research institute so they might learn what provoked it. Less than an hour ago, I was talking to a place in Idaho that seemed willing to take it."

"Did they know it killed your daughter?"

His chin quivered and his head shook slowly. Talking about this was harder than he imagined. Fighting the lump in his throat, he finally said, "I told them it was trapped in the park and needed a new home."

"Randy, Warden Hollinger planned to take it up to the Sierras today. He had already tagged it and had every intention of releasing it. He was equally upset that it had to be destroyed. I also doubt that this research institute would take the animal once they learned it killed a human being. Are you going to be okay?"

Randy grimaced as his gut clawed him. Knuckling his steering wheel, he stared at the sky and said, "Sure. Why wouldn't I be? After all, the case is closed, right? Kerri's dead, the cat's dead, and life goes on." Following a lengthy pause, he added, "Does the press know about this?"

"Our public relations department is handling the press so you won't have to. Again, I'm sorry about your daughter. By the way, several of us would like to attend Kerri's memorial service if that's okay with you and Amanda."

Randy calmed down. "By all means, please come. Kerri's ordeal became a public event, so everyone's welcome. Thanks for keeping me informed, lieutenant, and I'm sorry for all the times I've taken my frustrations out on you. I'll call you with the arrangements."

While tucking his phone away, Randy spied a deer munching flowers in a private garden. He imagined a cougar wandering this street in search of prey. More innocent lives could be lost if they invaded this residential area. So far, none had been spotted. Hopefully it would stay that way.

Going to work was pointless now. His bitterness would only bring people down. Besides, he wasn't ready to face Bob or Jerry. He dialed his home, talking fast so his mother couldn't get a word in. "Please invite Amanda and her parents over. I'll be home in an hour or so. Thanks, Mom." He then hung up.

He could have called Amanda himself, but he needed some time to think. He returned to Skyline Gate, watching East Ridge Trail until he found the courage to walk it. The trail had been cleared, the washouts covered with tarps. From the overlook bench, the Sunol hills mocked him with a light coating of snow. No doubt Diablo had some, too. He begged God for an explanation that never came.

On his way back, he paused at Eucalyptus Trail to say a prayer for his daughter. Sunshine fanned the forest, a jay squawked, a lizard scurried across his path; nature's way of telling him that life went on. He moved away quietly.

Amanda's car was parked in front of his house when he pulled into his driveway. Everyone inside anticipated more bad news. He soon joined them in the living room. "Thanks for coming," he softly said. "I thought you should all know they killed the cougar. Its necropsy confirmed it was the right one. The nightmare is over."

"No," Amanda said, "it will never be over, but thanks for sparing us the details." Her eyes were glued to Kerri's picture; the one with the single strand wafting in the breeze. "By the way, Sam Razini called. I told him he needed to talk to the police. I couldn't face him again."

"I know what you mean. I feel the same way. Besides, Lt. Donovan said the Parks Police will handle the press. He also asked if he and several others could attend Kerri's memorial service. I said it was okay. I hope you don't mind."

"Of course not."

Amanda noticed some pine needles imbedded in Randy's carpet, just like in her house. Before Kerri disappeared, such things appalled her. Now, they no longer mattered. She thought about Kerri's memorial service and her anger broke loose. "Personally, I'm glad the cougar's dead. It didn't deserve to live after what it did. And don't give me any shit about how attacking her was nature's way."

Randy looked at her, surprised by her ferocity. He let her vent, uninterrupted.

"Aren't cougars supposed to be elusive?" she continued. "Run from people? That beast tore our lives apart. Think of all the suspicions, insinuations, accusations, and innuendoes that played out in the public's eye, and all the while it was a goddamn cougar!"

"I know. And like you said, it will never be over for any of us. I can't tell you how many times I've asked God to take that day back. Why did He send this beast to take our child? I support three nature organizations, for Christ's sake. That should count for something."

He slumped against the wall and shut his eyes. An angelic voice answered.

"*I'm okay, Daddy. I love you and Mommy.*" The voice was distant, fading. "*I have to go, Daddy. Don't worry about me. I love you.*"

Someone coughed and he opened his eyes. Everyone was staring at him. "Did anyone else hear her?"

"Hear who, dear?" said Evelyn, holding a coffee mug.

He shook his head to clear it. "I must be imagining things." Except it *was* Kerri's voice, more perfect than any human could mimic. Whether she was with God or a figment of his imagination made no difference; her soul lived in his heart, and her message was comforting. Sadly, he couldn't share his vision with his wife; at least not until time healed her. Perhaps this journey was intended to put more meaning in their lives. He couldn't bring their daughter back, but he could mentor a needy child or become a Big Brother. Maybe volunteer at an orphanage, too. There was more to life than existing through his work. Kerri always wanted to make the world brighter. He promised himself that he would do that for her.

Amanda grew concerned over Randy's odd behavior. "Are you okay?"

"Not yet, but I will be."

Confused and exhausted, she rose from her seat, slipped on her coat, and headed for the door. "We've got to go." Her parents followed her until she stopped short of the threshold. Her parents kept going. "I'll make an appointment with Highland Mortuary," she said to Randy. "You can meet me there."

He nodded, skewered by her sudden coolness. Suddenly, he felt very alone and sad.

Evelyn waited for their guests to leave before approaching him. "What's with you? You're acting very strange."

"I was just thinking about Kerri. Like I said, I'll be okay. I'm gonna lie down for a while."

He closed his bedroom door, troubled by his wife's gruffness. It was foolish to think she no longer blamed him. Even more preposterous believing they were getting closer. After all, it takes two to be in a relationship. She could be bitter for the rest of her life, and there was nothing he could do to change that. He lay on his bed, lost in thought over the angelic voice he heard. It must have been his imagination; a wishful vision, trying to convince him that Kerri was with God. Isn't that what they'll say in church? That she's with God now? He angrily sat up. *She belongs in my arms, damn it. Not God's!*

How many times would he hear "she's in a better place" at her memorial service? All of this heartache was the result of a moment's inattention. *His* inattention. That brief moment took his daughter's life and sentenced her family to a lifetime of misery. If Hell is a state of mind, then Randy's would forever lie in Diablo's shadow.

SIXTY-THREE

Eucalyptus leaves dripped dew from the fog-shrouded hills. The air was still; the packed church disturbingly quiet. Randy addressed his image in the mirror, rehearsing for his daughter's memorial service. Re-tying his tie six times wasn't enough. He wanted it perfect for Kerri.

The music started and his mother reached for the doorknob. "It's time, Randy."

He feebly slipped on his coat and moved next to her. "Mom, about the other night." He choked and started over. "The other night, when Amanda—" He coughed again, fighting to speak. He swallowed hard and downed some water. Her calm eyes encouraged him to continue. Finally, his words flowed.

"Kerri spoke to me, Mom. I know it sounds crazy, but I swear it was her. She said she was okay, and that she had to go. I thought I was dreaming until I saw everyone staring at me. I can't get her out of my head, Mom. The more I think about her, the more I'm sure it was her."

Evelyn kissed him on the cheek, whispering "I believe you" in his ear. She held him close, knowing Reverend Dole wouldn't start without them. "There are so many things we don't understand about beginnings and partings, but it's no coincidence that people around the world worship a Divine Being. It's the dimension beyond our reality that drives our faith. I know Kerri's alive; she's just in a different dimension. She'll always be with you, Randy, just like your father's with me. I'm glad she spoke to you."

He smiled thinly. "Does Dad still talk to you?"

"Of course he does."

His smile broadened; pleased to learn why she frequented his tombstone.

Footsteps paced the hallway and the music grew louder. He heard Amanda's family leave the adjoining room. It wasn't right to keep them waiting. He opened the door and escorted his mother to the front pew, acknowledging his manager Jerry Meshner and shop foreman Bob Underly with his eyes. Though unplanned, they were sitting with some of Amanda's co-workers. Stacey Webster and Mathew Bodine were sitting together. Lt. Donovan, Officer Rodriquez, Game Warden Hollinger, Fire Chief Hagley, FBI Agents Essex and Andredi, and Park Ranger Arandale were all sitting near the front. Across from them were Mr. and Mrs. O'Riley and Jessica Caruso; the first people to help with the search. Incredibly, every seat was filled, and people were lining the walls. Standing room only, as they say. It was inspiring seeing so many lives touched by this little girl with golden hair. No doubt, her passing was her gift to humanity.

An enlarged picture of Kerri riding the Tilden Park Merry-Go-Round was centered in the wreath placed near the base of the cross. Environmental law prevented them from scattering her ashes in the park, so her remains were scattered to the wind outside the Golden Gate, three thousand feet above the ocean. Taco the stuffed duck was included in her cremation because she adored him so, and it hurt too much having him around. Her airborne farewell seemed a fitting tribute for a fallen angel.

Randy sat next to Amanda, unable to face her. Karen and her parents sat nearby, but their eyes never met.

Reverend Dole raised her hands and the music stopped. She embraced her congregation, and gave special recognition to the parents she hadn't seen in years. "It's wonderful seeing so many here today," she began. "Your presence is a testament of your love for thy neighbor. Although Kerri's passing is heartbreaking, we find comfort in knowing that she's with God.

"Six years ago, I baptized her at this very altar, and since that time her love grew at an astonishing rate. With a smile that could melt a winter's snow, she cast an aura of warmth on all of us. We should all learn from her example."

Dole continued to praise the child who was prematurely taken, and when she concluded, a bagpiper played Amazing Grace while strangers said good-bye to their child of the park, the face they all knew, the girl they never met.

Kerri's picture held Randy's gaze. He yearned to hold her and say how much he loved her. He prayed to hear her angelic voice once more. When he couldn't hold back, Evelyn offered him a tissue. He gladly accepted it, and squeezed her hand.

Reverend Dole said her final prayer and the music played again. She waited for the family members to exit before inviting the guests to join them in the reception hall. Kerri's photos were displayed so that visitors could browse through them while standing in the reception line. Sharon and Evelyn partook in friendly discussion while Donald and Karen caught up with her life in the Silicon Valley. The foursome kept to themselves while Amanda and Randy greeted their guests.

Side-by-side, Kerri's parents were determined to stay until their last well-wisher left. They weren't prepared for such an emotional outpouring.

Mathew Bodine and Stacey Webster stood together wearing matching yellow ribbons on their coats. After offering their sympathy, they walked off hand-in-hand.

Oakland Tribune reporter Sam Razini was next in line. Randy shook his hand and said, "Thanks for omitting the details of Hollinger's dart incident."

"Be sure to read tomorrow's paper," he said. "My tribute to Kerri will add closure to the thousands who couldn't attend her memorial service."

Amanda smiled at him genuinely. "Thank you, Sam. That's very kind."

The wave of compassion continued with Lt. Donovan shaking their hands. "I'm truly sorry for your loss," he said. "I want you to know this memorial service touched me like no other. If you ever need anything, please call."

Agents Essex and Andredi followed Donovan, apologizing for the hell they put them through.

Bicyclist Jessica Caruso warmly greeted them. Randy couldn't help noticing her boyfriend Jerome wasn't there. Jessica read his look and said she hadn't seen him since the day Kerri disappeared. "I have you and Kerri to thank for that. Lord knows I'm better off without him. Thank goodness he showed his heartless self before our relationship got too serious."

"I'm glad something good could come from this," is all Randy could say to her.

Ranger Arandale barely looked up. "I'm sorry I didn't call for help sooner."

"Ranger, your inactions weren't responsible for Kerri's fate, but prompt action in the future might save someone else's life. I hope you'll remember that."

"I will." Arandale then melted into the crowd.

While all of their guests offered kind words, it was one of Kerri's classmates who brought them to tears. The eight-year-old girl in a wheelchair had waited forty minutes to meet them. When she had the chance, her tiny hand held Randy's as she said, "Kerri was special to me. I always got left out of the playground games until she made them change the rules. I liked her a lot. God should have waited longer for her."

They both hugged her, and her father wheeled her off. Randy and his wife parted company soon after.

He escorted his mother outside and pointed to the sky. "Look at that."

She clung to his arm, admiring it with him. "It's a fine rainbow, son."

Just as she slid into his car, Amanda called to them. "Would you two like to come over for an informal reception?"

Randy smiled at her and closed his mother's door. "That would be nice. Thank you."

Once his wife drove off, he admired the rainbow again. "Good bye, Kerri. I miss you. I'll always love you." He got in his car and closed the door, hiding his face from his mother while fastening his seatbelt. "Well, that invitation sure came out of nowhere, didn't it?"

"Don't read anything into it, Randy. It's just a reception. Accept it for what it is."

He looked at her, taken aback. "When did you get to be so smart?"

"Like they say, with age comes wisdom."

He thought about that as he started his car.

* * * * *

Amanda's family had barely walked inside when Randy pulled up to her house. Since he was clearly in no hurry to get out, Evelyn touched up her makeup. She capped her lipstick, tucked it in her purse, and folded her hands. The minutes dragged on. Finally, she looked his way. "Well? Are we going in or not?"

"Yeah, let's go."

Randy climbed out and opened her door as he always did. His feet dragged as they climbed the stairs. Before they reached the deck, the door opened and his wife invited them in.

Amanda's living room was adorned with the flowers and family photos from the memorial service. "Beth delivered them while we were greeting our guests," she explained.

Randy focused on some family photos of the three of them together. He was astounded to see several pictures of just him and Kerri taken after he and Amanda split. But his favorite photo was still the one he took of her in Redwood Regional Park with that single strand of hair splitting her forehead. Sadly, it was also one of her last. Amanda had it framed in a yellow ribbon bearing Kerri's name. He cradled it in his hands for several minutes before gently setting it down.

He felt sick and gestured to his mother. "Amanda, thank you for sharing these with us, and thanks for having us over. It means a lot to us." With that, he headed for the door. A moment later, she called to him and he looked at her over his shoulder.

"If you can spare the time, can you take me to the park tomorrow before work? I need to see where it happened. I need to understand."

He didn't have to think about that one. "I'll pick you up at seven."

He wanted to slink out the door, maybe hide under a rock, but his feet wouldn't budge. He couldn't leave without saying good bye to her family. He approached Donald first, but Sharon joined them before he could speak. "Sharon, Donald, I'm sorry for all the pain I've caused you. I don't expect you to forgive me."

Sharon embraced him fondly. “I’m afraid I’m the one who should be apologizing. I’ve caused so much ill-will between you and Amanda. I don’t know why I judged you so harshly. You’re a fine man and a good father, and Kerri was a free spirit. What happened wasn’t your fault. I hope you can forgive me.”

He hugged her back, grateful for her love and understanding. “It’s okay, Sharon. You were only looking out for your family.”

Donald shook Randy’s hand and patted him on the shoulder. “Only Kerri could bring everyone together like this. It’s her wish for us to part on good terms and keep in touch.”

Too choked up to respond, Randy nodded his thanks and went over to Amanda’s sister. He wanted to thank Karen again for the ribbons, but couldn’t form any words. Karen held his hand, but like him, was unable to speak. She covered her face and hurried off to the bathroom.

The persistent rainbow called Randy back to the bay window. It looked just like the ones Kerri painted. *Beautiful.*

SIXTY-FOUR

Randy arrived at Amanda's house at the exact time he picked up Kerri. It wasn't by coincidence, though. He wanted everything to be the same; especially the shadows. Thankfully, the sun was just as it was on that fateful Wednesday morning.

It stung not seeing his daughter waving from the window. Amanda was out the front door before he could get out of his car. He immediately ran to the passenger's side and held the door open for her, just as he did for Kerri. Amanda got in without saying a word. The drive to Skyline Gate never felt so long.

Amanda had her door open before he could set the parking brake. While zipping up his jacket, Randy counted five pickup trucks and three cars in the parking lot, none of which were emergency vehicles. A dog walker was leashing four dogs together while a woman wearing spandex stretched her legs against a post. The scene was typical, so where were they last Wednesday? He straightened one of Karen's soggy ribbons while his wife read a faded cougar warning. It had been there for years. No one took it seriously until now.

He kept his hands in his pockets as he led her down East Ridge Trail. He stopped when they were half way to Eucalyptus Trail. "This is where I sensed someone was watching." The stirring leaves and clanking branches seemed perfectly normal today.

Twenty yards later they stopped again. "Kerri found some ladybugs here."

Amanda looked for them, but there weren't any today.

They walked another twenty yards and they stopped again. "Have you ever noticed how indifferent nature can be?" She looked at him, puzzled. "Look at this place, Amanda. People annihilated these canyons over a hundred years ago, but now this park flourishes. Remember how Reverend Dole commented there is no death, only renewal? Well, I never understood that until now."

"Randy," she said, choosing her words carefully, "I came here to understand what happened to my baby, not learn about renewal." She walked with him, torn between resentment, pity, and sorrow.

He stopped where East Ridge Trail sloped downhill and curved to the left. "This is where Kerri took off running. She wouldn't stop, no matter how many times I called her name. She kept laughing that high-pitched giggle of hers. Warden Hollinger said that might have attracted the cougar because her sounds mimic a distressed animal. I ran after her, yelling for her to stop. After that, I never saw her again."

Amanda took in the dense foliage, the budding flowers, the wind rustling the leaves. The forest was indeed intimidating, yet it was also beautiful. "I can see how a cougar could stalk you without your knowledge." She quietly moved on.

They stopped at the intersection of Eucalyptus and East Ridge trails. "They believe this is where she was ambushed," said Randy. "They found her less than a hundred yards from here on East Bay MUD property. Apparently, their initial search never went in far enough, and the helicopter's infra red scan couldn't pick her up because she was already cold. Somehow, Stacey Webster and her dog were the only ones that had a clue. Whether Tracker was drawn to the cougar or Kerri is a moot point, but Stacey knew something was up and kept insisting they go back.

"Warden Hollinger says cougars plan their attacks while stalking their prey. They have to make their first strike count because they don't have much endurance. He believes the animal disappeared up this deer trail, but I'll never understand how he did it without leaving a trace."

"I've seen enough," she said, cutting him off. "Thanks for showing me, Randy. You couldn't have predicted this, and Kerri always bragged about how she could outrun you. Hopefully, she never saw that cougar. I couldn't bear her suffering."

She closed her eyes to hear the wind waves and smell the eucalyptus trees. There were no sirens here. No freeway noise. Only birds, lizards, nature. No wonder Kerri loved it so much. "Let's see if we can get a memorial bench placed here in Kerri's name."

"That's a great idea. She'd like that."

Amanda spotted a ladybug on her coat and let it crawl onto her finger. She slid a leaf near it and patiently waited for it to climb aboard. Finally, a smile crept over her sad face. "I wish I could thank Kerri for bringing me here. I've missed this place. I'll be coming back."

Randy chewed on his lower lip. "Call me if you want some company."

She didn't respond. Instead, she hugged her chest and eased out a breath. "I need to see my folks off. Thanks again for showing me, Randy." She reached for his hand, her touch deepening her words. "It's not easy for me to say this, but her attack was a fluke. God, I miss her."

"I know. He gently wrapped his arms around her and she melted into him.

* * * * *

Sharon rode with her daughter while Donald drove the rental car. After returning the rental, Amanda drove them to Terminal One at Oakland International Airport. Having said their good-byes in the car, she left her parents at the curb and parked where she could watch silver-winged planes reach for the heavens.

Reverend Dole was right; there is renewal. She and her husband were speaking again, and she and her sister were traveling to Florida for Christmas as their parents' treat. She noticed a wildflower stemming from a crack in the road and thought about what Randy had said about nature being stronger than mankind. A loudspeaker demanded that she move her car. She looked in her mirror and noticed a police officer was waving her on. She waved back and merged into the traffic, thinking about her job. It wouldn't be easy going back, but she had no choice.

Dropping her parents at the airport spared her the usual morning gridlock. The Nimitz Freeway was moving well enough for her to enjoy the scenery. To her right, the elegant Claremont Resort rose brightly from emerald hills. To her left, a faint rainbow spanned the Golden Gate Bridge. She smiled.

SIXTY-FIVE

Randy scanned the *Oakland Tribune* searching for Sam Razini's article. He found it on page 4, section D.

> "...A gentle mist hid the tears from the hundreds of attendees at Kerri Connifer's memorial service...Kerri captured the hearts of the nation as her parents launched a national campaign...No one could have predicted her tragic end."

He trembled as he thumbed through the paper. Not surprisingly, her story had been replaced by terrorist threats, war dead, street crimes. He went to the obituaries and found her picture, saddened by the few sentences that summed up her brief life.

He reflected on his own mortality and realized how few interests he had except for Kerri. Once she was born, his hobbies took a back seat as she became his world. He depended on her for his happiness. It occurred to him that Amanda had done the same, leaving no emotions for him. It's no wonder they drifted apart.

Evelyn joined him at the table, preparing to go home. He set the paper down and kissed her on the cheek. "You're amazing, Mom. I don't know how you became so brilliant at matters of the heart, but I thank you. Every time I hit rock bottom, you're there to pick me up. I couldn't have gotten through this without you."

She sat down and took his hand. "You know it won't be easy living without her. Only a fool could deny that. I've never stopped mourning your father, but I did learn three rules that helped me, and might help you, too. First, don't make any drastic changes in your life right now. Second, don't dwell on Kerri's death. Finally, lock your heartache away because most people can't handle it."

"Those are good lessons, Mom. I wish you had shared them when I was first having problems. Especially the last one. I bombarded Bob Underly with my side of the story and unknowingly turned him against my wife. Bob didn't deserve my abuse, and Amanda did nothing to warrant his bias."

"I see you've already forgotten rule number two—don't dwell on the past." She let him stew on that while rinsing out her coffee mug.

He watched her, dumbfounded. She sounded confident enough, but she was also having trouble setting her mug in the dishwasher. "Penny for your thoughts, Mom."

"I was just thinking about your father. You have no idea how much better he listens now that he's gone."

They shared a laugh and he kissed her on the cheek. "Thanks again for being here. I love you, Mom."

SIXTY-SIX

Amanda's co-workers were supportive and didn't pry. Working proved to be good therapy, but when she got home, there was an uneasy silence. She sank into her favorite chair, kicked off her shoes, and wiggled her toes. Until now, she never noticed the ticking clock, the cycling furnace, the dripping faucet. She was about to turn on the TV when the phone rang.

Randy would have hung up except her caller ID had already identified him. Before losing his nerve, he said, "I don't mean to bother you, but have you had dinner? I understand if you'd rather be alone."

"No." Realizing that came out wrong, she nervously tucked her hair behind her ears. "What I mean is no, I haven't eaten," she said, racing to cancel her microwave dinner. "What did you have in mind?"

He heard the microwave beep in the background and grinned. "Well, today is the first day I've felt like eating in a week, so I was planning to go to the Chinese restaurant in Orinda. If you don't want go, I can bring something back for you."

"I'd love to go," she said, certain he was talking about the restaurant they used to visit. The family-run business had always treated Kerri to a peeled orange while they awaited their dinners. She checked her face in the mirror. It wasn't perfect, but it would do. "I can go any time."

"Great. I'll be right over."

He was sweating, overwhelmed with first-date anxiety. He drove off believing Kerri wanted him to go. He had to believe in something, and he was still having issues with God.

This time, Amanda was waiting for him at the front door and walked with him down the stairs. They both noticed the empty back seat and thought of Kerri, but neither mentioned it for fear of ruining their outing.

Not far from Skyline Gate, Randy turned onto Grizzly Peak Boulevard, slowing to a crawl where it offered an unrestricted view of San Francisco Bay. He pulled into the turnout above the Caldecott Tunnel, admiring the red and white car-streamers on the Bay Bridge. This is where they parked on their first date. He wondered if she remembered. "It's beautiful, isn't it?"

"It is."

"Would you like to get out or keep going?"

"I have plenty of time." She said that, knowing he wouldn't have stopped if he didn't want her to get out. At fifteen hundred feet above the city, it was a favorite spot for lovers and photographers. The wind tossed her hair as she leaned against the railing. Tires sang from the highway below. Cars passed behind them on Grizzly Peak Boulevard. She shifted her weight and gave a furtive glance. "So, how was your day?"

"It was okay."

A headlight caught her profile. She looked lovely as always, except her eyes had a grave sadness to them. He longed to hold and kiss her, but respectfully kept his distance. Like Mom said, they were both vulnerable right now.

He kicked a pebble over the slope and listened to it tumble. When it stopped, he faced her. "Jerry did a great job managing the business in my absence. I should give him a raise. Bob, too. By the way, they managed to land the Wilson account in spite of me."

"Really? Congratulations."

"Thanks. I'm just sorry it took me so long to figure out that I don't need to be there all the time. In fact, this last week has proven that the place runs fine without me. How about you? How was your day?"

Alcatraz' beacon speared the moon's reflection in the indigo water. A train whistle blew. A siren blared. The distractions made her re-think his question about her day. "It was okay, considering I'm a slave to this perpetual motion machine. While driving to work, it occurred to me the other commuters could care less about the weather, road conditions, or people's tragedies. I wonder how many of them noticed the rainbow this morning."

"We had another rainbow?"

"It was faint, but it was definitely there. I thought about Kerri."

"Oh, it was her, all right. I'm sure it was her."

She reached for his hand, cool to the touch. Today, the man standing beside her was much more than the football star she fell in love with. He was the man who suffered with her, yet made her feel like she belonged in this world. She glanced his way and briefly met his eyes. "Anyway, back to my day. Everyone was glad to see me and did their best to make me feel comfortable. It was good going back."

"I'm glad to hear that."

Another car drove by and disappeared into the darkness. Randy gently freed his hand and folded his arms across his chest. "Did you happen to notice Matt Bodine and Stacey Webster after the memorial service?"

"No. Why?"

"Remember how I told you Stacey couldn't stand Matt after she learned what he did for a living?"

Her lovely eyes fixated on his. "And?"

"Well, after the service they were holding hands, talking like old friends. Matt even had his arm around her." She looked away and his stomach tensed. "Oh, never mind. It's not important."

"But it is. Go on."

"I was just wondering what Matt said to her because Stacey was all smiles."

"Maybe he promised to change his ways," she said, gazing at the radiant city, alive with a million lights. "So, do you think they're together again?"

"I don't know. Maybe."

"Well, stranger things have happened. It's always nice when people get back together."

She cautiously smiled, patting his back; a peace offering of sorts. She dropped her hand and smiled at him. "I don't know about you, but I'm starving—"

POSTSCRIPT

The chance of sighting a cougar in its natural habitat is as remote as the wilderness itself. Still, our world is constantly changing. Hunting restrictions and preservation efforts have not only reversed the extinction of some species, but in some cases, have overpopulated them. Where urban areas attract deer, raccoon, opossum, skunk, rabbit, ducks, and geese, predators such as cougar, coyote, fox, and wolf are likely to follow. While these carnivores once controlled animal populations, man's interference has changed the course of nature. Although cougars normally sustain themselves on deer, some have developed tastes for cats, dogs, pigs, and chickens. However, there is no evidence that suggests they intentionally seek out humans. Since predators only respect rival boundaries, we should expect more encounters as we encroach upon their territory.

Like habituated deer, cougars have learned that humans and their dogs pose little danger. Increasing day encounters have demonstrated that today's cougar is bolder than those from a century ago. Cities like Boulder, Colorado, that have frequent cougar encounters have trained their police officers to drive the animals away using rubber bullets and bean bags to teach them to fear humans as they once did. Once this fear is passed on to their cubs, urban encounters are likely to decrease. Sadly, too many police forces overreact, firing their weapons, even if it poses a greater danger than the animal itself.

At best, wildlife management is a gamble. In some areas, relocated wolves and bears have become a nuisance, and are now being hunted. There is no question that the thriving cougar population will lead to restricted hunting permits.

Conservationists, hunters, politicians, and wildlife managers will never agree on how to handle the carnivore problem because man cannot control nature. Unfortunately, every attack on humans results in the death of that animal, and far too many animals die because of human ignorance.

For those wishing to learn more about cougars and wildlife management, I recommend reading *The Beast in the Garden,* by David Baron. It is a compelling read and startling glimpse into the future. Understanding animal behavior can certainly reduce human encounters. Precautions should always be taken when entering cougar country. Above all, cougars, like all carnivores, deserve our respect.

MARK W. DANIELSON grew up in the San Francisco Bay Area. He now lives in Denver, Colorado, with his wife, children, and faithful pooch, Lucy. He is an international airline pilot as well as suspense novelist. *Diablo's Shadow* is his third novel.

www.NightShadowsPress.com
www.markwdanielson.com

www.ingramcontent.com/pod-product-compliance
Lightning Source LLC
LaVergne TN
LVHW091042080826
845145LV00002B/594

9780979916755